LOVE'S BURDEN

Richard English put his arms around Hevatha and she tensed. He drew her to him and kissed her mouth, feeling her lips part, seeing the surprise and warmth in her eyes. She clung to him briefly and then stepped back, cocking her head curiously.

"Come on," he said, and his voice sounded much rougher than he intended. "We have to keep moving if we want to escape. Which way?"

Hevatha thought again what a strange man this yellow-haired one was. Strong and weak, intelligent and yet ignorant of so many things. How could he survive when already he moved stiffly and was breathing hard, while Hevatha thought nothing of running all day through snow and mud, as did their pursuers?

In this wilderness where one mistake meant death, she had to provide wisdom enough for two. . . .

NORTH STAR

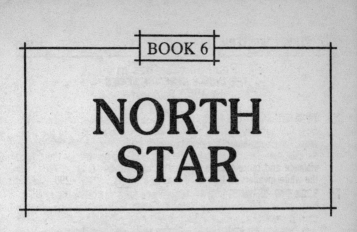

BOOK 6

NORTH STAR

THE INDIAN HERITAGE SERIES

by

Paul Joseph Lederer

A SIGNET BOOK

NEW AMERICAN LIBRARY

Copyright © 1987 by NAL PENGUIN INC.

Grateful acknowledgment is made for the following material:
"The Sleeping Place," copyright © 1981 by Malcolm Margolin, Heyday Books, P.O. Box 9145, Berkeley, CA 94709.

Ⓞ

SIGNET, SIGNET CLASSIC, MENTOR, ONYX, PLUME, MERIDIAN
and NAL BOOKS are published by NAL PENGUIN INC.,
1633 Broadway, New York, New York 10019

First Printing, June, 1987

` 3 4 5 6 7 8 9

PRINTED IN THE UNITED STATES OF AMERICA

The sleeping place
Which you and I hollowed out
Will remain always,
Will remain always,
Will remain always,
Will remain always.

   —A Wintu Indian song

With the fury of a lost longing remembered the sea thundered through the inlet and flung itself against the sentinel cliffs, frothing into the air before it forgot itself and withdrew, leaving a lacework of foam against the white-streaked gray stone.

Hevatha spat into the sea to appease it and crept nearer. The fur seal lifted itself from the sinkhole and waddled toward her.

The wind from the far islands was cold and fierce, twisting her long hair and drifting it across her face. The shaft of the harpoon she held was polished by time and use. Its tip was serrated whalebone.

The seal lifted its whiskered muzzle, scenting or sensing something which did not belong in its world of green-gray seas and stark stone rookeries where bulls clamored and cows bellowed to protect the nesting young, and where terns and screeching gulls wheeled raucously through the skies.

The seal turned and the sea roared in again. When it retreated the seal was gone, leaving no more trace than the ocean spray.

Hevatha stood, lifted her face to the sky, shook her head, and laughed. She put one hand on her hip and pointed at the sea. "You have fooled me this time. This time you are free, *natook*. This time I will have no new seal jacket."

The old seal jacket she wore, the one with the glass trade beads sewn to it, was worn at the elbows. Her matching skirt, made by old Aunt Godak, was frayed and thin now. Hevatha wiped back her unruly black hair, rubbed her elbow which she had skinned stalking the *natook*, and laughed again.

"Next time," she said. "Next time."

The sea rushed in again and with its roar drowned out her laughter. She looked seaward, to the source of all things: the sea, avenging, bountiful, kind, evil, and endless. A mile offshore, mountainous islands lifted craggy amber heads which glowed softly in the low sunlight of Tlingit summer. There the seals had their breeding grounds, and there was the island of the dead where the honored Tlingit slept eternity away in their totem-fronted grave houses. There the last great shaman, Dah-chet-jah, dreamed awhile of mortality before he rose to resume his ancient feud with the sea.

Hevatha raised her harpoon, spat once again at the sea, and turned, walking back toward her village, the one called Klinkwan, which means "the town where people get things at low tide."

For at low tide the wreckage of fishers and of storm-torn towns like Sukwan to the north drifted onto the rocky beach below the village. The salmon were left flapping on the beaches, silver shimmering things, grudging gifts of the sea.

Steaming piles of moss burned to keep the mosquitoes away from the village of wooden houses crowding the inlet. Green-budding highlands lifted above the town. Hemlock grew there, and fir, thimbleberries, and skunk cabbage taller than a woman's head. Bear prowled there and the spirits of the Tlingit dead, wishing to return to their home by the sea.

On this day festive songs filled the air, nearly drowning out the constant snarling and yapping of the sled dogs. The great man, Gunyah, was preparing for potlatch and the villagers prepared with him. Gunyah was wealthy and proud and the potlatch was his chance to demonstrate to the Tlingit of the neighboring towns just how wealthy he had become.

For the next three days the people of Tuxican, the winter town, of Sukwan, the grassy town, and of Kasaan, the pretty town, would gather at Klinkwan for feasting, dancing, for the gift-giving. Gunyah would give away half of what he owned, perhaps more, and by doing this gain prestige and still more power and wealth, for the chiefs of Tuxican and Sukwan and Kasaan would be honor-bound to hold their own potlatches and return greater gifts to Gunyah.

Hevatha, who was not Tlingit by birth, would receive no gift, not even a hide scraper. All the same, she loved the time of potlatch, the dancing, the competing clans in their costumes, bear clan against raven, whale against salmon. The men drank *hootch-i-noo* and got very drunk, telling tales of ancient battles while the dancers chanted, twisted, straightened, crouched, and crept, singing songs of valor and lost love to the thumping of the constant drums and the jangling of rattles.

Everyone ate more than he wanted, filling bellies with *eulikon* from the big canoe where butter and fat and candlefish had been allowed to age, stuffing down the elongated snouts of salmon smoked on the racks, and pounds upon pounds of fish roe eaten like candy from long colorless strings.

And then the slaves would be killed.

This wasn't something Gunyah had to do, but it pleased him. He had many slaves in his house. His four wives couldn't be expected to do common labor. The slaves were of the Kwakiutl tribe and the Kaska and the Chugachigmiut. Some of these would be given away to the other Tlingit chiefs. Some would be killed outright so that Gunyah could demonstrate just how wealthy he was, so wealthy that even his slaves didn't matter to him.

"Vatha!" someone called from across the camp, but Hevatha kept walking. To the Tlingit she had always been "Vatha." They had difficulty pronouncing her real name and many had simply forgotten it. Hevatha hadn't forgotten. It was the name her dead mother had given her, her dead mother, the Cheyenne woman.

"Vatha!" The young man was running toward her. He wore a raven's-head hat and a striped shirt, trade jeans, and high-top moccasins. Hevatha stopped and turned toward him, hands on hips, her left hand still holding her harpoon. She blew a strand of hair from her face with a puff of breath and then put one hand at the crown of her head, waggling her fingers at Ganook.

"Vatha, wait! Hevatha, wait!"

Hevatha wiggled her fingers again and laughed, walking on, but Ganook caught up with her.

"I've decided," the eldest son of Gunyah said.

"Good." Hevatha kept walking. Ganook half-ran beside her, his raven's-head hat swaying on his head. Ganook was short, dusky, powerfully built for a man of his age. He was also self-important and arrogant.

"You don't know yet what I have decided, Vatha."

"No," Hevatha said, still walking at a furious pace toward Aunt Godak's house, where smoke rose from a square hole in the roof.

"Stop! Will you stop, Vatha!" He grabbed her arm, turned her, and had his hand slapped away. Ganook tensed and his hand reached out for her again, not quite touching her. "At least walk more slowly," he said at last.

"I am in a hurry."

"But something important has happened. I've made my decision. I'm going to have my father buy you for me. You will be my wife."

Hevatha stopped again. She looked at the young man with bright, inquisitive eyes. And then she laughed. She laughed until she doubled up with the laughter, holding her belly. Ganook stood seething with anger. He was the son of the Tlingit chief. He was a man of rank, a member of the raven clan, and this woman of no rank had refused him, mocked him. He was angry, and then, watching her, he was only cowed. He felt impotent and lost.

There was no one like Hevatha in the town of Klinkwan, no one like her in all the Tlingit lands. Proud and tall and overflowing with a vibrancy which might have been sexual yet wasn't. Her soul had its own source of light and sheltered its own secrets.

She was classless, or would have been except that Yakwan, who had been called the long rover, had adopted Hevatha years ago. Hevatha was from a land to the south, a land where there was no sea. Ill and lost, she had been brought to Klinkwan by the long rover and raised by Aunt Godak. But she had not been raised properly. She had no respect for rank.

"Do you know what it cost me to talk to my father about you?" Ganook continued almost desperately. "I wouldn't have dared it except he's in a fine mood because of potlatch. Do you know what he thinks of you, Vatha?"

"I don't care," said the young woman with the man-haunting eyes, willowy body, and foreign ways.

"Look at your jacket, look at your skirt! Don't you know how much I can give you, Vatha?"

"Well then," she said, "give it to me. Leave the presents on my doorstep."

"I am willing to marry you."

"I am willing to accept your presents," Hevatha said, and Ganook just stared, stared until he realized that she was laughing inside, still laughing. Then he turned sharply and walked away across the gray rock beach and was swallowed up by the smoke from the smudge heaps.

Hevatha watched him for a minute and then shrugged and walked on. She walked silently through the burning ground for the dead, which separated the two halves of the village, and to Aunt Godak's house. The house was rectangular, of log and bark. A flight of outside steps had to be climbed to reach the doorway, which was covered with a curtain woven of bark.

Hevatha entered the smoky house, yawned as the sudden warmth overcame her, and walked to the nook where weapons were kept. From the platform which ringed the interior of the house she could look down to the central sitting room, where cooking was done. Skins hung on the walls, and from the smoke-blackened ceiling hung salmon and deer and seal. Near the fire sat Aunt Godak and her three blanket-clad cousins. Their naked grandchildren rolled in a tangle of limbs in the corner as three white spitz puppies yapped approval.

Aunt Godak lifted her eyes and her seamed face beamed. "So where is the *natook*, Cheyenne hunter?"

"With her pups in the green sea," Hevatha laughed.

She waved a hand and walked along the familiar platform to her bed in the corner of the clan house. She sat on her cedar trunk and tugged off her boots, rubbing her feet.

A huge dog lay on a blanket watching her with yellow eyes, his massive head resting on gray-and-white paws. Hevatha cocked her head and made a mock growl in her throat and Tyee rose, wagging his thick curled tail.

The sled dog went to Hevatha and had its pointed ears scratched. "Are you good, Tyee? Are you a good dog or is your wolf grandfather stirring in you today?"

She held its head on her lap, looking into the yellow eyes. Tyee was hers. The malamute would go to no one else and never had since Hevatha had plucked it from the litter of eight which its mother, Kloosha, had delivered. Tyee weighed more than most grown men. He was a wolf dog, as were most of the dogs in the village. Every few generations when the blood of the sled dogs was judged to have become thin, the bitches were taken into the woods and tied there to await the coming of the wolves. Tyee's blood was wolf. He was strong and patient and loyal.

"There is no *natook* liver today, nothing to give you." Tyee's great tongue wiped itself across Hevatha's hand and he turned to lie down again, circling three times on the blanket before settling with a groan.

Hevatha took out her house moccasins and put them on. Then she went down the interior staircase to where the women sat around the fire, discussing the politics of the tribe, which they controlled, and the marriages they must decide.

It was the Tlingit women who held power, except in the case of a great chief like Gunyah, who was a law of his own. Women could not be chiefs but they settled all family matters and controlled clan politics.

Marriage was one of their chief concerns, marriages ordained by the shaman, the "Iht" with his magic sticks, marriages dreamed of or promised as payment for a clan debt. It was not unusual for a young girl to be given to an old man or for a young boy to be given to an old woman. If these things were judged proper, they were done.

"So Ke-an-Kow did not smile on you today, Hevatha," Aunt Godak said as the young woman crouched to fill her bowl at the hearth. "The Great One Over All has sent you home without meat."

"The sea had eyes and it warned the *natook*," Hevatha answered.

"A Tlingit woman would have brought *natook* meat," one of the other women, Aunt Kawclaa, complained.

Hevatha had to swallow her mouthful of salmon stew before she answered with a smile, "A Tlingit woman would have sent her slave to hunt *natook*, and before the slave returned to the house there would be nothing left but bones."

Aunt Kawclaa didn't like that. "When I was a young woman I went hunting often. I was the best hunter of all the young women."

"That was before you had six slaves," Godak said. "Hevatha is right. What Tlingit woman needs to hunt? What Tlingit woman of a certain class?"

"Work is for slaves," the other aunt, Shak-ish-stin, agreed. "Give me food, Hevatha." She handed a bowl to Hevatha, who filled it for her.

"I used to hunt, Kawclaa said in an undertone. Hevatha thought she felt guilty about having slaves. Once a white missionary had come to Klinkwan and he had told them they were sinning by keeping slaves. Kawclaa was one of the few who had listened to the missionary's strange ideas. For a time Kawclaa had even worn a little ivory cross around her neck.

Godak changed the subject. "We have decided to marry Ska-wat-klan's daughter to Duktat," the aunt announced.

Hevatha made a face. "Poor girl."

"She will gain much. The bear clan is dying out. Duktat will be their wolf."

Hevatha made the face again, mouth tightening and turning down, eyes squinting shut. Duktat's name meant "dirty face." It was a little boy's name but he had carried it all his life. His face was discolored at birth and had remained so. He was big, well-tattooed, and wealthy. But Ska-wat-klan's daughter was only twelve and very shy. Hevatha knew she would not want to share Duktat's blankets, and she said so.

"Duktat would not want you either," Kawclaa sniffed. "Classless thing."

"How will you marry her off?" Skak-ish-stin asked, looking Hevatha up and down. "What will you do with this pup you have taken in? Feed her forever?"

"She is my daughter," Aunt Godak said stubbornly.

"A good daughter should marry to bring wealth to the clan," Skak-ish-stin answered stiffly.

"Perhaps," Aunt Godak said with a sly smile, "Hevatha will make a better marriage than even Ska-wat-klan's daughter, who knows?"

"Better than Duktat? Who would that be, Godak?"

"Just wait," the old woman said with a smile which now had broadened to reveal most of her worn front teeth, "perhaps Hevatha will tell us soon."

"If you mean Ganook," Hevatha said, placing her bowl aside, stretching and yawning, "then you are wrong. He asked me today and I refused him."

"Refused him?" Godak asked in dismay. Her smile faded and she shook her head worriedly. "That would be good for the clan, Hevatha, very good for us."

"I won't marry him."

"Did you hear that!" Kawclaa wailed. "She refuses to make a marriage for the clan! Beat her, Godak. Let the three of us gather around her and beat her."

Godak shook her head wearily. "It would do no good," she sighed. "No good to beat Hevatha. She does what she wills. She has always done so."

Hevatha was through with her meal. The three older women got back to their business of matchmaking and she rose, whistling for Tyee, who lifted his great head and lumbered to meet Hevatha at the top of the steps.

It was growing cool and so she put on her fur boots and bearskin coat before going out, Tyee at her heels. Near the exit her bow and arrows hung and she took these along. She was not through hunting for the day.

She had seen grazing deer among the wild celery on the wrinkled bluff beyond the red inlet and she meant to bring meat to the house.

No matter what her aunts believed, Hevatha was grateful to the clan, to the Tlingit. Most of all to the long rover, Yakwan, who had found her in the southern lands, fevered, freezing, half out of her mind, and brought her to his home. Yakwan was dead now, but he had raised Hevatha as a daughter, he and Aunt Godak. She had always tried to please the two of them, to contribute to the clan needs.

She would hunt for them, sew for them, scrape hides, make tallow, cook, and scrub. But she would not marry for the clan. At heart she was still Cheyenne, still her mother's daughter.

She was a remarkable woman—Amaya was her name. From her Hevatha had learned self-reliance and independence. She had learned to endure.

Hevatha walked into the highlands with the brisk sea air swirling around her, carrying the scent of salt and of kelp. Tyee started a hare and bounded after it, racing through the long grass.

At the top of the bluff Hevatha paused for breath, sitting cross-legged on the sandy earth, looking out at the gray sea, the golden islands in the distance, at the low sun which slowly circled the sky, never setting at this time of year.

"Hevatha!"

She turned and smiled, rising to meet the young man with the infectious grin and nearly flat face. He had a basket of cranberries slung around his neck. The hood of his worn sealskin parka was down, allowing his straight fine hair to drift in the sea breeze. Tyee, back from his fruitless hunt, leapt up and put his massive paws on the youth's shoulders.

"Hello, Koosh," Hevatha said. Koosh was a slave, a man of the far north who had been blown to the southern coast by a winter storm. He had been hunting whales with his father and uncles. Only Koosh had survived when their fragile boat had been wrecked.

Koosh put Tyee's paws down, set down his cranberries, and looked to the village below. "Potlatch," he said with a grin. "A good time. Tonight we will eat *eulikon* and salmon wrapped in skunk cabbage and strawberries until we burst."

"Tonight," Hevatha repeated. "Why don't you leave tonight? Run away, no one will see you. Everyone will be watching the dancers."

"Run away?" Koosh's broad face wrinkled into a grin. "Why would I run away, Hevatha? Why would I run away at potlatch time? Perhaps I shall be given gifts by my master, Gunyah."

"I want you to go," Hevatha said. She had been thinking of Koosh for days. Koosh was her hunting companion, her friend. "I want you to go so that something evil doesn't happen to you."

"So that I won't be killed!" Koosh laughed. "Gunyah would not kill me. I am too valuable." He tapped his chest and laughed again. "Who would bring meat to his house if not Koosh?"

"Koosh," Hevatha said, taking his face in her hands. "I want you to go. No matter what Gunyah has told you, no matter how valuable you think you are. The *hootch-i-noo* will be poured and it makes its own laws."

"What do you mean, Hevatha?" Koosh asked. Poor Koosh only trusted. "*Hootch-i-noo* makes the men happy."

"Too happy," Hevatha said.

"Where could I go?" Koosh asked as Hevatha's hands fell away from his smooth cheeks. "I am Aleut. Should I swim across the sea to my home in the islands? I am happy here. I work and at night I'm warm in Gunyah's big house. One day soon perhaps you will marry Ganook and you will live there with us, singing your songs."

"I want you to go," she repeated. "This will be a bad night."

"It's against the law!" Koosh said ingenuously. "If I ran, they would hunt me down and kill me. Where am I to go, what am I to do? Go inland among the wolves, inland where no one lives but the Nahani? What would the Nahani do to me, Hevatha? If they did not kill me, did not find me, then I would live alone until I was an old man, fighting the animals for carrion. No," he said, shaking his head heavily, "there is nowhere to go. Besides, I am happy here. Happy to sing, to have a warm bed, to be where you are, Hevatha."

"Do this for me then," Hevatha said, her eyes shuttling briefly to Tyee, who was digging a massive hole in the ground, pursuing an unseen prey. "Don't drink *hootch-i-noo* tonight. Stay away from the festivities, away from the banquet mats."

"But, Hevatha, that is why I want to be at potlatch!"

"Hold yourself back, Koosh, and watch. Watch and wait—and have a dogsled ready."

"If you tell me to do this, I will," Koosh said. There was childish disappointment in his eyes. "Only for you, for no one else."

"Promise it."

"Very well, I promise it. But you don't know my master, Gunyah. He has promised me that nothing will ever happen to me."

"I know Gunyah," she said quietly. "I know him very well. Just do as I ask, please."

"I will do it." Koosh shrugged with one shoulder and then grinned. "But I will not like it, Hevatha." He hefted his cranberry basket, shouldered it, and started on, waving a hand. Tyee followed him for a way down the bluffside trail and then turned to trot back to Hevatha.

Hevatha went on across the wooded bluff. Wild celery flourished there, and salmonberries, skunk cabbage, and blueberries. The blueberries were prized more as a source of purple dye than as a food, and the Tlingit ate few of them—the bears who roved the bluffs did, however. Hevatha saw the fresh sign of a grizzly, a very large grizzly, and found his clawmarks ten feet up the trunk of an alder where the bear had stretched himself and sharpened his claws.

Deer moss hung from the trees and there was plentiful deer sign in the sandy earth. They too had scarred the trees as they reached for yellow-green morsels.

She thought of the missionary again then. The missionary had wanted to try hunting deer with a bow and arrow. He was so bad at it that Hevatha had laughed half the day, frightening away game.

His name had been Johnson, which meant "the son of John." He spoke of things which made no sense, of taboos and punishment at the hands of Ke-an-Kow. But the Tlingit had laughed, knowing that the Great One Over All did not punish someone for being a human being. Gunyah hadn't liked Johnson, nor had the Iht. The shaman had placed a hand on the missionary's head and said the word of death and then no one had seen him again. The Iht had proven his power.

Johnson had brought no gifts with him which offended the Tlingit, especially Gunyah. But he had brought his language, the English which only Hevatha understood. Her mother, Amaya, had taught her some English when she was young. Amaya had been raised on a white reservation and she knew the words. The missionary had taught Hevatha more words. Now there was no one to speak the words to. They lay uselessly in the back of her mind like scattered dreams.

The mule deer was in the wild celery and it lifted its head with its magnificent rack of antlers as Hevatha moved silently through the alder wood. She held herself still, slowing her breath, looking slightly away from the deer so that the spirit inside the buck wouldn't feel the waiting death in her eyes.

Soon the deer lowered its head again and began to feed on the celery. Hevatha notched her arrow and stepped softly forward, ducking beneath the tangled alder branches.

She lifted her bow, letting out a little breath and then holding it again. She looked down the length of the arrow's shaft, fixing the bone head of the arrow on the spot she meant to strike, just behind the deer's shoulder, where the arrow could penetrate heart and lungs and bring it down cleanly. A missed shot would mean a long trek through the woods, perhaps to face the injured deer in a snarled thicket of berries and brush. There is nothing so harmless as a deer, nothing so dangerous as the hooves and antlers of one cornered and hurt.

Hevatha's fingers uncurled slightly. The sinew bowstring strained at her fingertips, a living thing anxious to do what it had been designed to do, send death hurtling through the space between Hevatha and the deer.

The mule deer lifted its head again and bounded sharply away.

Hevatha lowered her bow, her eyes narrowing. The wind had not shifted, carrying her scent to the deer's nostrils. Tyee lay obediently, silently beside her. What had startled the deer?

Then she saw him. The Iht.

The shaman had a rattle in either hand. On his head was the four-horned hat of his rank. He wore buckskins, fringed, intricately embroidered, and his labret, a large copper ring which hung from his nostrils, catching the low sunlight, dully gleaming.

He came slowly through the vines and trees toward Hevatha, shaking his rattles, his tattooed face hollow-cheeked, dark as ash. Hevatha put her hand to the crown of her head, wiggled her fingers at the Iht, stuck out her tongue, and ran as fast as she could, Tyee bounding at her heels.

The shaman would not put his hand on *her* head. He wouldn't curse her with his magic word. She looked back across her shoulder, saw the man struggling to keep up with her, rattles raised, and she laughed. Hevatha laughed until she could scarcely run.

"Old skunk, old badger, old liar," she said, and then she slowed. The Iht had given up chasing her. Hevatha wriggled her fingers at him one more time and then strode on, bow in hand, Tyee beside her, his pink tongue lolling from his sharp-toothed mouth.

The Iht claimed to heal, but he only cursed his enemies and then they died. He hated Hevatha, hated her for being classless, neither Tlingit nor slave. He hated her for the laughter which constantly bubbled from her lips, for her lack of respect, for having been a friend of Johnson, the missionary. Perhaps he hated

her for her youth. Perhaps he hated everything because he had never learned the secrets of the last great
shaman, Dah-chet-jah, who had known all of nature's
whims and moods and had controlled them.

This Iht shook his rattles and perhaps someone lived.
He placed a hand on your head and said the word and
you died. His magic was dark and crimson with blood,
and if you did not believe in the Iht, he saw that you
died.

He lived only to see that other things died and he
encouraged the excesses of others like Chief Gunyah.

Hevatha had come to the rim of the bluff again. The
long salt grass reached to her knees and it furrowed
and rolled in the wind. For a time she watched the
sea, its incoming white rush, its slow, defeated with-
drawal. *There* was magic, not in the Iht's medicine
bag. What the magic might have been, she could not
define. She thought only of a word, distant and alien,
a word brought by the missionary when he had spoken
of his God.

"Ineffable," Hevatha said, and it was a word which
brought both wonder and amusement on its heels.
"Ineffable," a word laughable with its strange English
sounds, a word nearly magical, meaning, as the missionary had said, nothing and everything at once.

Hevatha stood for a long while, lost in thoughts
without definition. Then, laughing at her own foolishness, she wandered to the village below, where the
sounds and smells and activities of potlatch filled the
air with excitement.

The midnight sun glowed softly when Hevatha again
emerged from her clan house. From the north and the
south and the east the neighboring tribes arrived,
banging drums, dancing, shaking rattles. It was the
middle of the night and potlatch had come with a good
omen—the northern lights shone and shimmered and
the sea which had been raging ceased its pounding
against the rocky beach of the Tlingit village.

"Put on your good dress, put on your new moccasins," Aunt Godak called as she hurried past Hevatha

down the bare outside steps to the beach. "This night won't come again."

Hevatha waved a hand and stood leaning against the wall of the clan house, watching. As the frog clan and the ravens danced in mock warfare, the fires were started along the beach and the people of Tuxican and Sukwan streamed into the village, waving clan poles, wearing raven hats and bear masks, shouting to old friends, raising fists to old enemies, protected by the bans of potlatch. The great chief, Gunyah, emerged from his house in his raven hat and furs, Ganook beside him, to lift his arms to the arriving people.

Iht was there, dark and somber, shaking rattles, the four-horned hat covering his gray hair, his eyes bleak and hollow, jaw clenched, anger and power emanating from his body, his rigid stance, and his hollow-cheeked tattooed face.

The *hootch-i-noo* in clay jars was already being drunk, copiously, steadily. The eating hadn't yet started, for before the potlatch actually began Gunyah had various tribal matters to settle. The first was the murder of a woman named Yak by a man named Kay-ish-tik. Yak was of the bear clan, Kay-ish-tik of the eagle. The bear clan demanded a price for the death of Yak.

Hevatha wandered nearer, looking around for Koosh. She saw him nowhere so perhaps he had heeded her warning. Gunyah was listening to the charge of murder against Kay-ish-tik. Yak's brother had seen the murder and he was describing it.

"Yak was angry. Kay-ish-tik had walked through her cooking place, spilling things everywhere. Yak took a stick and hit Kay-ish-tik with it and he turned and killed her with his hands."

Kay-ish-tik had no defense. He stood before Gunyah, arms folded, wearing his eagle-clan dancing costume.

"Yes, I killed the woman," Kay-ish-tik finally said, lifting his arms to his chief. "It was a bad thing, but it isn't right for you to take my life for that of a woman, Gunyah. Take my sister instead and kill her. The law says a man's life for a man's, a woman's for a woman's."

Kay-ish-tik's sister began to wail. She tried to turn and run away but the men of her clan grabbed her and held her. The Iht and Gunyah conversed privately and then the Iht came down from the platform, moving through the crowd, which fell back as he approached. The Iht walked to Kay-ish-tik and then past him to his sister. As Hevatha watched, the Iht put his hand on the woman's head and said the word. It was justice and the people of the eagle clan embraced the people of the bear clan.

Hevatha turned away. She walked slowly from the camp, following the line of the bluff which overlooked the village. Here and there were patches of snow. Beyond the bluff, in the mountains and valleys beyond, the snow was heavy. The sea rushed against the beach, hissing and groaning, drawing small rocks after it as it receded. From the camp a cheer went up and Hevatha winced. The cheer rose again, mingled with the roar of the surf, and fell away.

Hevatha climbed a small dune and walked to the private place of her clan women. A pit in the ground covered over with sea grass, poles, and woven mats had been dug. Around it clay jars of fresh water and baskets of food rested.

Hevatha went to the hole and crouched down, crossing her arms on her knees.

"Who is it?" the voice from the pit asked.

"Hevatha. Are you all right, Kaish?"

"Yes, Vatha, thank you. I hear singing sometimes. What is it, potlatch?"

"Potlatch, yes." Hevatha parted the poles and bark mats and peered down into the hole. Ska-wat-klan's twelve-year-old daughter looked up and smiled. She had reached her time of womanhood and so the clan hid its shame by placing Kaish into the pit. She would remain there for between four months and a year. When she emerged she would no longer be a girl and the clan would welcome her back.

"Do you want me to get you anything?" Hevatha asked.

"No." The voice was small, weary, resigned. "Did you hear about my good fortune, Vatha?"

"Duktat, you mean?"

"Yes. I am going to be married to him. One day I will be a powerful woman." An undercurrent of some emotion, perhaps vengeance, rippled through her words. Hevatha saw that Kaish's fist was clenched tightly. And when she was a powerful woman, would she remember the frightened girl who had lived in this hole in the ground for so long?

"Duktat will be a strong husband," Hevatha replied.

"I know that." Kaish's voice had grown small again.

Hevatha asked, "Don't you want me to get you something? To do something for you?"

"No. There's nothing. Just tell me sometime about potlatch. Tell me the songs they sing, tell me how Duktat looked in his raven costume."

"Yes. I will tell you all of that when I come back."

"Vatha, you are my friend."

"Yes." Hevatha rose, covered the pit again, and stood for a minute looking at the private place. "I am your friend."

She turned then and walked on, the sea in her ears, the wind casting sand from the bluffs against her cheeks. She came to the river where the salmon would run and watched it flow into the sea, be repulsed by inrushing tide, and flow on. Along the riverbanks pine, birch, and poplar crowded the beach. An owl hooted once and then took to wing, a snow-white bird with huge yellow eyes. It was Kay-ish-tik's sister flying away toward the midnight sun.

The sounds of potlatch rose up out of the glow of the fires and softer golden glow of the beach as Hevatha returned to the Tlingit camp. The dancing continued, rattles shaking furiously as the clans in costume—bear, eagle, frog, and raven—competed. Old men chanted old songs. Children shrieked and imitated the dancing of their elders. The Iht stood upon the platform yet, decrying evil, like the bloody Kwakiutl, praising the good, the Tlingit and their great chief, Gunyah. People would pause to listen for a time and then wander away to drink *hootch-i-noo* and listen to the songs, to fill their bellies with herring, salmon, honey, abalone, and mussels, halibut heads, wild celery, cranberries, and soapberries.

Hevatha walked among the people, listening, watching, lifting a hand to friends and clan members. The Tlingit dancers moved like shadows, raven and bear, eagle and frog, whale and mink, mingling with raw nature, displaying communal strength and purpose as they released tensions and secret deviltry.

"Vatha!"

Hevatha glanced at Ganook, Ganook with his labret through his lip, his raven's head hat and painted face, but she walked away from him, hearing a sharp exclamation of disgust.

The Iht had finished his droning speech which praised the great Tlingit nation, praised each tribe and clan and chief by name, and derided the enemy tribes by clan and name and village. Now Gunyah emerged again from his great house.

The people fell silent and started toward the house, crowding together beneath the platform where Gunyah was surrounded by his gift-bearing slaves. His four wives stood at a respectful distance in their finest dresses, looking, Hevatha thought, considerably abashed. They had reason—their husband, the great man, the good chief, was about to give away the majority of their wealth, from household belongings to items of clothing, from slaves to canoes, from finely woven baskets to jewelry of copper and silver, opal and pearl.

Hevatha stood on the fringe of the mob, listening with the others to discover who would be honored first, with which visiting tribe, with which great chief Gunyah most wished to seal an alliance—or whose reciprocal goods he coveted the most.

"It is potlatch," Gunyah said in his gravelly voice. His tattooed, labret-decorated face was nearly immobile as he spoke. "It is time to forge friendships and to share the wealth the Ke-an-Kow has bestowed upon his most favored. Like the Great One I must chose a most favored among all of the friends of the people of

Klinkwan." He paused, rocked forward on his toes, and then said, "I invite the chief of Tuxican, the winter village, my ally and brother, Hultish, to come forward and stand with me. I invite him to choose among my fine slaves a man he wishes, I invite him to chose from my war canoes the one he wishes; I invite Hultish to stand beside me as a brother and take from the house of Gunyah whatever his wives desire, to choose a sled and a team of dogs, to accept the gift of white bear hides and steel knives I offer him."

Hultish was old and needed help to mount the platform, but his greed and the greed of his wives was strong, and in minutes they had taken away Gunyah's gifts, including the slave Tak-shoo-tik, who left behind a daughter and his own wife.

"Next, my ally Ka-uh-tan," Gunyah intoned, spreading his arms to indicate his own magnanimity. "I wish for him to take what he wishes from my food stores, to take the second-best war canoe . . ."

It went on, but Hevatha did not listen. The others, the people of Klinkwan and the visitors from the other Tlingit villages, pressed even nearer, hoping that their own clan leader might be next, expecting some gift, for even the lowest-ranking member of the tribe might receive something. Hevatha expected nothing, wanted nothing. She yawned and turned away—and nearly walked into the Iht.

He had one braceleted hand raised. The other shook a rattle menacingly at his side. As Hevatha turned, the Iht tried to touch her head, tried to say the word of death, but she ducked away and sprinted off, pausing after four strides to put her hand behind her head and waggle her fingers.

The Iht shouted the death word at her, but it had no effect unless you were touched by his hand, and Hevatha, hands on hips, thrust out her tongue and walked on, the death word ringing in her ears as the shaman shouted it over and over.

"Thing," she answered, using the missionary's language. "*Thing!*" and then she forgot about the Iht and went to a nearly deserted food mat to collect scraps for Tyee.

The big dog devoured the food with habitual growls and throaty warnings, though there were no other dogs from the pack near. Hevatha crouched near Tyee, speaking softly to him. "Your manners are no better than a wolf's. No one wants your filthy salmon heads. You are worse than your grandfather."

Tyee paid no attention to her, but when he was done he came and sat beside Hevatha, licking her hand and neck as she scratched the thick hide beneath his shaggy silver-gray coat.

"What will happen to you if the Iht kills me?" She took his head and looked into his yellow wolf eyes. "Who will feed you then? You go to no one, no one but Koosh, and after tonight perhaps Koosh too will be gone."

Tyee looked deeply into her eyes, trying to understand her, to know what she wanted. "Ah, you are nothing but a fat wolf. Go and sleep some more. Sleep now and grow fat—the snows will come and then you will be sorry that you have grown so fat and lazy. Then you will be a sled dog again and have to work. Then the dogs you lead will eat you up like whale blubber, fat thing!"

Tyee's mouth opened and his huge tongue, hot and damp, dropped out. He sat contentedly as Hevatha stroked his huge head. She scratched his ears and teasingly scolded the dog, but her mind was elsewhere.

It was with Koosh; Koosh, who wanted to be at potlatch, who must not be. "Come," Hevatha said to Tyee, "let us see if our friend has his sled ready."

Why she felt sudden urgency about Koosh, Hevatha couldn't have said. She only knew that anxiety for her friend rose like a fluttering bird in her breast, trying to force its way into her throat.

"Come, Tyee! Don't dawdle," she snapped.

Outside, potlatch continued; Gunyah's endless speech-making and gift-giving stretched on. The Iht had re-taken the platform and at any gap in Gunyah's own speeches the Iht moved forward to declaim against evil and neighboring tribes, against any and all of creation which did not please the Iht.

Hevatha walked behind the great ceremonial hut, which had a totem pole at each corner, raven on eagle, bear on turtle, whale on frog, and went into the tangle of berries beyond, moving certainly through the thorny vines along a hunting trail, Tyee padding silently at her heels until she reached the bluff.

She saw the sled lashed to a young alder, the team of dogs lying curled on the ground. They rose and yapped as Tyee walked past them, but the big dog paid them no more attention than Gunyah normally paid his slaves.

Koosh was not there.

Hevatha looked back toward the potlatch, tugged nervously at the sleeve of her bearskin coat, and looked again to the alder woods.

"Koosh!" She called out several times but there was no answer. "He went down there after all," Hevatha said. Tyee cocked his head and looked up at her expectantly. "Come on, dog, son of a wolf."

Hevatha started down the bluff again, slipping once, sliding into a coil of thorny berry vines. Tyee got down on the ground and rolled playfully beside her, thinking it was a game. Hevatha slapped at him and got hurriedly to her feet again. Below a cheer went up at some unexpected gift. The dancing had begun again and now impromptu dancers, prodded by the *hootch-i-noo* in their bellies, began to join in. Hevatha saw Koosh. He was behind a fox-clan house, clapping his hands as the song went on, wearing fur boots and parka for traveling, his face split by a wide grin.

"Koosh!" Hevatha called out, but the slave couldn't hear her above the drums and rattles. "Koosh!"

Finally Koosh did turn, his eyes widening with pleasure and then withdrawing with shame as he saw the expression on Hevatha's face.

"Hevatha . . ."

She didn't let him say any more. She reached him, panting, her mouth hanging open, and she pushed him on the shoulders with all of her strength. Koosh took a step backward to regain his balance.

"Get out of here! What did I tell you? Get to your sled and go!"

Koosh looked at her with hurt in his dark, liquid eyes. He glanced once toward potlatch and then turned and trudged away, pausing only to let a hand rest momentarily on Tyee's head.

Behind Hevatha a roar went up. She watched until she could see Koosh no longer as he wound through the berries, and then she walked into the camp. The dancing had stopped. The people were only dark silhouettes in the golden sunlight, dark totems bathed in liquid honey. On the platform stood the Iht, his hand resting on a slave's head.

The slave tried to break away at the last minute but Gunyah was waiting. The chief of Klinkwan village stepped forward and Hevatha saw his arm fall, heard the dull, heartbreaking sound of stone meeting skull, and she heard the crowd cheer as the slave was pushed forward to fall from the platform and lie on the rocky beach, his body twisted into a macabre pattern. Another slave, yelling, struggling, was dragged forward and the Iht put his hand on the man's head. Gunyah lifted his club again, and again that sound reached Hevatha's ears. The sound of death.

She turned and walked away quickly, so quickly that she nearly fell. She crossed the inlet to the south on the rocky bar and waded through the sweet creek to the pine woods beyond. She climbed the hill there, climbed until she could no longer see the village, no longer hear the cheers, the death sounds.

Then she sat, arms around her knees, breath coming dry and ragged, watching the sea. The constant sea, the endless thing, gold and gray in the midnight sun's light. She lifted her eyes to the far islands, craggy and broken, and then looked beyond them to the farther points that only thought can reach.

2

THE schooner *Cormorant* lifted its bow, slewed sideways, and began a sickening roll before it plunged down the far side of the foaming mountain of water. Every plank and bit of rigging groaned with the effort of the three-master's effort to stay afloat. She wallowed through the frothing valley between two walls of moving water, lifted her head slowly again and again, wearily climbed a vast pyramid of rolling gray water.

The storm had lasted most of the day and into the night as the *Cormorant,* bound for Sitka out of San Francisco, breached the Hecate Strait futilely seeking shelter on the lee side of Graham Island.

The storm gave no quarter, however; it rolled on from out of the north, blanketing the sea with storm clouds from Vancouver to the 60th parallel.

The Swede dropped down through the companionway, followed by a rush of wind and the silver wash of rain. The hatch dropped shut behind him and he walked into the galley, his oilskins dripping water, his blue stocking cap covering his shock of bright red hair. He carried a storm lantern which cast shadows before the figures of the men crowded around the oak table.

"Cap'n says it'll ease off by morning."

"The captain is a weather prophet?"

"No, sir, Mr. Butler," the Swede said blankly, "but Cap'n Aronson has seen some seas and some storms."

"We've been seeing this one for three days," Butler said, stretching. He was meaty man with a sallow complexion, pockmarks on his cheeks, and a thick, unruly black mustache.

That wasn't strictly true. The Swede doubted if But-

ler had seen more than five minutes of the storm. He
had been rooted to his chair watching the cards for
most of the last three days.

"Yes, sir," the Swede muttered with grudging servility.
The captain had told him to show respect to these
men, such as they were. Butler, English, Landis, and
Demarest. The four of them had had the money to
pay first-class passage on any ship sailing for Sitka, but
they had chosen the *Cormorant*. She was a sealer and
not a passenger ship, but she was fast and she had
been leaving the night these four made their inquiries.
"Let them complain," Aronson had said, "let them do
whatever they want. They're worth half a thousand
sealskins to us."

Maybe they were, but the Swede didn't like them.
He didn't like carrying passengers and he didn't like
kowtowing to them. He watched the game for a few
minutes more, bracing himself as the *Cormorant* dipped
into another trough and began her slow rise to the
crest of the following wave. His lantern intermittently
flashed on the features of the sealer's four passengers.

Landis was a San Francisco financier. For all that,
he didn't know an ace from a trey and shouldn't have
been in a card game with a man like Aaron Butler.
Charles Landis had been an Indian fighter, a ship-
builder, a mine owner. He had been involved in some
nebulous, possibly illegal China trade for years. Despite that, the white-haired man was somewhat simple,
uneducated but proud. Raised on a Kentucky farm, he
had made himself wealthy by a lifetime of effort. He
took the government's policy of laissez-faire as a personal mandate and was doing his best to grow as
wealthy as was humanly possible.

Sitka, Juneau, the the Yukon were new, explosively
developing fields of opportunity for Landis. He owned
three of the only four lumber mills in a thousand-mile
radius from Vancouver and he meant to solidify his
position on this trip. In his cabin trunk was a small
chest which, if filled with gold, must have been worth
ten thousand dollars, and the Swede, who had loaded
it, had hefted gold in his time. Just now Landis seemed

intent on losing some of his vast wealth to Aaron
Butler. There were spots of high color on Landis'
pallid cheeks, and if the mate of the *Cormorant*
noticed them, then surely Butler did. He threw in his
cards, refusing to meet Charles Landis' raise.

"Damn," Landis muttered. He took the pot unen-
thusiastically, and like the inexperienced player he
was, couldn't resist showing the others the hand he
had held: aces and tens. "That didn't bring much
home," Landis said.

Aaron Butler yawned. He glanced at the Swede as
he did so, and the mate looked briefly away. Butler's
eyes had that effect on a man.

The Swede had been twice around the Horn, had
sailed the Madagascar Channel off Mozambique, out-
run a fleet of Indian pirates, been involved in more
waterfront brawls and knifings than he could remember, but still the dark, deliberate eyes of Aaron Butler
could push away his steady gaze.

A part of that had to do with what the mate knew
about Butler. It was little enough, in fact. Butler's past
was as murky as his eyes when he turned them back to
his new hand of cards. As murky and as violent. They
knew Butler in San Francisco, and what they knew of
him was enough to get him run out of that usually
tolerant city. He was always near cards and women
and violent occurrences, unusually near. What his hurry
was to reach Sitka, where the weather was hard and
the work a man had to do just to survive even harder,
was a matter for the Swede's dour speculation.

"Fold," was the first word Demarest had muttered
the entire time the mate of the *Cormorant* had spent
watching the card game, trying to warm his bones,
which seemed frozen and fiery at once after a four-
hour watch on the dipping, rolling deck of the schooner.

Demarest threw his cards down, leaned back, and lit
a stubby pipe. The blue rings of smoke rose through
the shadowy light. They could hear the wind and sea
above, a muffled ceaseless roar inside the galley. From
time to time booted feet stamped overhead on the
deck. The endless complaining creaks of planking and

fittings punctuated each thought and remark. The cook, Chinese and quite old, worked beyond the card players, bracing his feet expertly with each tilt and swing of the ship, tending his chopping board, ovens, and black iron pots with instinctive dexterity. From time to time a small catastrophe brought a mandarin curse to his lips.

"It was only a two-dollar raise, Demarest."

"That was plenty, Butler," Demarest said. He had his hands behind his neck and was tilted back in his wooden chair. Butler frowned, kicked the pot up another five dollars, and sat looking at the other players, an unlighted cigar in his mouth. It seemed to amuse Demarest.

He had been a prospector, a carpenter, a cowboy, a sandhog, and too many other sorts of laborer to recall. He was thick in the neck, placid around the eyes, and constantly smoking. This one the Swede could understand. He was going to the Yukon for yet another try at riches. Demarest was nearly sixty but as a young man he had done his time in the California goldfields, making enough despite robber traders and crooked partners to support himself in high style until he had made the mistake of marrying a Denver lady who knew all there was to know about spending gold.

"Well?" Butler growled. The young man across the table lifted his eyes. This was the one the Swede didn't understand at all, the fair-haired one with the blond mustache and blue-gray eyes. They said he was a writer of some sort, a man from the East. His hands and arms showed signs of some labor, but his eyes reflected no understanding of a man like Aaron Butler, of the world of cutthroats and gougers, pimps, bullies, cardsharps, and liars.

Or perhaps they reflected a knowledge that had deepened into a sadness near despair. Such judgments were beyond the mate of the *Cormorant*.

"What's it going to be, English?" Aaron Butler demanded.

Richard English shrugged as if it made no difference at all and chipped five more silver dollars into the pot.

The ship canted to one side and the coins slid away, forming a disconnected chain.

Charles Landis was hunched over his cards protectively. His eyes were still, but those spots of crimson had appeared on his cheeks again. Butler knew Landis had a good hand, but Butler, as the dealer, knew he himself had one better.

"A hundred," Landis said, and Butler's eyes flickered appreciatively. The mate looked at Butler, at the lumber-mill owner, and then to Richard English, whose eyes weren't even on his cards. The *Cormorant* hit a huge trough and the deck fell away from them. Butler muttered an oath.

"Damn all, doesn't Aronson know what he's doing with this ship?" More impatiently he looked to Landis, pushed in his own hundred dollars, in gold this time, and glanced at English.

"Don't have it," Richard English said.

"You don't have the cards or don't have the money?" Butler demanded.

"It doesn't matter—I'm out."

Butler growled something as English placed his five cards, faded red backs up, on the table and idly fanned them out.

Demarest had begun a tale. "I recollect in Leadville a miner without a cash dollar. Put up his claim on three sixes . . ."

English lifted vaguely interested eyes to the prospector. No one else paid any attention and the Leadville miner passed into the vague mist of Demarest's memory, to sleep for a time.

"What are you going to do, Landis?"

Landis' eyelids flickered slightly and the color in his cheeks heightened. He was a man of some stature and he was used to being addressed as "Mr." Landis even by men of Butler's class.

The Swede thought that Butler had done it on purpose, goading Landis further than he might otherwise have gone. It seemed to the mate of the *Cormorant* that this was the single hand Butler had been waiting for. Butler had his hand closed up, but the mate could see the king of diamonds, half-curled, peering back at him. Butler glanced at the mate and placed his card hand flat on the table.

"Well?" he asked Landis.

"What's on the table?" the lumber-mill owner asked.

"Two-fifty."

"I'll raise you that again."

Butler's shoulders seemed to relax a little. Richard English looked quickly, penetratingly, at the dark-eyed man opposite him.

"You got it?" Butler asked.

Landis was indignant. "You know I do."

"I don't see the money."

"Mr. Butler, I'll have you know—"

"I don't need to know anything but that your money's good. Mine's there," he said, lifting his chin. "Hard cash."

Butler's stubby finger reached out and tapped the table. The Chinese cook swore as the boat yawed crazily, spilling yet more food. Landis sat slowly reddening at this affront.

"My check, sir," he began stiffly, but Butler wagged his head.

"Table stakes. You going to put up or fold, Landis?"

Landis was content to sit smoldering in the heat of his own indignant anger for a time. Then, looking again at his cards, again at Butler, he slammed a bony fist against the table so hard that the cook looked around in surprise.

"Damn all, sir! I won't be spoken to this way, but I won't be bullied out of a hand either. I trust you'll let our young friend hold my cards while I'm gone?"

Butler glanced at English and shrugged. Landis shifted his hand to Richard and rose, swaying as the *Cormorant* nosed down into a trench once more. Butler's eyes were feral, watching closely as the older man walked steadily toward his cabin.

The Swede thought: That's cracked it. Now he knows that Landis has gold in that trunk.

Butler, apparently self-satisfied, leaned back, finally lighting his cigar. Floyd Demarest began his story again, but no one was listening. Richard English sat looking at the cards he held without fanning them to see what Landis held. A jack of spades looked one-eyed into the margin where a milkmaid or queen or fortune in gold hid away from human vision.

Landis was weaving his way back. The cook turned to watch him, ladle in hand. Butler's cigar had grown half an inch of ash. Demarest's miner had lost his claim back in some long-ago fabled game of poker. The Swede, due back on deck, clung tightly to his lantern and watched as Landis sat, plunked down a stack of gold double-eagles, and recovered his cards from Richard English.

"There, sir," Charles Landis said, "is your two hundred and fifty. Permit me," he went on, "to raise you another one hundred."

Butler didn't even blink. He must have been expecting that. He didn't give Landis the satisfaction of seeing him express any emotion. He took a small chamois purse form his coat pocket and counted out the money, sitting back in a way which baffled and irritated Landis.

"Another hundred?" Landis suggested. Now the cook had forgotten his work completely. The mate's watch duties seemed a thousand miles away. Demarest leaned his forearms on the table and waited expectantly. The young blond man to his left glanced at Landis, showing some interest now.

"You saw my cards, English?" Landis asked pleasantly.

"No, sir."

"I'm not wrong, am I?" he said, as if English hadn't answered at all.

"I think you are wrong, Landis," Aaron Butler said. "I think you're wrong enough to call." Butler placed five more gold double-eagles into the pot and leaned back, tugging at his shaggy dark mustache. "What have you, Landis?"

"Full house, jacks and tens," Landis said, carefully spreading his hand. English was watching Butler, watching him tense and lean forward, his mouth forming into a rictus of fury.

"By God, you . . . English changed cards," Butler raged.

"You know I didn't," the blond man said.

Butler's hand clenched and raised above the table. For a moment English thought Butler was going to club him with it. "You had to!"

Butler's eyes moved around the table, seeking out the man who had deprived him of Landis' gold. Finally he rose, filling the galley with his bulk. Then, wordlessly, he turned and walked toward the hatchway. Eyes watched him silently as a gust of wind hurled rain into the galley. The hatch banged shut and he was gone.

Landis was chuckling as he collected his winnings. English had been holding his breath without realizing it. Now he let it out, lifting his eyes to Demarest, who was smiling distantly.

"What do you think, Swede?" Demarest asked.

The dour mate nodded, staring at the faded deck of cards left scattered on the table.

"What is it, gentlemen?" Landis asked. He was still chuckling, trying to stack the gold, which toppled with each list of the *Cormorant*.

"It went wrong for Butler," Demarest said. The old miner lit his pipe again. "He was cheating, I'm afraid, but he misdealt somewhere down the line."

"Cheating?" Landis shook his head. "Nonsense—I won, didn't I?"

"You won, but Butler wasn't disappointed or angry. He was furious. Didn't you see the way he turned on young Richard here?" Demarest jabbed at English with his pipe stem. "He was sure it was impossible for him to lose, certain that he knew what cards you were holding. The only explanation was that you and English were somehow accomplices, that English had given you a card or two. A swindle went wrong, and it cost Butler money."

"I wonder," Landis said thoughtfully, biting at the tip of his white mustache. "If it's true . . ."

"If it's true, let things lie," Demarest said. "He's got his lesson. It won't do any good to tangle with a man like Aaron Butler over this."

"No, probably not." Landis looked to the mate. "You said something, Swede?"

"No, sir, not me."

"You indicated that you saw something. Did you see him try to cheat me?"

The redheaded mate shook his head again. "I didn't see anything, sir. I'm a sailor." He tugged the hood of his rain slicker up, turned around, and started up the hatchway himself.

Landis leaned across the table, which tilted away from him toward Demarest. The lanternlight shadowed his narrow face and highlighted the cheekbones. "You're sure of this, Demarest?"

"I've seen cards played," was all Demarest would say. "But if I were you, I'd lock that gold up tight. Maybe in the captain's trunk."

Landis was indignant. He, too, had lived a long, rough life. "By God, I've got a .44-40 pistol in my cabin, and I have used that gun before. You don't think he would try to take it back by force?"

"I don't want to guess what a man like Butler would come up with. But I wouldn't sit at a card table with him again."

"No," Landis said soberly, straightening up, his hands on the table before him, flanking the gold.

"And you, young man," Demarest said to Richard, "I'd watch my step as well, if I were you. Butler seemed to believe that you conspired against him."

"He can believe what he wants," English said sharply.

"He will," Demarest said with a wink. "Just take this advice, son, it's well-meant."

The cook was hovering around the table now and English looked at him. "I think he wants us to clear out." He tugged a gold watch from his pocket and glanced at it. "Second watch will be coming in to eat."

Landis had scraped his gold together and deposited it in his pockets. He looked older suddenly, as if Demarest's warning had brought a touch of mortality to him.

English put his gold watch away and yawned. "I'll hit my bunk, I suppose . . ." The ship lurched crazily, and he paused. "Nothing else to do. How many days to Sitka? I've lost track."

"If the Swede was right and this breaks by morning," Demarest said, rising, "three of four days, depending on the winds."

"Eternity," English said with a frown.

"If you don't mind my asking," Demarest said as they started toward their cabins, leaving the cook to set the table the best way he could, "what exactly is it you're going to do in Sitka, English? You've never made that clear."

"Haven't I?" They had come to Richard's cabin door and he leaned against the bulkhead. He might have smiled, but the expression was so faint and fleeting that Demarest couldn't be sure. "Good night, Demarest. Landis."

Then he opened his door and went in, leaving Demarest without an answer. Landis said to the closed door, "If you want me, just knock. You too, Demarest."

Then the lumber baron was gone, shuffling into his own cabin, leaving Demarest to shrug, glance at his cold pipe, pocket it, and head toward his own bunk.

Richard English didn't bother to light the lantern in his small, musty cabin. He found his bunk by feel and lay down, arm flung over his face to listen to the groaning of the *Cormorant* as she made her slow way northward.

Demarest's question rang in his head endlessly. What exactly was he going to do in Sitka? Make his way to Dawson and the goldfields, but why? English rolled onto his side and stared out at the nearly complete darkness of his tiny cabin. A rat scuttled away, scratching its way across the tilted decking. The ship raised its bow again and slapped down into a trough. Maybe it would tear itself apart against the walls of water and the *Cormorant* would join the fleet of dead ships beneath the icy northern Pacific.

It couldn't have mattered less. English turned onto his other side and stared bleakly at the darkness. Thoughts, muddled and empty, surged up in his mind and fell away before he could grasp them, organize them, make any sense of them.

It amused him. He was supposed to be a writer. He was supposed to know what to do with fleeting images, with the hums and whispers of eternity and the shards of ideas his consciousness touched.

He wiped at his forehead, sat up, and felt under the bunk for his whiskey. He drank from the bottle until it lifted his stomach in protest. Then he lay back again, still hearing the storm's muttered threats—impotent threats. What threat can death hold when there is no will toward life to give it power?

He was still young, barely past thirty, and his powers were at their peak. Or what were called powers. The ability to put one word after the other, stringing them like dark beads across a line on his yellow ruled tablet. Add punctuation and the thought is ended, the usefulness of the author ended. The book is closed, then a yawn, the fire banked, the light put out, and on to bed.

But the author lives on somewhere, a real person with demands on his soul, with obligations and debts. And needs—some undefined and vague, as nebulous as the thoughts which sang through the darkened interior of the *Cormorant*. Others well-defined, blond, pert, and haughty, filled with a delight in life.

"Laura." He said her name aloud and the ship plunged downward again. The name, spoken aloud like an invocation, stirred every old agony, desire, and hatred, bringing English to uneasy alertness. He reached again for the bottle.

"There is nothing," he said to the darkness, "like the life of a fool." He lay back to watch the night, the bunk rolling beneath him as the *Cormorant* strove madly on through the stormy sea.

Morning was clear and bright, cold. The captain's promised end to the storm had come, the sea transmutting itself from a prowling gray beast to an endless sweep of sunlight-polished glass. The coastal mountains were blue, hazy monuments on the starboard, Graham Island a vanishing emerald extravagance of nature to the port.

Richard English went forward on deck, standing at

the bow rail as the cold mist broken by the *Cormorant*'s cutting edge washed over him.

"Everything quiet in the night?"

English lifted his pale eyes to Demarest, who, pipe in mouth, had come to stand beside him, arms resting on the varnished rail of the ship.

"Quiet? Yes, why?"

"Don't know. Still thinking about Butler, I suppose," the miner said.

"I can't believe he'd try anything on shipboard. Everyone would know what had happened. He couldn't run away, could he? It was just momentary anger. He'll come to his senses."

"Butler?" Demarest wagged his head. "I know his kind. He'll take the loss of gold as a capital offense."

English wasn't listening. He stared at the vast stretches of jeweled sea, the wind lifting his fine blond hair. His hands were wrapped tightly around the rail, but not from any sense of fear.

"Who is she?" Demarest asked, and English turned slowly toward him, the hard light in his eyes revealing that Demarest had guessed right.

The answer was tight-lipped. "That is none of your damned business."

Demarest watched the young man for a minute and then nodded. "No, I guess it ain't."

There was a silver flask in English's coat pocket and he took it out now, offering it first to Demarest, who refused. "At two bells? Not for my stomach. Want some advice?"

"I don't," English said.

"A man who uses his mind for a living has no business pouring that stuff into his belly."

English's reaction was defiant. He emptied half the flask before his body began to reject the effort. His eyes were watering and red, as he tucked the flask away.

"It's none of your business, Demarest."

"No. You're right. It's none of my business." The older man briefly placed a hand on English's shoulder and then turned away, stumping down the gently sloping deck of the *Cormorant*. He glanced back only once, to see English at the rail, his head on his arms.

Demarest passed Butler near the foresail, but the gambler didn't even look at him. He was deep in conversation with one of the *Cormorant*'s sailors, a Kaska Indian named Wejah. Demarest walked on, hands thrust deeply into the pockets of his red-and-black mackinaw.

Butler was up to something, Demarest knew, but he wouldn't attempt it in broad daylight. He was a creature of the night, of dark and hidden places where a man's actions didn't weigh upon his character.

Landis hadn't been out of his cabin all morning. Demarest didn't blame him. He waved to the captain, walked aft to the taffrail, and leaned against it, watching the sea and the day slip past.

Landis still hadn't made an appearance at lunch. Nor did he come from his cabin at dinner. Demarest and English, the only passengers to appear, sat across from each other at the table eating silently until English said: "The old man is going to starve to death."

"He'll be out when his hunger outweighs his fear."

"Fear! Of Butler? That old land pirate!"

"That's right," Demarest said, "fear. Landis is an old pirate, too, and like all old pirates, he fears for his gold. He's spent a lifetime collecting it, maybe in ways we wouldn't like if we'd been there to witness it. But he's in there shivering, his revolver in his hand, waiting for Butler."

"Then Butler's already had his revenge," English said.

"Maybe. Maybe so," Demarest agreed. "But from what I know of Butler, it takes blood to satisfy him."

"Christ," English said, "it was only a card game!"

"Only that. Only gold," Demarest responded softly. "I've known a few men who were killed for gold, haven't you?"

English didn't answer. Landis had just made an unsteady appearance, looking haggard and worn, as if he hadn't slept since they had last seen him, but had sat hunched over the trunk of gold in his cabin. The flap of his coat bulged where his huge ancient navy revolver rode in his belt.

Demarest tried to liven things up with a few old stories and a few jokes, but no one smiled or listened to the slow unraveling of his tales. Landis, furtive eyes darting in all directions, hunched over his soup and slurped it quickly, noisily. English, who had been at his whiskey most of the day, was trying to float the spoon he had been given by the Chinese cook in his barley broth. Butler remained absent.

"I finally remembered," Landis said, wiping his mustache with his linen napkin.

English lifted his head. "Remembered what?"

"Where I've heard your name. Why, you were quite a celebrity in San Francisco's cultural circles for a matter of months, weren't you?"

"Yes," English said dryly, "for a matter of months."

"*Scorpio Rising*, wasn't that the title of your book?"

English looked as if answering were distasteful. "That was the title."

"Summer love," Landis advised Demarest, who appeared puzzled rather than interested. "That was the subject of the novel."

"Oh?" Demarest said. English had returned to trying to float his soap spoon.

"The ladies quite devoured it. One of my acquaintance . . ." But Landis wasn't getting any more of a hearing than Demarest had to his tales. The author in question seemed bored, and Demarest was only amused at the idea of anyone finding fascination in a book.

"Well," Landis said, "I finally did recall it. Quite good, they say . . . never read such things myself."

English played with his barley broth until the main course came. Then, looking from the cook to the salt pork and beans, he rose and put his napkin on the table. He went up on deck, where the stars shone through the shifting sails and rigging of the *Cormorant*. He put his back to the rail, took a drink of whiskey, shuddered, and put it away. A fleeting thought drifted through his mind. Something useful, something to yank from his entrails and slap down on paper, but again the notion was gone before it could coagulate into thought in words.

He was done. Washed up at thirty. Finished. Well, what did it matter anyway? He could write until he was eighty and it wouldn't extend or enhance his life, wouldn't brighten it or rid it of the nameless sin which haunted his existence, the nameless blight which had caused Laura to . . .

She was cool and almost too beautiful. The moon silvered her pale hair, and she smiled with the deep smile of woman-knowledge. She was far above and distant from English, like a fleeing nymph glimpsed briefly through a summer wood, a spectral image of what a woman should and cannot be. His work had given him entrée into her world. A summer lawn party, all parasols and pastel dresses, dourly chaperoning matrons, balloons floating above the great yellow-and-white house.

And Laura watching in fascination, arms around her knees, listening as he read from his book, a book which might have been designed to conquer her. English's throat had gone dry as he read, and she had risen to come nearer, offering him cool water in a crystal glass, regal and aloof.

She had kissed him by moonlight, a sensual, mocking kiss such as only Laura could give. A kiss which teased, promised, delighted, flooded with desire, and then turned to sudden laughter.

That was Laura, but she had grown tired of art and poets and novelists and turned her capricious eyes to a French nobleman, a Welsh prizefighter, and an Argentine cattle baron. English had stayed on, haunted and obsessed. Work meant nothing any longer, only Laura, and she had only laughed.

"There was nothing to it, Richard. It was fun, but how could you support me? Besides," she had added, her voice sophisticated and childish at once, "Father finds you unsuitable."

He lifted his eyes to the great house, to the white-fenced corrals with their herd of Arabian horses, and repeated, "Unsuitable. It's money, then, isn't it? Nothing but money?"

He had reached for her, pulling her against him, trying to flood her with his need and his want until she could feel it physically, but Laura had stepped back, laughing. "Yes," she said, "of course it's money, Richard. What else is there?"

And then Laura had lifted her skirt and departed, walking across the long expanse of green lawn to the massive iron gate. A dark, slender figure of a man waited at the gate and English watched them ride off in his yellow-wheeled surrey. He watched them go and then returned home to sit, to stare, to watch his numb, useless hand as it crushed a broken fountain pen. . . .

Landis was walking forward now, his head thrown back to allow him to breathe in deeply, to watch the stars above the treetops. The wind gusted and slackened. The halyards grew taut and then sagged. The three rows of reef-points slapped against the canvas of the mainsail forward. The sea was alive with phosphorescence, the low midsummer sun was a ghostly sheen in the southern sky, scarcely brighter than the stars and pale half-moon.

Landis looked weary, and his deep breathing seemed to be a futile attempt to revitalize his aging body. English felt the same urge. His soul was aging far too rapidly. The universe above him seemed to explode with endless vitality, but nothing he could do filled him with spiritual youth.

Some deep empathy toward a man he scarcely knew drew English forward. He lifted a hand and started to call out to Landis, but before he could speak, dark figures, primitive and ominous, yet insubstantial, leapt from the shadows toward Landis. A club was raised, and English called out too late.

"Landis!"

English was running toward the fray, and he recognized one of the men, the Indian crewman, Wejah. The other man rose and spun—there was a gun in his hand.

"You," Aaron Butler shouted, "you switched those cards!"

English had halted abruptly. He stumbled over some unseen bit of ship's hardware and began to back away.

"What are you doing?" the young man asked.

"What do you think?" Butler walked after him, gun still in his hand. In the background English saw Wejah club Landis again. Landis wasn't moving. English looked around, but no one seemed to be stirring on the deck. The masts of the *Cormorant* swayed and creaked, their canvas snapping brightly in the wind.

English had reached the rail, and he stood, arms outstretched, watching the implacable Butler. "You can't get away with this!"

"No?" Butler just laughed. "Why not? Where're the witnesses?"

"I saw it."

"In a minute you won't count," Butler said, and he raised the pistol.

"Are you mad?" English screamed.

"Just unforgiving," Aaron Butler replied, or might have replied. English was never sure afterward. The gun in his hand exploded with flame and sound, and a shocking, searing pain bored into his shoulder. Whether he leapt or fell, English never knew either; all he knew was that he was suddenly over the rail of the *Cormorant*, tumbling through a fiery tunnel before he plunged into the dark and depthless sea.

English stayed underwater in the frigid, moving sea for what seemed an eternity, and when he at last bobbed to the surface, the *Cormorant* was a quarter-mile distant, a toy ship leaving a crescent wake behind her as she sailed on toward Sitka.

The water numbed English's legs and arms. His heart leapt in his chest, protesting the effort of beating. His shoulder ached more than burned, and he had difficulty lifting that arm. It didn't matter. In a few minutes he would be dead, drowned in an empty sea.

He shook his head, looked toward shore or where the shore had been. It was nowhere in sight over the dark swells of the ocean.

"East." He looked to the stars, searching for the Dipper, for Cassiopeia, any of the familiar constellations, but the stars swam and faded, dimmed by the light of the moon and the glow of the midnight sun. He was unable to reconcile the relative positions of the moon and the low arctic sun. In the end he struck out, not knowing how far he had to swim, not certain that he was swimming in the right direction.

English swam on his back, conserving his energy. His body was numb from toes to fingers. His teeth chattered constantly. He moved through the swells, an occasional wave washing over him, filling his nostrils and mouth with salt water.

He would die. He waited for his life to pass before his eyes, but nothing so dramatic happened, fortunately. His life had been bleak and murky and tangled with deception. He wondered if the San Francisco papers would note his passing, or if anyone would.

His head struck a solid object, nearly knocking English unconscious. He went down, flailed to the surface, and reached out. The object, dark and heavy, drifted away. English found it again and wrapped an arm around it, clinging to it for a long minute by instinct alone.

He forced his thoughts to clear, forced his ringing head to reason.

A canoe, he decided. He looked again, not daring to believe it. It was some sort of dugout canoe made of solid cedar. If he could upright it somehow—but that proved impossible with his waning reserves. He simply clung to it, surprised that he could summon the life-urge necessary to hold to the canoe so tightly, to let it take him, drifting, to wherever the currents of the cold dark sea decided.

3

THE roaring in his ears meant something, but what? It was like the chanting of a nation of warlocks, the sound of a blizzard twisting through the stands of aspen in the Rocky Mountain wilderness, the vague, methodical humming of time.

He opened one eye. The world was not quite dark, not quite light. The moon had gone but the golden sun still hung in the sky it shared with the dim stars.

Another breaker slammed its frothing head against the beach and reached out for English with cold talons. He could see the dugout canoe shifting in the grasp of the tide, see the long stretch of kelp-strewn rocky beach. He tried to rise but his body wasn't capable. His shoulder ached dully and his head throbbed in sympathy.

He rolled onto his back and slept, wandering through broken, watery dreams. When English opened his eyes again the stars were gone, the sun brighter, somehow colder.

The Indians were standing in a circle around him.

The first man he was able to focus on out of the haze of pain and exhaustion was vast and painted, wearing a ring through his nose and a bear-claw hat. He had a spear in his hand and he said something to Richard.

"I'm sorry," English said, struggling to rise to a sitting position. "I don't understand you. I can't speak your language. If you could help me find a white settlement . . ."

The big man spoke again, and English was jerked to his feet, his shoulder reacting to the rough treatment with a silent scream of pain. His mouth opened with the shock and he struggled briefly, feebly.

"Please . . . I've been shot."

The Indians didn't respond except to take him by his arms and drag him down the long rocky beach. English looked from face to face.

"I'm a friend," he said. "Just a wounded man."

The faces, broad, dusky, tattooed or painted, didn't change. Overhead a cloud of white gulls cried out derisively. Ahead stood an Indian village built up against a low, sandy bluff, and from the wooden houses dozens of people emerged, pointing, calling out, running toward the incoming party.

English passed out once, momentarily, and when he looked again he was nearer. Dogs were everywhere, yapping and fighting in tangles of fur and fangs. The Indians clubbed them aside.

They waded across a bog filled with spongy decaying vegetation and crossed a narrow inlet where a freshwater stream flowed out of the highlands to duel briefly, futilely with the tidal flow. A man with a hat made of wood and leather in the shape of some wild-eyed bird danced around them, and another with rattles in either hand approached, shaking them, shoving them in English's face.

All around them now were women in skins, children with mocking eyes, men with tattooed faces and brass or bone rings in their noses. Something terrible was cooking in great pots along the shore. Totem poles with strange beasts and birds, painted with gaudy reds and blues, yellows and fading green, rose up before the houses. Eagles, frogs, bears, ravens, and whales were frozen in eternal wooden tableaux.

The dogs had followed along in a constantly snarling pack, still yapping, still fighting. The Indians danced and chanted and spun like dervishes, their faces heavy with paint. English screamed at them. "I'm a friend! What is it you want?" To the man on his right he said, "My arm! For God's sake! Doesn't anyone here speak English?"

They had stopped before a large house with a platform built between the first and second stories. The people fell abruptly silent. Even the dogs had quieted. English could hear the sea again, the sea and the calling gulls.

The man to English's right shook him, bringing a shock of pain back. English stood up straight, guessing that this was what his guard wanted. He stood staring into the glare of the sun off the sand, watching the big house through a shifting veil of near unconsciousnes.

It was an eternity later when the big man with the staff in his hand, a bearskin cloak over his shoulders, emerged from the house and stood on the platform, peering down.

"If you speak English," Richard began, but his guard shook him again and he simply hung there as the man on the platform asked a question. What the question was, what the answer might have meant, he had no idea.

It lasted only a minute or two and then English was turned roughly and half-dragged across the camp. Behind a scraggly, denuded hemlock tree there was a small windowless structure no more than ten feet square, eight feet high. English was taken to this, held while the door was opened, and then shoved inside, to fall ten feet to the bottom of a pit.

"Just a minute, please," he said, too stunned to rise. But he had only a last glimpse of a red-painted face and then the door slammed shut, leaving him in near-darkness. A little sunlight winked through the chinks in the walls of the house above him, but this did nothing to alleviate the gloom. It never touched the floor of the pit where English sat.

It took him a long while to get to his feet, to walk in a slow circle around the perimeter of the pit, looking up at the ledge above him, the locked door and windowless walls. The pit was dug so that it was wider at the bottom than at the mouth. The soil was damp and soft. There was no way to climb out and nowhere to go if he had been able to. Beyond the walls some sort of song went on, raucous, endless, and English, holding his wounded shoulder, sagged back to the earth and sat waiting for whatever might come.

"Hello?"

English's eyes flickered open. Somehow he had fallen asleep—for how long he couldn't tell. Blue light flooded the open doorway above him and he jerked to his feet enthusiastically.

He stared upward, hands on the walls of the pit. The woman, slim and tall, entered the house and crouched down at the edge of the pit.

"Please," Richard said, "help me get out of here."

"Hello," the woman repeated, and Richard slapped at his head in anguish.

"For God's sake, is that the only word you know?"

"For God's sake," she answered, "no."

"I have to get out of here. I was on a sailing ship headed for Sitka when I was assaulted and fell overboard. I've got to get out of here and to Sitka, and from there to Dawson."

"I don't think so," the woman said.

"What in God's name do you mean?"

"No one can go to Sitka, no one can leave," the Indian woman said. She lifted her head and shook her hair. English could see her fine profile in the rectangle of blue light behind her.

"What are they going to do with me?" he asked, peering up at the woman.

"I don't know."

"You don't *know?*"

"No one knows until the Iht tells us. Maybe he will kill you."

"Kill me?" English tried to laugh but couldn't. His throat was strangled with emotion. The woman spoke casually, as if life and death were unimportant matters, matters of total indifference to her.

"Where am I?" English asked.

"Klinkwan village. I am the one who speaks the white language and so here I am." She shrugged and seemed to smile. The light wasn't good enough to be sure.

"What kind of Indians are you?"

"Indians?"

"What do you call your people?"

"Tlingit."

"I see," Richard replied, forcing himself to stay calm, to fight back the urge to demand, to scream, to curse. "And where are we exactly? Where is this town?"

"Klinkwan," the woman said, and there was amusement in her voice. "Don't you listen to me?" She paused and then said, "Did you know your hair has gone yellow?"

In spite of himself Richard laughed. "It always has been, I'm afraid."

"Yes? I have seen whites. I never saw yellow hair."

"Well, be that as it may—look . . . what is your name? Have you a name?"

"Hevatha," the woman answered. There was still amusement in her voice, although what she could have found amusing about a man being imprisoned was beyond English's understanding.

"Look, Hevatha, I must get out of here. I am wounded, I must get to a white town."

"Maybe," she said infuriatingly.

"Maybe! Maybe *what*, for God's sake!"

"Maybe, for God's sake, you will get out of here. Maybe you will be killed, maybe you will be a slave. The Iht and Gunyah must decide that."

English stepped away from the wall of the pit, stared down at his feet for a minute, and ran his left hand through his hair. "Who is this Gunyah—some sort of chief, I imagine? Can I talk to him?"

"Gunyah can't speak to you until the Iht tells him he may."

"What is the Iht? A medicine man? Look, Hevatha, I have to get out of here. Isn't there some way?"

"The decision must be made. Maybe"—she shrugged —"if you gave Gunyah a gift."

"A gift? But I have nothing . . . Wait, I do." English reached into his pocket and found his gold watch. He held it to his ear. It still, incredibly, was ticking.

"Will this do?" He tossed it to Hevatha, who caught it and turned it over in her hands.

"Maybe. I don't know. Someone will say."

"Someone, when . . . ?"

But the woman had risen and now she turned and walked out of the jail, closing the door behind her. English stared at the dark wall of the prison and then with a vicious muttered curse sank to the ground again to sit brooding.

I'll kill you, Butler. Kill you if I get out of this alive.

He was surprised at the savagery of his own thoughts, but analyzing them did nothing to chill the fiery urge toward vengeance. Butler had killed Landis, tried to kill English. Now English was a prisoner of these painted savages. Butler would pay. One day he would pay for this.

It was hours before anyone returned. When the door did open again, it was Hevatha who entered. She carried a long ladder, which she lowered to English, who clambered up, using his one good arm.

"What happened?" he asked as he reached the ledge. He was surprised to find the woman was nearly as tall as he was, and to find that close up she was extremely beautiful, not thick or featureless as most of the other Indians had seemed, but well made, with a fine skull, a delicately arched nose, a somewhat wide, curved mouth, and wide liquid eyes which held laughter.

She was looking at him as he examined her, and it was only when she finished her inspection that she answered. "Well, for now you are to live. Gunyah liked the watch."

"Then I am free to go."

"No. The Iht said you should not go."

"Then," English said, "I'm still a prisoner."

"No. The Iht wanted to make you a slave, but Gunyah said we should keep no white slaves. It might mean trouble."

"You're damned right it would!" English said indignantly.

"So you are free," Hevatha said. "Did you know your eyes are the color of the sea?"

He smiled. "Yes. I knew that."

"I thought fear made your hair yellow and your eyes pale."

"No. They've always been that way. Look, Hevatha, if I'm not a prisoner, then I must be free to go."

The woman shrugged. "Where would you go? To the land of the Nahanis?"

"I don't know where that is. I don't know where I am. But one of your men must be able to guide me, to take me to a settlement. Dawson is where I wish to go," he told her.

"No one will take you."

"I can pay them," English said, but Hevatha shook her head.

"You have nothing to pay them with."

"I can get it—in Dawson."

"No one is allowed to take you."

"The Iht," Richard said with disgust.

"Yes, the Iht. He hasn't decided yet."

"Decided what? I want to talk to this man."

Hevatha said, "He will not talk to you." She pulled up the ladder and carried it outside, placing it on the roof of the jail as English watched her. The sea breeze was fresh, lifting his hair, cooling his body. His clothing, he realized, was still soaked, and he was bordering on becoming feverish. "What's wrong?" she asked. "You are cold?"

"Yes, very." He crossed his arms and stared at her. He was still staring when he folded up, fainting, and fell to the rocky earth, to lie there as darkness swallowed him up.

When he awoke again his head was still ringing. Slowly opening his eyes, English saw that he had been moved inside a house of two stories. He now lay beneath a pile of blankets. Smoke flooded the interior of the house. If there was a chimney or vent hole, it wasn't doing much good. Around him others slept. A circle of Indians sat hunched near the smoky fire, jabbering away. Three naked children were wrestling, a litter of young pups biting at them when the opportunity presented itself.

The air was rank and stifling. There was no light but that of the fire. Salmon by the dozens hung from the roof above the fire, as well as at least two whole deer carcasses. English sat up gingerly. Someone had bandaged his shoulder. A bit of yellow moss protruded from the bandaging. Good, he thought. They'll have infected it and I'll die.

He was aware of the woman's presence before she had gestured or spoken. Hevatha was on the landing above him, looking down. Now she smiled and stared down the stairs to where he lay. None of the others paid any attention to him, even after realizing he was awake and sitting up. He had apparently ceased to become a curiosity.

"Hello," Hevatha said. She crouched down, draping her arms over her skirt-clad knees. "Now you will wish to eat."

"Eat?" His head still wasn't clear. The smoke wasn't helping any. When had he last eaten? His stomach began to respond suddenly as the idea burrowed itself into his consciousness. "Yes, I am hungry."

"Good." Hevatha rose and walked away toward the fire, her hips swaying fluidly. Her body was a study in grace. English was again taken with her beauty, with her difference from the other woman he saw. She returned with a bowl, noticing his eyes on her. She crouched down again and handed him the bowl and a horn spoon.

English tasted it cautiously and then swallowed it with difficulty. He never took a second spoonful. "What in God's name is that?" he asked.

"*Eulikon.* Very good. From potlatch."

"It's terrible. How's it made?"

"*Eulikon* is a good fish. They run in the summer," Hevatha explained.

"This is not fish," English said, poking at the gelid mass in his bowl.

"First, for God's sake, you take the fish and bury them in the ground so they get ripe," Hevatha explained patiently. "Then when they are ready, we dig them up, put them into a canoe. Red-hot stones are dropped in so that they cook. When the oil rises, we call that *eulikon*. That is the oil in your bowl. Very good."

"Not very good," English said. "Oil from putrid fish."

"Do you eat your fish alive or dead where you come from?" Hevatha asked with a teasing smile.

"Not this dead," English said. "I hate to be an ungrateful guest, but haven't you got anything more palatable?"

"Salmon snouts and tails?"

"Not cooked like this."

"No," Hevatha answered, "not cooked at all."

"Never mind."

"You aren't hungry anymore."

"No one would be," English muttered. "You have deer meat. Could I have some of that?"

"If it pleases you." Hevatha took the bowl, tasted it, and shrugged. English leaned back to watch the playing around him. There had to be a way to get someone to guide him out of here. The *Cormorant* was bound for Sitka, and it was likely there by now. Butler's destination had been Dawson, hundreds of miles overland into the Yukon from Sitka. Now that was Richard English's destination as well. There Butler would be turned in to the authorities—turned in and hanged.

Hevatha had come back with strips of venison prepared with some sort of spicy berry and corn. It was smoky, sweet. English began to eat, the woman watching him.

"I have to leave, Hevatha."

"There is no way."

"I want either a boat to Sitka or guide to Dawson."

"Dawson is far away, over the white mountains. No Tlingit travels that far. None but the long rover."

"The long rover—let me talk to him, then."

"Dead," Hevatha answered. "He was Yakwan, my Tlingit father. Now he's dead."

"Your Tlingit father? Have you more than one father, Hevatha?"

"Once another, long ago, far away. He was Cheyenne."

"You're Cheyenne! What in God's name are you doing here?" English lowered his bowl and watched the woman before him with narrowed eyes, understanding now where she had gotten her distinctive features.

"Yakwan brought me," was her answer.

"Yes, but . . ." English began to cough. The air inside the house was stifling. "Can we go outside, Hevatha?"

"We can go where we like." She smiled. "Except Dawson."

Rising with some unsteadiness, English followed Hevatha through the dogs and children to the upper loft. There she put on a parka of sealskin lined with bear fur and handed English a similar garment, worn and much repaired.

"This was Yakwan's," she said. A huge dog with a massive head and a set of wolfish yellow eyes had come to them, growling deep in its throat. Hevatha slapped the dog's head and it turned away, still growling.

"What's that thing?" English asked. He had seen dogs, and large dogs, but never a *thing* like that.

"Tyee. My dog."

"I thought for a moment he was going to tear me apart."

Hevatha shrugged. "Maybe he would have."

They went out then, the dog following. English felt a compulsion to keep his eyes on the furry beast. Hevatha's words hadn't exactly been reassuring.

Outside it was cooler, yet the wind seemed lighter. Offshore masses of gray clouds swept toward them, forming great battlements and towers. Distant thunder rumbled.

"This Yakwan," English asked as they walked the rocky beach away from the village, "how did he come to bring you here? Were you some sort of captive? A slave?"

"No." Hevatha took a deep breath and let it out. She swept her fingers across her forehead, tugging her hair aside. "You see, there was a war where I lived. All the white soldiers came and they killed all the Cheyenne. I ran away. It was snowing very hard, very hard, and I fell down. I could run no more and just lay in the snow. Yakwan found me there.

"He knew there was war, and that I would be killed. I had a fever for ten days and Yakwan took care of me, Yakwan and his brother that the Kaska killed. They brought me north, and here I live."

"You saw your family massacred?" English had stopped. His eyes were filled with sympathetic pain. Pain the young woman had to still be feeling. But he saw no sign of anger or of pain in Hevatha's own dark eyes.

"I saw the war. I was very young. Yakwan said no one was left alive."

"You never tried to go back?"

"To see the dead?"

"No, I suppose not." They started walking again, slowly moving along the gray beach as the thunderclouds moved toward shore, wind rippling the long grass on the low sandy bluffs to the east.

"Yakwan brought me, my Aunt Godak raised me. I am Tlingit now."

"Yakwan was a good man."

"Yes," Hevatha said. "Very good man. A strong man, a good hunter. Not *halo skookum*."

"*Halo skookum*—what's that?"

"Like you, you know." Hevatha pinched his arm above the elbow. "Weak."

"I've hardly been called that," English objected. "I've done hard labor in my time."

"Not for a long time, I think. Not for a lifetime in a hard land."

"No."

"Yakwan took me everywhere. That's why I'm strong. I can hunt or fish, paddle a canoe, drive a dog team, pack snow for a sled. I can do everything!" she said positively.

"You say Yakwan took you many places. Where?"

"Everywhere," she answered. "The land of the Tsetsaut, to the Stikine in the Nahani lands, to Huna and the white mountains."

"The white mountains? Where are they?"

"Oh, over there." Hevatha waved a hand vaguely inland.

"You don't mean the St. Elias range, do you?"

"I don't know," Hevatha said. She had stopped to wing rocks toward the inlet ahead of them. Tyee bounded into the shallow water, chasing them.

"You've been nearly to Whitehorse! You know the way to Dawson and you could take me there, Hevatha."

He took her arms, gripping them tightly, but she shook him away. "No, I can't take you. No one can."

"Because of this Iht?"

"Yes."

"Does he have that much power over you all?"

"Maybe over some. I can't go away, though. If I went, how could I come back? I would have no home at all then. Besides, it is late in the year already for that journey. I don't want to go to Dawson. What for?"

"I could pay you after we got there." English looked intently into the woman's eyes. "You would have all sorts of goods, cloth and steel knives, beads, whatever you wanted."

"I want to stay here," she said. "You are better to stay here too. You are not strong. You could never cross the white mountains. You are just *halo skookum* and worthless for such things."

"How far is it?" he asked, looking to the north and east. "How many miles, Hevatha?"

"Two months for good sledders with a good team if the Nahani or Han don't kill you or the dogs don't get killed crossing a river of ice or rabid wolves don't bite them or you don't break a leg or your sled doesn't break. Two months—or forever to Dawson."

"There must be a way."

"Not for you," she said. "There is no way for you. What makes you want to go there anyway?"

"You wouldn't understand."

"No?" Hevatha laughed. "I understand you—you are a man. You want wealth or a woman or power."

"None of those," English said with irritation.

"No?" She looked at him closely, crouched, hurled another rock into the inlet, and said, "Then you wish to kill someone. That is a mad reason to go to Dawson. To go anywhere."

English didn't respond to that. He was watching Hevatha as she crouched, straightened, and skimmed rocks across the inlet's face. Lithe, clever, totally without malice or artifice. How had this civilization formed such a creature? How did any?

"Where did you learn your English?" he asked her.

"Oh, long ago." She briefly told him about her mother, about Amaya, who had been raised on a reservation. "And then the missionary taught me words."

"The missionary?"

"Johnson. He's gone now."

"I thought I was the only white man the people here had ever seen. None of the others speak English."

"They know some. They don't care to speak it. They didn't care for Johnson. The Iht put his hand on the missionary's head and said the word."

Tyee had come back, shaking the water from his gray-and-white coat, waiting hopefully below Hevatha's hand for a pat or scratch. The woman was watching the clouds roll in.

"The Iht put his hand on Johnson's head—did that mean something?" English asked with a bewildered gesture.

"It meant he would die. And he did," Hevatha said.

"The Iht said a magic word and the missionary got sick and died?" English asked with a disparaging laugh. "Something like that?"

"No." Hevatha turned toward him. "The Iht said the word and then they killed him."

"They murdered the missionary!"

"Oh, yes," Hevatha replied casually.

"Doesn't it bother you, for God's sake? It was a

crime. A terrible crime. Didn't you like this missionary, this Johnson?"

Hevatha thought for a moment. "I don't know," she said. "He never brought me any gifts."

"Just when I thought . . ." English began, but he fell silent, frustrated. He thought he fathomed Hevatha, thought he had found a "civilized" Indian, but the death of the missionary seemed to mean little to her. All she could comment was that the man hadn't given gifts to her. Was that his crime—not having given gifts? To Hevatha, to the Iht, to this Gunyah?

"This is madness." English removed his parka hood and ran a troubled hand through his pale hair. "I've got to get out of here. Someone has to take me to a white settlement."

Hevatha didn't answer except to smile. How many times had she explained to this white man that there was no way to get to Dawson, that the Iht didn't want the man to go, that he was too *halo skookum* to make it on his own, that no one would risk disobeying the law of the Iht to take him? Not without great gifts, anyway, and the man had none, despite his promises.

Her eyes flashed with some angry emotion and lifted to the bluff above them. English looked that way and he too saw the man, stocky, painted, wearing a colorfully woven blanket.

"Who is that? I've seen him before."

"Just Ganook, only Ganook. He wants to marry me," Hevatha said.

"I see." A tolerant smile had begun to lift English's lips.

Hevatha added, "Now he will want to kill you."

"Kill me! What for?"

"Being with me."

"This is hardly what I would call . . . being with you."

"Ganook slays wolf pups," Hevatha said.

"I don't understand you—what does that mean, Hevatha?" English asked with growing frustration. The Tlingit on the bluff still stood staring at them.

"He kills the pups before they can grow and threaten his dogs."

"Oh, I see. But the chief accepted my gift, didn't he? Surely that means I'm under his protection. Gunyah wouldn't let this Ganook kill me, would he?"

"Ganook," Hevatha told him, "is his son."

They walked back toward the village. There was some excitement on the far side of Klinkwan, but it appeared to have nothing to do with English. Men and women were huddled together pointing out toward the sea. Perhaps, English thought, they were afraid of the storm and what it might do to their village.

They passed a clan house—which one, English didn't know—and Hevatha stopped next to the totem pole which fronted it. She said a few words in the Tlingit tongue and then waved, apparently at the corner of the house.

"What was that?" English asked as they walked on.

"I was saying good day to Washto."

"Oh? A spirit?"

"Now," Hevatha answered after a minute's thought. "Yes."

"What do you mean, *now*?"

"Washto was a slave," she said, as if that explained anything.

"Yes?"

"When the house was built, he was buried beneath the corner post."

"He had died?" English asked.

"Not then, no."

English stopped and took her arm. Tyee growled at the action and so Richard let his hand fall away. "Do you mean," he asked with sickening certainty growing in his stomach, "that a man was buried alive beneath that house?"

"Yes." Hevatha nodded. "I told you. Washto." She looked at him as if he were stupid.

"A man . . . It's barbaric, Hevatha. Don't you see that? It's a sinful, pagan act."

"Now," she said, "you talk like the missionary. Be careful who hears you. Some of the people understand your language, believe me. Enough to know the words of sin and evil.''

"Is that why the Iht had Johnson killed? He told you that you were evil?''

Hevatha said, "He told the Iht that the Tlingit laws were wrong. He told Gunyah that the ways of our people were bad. He told us all that only his way was right.''

English was too numb to answer. He walked on with his guide, mute and overwhelmed. He had to get out of here. Had to. The nineteenth century was rolling to a close and these people were still living in the Stone Age, worshiping animals, burying men alive, killing visitors. God knew what else they did. There had to be a way out.

A shout went up from the gathering across the camp and Hevatha turned excitedly to English, gripping the parka sleeve. "Now a good thing is going to happen. Come with me, English, and we will celebrate.''

What, he asked himself, could there possibly be to celebrate ever in this godforsaken, primitive village pasted to the gray coast of Alaska a thousand miles north of San Francisco?

"Are we going to murder someone?'' he asked coldly.

Hevatha paused, looked at him with a peculiar smile, and answered, "No. It is fish-egg time, English, fish-egg time. Come running and see.''

The Tlingit were setting to sea in canoes and chanting as they rowed. Children ran screaming after their elders, leaping for the boats, sometimes swimming after them through the icy surf.

"Where is everyone going?'' English panted as he broke into a trot to keep up with Hevatha.

"To the island, the little island. Hurry up, English.''

A canoe was being held to shore, and in it were Hevatha's adopted aunts, children, and two old men. They reached the canoe by splashing through ankle-deep water, English clambering in just as the Tlingit with a great shout pushed off into the sea. Then they were paddling furiously, the wind sweeping over them. The oldest man sat in the bow, pointing southward.

Ahead a fleet of canoes pointed their bows through the green sea and frothing surf toward a small, barren island.

The island appeared dead and lifeless, but the water around the canoes had come to thrashing, clotted life, and the sky above them was swarming with terns and gulls, flying so closely together that they formed turgid white-gray clouds.

A sleek, thick neck appeared in the water next to the canoe, and then another. Sea lions swimming shoulder to shoulder pressed against them. Now and then one would bellow from deep in his entrails, the sound a roaring trumpet. English had never heard that sound before; now he knew how the sea lion had gotten its name.

It was a mad dash toward the island ahead, sea lions, Tlingit, gulls on the wing. English lifted himself up and looked over the bow as the Indians rowed furiously. Then he saw the silver mass of fish like a living sea moving toward the island.

"Herring," he said. "Millions of them."

Now and then the gulls would dive, not one at a time, but by the hundreds, rising into the air with herring in their beaks, swallowing them as they flew before other birds could snatch them away in midair.

The canoe moved through the swells, and riding up over one rolling breaker, reached the rocky beach of the small island. The Indians leapt from the boat before the old man had tied up to a craggy boulder. All across the face of the island the Indians moved, cutting at the hemlock trees which grew there. In the water where the spawning herring swarmed in a thrashing mass, immeasurable quantities of eggs floated, clinging to rocks and seaweed.

"Come on," Hevatha said, gesturing. "Not here—this belongs to the eagle clan. Our beach is this way."

English followed along. Indians rushed everywhere. There were many small unused huts along the shore, and now, as the Tlingit began to wade into the water, recovering the fish eggs, which were strung together in long strands like colorless pearls, the huts were covered with the roe. Like translucent moss, poles, roofs, trees were draped with fish eggs.

People stuffed the roe into their mouths and waded out, driving the hemlock branches into the rocky bottom of the inlet. In minutes each pole was coated with pearly roe.

"Here." Hevatha, breathless, had finally stopped. Around them Aunt Godak, Aunt Kawclaa, and other Tlingit English didn't know waded into the water, rushed to their own huts with long strands of eggs. The water was thick with eggs, frantic herring, sea lions which rose up and swallowed dozens at a time, and the Tlingit.

English took the stick Hevatha had given him and waded into the water himself. It was icy, alive with the spawning herring. He followed Hevatha's shouted instructions and swirled his branch around in the shallow water, feeling the constant press of herring against his legs and once the solid thump of a pursuing sea lion.

He raised his stick from the water to find it coated with long strings of roe. Like a hod carrier he waded from the water and followed Hevatha up the beach to a hut. She clambered on top and took his stick, spreading the roe out to dry. Everywhere the Indians were singing and cheering, the children screaming as they ran up and down the beach, eating the roe like candy.

"You have tried it?" Hevatha asked as she shinnied back down. She held a string of fish eggs in her hand. Plucking one, she handed it to English, who tasted it warily. Outside of a slight saltiness, it was nearly tasteless. Hevatha was watching him eagerly for his reaction.

"Very good," he told her.

That didn't seem to be enough praise. Hevatha shrugged and grabbed his hand. "Come on. Work while there are eggs."

They ran to the water with new sticks. Hevatha was still holding his hand and it was pleasant, very pleasant. The day passed in vast cold confusion, the constant swarms of gulls raucously competing with the cries of the Tlingit and the bellowing of sea lions.

There was no end to the herring school, it seemed, no end to the roe or the Indians' enthusiasm.

Within an hour English was exhausted and cold. He staggered out of the water with his last load of roe, hung it on a cross pole hastily constructed for that purpose, and sagged to the sand of the beach to watch the limitless vigor of the Tlingit.

For them it was a good time, an important time. A delicacy of the sea had been given to them. Dried, it would help see them through hard weather and less plentiful times. There was something raw and beautiful about it, something which nudged at English's mind until he forced the feeling away with thoughts of the primitiveness of it all.

Hevatha walked toward him burdened with roe. She hung her fish eggs on the pole like a woman hanging wash, and then sat down beside him.

"What's the matter? You are tired?"

"My wound, I think," English answered.

"Later I will look at it. Later I will put more moss on it."

Hevatha sat silently beside him then, watching the people work, watching as Ganyak, the old man, tripped and fell into the water. Everyone laughed and Hevatha clapped her hands in enjoyment. He rose shaking his head, calling a sea lion outrageous names. Then Hevatha turned her head to look at the yellow-haired man beside her, at his narrow face and pale eyes, his lips compressed in concentration. What was he thinking? She didn't understand his mind any more than she had understood the missionary's.

But this one was different from the missionary. She watched him, looking at his pale hands, at the golden hair on them, and she felt a vague uncomfortable stirring.

"What is it?"

English turned to look at her, and his eyes met hers. A sudden knowledge seemed to appear in his eyes, quick, darting shadows moving behind the blue-gray of them, passing away as quickly.

"I have to work," Hevatha said. She rose abruptly

and walked away. Glancing back, she saw that the white man's eyes were still on her, and Hevatha shook her head, not liking the embryonic notion that was living within her now.

She turned, shouted happily to Aunt Godak, who was wearing strings of roe like beads around her neck, and waded into the water once more.

Neither Hevatha nor English saw the man among the rocks and broken hemlock trees, the man with the fishing spear in his hand, the man with the cold obsidian eyes and tattooed face, but Ganook was watching them, watching them with a cold fury which caused his hand to tighten on the shaft of his spear and his heart to swell with anger.

Ganook drove the head of his spear into the sand. Once he did it, and twice and three times, looking down as if he expected crimson blood to seep from the gray earth.

This *thing* cast up by the sea was evil. He was evil as the missionary had been evil. For one gold watch Gunyah had given the white man his protection. One gold watch which meant nothing with its ticking and movements in a land where the sun never set. The Iht could be approached. The Iht knew that whites were no good, that they came only to change the Tlingit way of life. The Iht could say that word and then there would be no more white man to hold Hevatha's hand or follow her movements with his sea eyes.

Ganook looked again at the head of his spear buried in the sand. Then he yanked it free and turned sharply, walking up into the island highlands. When fish-egg time had ended, something would be done. Something to dull the white eyes, something to still his heart. Hevatha would be taught, taught that she could have only one man ever.

4

FISH-EGG time lasted for ten days. The Tlingit moved into the huts on the tiny island and gorged themselves on roe and on herring. The island was draped in fish eggs drying in the sun. The herring still ran and the gulls and sea lions still pursued their limitless prey.

Richard's arm was nearly healed. There was only a smoky blue hole beneath his shoulder, a jagged red scar behind it to mark the passage of Butler's bullet. He sat by the sea watching the Tlingit, from time to time seeing a distant sailing ship dark and miniature on the horizon, making its way toward Sitka or Juneau and the Yukon.

"Can you paddle?" Hevatha asked him, looking at English's arm.

"Paddle? I suppose so. Why? Aren't you fishing today?"

"Not today, it is the anniversary of Yakwan's death. I want to go to the far islands."

She looked to the craggy, golden offshore islands and then to English. "You don't have to go."

"I want to."

"Yes?" She looked at him inquisitively, seeing again small darting shadows in his eyes. "Then get up, lazy *halo skookum,* we shall go."

English rose to walk with her to the beach, but Hevatha, in high spirts, ran ahead of him, her lithe young body alive with the eager forces of nature, her dark hair floating in the wind. He walked after her, feeling old and worn.

The canoe was unpainted, made of cedar, hollowed

out from a single log. It was beautifully formed with a unique technique. After the log was hollowed out, the canoe was filled with water and red-hot stones. The heat expanded the wood and braces were placed inside to cause the canoe to bow out. After the water inside had cooled, the braces were removed and the canoe retained its shape. The canoe was then rubbed with blocks of hardwood until the cedar grain leapt to life and the wood was as smooth and gleaming as if it had been varnished.

Richard English looked to the far islands. They were easily two miles away, and the canoe was heavy. It would be a day's work to get there, but Hevatha seemed to have no doubts about their ability to make it. The woman knew the currents, and riding a riptide, she guided the canoe half the distance, with only an occasional stroke of her wide paddle to correct their course.

The sea was endless, the sky cold, still crowded with storm clouds. The fish-egg island fell away. Klinkwan, to their right, was small and from this distance apparently unpopulated, though English knew that some people were there—slaves and a few overseers. The slaves worked on, having nowhere to go, no hope of a future. They cleaned the houses and hunted and chopped hemlocks and firs for firewood, dried fish on racks, and waited for some undefined, perhaps violent end.

"Gunyah has slaves?"

"Not so many now," Hevatha answered. "Some were given away, some killed at potlatch, but soon he will have more. The other chiefs will have to have potlatch too. Gunyah will be the first to receive gifts and then he will have slaves. His wives will be happy again, they will have many new goods."

"Barbaric," English said almost under his breath.

"Yes, yes," Hevatha said, still rowing. "The missionary said so. The Iht asked him if whites never had slaves. He said not for a time. So what is barbaric is something that one man has stopped doing. I have seen white armies, I have seen Indian armies. I have heard of slaves everywhere. Everything is barbaric. The sea lions eat the herring. We kill the sea lions. Barbaric. You kill a cow or a chicken. Barbaric."

"Hevatha, you are right, but don't you believe in the progress of the soul?"

She smiled. "What is that?"

"Finding the best that man can be. Advancing through civilization."

"Now, that is more missionary talk," Hevatha said.

"No, it isn't." A swell washed over the canoe and English turned his head. "I'm talking of the essence of man, of his soul and his heart, his mind."

"The essence?"

"What makes a man a human being. His higher thoughts."

"His brain. What good is a brain if it can't keep him alive, Richard English? Your brain couldn't keep you alive here for weeks, days. The essence of a man is the entrails. I met civilization, if I know what you mean by that. It seeks many things, like a magic world, but it turns dark and stormy when there is hunger and need."

English just stared at her. Perhaps the woman was right. She had a grasp of ideas that was incredible for one with her small English vocabulary. Had someone filled her with these thoughts? Certainly not Johnson. Her distant, dead Cheyenne mother?

The island was above them, stark against the sky. Fir and cedar clung tenaciously to fluted columns of solid granite. The beach, narrow, long, was clotted with berry vines and skunk cabbage, poplar and cotton grass.

The houses, well maintained, rested back from the water's edge some fifty yards. Hevatha and English tugged the canoe up onto the beach and stood silently looking at the peaked roofs, the totems, listening to the voices of the wandering wind as it swept across the island.

"Come on," Hevatha said, and she started off toward the village of the dead.

"I thought the dead were burned," English commented. "That patch of ground in the village. Isn't that where the people are cremated?"

"Yes, most people. The honored sleep here," Hevatha said with evident pride. "Yakwan was a much-honored man. A fearless man."

English wasn't a superstitious person, but walking toward the weather-grayed, silent houses, the tombs of the Tlingit dead, he felt a chill that wasn't caused by the wind creep up his spine and into the base of his skull. Hevatha didn't seem awed or fearful: she was smiling.

"Here it is," Hevatha said cheerfully. She had stopped before the broad single step of the death house, waiting for English. "Inside is where Yakwan sleeps."

And inside he did sleep, waxen, embalmed in some mysterious efficient way. A man just past middle years, with a lean face, broad nose, and thick lips, lay with his arms crossed on his chest. His hair was long and thick. He wore a copper ring through his nose and a bear's-head hat. His clothing was deeply embroidered with unintelligible, flowing symbols. The shirt was red with black stitching, the trousers of buckskin. At his side lay a spear, a quiver of arrows and a bow, and an ancient musket.

"Hello, Father," Hevatha said, not quietly as people normally speak in the places of the dead, but brightly, cheerfully. "I have come to see you. I have brought a white man. I hope this doesn't offend you, but I know that you had white friends among the trappers. He has come from the sea to stay with us."

Then, as English shifted from foot to foot, Hevatha crouched by the dead man's side and began to tell him everything that had happened in the village, of marriages and murders and family quarrels, of births and successful hunts, of fish-egg time and potlatch.

It took her nearly an hour as she recalled each event in detail, sometimes laughing at a memory. English looked around the house at the carvings, the hunting trophies, skins and weapons, bowls and baskets, at the broken sled in one corner.

When Hevatha finally rose, he was more than ready to go. The place was oppressive and disturbing in ways he couldn't define. Perhaps he knew he shouldn't be

there, that he was an intruder in the house of the
dead, an intruder in the culture of the Tlingit.

Outside, it had begun to rain. The storm had finally
gotten a foothold on the land and it drifted over the
island and toward the coastal village like a steady,
endless beast.

Hevatha didn't seem to mind the rain or the wind.

"That was a good visit," she said as they rowed
away from the beach. She was thoughtful for a while
and then repeated, "A very good visit."

"Does he . . . speak to you?" Richard asked, and
Hevatha looked up at him sharply.

Then she laughed. "I don't think dead men speak,
do you?"

"I just wondered what you thought," he explained.

"I think that Yakwan is dead. I think that one day
far in the future he will come back to life and walk the
earth again because he was a good man, a strong man,
a brave and honored man."

The wind shifted her dark hair. She paddled rhythmi-
cally on, and the sea grew grayer, the swells growing
in size. English said nothing more on the subject of
the dead.

"The village, Richard," she instructed, "not the fish-
egg island. The sun is gone and the eggs can dry no
more. The people will be coming home with the eggs."

"All right." He adjusted his paddling and together
they aimed the bow of the canoe toward Klinkwan:
toward home. The notion disturbed English, disturbed
and angered him. The fish-egg hunt had distracted him
briefly, the visit to Yakwan's tomb had occupied his
mind, but as the village grew larger through the steely
mesh of the downpour, he realized that he was still a
virtual prisoner, that ahead lay his prison.

His arms ached but Hevatha, singing under her
breath, rowed tirelessly. English tried to feign the
same sort of strength, but Hevatha knew. She knew
and she smiled.

"You are always smiling, always laughing," English
shouted.

"It makes you angry."

"Not angry, but can't you be serious?"

"Yes, very serious. And then," she added happily, "I smile."

And she did. The rain fell down coldly, the storm tossed their canoe. The paddling had brought a glow of pain to English's shoulders and chest, yet she sat smiling, pleased with herself and nature.

English could see other boats now, returning from the small island. The canoes were dragged ashore and weighted with rocks. English jumped out of the canoe as they approached the shore and towed it onto the rocky beach. Hevatha climbed out and pushed. Together they pulled the heavy cedar craft to its resting place.

Everyone was scurrying for shelter. There were already fires lighted in many of the houses. Hevatha looked at English, who was obviously exhausted, and said, "Go home now. Rest and eat."

"Where are you going?"

"To see another friend."

"A friend?"

"Yes. Up there." She gestured toward the bluffs.

"I'll go with you."

"If you want." She shrugged. They walked swiftly, silently, away from the village, the rain gusting against their bodies. English lifted his face to the rain and breathed in the cold air.

Hevatha said, "I was born a twin, English. It was foretold that I would come north. A falling star was seen to break in half. One half fell to the north, the other to the south. My sister, if she is alive, is in the southern lands. You ask why I laugh so much—I don't know. There is no room for sorrow in me, that is all. My sister's name was Akton. When we were young she was always serious, I was always having fun. The old women in the tribe said that while we were in my mother's womb something happened—Akton was burdened with all the seriousness while I received all the laughter."

"Do you remember much about your girlhood?"

"Cheyenne times?" Hevatha leapt a rock. "Sometimes I don't remember much, but then at night I will think and recall many things. My mother, my father, whose name was Indigo and was very strong, our little brother, Dark Moon. The buffalo. The long plains, the tepees, the fun of being young in those days of freedom, the fear of the white soldiers." She broke off. "Up there is where my friend is."

They climbed to the secret place where Kaish was kept away from the tribe in her underground home. "A man shouldn't go near her," Hevatha said, "but since you are white, it doesn't matter."

"Near *her*?" Richard said, stunned. "Do you mean a human being is living here, in this hole in the ground?"

"Yes," Hevatha answered. "She must. She is approaching womanhood."

"My God!" English murmured. "Out here."

"Some of the young women live in pits in the clan houses—I will show you Hawwat sometime," Hevatha said, as if nothing could be more natural. In her world, English supposed, nothing could be more natural. "Bear-clan girls stay outside, though. But they have food and furs and blankets, and friends bring them songs."

English could not respond. He watched as Hevatha crouched down in the rain and uncovered the pit in the ground. The rain twisted and drove down in the wind off the ocean. Hevatha began to speak to the young girl in the hole, telling her about potlatch and fish-egg time. English kept his head turned away. Where *was* he? On what planet, in what time?

It was an hour before Hevatha had finished and covered the pit once more. She stood up, smiling, and said, "Now I have done my duty for the day."

English muttered something unintelligible. His impulse was to pull the girl out of the hole in the ground, but what would that accomplish? The poor creature probably wouldn't come anyway.

They walked slowly back toward the camp. Once Hevatha said, "I wonder if this storm is touching Koosh." English had already heard about Koosh, the runaway slave.

"At least he is free," English answered.

"And you are free, English."

"Free . . ." English choked on the word.

"And alive." Hevatha had stopped. Now she faced English, her rain-bright face lifted to his. Her hand touched his coat at the wrist and she smiled.

English put his arm around her waist and drew her to him. His lips met hers, tasted them, sought a deeper response.

She pushed him away and stood looking at him curiously, knowingly. "Yes," she said, "you are a man, aren't you?"

And then she laughed, laughed until English felt the tips of his ears burning. She turned and started away, and as he reached for her she began to run through the cold gray storm.

At last she slowed, looking back to where the yellow-haired man stood watching her. Then, pursing her lips thoughtfully, Hevatha touched her mouth with her fingers, smiled, and walked slowly on. It had been a full and unique day.

English watched the woman until she vanished through the misty haze of the rain. Then he bit angrily at his lip. What sort of fool was he, anyway? Just a creature of his own needs, of nature's urge to approach itself, male and female? She had so much as mocked him, this savage creature of the north, this huntress, wilderness child, absurd thing. But he could not be sure if his anger was with himself or with Hevatha, with his own natural needs or his sense of isolation. The rain washed down around him and he started toward the village.

If Hevatha resented the kiss, remembered it at all, he could not tell. In the morning the storm had become a cold drizzling sky and feeble breeze off the northern islands. Hevatha came to him while the rest of the clan house still slept and shook his shoulder.

"What is it?"

"I am going hunting. Do you want to come?"

Stiff from the rowing, sleep-fogged and weary, he rolled out of his bed of skins and climbed to where

Hevatha waited on the landing. Tyee was with her and his yellow eyes flashed as English approached, slipping into the parka which had belonged to Yakwan.

"Yesterday," English began, but Hevatha shook her head. Nothing had happened; there was nothing to speak of.

"Can you hunt?" she asked English.

"I've done my share."

"With a bow?"

"No," he admitted.

"It is different, English. When I traveled with Yakwan I saw white hunters. They hid in the bushes and waited for game. From a long walk away they shot and killed what they saw. We must stalk, carefully, silently, keeping the wind in our favor. Can you do this?"

"I'll try," English said a little stiffly. Did she have to assume that she knew everything and he knew nothing at all about life and survival?

"The dog's not going, is he?" English asked, nodding at Tyee, who watched motionless and primitive.

"Tyee knows how to hunt." She picked up her quiver and examined her bow. "Are you ready?"

"Don't I get a bow?"

"Not this time," she said, and English had to swallow a response. Did she think he was nothing but a boy to be raised with Tlingit wisdom?

The rain spattered down, drizzling and then clearing away entirely before coming in with brief squalls. The alder and pine trees were thick with water, the long grass bent under the weight of the rain. Tyee bounded ahead of them and then circled to walk at their heels as they climbed through a tangle of berry vines, followed a sandy path to the bluff, and walked deeper into the interior than English had been before. Once the clouds parted briefly and he had a glimpse of wide valleys, grass-green and empty, of snowfields which stretched away to the purple-gray mountains, of long forests which seemed virtually impassable.

Hevatha led them surely through huge stands of skunk cabbage, through deep fir forests to an icy river where water sheeted over gray stones forming three-tiered falls. The river twisted away through vines and underbrush and was lost in the deep blue-green forest. Hevatha motioned to English and crawled out onto a mossy ledge. When Richard caught up with her he was able to look down at a quiet fern-lined pond below.

Without saying anything, Hevatha put both thumbs in her ears and held her fingers up. The deer would come here to drink. She placed her quiver of arrows on the rock, withdrew one, and sat cross-legged, waiting.

English sat a little way behind her, watching the forest, the slim back of the woman before him. To his right Tyee lay chewing on a green twig, yellow eyes half-closed in concentration.

The rain had stopped and here and there a patch of clear sky showed through the masses of clouds. The forest below trembled in the wind. English would lift his eyes to the interior time and again, looking toward the white mountains, toward Dawson.

The buck walked slowly to the water, graceful and delicate in its tread, great rack of antlers shadowing his face. Hevatha had yet to move. She sat watching with all the patience of a wild thing.

As the buck bowed its neck to drink from the pond, Hevatha's hand reached out and drew her bow silently to her. She nocked the arrow and raised her bow without disturbing the buck, which drank, then lifted its muzzle, looking around cautiously before drinking again.

An arrow flew past Richard's head from behind, and the deer was away in three bounding leaps, lost in the forest. Hevatha rose and turned and Tyee leapt to his feet, snarling. English sat immobilized, unsure what had happened.

"Get down. Down here," Hevatha commanded, and English, still uncertain, followed her directions obediently, rolling down the rocky ledge to a shallow hollow nearer Hevatha.

She stood over him like a savage sentinel, bow in her hand, the arrow half-drawn. Finally she said, "He won't do it again, not while I'm here."

"Who?" English rolled to a sitting position and then stood, dusting off. "What happened, Hevatha?"

"Ganook. Only Ganook."

"He tried to kill me!"

"Yes." Hevatha shrugged and lowered her bow, releasing the tension of the string. "Now he has made up his mind that you will die."

English stood a moment, frowning without answering. It sank in slowly and he began to feel fear breathing on his neck. What defense did he have if the Tlingit decided to kill him? None at all but Hevatha.

She was looking to the pond below them, her eyebrows drawn together. "It was a fine buck," she said with regret.

"Yes, it was a damn fine buck, Hevatha, but what about me? What about my life?"

"You are alive," she answered lightly.

"Yes, for now," he said hotly.

"Now is all we can be sure of, Richard. However, I will speak to Gunyah. Perhaps he has not given permission for Ganook to kill you."

"You say that all so matter-of-factly," English said with cold anger. "And what if he has given permission, what if Ganook doesn't care about his father's permission? What then?"

"You could kill Ganook," she said brightly.

"I could . . . Hevatha," he said, taking her by the shoulders. "I don't want to kill the man. I want to go away. Don't you see that I'm a slave here? *You're* a slave."

"I am no slave," she said positively.

"As much a slave as Koosh was. You aren't free to go. All you are allowed to do is hunt and work and eat and sleep."

"What else is there, English? What else is there?"

Richard's hands dropped away. "I saw the inland," he told Hevatha. "Through the clouds. There's not much snow there. It looks passable to me."

"Not in the mountains," she answered. "Besides, it is already nearly Moon Child Time."

"It's *what?* Please, no riddles, Hevatha."

"A riddle? A joke?" She looked at him with pity. "Don't you even know what time of the year it is? What good was that gold watch of yours? It's a good thing you gave it to Gunyah. It served no purpose but to confuse you. Every Tlingit knows the days of the year, the way nature changes.

"First," she told him, "there is the Time When Everything Is Born. That is the warm time of the year. After that comes When Everything Commences to Fatten; when When All Birds Come Down from the Mountains. That was when you arrived here, English, but it is nearly ended. Soon will come Moon Child Time, when the first snow falls on the mountains and the bears begin to get fat. Later we will have When the Snow Has to Be Dug Away from the Doors. Then When Every Animal in the Mother's Womb Begins to Have Hair. Goose Time comes next—that means that soon there will be less snow, that the sun will return. There are Flower Time and Salmon Time later, but they are far, far away—no one can travel until then."

"I must," was all English said. His gray-blue eyes were on the distances. "I must."

"Because of Ganook?"

"Because life is out there. I am going to die here, Hevatha, perhaps not at Ganook's hand, but I will surely die of this."

"Don't men die in Dawson, Richard English?" Hevatha asked. When he didn't answer, she went to tiptoes and her cool lips brushed his cheek. She turned and walked away, hands behind her back clasping bow and quiver, the great gray-and-white dog behind her, leaving English to look toward the mountains until the clouds again closed off the view and left him locked in the land of the Tlingit.

When English got back to the village, the people were in the middle of frantic packing. He stood in the middle of the beach looking around in incomprehension. Women were bundling children in furs. Men ran across the beach from house to house, dogs yapping at their heels.

Was some invader making his way into the Tlingit

land? Not until he found Hevatha at the clan house
did he manage to dispel that unhappy idea. She too
was packing, and he approached her, watching silently
for a minute.

"I have fur boots for you, English," she said without turning from her cedar trunk. "Maybe too small.
You try them."

"What is going on, Hevatha? Is it war?"

"War, no! Potlatch."

"Again? I thought Gunyah just held potlatch."

"Yes, but now it is someone else's turn. Hultish of
the Tuxican village has send word. Aunt Godak says
the old man is impatient to return potlatch before it
snows. He doesn't want to spend the winter brooding
about Gunyah's success. Anyway, we are going. Everyone. Walking to Tuxican."

"How far is that?"

"Not far. Half a day. Then everyone will eat and
dance. The men are gathering their costumes, hoping
for great gifts. Hultish is even richer than Gunyah.
There will be much."

"We have to go?" English asked wearily. He sat on
a carved bench beside Tyee, who growled perfunctorily.

"Have to go?" Hevatha turned curious bright eyes
on English. "Why would someone not want to go?"

"I don't want any gifts and won't get any—nor will
you. It's a long walk for a meal."

"But we meet all of our old friends, speak to our old
enemies, seal the bonds of blood between Tlingit and
Tlingit. Why would someone not want to go?"

"Maybe someone is not Tlingit," English said dourly.
He dropped his hand onto Tyee's head and the dog
growled again, but as he scratched its ear abstractedly,
the malamute allowed his familiarity.

"We are going. I am going. Do what you like,"
Hevatha said.

English watched her for a minute longer. "Hand me
the fur boots," he said. "Let's see if they fit."

They walked north in a long column, strung out
behind Gunyah and the Iht, who led them in full

regalia toward Hultish's village. The Tlingit were mad with glee, a response that completely eluded Richard. The entire idea of potlatch was one which he couldn't come to grips with. One chief gives all his goods away to another chief and his people. The other returns the favor. Nothing much has changed, but somehow the chiefs have gained stature.

The clans practiced their songs endlessly, wearing against English's nerves. The toneless singing, the constant clatter of their rattles, was enough to drive him mad. The Tlingit, on the other hand, seemed to enjoy it immensely.

"Perhaps you should know the stories," Hevatha said, "then they mean something. Listen now to the raven clan. They sing, 'Once the raven was white. This was in the days when there was no sun in the world. Before raven brought light there were no stars, no moon, no sun. Then raven flew high beyond the veil and brought back light.'"

That was all there was to the song. How the raven had brought light to the world, English didn't understand. "How did the raven get black, then," Richard asked, "if he was once snow white?"

"The evil Iht," Hevatha said. "He was angry because raven had such powers and locked him in his hut. Raven tried to fly out of the smoke hole but the Iht's spirits kept him inside until smoke from the fire blackened raven." She looked at him happily, sure that now English understood the importance of the raven song. English understood nothing, but it seemed that the legend reinforced the idea of the Iht's power while giving the clan something to be proud of. Other than that, it was a foolish legend, childlike, scarcely intelligible.

The village of Tuxican appeared out of the low mists that had drifted in off the sea. This Tlingit town was set higher on the bluff than Klinkwan, but otherwise it looked much the same, fish eggs drying, totem-decorated square houses, yapping dogs everywhere.

The people of Klinkwan entered the town and were met by the people of Tuxican. There was much formalized embracing, the shaking of rattles, the piping of bone whistles, the thumping of drums.

English removed himself from the clamor. The Indians made more noise than the surf that drove its head against the sea rocks behind him.

There was a joy in their meeting which he wasn't capable of fathoming. Now and then he saw poorly dressed men or women on the fringes of the activity and he guessed them to be slaves. People who might not survive the display of largess their chief had planned.

Richard went to the sea and stood looking. He was surprised to find Tyee beside him and he patted his head. "There's nothing much for the Tlingit dogs at potlatch, is there, Tyee? More scraps. That's all."

Tyee suddenly bounded away, running for no good reason through the surf with seeming effortlessness, amazing strength, and great exuberance. A breaker five feet high crashed over the dog, burying it in a wall of water, and English started that way, worried for Tyee. But as surely as if he were a sea lion, Tyee rode to shore, stepped nimbly across a field of pocked gray rocks, and shook himself, sending a vast spray of cold seawater everywhere.

Tyee was in his element. That was the difference between them. If Tyee cared nothing for potlatch, he would endure it with a canine interest. English wasn't capable of such endurance.

When Hevatha found him he was in a somber mood, standing on the beach, a length of driftwood in his hand, writing in the gray, trackless sand.

Hevatha stood beside him a minute, staring down at the characters etched there.

"Can you read, Hevatha?" English asked, still staring at what he had written in the sand.

"Read? Yes, I can read," she answered.

"The missionary taught you?"

"No. Not him. No one taught me to read *that* language."

"What do you read, then?" he asked. English's voice was nearly toneless and she looked at him closely.

Some old spirit had come to haunt the yellow-haired man.

"I read all the symbols."

"The Tlingit don't write anything down," he said sharply.

Hevatha looked puzzled. "Things are written everywhere. There are symbols on the totems and on the masks and sewn into the clothes we wear."

"How did you learn to read?" he asked as if with exhausted patience.

"I listen while someone tells me what the symbols mean. Then I say it again when I want to—how can I read anything if someone hasn't told me what it says?"

"Never mind," English said sullenly.

"You mean some other kind of reading, English?"

"Yes." He hurled his stick into the sea and saw it bob away. "Some other kind of reading, Hevatha."

"Well, don't worry," she said with a smile, gripping his arm tightly. "No one has to read that way here. Don't worry for me."

"No." He looked at her, ran his hand over her sleek head, and said, "I won't worry for you."

"Come on, now, potlatch is now. There is much to do, much to celebrate."

She took his arm and turned him away from the single word he had written in the sand: "Laura."

Hultish, the ancient chief of the Tuxican, was on a platform much like that used by Gunyah. He was making a long raspy speech while the visitors watched with apparent great interest. The Iht was there, Gunyah and Ganook. The Tuxican's own shaman, very fat and owlish, stood by in an elaborately decorated blanket, a labret of whalebone through his lip, arms folded.

Hultish spoke a name Richard recognized, and he glanced that way as Gunyah climbed the steps to the platform. Gunyah's voice droned on endlessly until Hultish embraced him and pointed toward a long sled, a carved canoe, pots of iron and of copper. The giving went on so long that English yawned and turned away. A Tuxican was staggering toward them. He carried a huge clay jar and he stopped before Richard, peering at him out of befuddled eyes. The Indian spoke and touched Richard's hair.

"What did he say?" English asked Hevatha.

"He says he had a dream a yellow-haired man would come."

"Oh." Richard nodded amiably to the Tlingit.

The Tlingit hoisted his jar and offered it to English. "Now what?"

"He wants you to drink *hootch-i-noo* with him. Don't do it, Richard English, it is bad drink. Makes men stupid."

"Liquor, you mean?" English asked.

"Yes. Very bad poison."

Hevatha looked concerned but English took the jar and said, "Tell my friend here that there is nothing in all of God's world that I would rather do just now than drink *hootch-i-noo* with him. Drink it until I can't stand."

He lifted the clay jar and poured the raw liquor into his mouth. It tasted terrible, burned horribly, but English swallowed it, handed back the jar, and wiped his mouth.

"Richard, please," Hevatha said, "not too much."

"No? And what else is there for me to do here, Hevatha, what else in this land God has forgotten?" The Tlingit, pleased to find a new drinking friend, gave the jar again to Richard, and English drank again, even more this time, until his nostril and eyes burned with the stuff. He put his arm around the shoulder of the drunken Tlingit. "My first friend. My first Tlingit friend, you see,, Hevatha. Aren't you happy for me? Drink again, friend, and then give the jar back to me. Let's drink potlatch away, drink time away, and then we'll sing songs together."

Hevatha turned away. She had other things to do than watch men get drunk. "Tyee—come with me," she called, but Tyee remained rooted where he was, watching English drink. The Tlingit had taken his fox-head hat with its matching cape from his own head and had put in on English's. Hevatha, fighting back a smile, walked on, lifting a hand, calling out to an old friend who stood talking to Aunt Godak.

The dancing had begun in earnest, although gifts were still being given. A team of beautiful white sled dogs had been hitched to Gunyah's gift sled and the chief of the Klinkwan village briefly rode the sled along a patch of white sand before he decided it was beneath his dignity. Then the team and sled was led away.

Richard's friend was named Not-ti-sha, at least that was how it sounded to English's ears. At first they tried to introduce themselves, to talk in a primitive fashion, but that was too much trouble and so they returned to simply drinking.

A long train of dancers wound past where Not-ti-sha stood, and with a whoop he joined them, tugging English after them. English's fox-head hat slipped over his eyes and he pushed it back from his forehead, drinking as he danced among the painted, tattooed Indians. All of them wore some bit of fox fur, a cape, a tail, a head. English decided he had been adopted by Tuxican's fox clan and he danced wildly with them, following their winding path up the beach, passing the jar of liquor to new friends, who drank it down happily, rubbing bellies, slapping English on the shoulder as if he were the finest man on earth.

In the middle of the camp the fox dancers joined the men of the other clans, the men from six different Tlingit villages. They began to dance in opposing circles around the fire, five hundred men, English among them, his ears roaring with drums and with *hootch-i-noo,* his vision vague and deceiving. He had lost Not-ti-sha and was dancing beside a man in a bearskin. A fresh jar of *hootch-i-noo* was passed to English and he drank again, laughing, signing in his own language, "Oh the raven was white and he brought the light . . . black bird. The fox clan ate him up!"

Those around him seemed to approve of the song. It didn't matter that no one understood a word of it. "We are fox clan!" he shouted, moving the jaws of his fox hat. "We dance the loudest and sing the . . . sing the loudest . . ."

He was suddenly out of breath, vastly confused, though still exhilarated. He staggered away from the crackling bonfire, which shot flames thirty feet into the air, moving through the endless ranks of potlatch dancers, ravens and bears and eagles. Not-ti-sha was gone, the fox clan was gone. The liquor was gone.

Looking around in befuddlement, English saw the fox-clan members dancing toward their chief's house, and he ran to catch up, falling once, to rise with scraped knees and elbows. When he again joined the fox-clan dancers, they laughed, held him up, handed him a jar of liquor, and danced on. Tyee was with them, leaping and turning, following English as they moved back across the village.

Beneath a row of hemlock trees the fox-clan men stopped and sagged to the ground. English was tugged down to join them. Still more jars of liquor were produced and someone started a fire. An old man stood, bowed to English, and said something that made everyone laugh. English bowed in return and they laughed louder.

Then the old man began to recite a tale—the origin of the fox clan, English guessed. He watched with steadfast attention, listening in earnest. If one listened hard enough, one could understand somehow. But he didn't understand it, nor did it matter. It was good to sit with the men of the clan, good to drink their liquor and wear the fox-head hat. Good to have a dog beside you and a low fire.

Hevatha had appeared from somewhere and she stood, arms crossed, watching him tolerantly. Richard lifted a hand and pointed at his fox hat and she smiled, nodding her head.

The woman seemed pleased. Perplexed, but pleased. Perhaps she was thinking that *hootch-i-noo* was good for something after all. The old man spoke on and Richard watched his gestures, glancing from time to time at Hevatha. Later she would tell him what the story meant.

Richard was watching intently, his head cocked to one side. The liquor was warm in his stomach. He heard Tyee growl and reached out to quiet him. As he did so, he felt a hand rest lightly on his head, heard someone behind him speak a single word.

Then Hevatha screamed and the fox-clan men leapt to their feet. Richard rolled to one side and looked up to see the Iht standing over him.

"The death word," Hevatha cried out. She rushed across the fire ring to where Richard sat. He came to his feet, anger flashing in his eyes. The Iht, pleased with himself, shook a rattle in Richard's face as Hevatha watched with horrified eyes.

"Damn you, you old faker," English thundered. His hand reached out, snatching the rattle from the Iht's hand, flinging it into the fire as the fox-clan men of Tuxican stood watching motionlessly, shocked and awed. "You sneaky, dirty old devil," English said, and he started walking toward the Iht, who backed away.

"English!" Hevatha screamed. "Don't touch him. Don't put a hand on the Iht!"

She was to his side, trying to push Richard away from the shaman. The Iht reached out, grabbed her arm, and hurled her to the ground. Before Richard could react, he heard a low growl, saw a single yellow eye bright with firelight, a mass of thick gray-black hair fly past him and into the body of the Iht, who went back with a cry of fear, Tyee on top of him, slashing at his face and throat with his terrible white fangs.

"Tyee! Tyee!" Hevatha shrieked, but it did no good. She grabbed the scruff of his neck and pulled him away, still snarling and snapping.

English, suddenly sober, looked from the Iht, dead or badly injured, his face and chest bathed in blood, to the fox-clan dancers, who for now remained immobile, incredulous.

Hevatha suddenly had his hand. "Run," she said. "Now!"

"Where . . . ?"

"Run. After me, English. Run now before they kill us."

English took to his heels. From somewhere a shout went up. He didn't pause to look back to see if they were being followed. He had the feeling they were, had the feeling that death was just behind him, but the liquor still fogged his mind and the Tlingit camp, the people, buildings, trees, passed in a blur.

Hevatha was ahead, sprinting toward the darkness beyond and above the camp. He followed her blindly. A painted man in a bear's head stepped out from behind a tree and held up his hands. English just ran by him, feeling a hand tear at his arm. The firelight was still in his eyes, and before it he saw moving ravens, eagles, bears, and foxes. He tore the hat he wore from his head, wove through a small knot of people, and followed Hevatha on, his head throbbing, his lungs ready to burst.

He had lost Hevatha in the darkness now but caught a glimpse of Tyee and ran that way. They were behind the chief's house, Hevatha pausing to grab his arm and shove him.

"Keep running."

Instead he stopped, looking behind them. Now there was pursuit, a mob of Tlingit carrying spears and clubs, still dressed in their potlatch costumes, rushing after them. English recognized Ganook at their head, spear hoisted overhead. Hevatha was fooling with something on the ground behind Hultish's house, English couldn't tell what. He walked that way and was met by a chorus of low growls. The night had come to life with dozens of yellow-eyed beasts. English backed away.

"I told you to run on!" Hevatha said.

"What are you doing?"

"We will need this. Go on, now." At last he perceived what she was doing. Gunyah's gift sled packed with his presents was behind the house, and now the dog team, also a gift from the Tuxican chief, was hitched to the sled.

A shout went up behind them and English, glancing

back toward the village, saw Ganook increase his speed, urging his fellow Tlingit on.

"We've been seen!"

"Run, for God's sake," Hevatha said.

Hevatha had the sled upright now and she lashed at the dogs. Tyee ran to the lead dog and started biting at him, forcing him to his feet. The sled shot off up the grassy slope, Hevatha running beside it. English belatedly started to run as well, his stomach threatening to heave up its contents, his legs moving leadenly, uselessly. An arrow from behind flew past, within inches of his head, and embedded itself in a fir tree. A crazed shout of anger—Ganook's shout—sounded shrill and terrible, wolfish in the night.

They were into the trees now, weaving through the massive pines and cedars, Hevatha running beside the dogsled. "Here!" she called, and Richard staggered that way, running drunkenly, his hands hanging limply, his mouth agape.

He saw the patch of bluish snow beyond the trees, saw the deep valley dip away and run toward the far river, and he ran crazily toward the dogsled, hearing the dogs yap, the Indians behind shouting to each other. He grabbed the rail and leapt onto the sled, and as it hit the snowfield it seemed to accelerate, to glide away at double its former speed, to sweep down the blue, packed snow, the dogs barking excitedly, Hevatha still running beside the sled, whip in hand.

Looking back, English saw the Tlingit slow, form a long line out of the bunch they had been in as the swifter runners began to outdistance the slower. But the sled plunged on, kicking up tiny whirlwinds of snow, and Hevatha, tireless and quick, guided it toward the long river that was the boundary of the Tlingit land and the beginning of the endless wilderness.

5

THE sled with the woman running beside it and the exhausted man riding crossed the river at a shallow ford and made its way up the wooded slope beyond, the dog team working silently now, the great yellow-eyed malamute running before it as they gained height and distance.

Hevatha slowed the team, jogged on for another half-mile, and then, on a treeless rise, halted the team to stand bent over, hungrily breathing in the cold air.

English rose stiffly from the sled and walked to her. Before he could speak to her a violent need to turn away and be sick overwhelmed him. The raw liquor gurgled back up, fiery and rank. English straightened, his head aching, feeling as if he had died and been reborn in some snowy purgatory.

"No more *hootch-i-noo*," Hevatha said, panting.

"It doesn't look like I'll ever have the opportunity again," English said. He looked back across the valley, seeing the twin grooves their sled runners had cut. "Are they still back there, Hevatha?"

"Oh, yes. I think so. I think they will come for many days, maybe forever."

"Until they've killed me?"

"You and me, yes."

"You? What have you done?" English asked.

"A terrible thing." She nodded toward the sled. "Taken Gunyah's gifts."

"Yes," English said meditatively. "Gunyah's gift sled."

"He won't forgive that. No one will forgive the murder of the Iht."

87

"Murder?"

"Yes. Tyee murdered him. Tyee is a criminal, you are a criminal. I am a criminal."

"You didn't have to save me, Hevatha. You could have let them take me and kill me."

"And let them kill that wolf-son of mine?"

"You didn't do it for Tyee."

"Maybe so." She shrugged.

"You've lost what you said you were afraid to give up," English said, breathing in slowly, deeply now, trying to clear his aching head. His eyes remained on the blue valley below. "Your home, your people, your way of life."

"Well," she said, smiling, "there are other people. We will go to Dawson and see them."

"To Dawson?" English frowned. "I thought you said it was impossible."

"Maybe not impossible for Hevatha," she said. Then she turned and looked toward the far mountains. "I am the daughter of the long rover."

"I'm sorry—" English began, but Hevatha silenced him.

"You have said that. The old world is already gone, though. Now we live in a new world. Now let us survive and be happy in it."

"All right." English smiled briefly in return. "We'll try."

Hevatha was silent, listening. "I think they aren't far away now. I think they returned for sleds."

"We have a sled as well, and we're far ahead."

"We have a sled, but each man of the Tlingit will have one. He will run and then ride—while you will have to ride all the while. The dogs will grow tired."

"I'll run too," English said with determination. Hevatha didn't answer him, but her thoughts were obvious—how far could this man run, and when Hevatha had to ride, when exhaustion overtook her, how would he drive the dog team? He knew nothing, this one; he was a man of mind and soul, not of entrails.

"The sled is too heavy," Hevatha said abruptly.

"Let us lighten it. We will see what gifts we can use and which are worthless to us."

English glanced at the sled and nodded his understanding. Perhaps finding a few of those goods would even slow down the pursuing Tlingit. He walked toward the sled, had a dog snap at him, and was surprised to see Tyee leap in and bite the smaller animal.

"Now Tyee knows you are his friend, now we three know we are friends," Hevatha said. "From here on Tyee will lead the team. They know now that he is the leader. They know he is the pack wolf."

English, rubbing at the arm the dog's snapping bite had narrowly missed, went to the heavily packed sled with Hevatha. On top of the goods uncovered when a long ceremonial blanket was untied were a half-dozen iron pots. Hevatha hissed with disgust and threw these aside.

"We'll need something to cook in, won't we?"

"Not these. Besides, we have nothing yet to cook," she added practically.

Hevatha sorted through the things, throwing away valuable cloaks decorated with beads and feathers, keeping several of the heavy furs, the good Hudson Bay blankets and fur boots.

"What's that?" English asked, pointing to a small object cast in bronze.

"Totem. Small totem. This is a medicine bag. We can't throw that away."

"Why not? It's Gunyah's medicine, isn't it?"

"That's why we must keep it," she said, tucking the small buckskin sack inside her coat. "And this . . ."

"I know what that is," English said with grim excitement, and he reached for the walnut stock of a Winchester .44-40 repeating rifle, model 1886. Brass studs had been driven into the stock to form an ornamental design, and the barrel had been wound with buckskin strips. "And I'll take it. Are there cartridges?"

"Richard, you should not take it," Hevatha said uneasily. English had spotted the green box of shells and he snatched that up, stowing them away in the pocket of Yakwan's parka.

"Why not? I have a use for it."

"I don't want you to kill. Not anyone. Not my friends and clansmen."

"You don't have a clan—and those men aren't your friends," English countered.

"I have a clan," Hevatha, still on her knees beside the sled, said. She spoke quietly, not looking at English, who had checked the rifle, finding it fully loaded. "They are my friends."

"Friends who want to kill you. And me. And Tyee."

"They must try, it is the law."

"There's a law called survival which says we have to try to prevent it, Hevatha."

"We can survive without death," she said deliberately. "Don't kill the Tlingit."

"All right." English was disgusted. "We'll let them take us."

"You can frighten them with that gun. No one else has one like it," she said hopefully.

"We'll try that, then. Try that first."

"Besides," Hevatha said, that smile of hers breaking through the momentary fear, "you might kill a member of *your* clan. You might kill a fox."

Then, despite himself, English laughed and Hevatha's smile deepened. She rose, finished with her sorting, and cut the lead dog of the gift sled free. In his place Tyee was strapped. The dog immediately behind the malamute growled once and Tyee turned like a thunderstorm in fur and bit it on the shoulder. It lay submissively after that, watching Tyee with hurt eyes.

"Here they come," English said tautly. Hevatha came to where he stood in the snow, and she too saw the Tlingit on their sleds racing down the long slope opposite, whips cracking above the heads of their laboring dog teams. English raised the rifle to his shoulder, settling the bead front sight into the notch of the rear sight. He followed the lead hunter down the snowy slope. Hevatha clung to his shoulder.

"Remember," she said, "do not kill them, English."

"It's Ganook," he muttered. "The man in the lead is Ganook."

"I know it is Ganook," she said quietly, reminding him of his promise without articulating it.

It would have been very easy. English was a good shot. He placed the sights of the rifle on Ganook's fur-clad chest and followed the man down the slope for a time as the Tlingit whipped and shouted at his dogs. Hevatha's hand tightened on his shoulder and he dropped his sights, putting a bullet into the snow before Ganook's lead dog. A small fan of snow sprayed into the dog's face. Startled, the animal veered sharply to one side, and the team, snarled in its harness, went down in a thrashing, yelping tangle. Ganook was thrown from the back of the sled. English aimed at a point five feet from the Tlingit and fired again.

The bullet struck much nearer to Ganook than he had intended, and English saw the Indian roll onto his side, covering his face with his hands. The following Tlingit had already slowed or stopped their teams, and now, without removing the rifle butt from his shoulder, Richard levered through half a dozen cartridges. The Tlingit turned their sleds hastily and retreated to the pines on the opposite ridge. Ganook had gotten to his feet and was running after them, his dog team towing his spilled sled behind him. English fired a parting shot and stood beaming.

"That's taken care of them," he said, reloading his rifle.

Hevatha shook her head. "They will come yet. More stealthily, but they will come."

"But why?"

"Why? English, you and I have killed their shaman. You and I have offended the tribe. You and I have stolen their chief's goods. You and I have had the death word spoken. We must die." She repeated, "We *must*."

"Then, by God . . ." English said, lifting the rifle again to his shoulder.

"No. No," Hevatha said, putting her hand on the barrel of the repeater, forcing it slowly downward. "No, by God, Richard English, we will not kill them."

"How far will they follow us, Hevatha? How far to

avenge the Iht's death? To the valley there, to the white mountains? To Dawson?"

"I don't know, English. Perhaps as far as they must."

English stood a minute longer looking at the snow-field crisscrossed by confused grooves and hollows cut by the sled dogs and Tlingit warriors.

"Then," he said, "we had better get moving."

They started the dog team, Hevatha guiding them, Tyee at their head. English, despite his pounding head, trotted alongside for nearly two miles through pine and cedar forest before he had to swallow his pride and hop onto the sled to ride.

Another four hours took them to the foothills which rose eventually to the reaches of the white mountains, now swathed again in mist.

They paused for breath on a barren rocky ledge where the wind drifted light snow over the tired dog team. English, rifle in hand, stood looking over the craggy trench beneath his feet toward the forest and the far valley. There was no sign of the Tlingit.

"We've lost them. We don't have to worry about their bows any longer," English said.

"Just the Nahani bows,' Hevatha said.

"What?" He turned slowly toward her. It was amazing; she was exhausted, her hair windblown. Without powder or rouge she was as beautiful as any woman he had seen in San Francisco. Her eyes, however, showed worry.

"We are in their land now. The Nahani do not like the Tlingit, nor, I think, do they care for the white man."

"We'll stay clear of them. Do you know where their villages are?"

"One, I think. They move sometimes to follow the game, and when the salmon run, they camp down on the Stikine River."

"We can only hope for the best."

"Soon we must camp, English. The dogs are tired. And they are hungry. You have never seen sled dogs when they are truly hungry. If we don't feed them, they will kill one of their own."

"Then we'll feed them." English lifted the rifle.

"If you fire that, everyone will know where we are. I have a bow and arrows. When we find deer sign, we will camp and I will hunt."

"Yes." He pursed his lips and looked at the useless rifle.

"English," Hevatha said, coming nearer, "did you know yellow hair is starting to grow out of your face?" She touched his cheek with the back of her hand, and English laughed.

"I knew it, Hevatha."

"I thought the Iht had put a curse on you," she said.

"No. It's something that happens to white men, and I'm afraid it's going to get quite a bit longer. I hope you don't mind."

"Maybe we can rub it off," she said hopefully.

"I'm afraid not. You'll have to get used to it."

Her hand still rested on his cheek. English put his arms around her and Hevatha tensed. He drew her to him and kissed her mouth, feeling her lips part, seeing the surprise and simultaneous warmth in her eyes. She clung to him briefly and then stepped back, cocking her head curiously, a small wary bird watching him doubtfully.

"Come on," he said, and his voice sounded much rougher than he intended. "We'd better keep moving. Which way?"

"Into the forest there. No game will be up here. We must find their forage to find them."

"Onward, then," English said cheerfully, but there was something in his gray-blue eyes Hevatha didn't understand, something which caused his eyes, on her face, to be also looking into the distances. She thought again what a strange man this yellow-haired one was. Strong and weak, intelligent and yet ignorant of so many things. How did he survive in his own land?

She went to the sled, brought the dogs to their feet behind Tyee, and started down the rocky, sloping ledge toward the verge of the forest below. English trotted alongside, stiff now and breathing harder.

He would die, Hevatha decided. English would die

before they ever reached the mountains. He was truly *halo skookum*. Hevatha had run all day through snow and mud. She had seen the long rover run for twenty-four hours, resting only when the dogs could go on no more.

"Ride for a time," she said. "It is downhill."

"No." He was barely able to pant out the word.

"Ride, English."

He nodded, giving in to the logic of exhaustion. Catching the rail, he swung aboard to cling to the gee pole. The snow began to thin and grow patchy. They were into alder and cedar now; salmonberries grew in profusion in the clearings. It was deer country and Hevatha began to slow the sled, to walk it through the trees.

"We still stop here. Leave the dogs in their traces."

English rose stiffly from the sled. "All right. You're going to hunt?"

"Yes. Watch the slopes above us. The Tlingit will be coming. When, I do not know, but Ganook will not stop hunting for us."

English stood with the cold wind whipping across his body. As they made their way inland away from the moderating influence of the sea, it was growing colder rapidly. His head still throbbed; his stomach still burned. English took up a position under a flourishing cedar and stood surveying the backtrail.

Hevatha took bow and arrows from the sled and with one quick glance at him she was gone, slipping silent as a shadow through the dark forest.

Tyee, eager to go with her, yapped once and then was silent. Hevatha wound her way through the trees, eyes searching for deer sign. The pack must be fed. The pack and the yellow-haired man.

It didn't take her long to find what she was looking for: spoor. The deer had been feeding on the berries. Three sets of tracks were delicately impressed in the inch-deep snow. A doe and her two fawns. Going to water now? The spoor was still warm; steam rose into the air. Hevatha crouched, held her hand over it, feeling the warmth, and then lifted her hunter's eyes to the deeper forest where fern and berries tangled haphazardly together, forming dense thickets. Perhaps they had gone to rest, to hide in their thicket beds.

She began to circle, nocking an arrow as she moved. She could hear water running now, and as she moved, she caught a momentary glimpse of sunlight on silver. A quick, narrow rill wound through the snowy forest, fell from a small ledge, and raced on, leaving the underbrush near the water's edge encased in ice.

She saw deer sign again now, much of it. The snow nearer the rill was overtracked by many hooves. A patch of grass had been pawed free of the snow and grazed at. Listening, Hevatha heard something moving in the brush. Not a deer; she thought a fox or perhaps a marten. They were safe from her arrows; she had no use for their furs.

She crossed a field of head-size boulders, moving along the bank of the little creek, and stopped abruptly. There was only one track, but it was clearly imprinted in the snowy bank. One footprint. The man had worn deerskin boots and he had come to the river to drink or simply to gaze at it. Then he had gone on. Or had he? Hevatha's eyes lifted to the forest above and around her and she drew her bowstring a few inches.

Compressing her lips, she went on. She needed deer meat. She came upon the doe suddenly. It was drinking at the water's edge. With it were two fawns, both more than six months old, well able to fend for themselves.

"Forgive me, deer spirit, for killing you," Hevatha said silently, "but I need your meat for my dogs and for my yellow-haired man. Do not take offense."

She raised her bow, the drawn string beside her ear, and holding her breath, released the grip her fingers had on the sinew. The arrow hummed lightly through the air like a homing insect and the doe leapt once and fell dead in the creek, the fawns darting into the forest on spindly, quick legs.

Hevatha looked around once more before she moved to the deer and gutted it. She could not conceal the entrails. Whoever was around would find them and know it was the work of a human being. So she and English would have to travel on tonight. Feed the dogs and move on deeper into Nahani land.

Hevatha bent, picked up the deer carcass and shouldered it, crouched to pick up her bow and quiver, and started on, moving quickly through the trees, her eyes constantly moving.

"Hevatha," English said exuberantly, "you're a marvel! I thought you'd be gone for hours!'"

"Be quiet, English, please."

He looked offended. "Why, what's the matter?"

"Help me put this down." She stood, hands on hips, breathing in deeply; then she told him, "I saw Nahani sign."

"Indians?" he said, forgetting that Hevatha was Indian too.

"Nahani. We are on their land now. They won't like it."

"Did they see you?" English asked.

"I don't think so, but maybe."

"How many?"

"One man. But there will be others. Stop talking now, English, let me butcher this deer."

English backed away obediently, taking up his post near the cedar tree again, his eyes now moving from the backtrail to the forest around him, only occasionally lighting on Hevatha, who skillfully, rapidly did her work.

The dogs began to yap and snarl, to bite at each other as they scented the raw meat. "Good God," English murmured. The noise they made would be audible for miles. There wasn't anything to be done about it.

Tyee was fed first; it helped reinforce his rank. The dogs behind him strained frantically at their traces, trying to get to Tyee's meat, a huge hunk of venison carved out of the deer's haunch. The big dog snapped once at them; then, growling deep in his throat, snuffling, he tore the meat to chunks with his powerful fangs.

The other dogs were thrown their meat, not handed

it. They scrapped among each other, fighting for each bite. English had never seen anything like it as they tangled their traces, yapped, and drew occasional blood. It was like watching a pack of wolves. That, he realized, was nearly what they were. Second- and third-generation descendants of timber wolves. No wonder Hevatha had told him it was urgent that the dogs be fed. They were capable of tearing one of their pack to shreds if need be. And capable, English knew, of turning on a man and doing the same thing. That sent a cold shudder through him.

Hevatha was rapidly packing the remainder of the carcass in a deerskin from the sled. Tying that with a length of hemp rope, she straightened, looked at English, and nodded.

"We will go now. Later we can eat."

"Yes. Hevatha, if there were no deer, they'd eat us if they could, wouldn't they?"

Hevatha laughed, putting her bow away, picking up her whip. "No, English. If there was no deer meat, we would eat them."

English looked at the dogs, revulsion twisting his mouth briefly. He rubbed his jaw and smiled at Hevatha. "Yes, I guess we would, wouldn't we?"

They started on, moving downslope again, aiming for a gap between the convoluted, snow-dusted hills ahead. Shifting gray clouds drifted toward them from the north, holding the threat of snow. From time to time Hevatha looked to them, not liking what she saw.

They crossed a narrow creek, nearly spilling the sled as English lost his grip, and moved up through another wooded slope.

The totem stood directly in their path.

Hevatha stopped the dog team and looked to English. It was a Nahani totem. Wolf and bear clans. Atop the pole, which had once been green and red but which now was nearly the color of cedar again, sat a raven with three eyes.

"What does this mean?" English asked.

"Mean? We are on their land, English. They are here, somewhere."

English looked at the forest, which was darker now, denser, and menacing. "Why would they harm us? We can give them goods. Maybe buy safe passage across their territory."

"Maybe," Hevatha agreed. "Maybe not, English. I don't want to have to try that. I don't wish to see them. They do not like Tlingit. Perhaps they won't kill us; perhaps they will only take us for slaves. I will not live as a slave."

"No." English gripped his rifle more tightly. A light snow had begun to fall, drifting through the trees. "I don't suppose there's any way around their land?"

"No way. Not between here and the white mountains. Unless we would turn back."

English looked back. Back to where Ganook and his warriors would be. There was nothing to do but go on. Wearily he nodded to Hevatha and on legs as heavy as logs he began walking unslope, following the woman and the sled as the snow began to thicken, swirling down on the currents of the gusting wind.

"Somewhere," Hevatha said, "we will have to stop. Look for a place of shelter."

"Yes," Richard panted. "I'll be looking . . . Hevatha! God, what is that?"

It was beside the trail. The *thing* was pegged to a pine tree, pegged there to hang and decompose. It had once been a man. Now it had no eyes. The mouth gaped open toothlessly. The face had been slashed with knives. The victim had been horribly tortured and then killed, hung up beside the trail. "It is a warning," Hevatha said. "A warning to those who would come this way."

English felt his stomach lift and he had to turn away. That had been a human being, that withered, eyeless thing. Animals had been at its feet, chewing them off nearly to the knees. On trembling legs English turned back.

"We have to go on. Let's go, then," he snapped. There was a fury in his voice, a fury born of fear.

"Yes. Let us go on." She paused still, paused and

silently said to the thing on the tree, "I am sorry, Koosh. Sorry for sending you away."

Then she slapped her whip stock against her leg, strode angrily to the team, and snapped the whip over their heads. Tyee rose and the sled lurched forward, gliding up the slope, deeper into Nahani land.

The spot they chose to camp was on a high bluff, a naked prominence jutting up from the surrounding forest. It was a treacherous climb up, an exhausting one, but they needed to be able to look around them, to see danger from any direction. The Tlingit were there; the Nahani probably knew by now that Hevatha and English were in their forest.

The dogs were left in harness except for Tyee, set free to lie beside Hevatha, who rested on a bearskin beneath a stunted, wind-twisted cedar, staring out over the endless wilderness ahead of them.

English stood watching the trail they had followed upward, alert for any sign of motion, for any bit of color, but the swirling snow drifting across the valleys obscured his vision and he gave it up, going to sit beside Hevatha.

"You are hungry," she said, looking up.

"So hungry I don't know if I can eat," he admitted.

"You will eat. You will keep your strength." She started to rise, to fetch the venison from the sled, but she slipped. English supported her arm, realizing that he hadn't given *her* hunger, her weariness much thought. It was Hevatha who managed the dogs, Hevatha who hunted, Hevatha who guided them. Hevatha who had admitted a white man into her life and paid the price of tribal ostracism—and would pay the penalty of death if they were caught.

"I'm sorry," English said at last. Hevatha's head rested against his shoulder as they sat together, the snow falling around them.

"You are sorry?" she said with surprise.

"This is all my fault, isn't it?"

"Your fault for being born. Your mother's for conceiving you, mine for coming north, the long rover's for bringing me, the Iht's for cursing you, Ganook's for wanting me . . . I don't think there is fault in the world, English. Only small tragedies."

Again English could only look at this woman with admiration and astonishment. Where had she come from? How had nature conspired to bring forth such a woman from the wild?

"At home," he said, "they believe all Indians are simple. Ignorant and savage."

"They are not?" she asked. "Those people who think this—are they not savage and ignorant? That is what we are, yes. That is what we all are."

"You may be right," English said, and he laughed, lying back to look up at Hevatha, at the snow moving around her head, dappling her raven-black hair with pure white. "You may just be right. You ought to see the goings-on on the Barbary Coast."

"What is that, English?"

He propped himself up on one elbow. "A place where San Franciscans go to display their own savagery and barbarity."

"They have special places for this?"

"Yes."

"So that their tribesmen don't see the evil things they wish to do."

"Just that, Hevatha. Just that, I'm afraid. So that wives and neighbors won't know that they have hearts of darkness, that inside they want to gamble, to whore, to see pain, blood . . . well, maybe we condemn them too much."

"Perhaps. They are, after all, only men." She reflected a moment. "I wonder, English, why the missionary came to the Tlingit lands when he had a place like this Barbary Coast to fight sin."

"I wonder," English said, but he wasn't thinking of the Barbary Coast any longer, nor of Johnson. His eyes were fixed on Hevatha's and he drew her down to lie beside him.

He kissed her, tasting the warmth of her mouth, the coldness of a snowflake. She was next to him, holding him tightly, almost protectively, as the snow fell and the wind gusted across the barren ledge. He pulled her

to him again, his hand going to her thigh, holding her
body against his.

"You are far from home, English," she said. Her
eyes moved and probed and shone.

"Yes."

"What would I be to you if you were in San
Francisco?"

English paused and then rolled aside, his hands
falling away from her body. He might have rolled back
toward her, taking her in his arms again, but Tyee
moved between them, a mountainous ball of fur, circled twice, and flopped down to lie with his muzzle on
Hevatha's stomach.

English had answered Hevatha with his silence. She
said from where she lay, "You have a woman in San
Francisco."

He was a long time responding. He lay with his
hands on his abdomen, staring up at the milky sky.
"Yes, Hevatha."

"Well, why shouldn't you? Probably they like yellow hair and yellow whiskers there."

"Yes," English said with a laugh, "they seem to like
it—or not mind it, at least."

"So," she said quietly, "that is right."

"Yes."

A vast silence as formidable and large as Tyee settled between them. English started to speak. He rolled
his head toward her, but Hevatha's eyes were closed.
Before he knew it, his own exhaustion dragged him
down into a dreamless sleep.

When he awoke, he was covered with furs. The
snow had stopped but the wind still blew. English
stretched. His limbs had gotten stiffer, so much stiffer
that he had trouble rising from his bed. Hevatha had
roasted venison for him. She looked up from her spit
and smiled.

"I didn't think you dared cook anything."

"With the wind, no one will see the smoke, no one
will smell the deer meat. Eat now, English, we must
travel on soon."

There was something in her eyes which caused him to ask, "You saw something, didn't you?"

She removed the venison from the spit before she answered, "Ganook. He is coming. Not more than five miles back."

"So near!"

"They travel quickly, English. They know their dogs, know their sleds."

"Yes." She didn't have to add that he was nothing but deadweight. A useless man.

He ate greedily. The meat, broiled over the open flame of Hevatha's fire, was smoking hot, burning his lips at the first bite. Within minutes it was cold. English himself was shivering despite the long rover's parka.

"It's cold," he said.

"Cold? This is the good time of year, English. But the bad time is coming. The time when the runners of the sled will freeze to the ground, when the dogs will howl with pain as their feet freeze, when there will be no creatures walking the earth, when the lungs will freeze and to step outside of a shelter is to die. This is what I tried to tell you before. This is what you do not understand about the white world beyond the mountains."

"And there's no way out of this, damn all! Damn it all!"

"You cannot damn creation. Ke-an-Kow's world is his world, harsh and good and beautiful."

"What can we do?" he asked, as if he hadn't heard her.

"Go on. Walk into tomorrow," she said cheerfully.

"Tomorrow. And tomorrow. An infinity of frozen bloody tomorrows," he said bitterly.

"Tomorrow is all that is given us, Richard English—if we are so lucky. No man has eyes to see the end of the long journey. We take each step as it must be taken."

"Each miserable damned step," he said, flinging the last of his meat to Tyee, who gobbled it up.

"You do not wish to live?" Hevatha asked with wonder.

"Of course I wish to live. But not like this."

"You wish to live or you do not," she said, rising to kick snow into the fire. "You do not choose the life you must live. Come now, you are being foolish and it is time we were going."

Hevatha placed Tyee in harness and started the dog team forward. The snow had intensified and they walked through a world of dark columns of trees and heavy white veils. English moved slowly and so Hevatha slowed the team still more, knowing that it was dangerous to do so, knowing that Ganook would be whipping his dogs, racing through the storm toward them.

In the trees there were eyes. How she knew that, Hevatha couldn't have said, but there were watchers there. The Nahani knew.

Why they didn't attack, she didn't know. Perhaps their shaman had to dream; perhaps the sight of a white man caused them to think twice. In the north country men in red coats carrying pistols now roamed, trying to protect the whites who were beginning to flood the land.

They were out there—that was all she knew. Yet she was the long rover's daughter and she kept on, taking the occasional fear which blossomed in her breast and placing it aside. English stumbled and nearly fell; Hevatha pretended not to notice. She had told him too many times that he was weak; perhaps it was time to tell him that he was strong and thereby make him strong.

She touched her lips and smiled. He was strong in his way. When he held her she could feel his strength, his differentness, his maleness longing for what was woman in her. His kiss was hard, yet eager to be responded to. Hevatha did not know how to respond, not really. Did she want to? Did she want to link her soul with this man who wandered lost in the north, stumbling toward some uncertain goal in the far country? He would never make a good husband. He would never be a hunter. What good was a man who would only be a burden?

Still her lips remembered, and her heart.

The snow deepened as they reached the long valley below the trees. Knee-deep, still it was packed well and the sled glided over it, following Tyee and the team, which floundered only a little. The big dog led the way eagerly; he would run until his great heart stopped.

They crossed an icy creek fringed with icicles and went again into forest. There the trees slowed the snowfall and the going was easier.

Hevatha looked at Richard English. His face was half-hidden by the fur of his parka hood, but exhaustion was apparent in each sluggish step. They would have to stop again, stop or the man with the sea-gray eyes would surely die.

"English!" Hevatha called. She had to repeat his name before his head lifted and his face turned toward her, peering at her through the falling snow as if she were far distant.

"We must stop to feed the dogs."

"All right," he said. "Yes, whenever you say."

Hevatha snapped her whip once to urge on the third dog, a black, blunt-muzzled thing which was trying to let the others of the team do his share. That one hadn't been a gift dog, but it was there when Hevatha had hastily harnessed the team and so it had come with them. The animal's eyes flashed as the whip cracked above its ear.

Hevatha looked behind them again. The snow was falling well; if it kept it up, it would cover their tracks in time. But Ganook wasn't far enough behind to give the storm time to erase the signs of their passing.

Seeing her look, English asked, "You think he's still back there?"

"I know he is, English."

"It's a wonder the Nahani haven't attacked them, isn't it? They look like a war party."

"Perhaps the Nahani are waiting," she suggested.

"For what?"

"For the Tlingit to kill the white man. Then they can kill the Tlingit without blame."

English's eyes showed comprehension. "Yes. That could be it." He had trouble getting the words out. He was trembling with weariness. When was she going to stop and feed the damned dogs?

How much of this was left to endure? A month of it, two? God, wasn't there a white settlement anywhere in this empty land? A place where he could find warm food, a bed, safety . . . Hevatha had achieved a narrow, crecent-shaped snowy bench above him and he struggled to it in time to see her slow and then halt the team. She was already carving chunks of meat from the deer carcass before English, exhausted, arrived and simply sat down in the snow to watch the dogs begin their ritual of snarling, biting, tearing at the bloody meat.

The snow washed down from out of a dark and shifting sky. The trees were gray behind the clouds, the land lost in deeper darkness.

"We can't travel on in this," English said.

"No." They could no longer see the trail if there was such a thing. Hevatha had been guiding them by the wind, which was from the northwest, always on her left cheek, but now the wind seemed to shift constantly and the snow obscured vision, making the eyes useless. "We will stop somewhere," she said, looking around, wiping at her eyes. "If we cannot see, Ganook cannot see."

Tyee was the one who found the cave. It was no more than ten feet deep, half that high, twenty feet wide, but it was dry, the stone cutting the wind, and Hevatha moved their bedding into it, leaving the dogs to sleep in the snow.

English was barely able to crawl beneath the furs and blankets before he fell asleep. Hevatha watched him for a time, his dark profile, the rise and fall of his chest, the strange, soft yellow hair. Then, listening to the wind, watching the snow twist past the cave mouth, she yawned, stretched, and herself went to sleep.

English slept in a tangled dream, a web of colorless

images composed of fears and needs and half-forgotten moments. He walked through a forest where all the trees were black relics of someone's nightmare. Owls clung upside down from the branches, chanting of a death in the wasteland. Dark schooners sailed across the endless sea of snow, their wolf figureheads snapping and snarling wolf oaths. Distantly a woman ran and English started that way through the deep sea where gold coins and playing cards floated. On a far bluff the minister chanted the fox-clan song . . . the ballroom floor was crowded and he swung Laura in gentle circles. She kept whispering into his ear. The dress she wore was of sealskin and silk. Her yellow hair was soft and scented with *eulikon*. He showed her the book he had written for her and she whispered again, "*Halo skookum.*"

English sat up suddenly. The man in the mouth of the cave had a spear. A fur parka wreathed his head. He seemed in that light to have no eyes. English dived for his rifle, turned and fired, and Hevatha leapt up.

"English!"

"Got him," Richard said. He was panting, fighting off the hazy echoes of his dreamworld. He crawled toward the cave mouth, levering another cartridge into the Winchester's receiver. "Got Ganook—he was going to kill me."

But it wasn't Ganook. English hovered over the body of the dead man, still on hands and knees, rifle still in his hands. He looked into the face of the dead Indian and then to Hevatha, who touched his shoulder uneasily. The dogs had begun to howl. Outside the cave a white moon hung in a broken sky.

"A Nahani, English. A Nahani, perhaps looking for shelter. You have killed him, and now I am afraid they will kill us."

"I didn't know. I thought it was Ganook. How would I know? I saw the spear." English rose to a crouch, wiping his hair back from his eyes. Something sticky and warm clung to his hand and he wiped it in the snow, staring in fascination at the dark spreading stain beneath the dead Nahani Indian. "What can we do, Hevatha? If they heard the shot, they'll come, won't they? Maybe this one wasn't alone."

English's eyes lifted to the moon-bright snow, the dark surrounding forest. Hevatha was snatching up the furs and blankets, calling to Tyee.

"We can run, English. That is all we can do. Run." She looked at the rifle and shook her head. "That is a bad thing. Not only will the Nahani know, Ganook will also know that you fired that shot. This is bad, English, very bad."

The sled was hastily packed, the surly dogs lifted to their feet. The black dog lashed out, snapping at the haunch of the dog in front of him. Hevatha rapped it on the skull with the whip stock.

"No trouble from you, Hahtik. English, we must go. Get on the sled."

"I'll run."

"It will be a long run. We can't stop until the Nahani are far behind."

"I'll run," English said stubbornly. "It's my fault we have to do this, isn't it?"

Hevatha said nothing. She simply lifted her whip, started the team off across the moon-glossed snow, and trotted forward herself. The weather had changed dramatically, rapidly. A chinook was building in the west. The temperature was rising; the air had a haunting palpability to it. The sun was still visible low on the gray southern horizon, but it seemed to cast no light. The moon was hard and bright.

The dogs labored on, lunging through drifts of snow. They crested a barren ridge and started down again, toward the vast valley below where nothing grew. Lifting his eyes to the night sky, English could see the mountains, still impossibly distant, stark and aloof against the gray background of the northern sky.

They traveled on, the dogs yapping, struggling, Hevatha surely guiding them toward the mountains, English running through his own dream of torment, of physical pain and mental suffering. Behind, there were Indians who wished to kill him; ahead, more hardship. His reality was made up of painful dreams of the past;

fear of the present endless, merciless wilderness; and
an unwillingness to face the future—if he had a future.
He could not have said which frightened him the most,
which cut most deeply at his soul and spirit. He ran
until his physical discomfort erased all reflective
thought, until only pain and exhaustion lingered, then
farther, longer, until a sort of dark euphoria overwhelmed him and he was only a bleak, spiritless or-
ganism endlessly chasing the dark figure of a woman
toward the white mountains.

6

THE chinook held for three weeks. The snows melted and brief-lived flowers sprang from the earth to flood the long valleys with pale, tragic color. The grass too returned, and the mountain passes, clotted with snow the week before, were open to them. They were ten days in the mountains, following sketchy, ragged trails up cliffsides and over windswept crests where still there was deep snow, snow which plumed into the air as violently gusting winds lashed at the gray stone monoliths thrust up by the giants of the aeons.

And then there was Whitehorse.

English stood atop the wind-buffeted crest looking down the long slope, past the timber to the dirty, jumbled, haphazardly formed town. He stood there and a tear formed itself in the corner of his eye.

"You did it, Hevatha. I did it. Tyee. It's Whitehorse, girl, and I'm nearly there. To see a white face again . . . God love you."

He held Hevatha, feeling the lack of response, her body leaning away from his as he hugged her. Looking down curiously into her expressionless eyes, he let her go. "What's the matter?"

"Nothing. Nothing is the matter," she said tonelessly.

"Then let's get down there. Damn all, Hevatha, let's have a look at Whitehorse!"

The Yukon River flowed past, cold and white, surrounded by empty tundra. Lake Laberge and Lake Marsh gleamed dully in the low sunlight. Smoke rose from every chimney as Whitehorse settled in for the long winter. Substantial buildings were few, but on the outskirts of town hundreds of log cabins and simple shacks had been thrown up. A steamboat, white and dark green, was tied up on the river. Everywhere were unruly, bearded, heavily dressed men in mackinaws and fur hats, most carrying pistols. The streets were a foot of mud with planks placed at the corners as bridges. Horses pulling huge freight wagons sloshed up the streets, steam issuing from nostrils and rising from their flanks. Men cursed and groaned, shouted from saloon to saloon, where hundreds of Whitehorse denizens fought off the chill of the day with raw whiskey. Pianos banged and now and then a woman shrieked with pleasure or surprise. Glass was broken and curses were hurled into the cold skies. Chinese, Indians, French, and Americans rubbed shoulders. Dog teams waited in the streets, snarling and howling.

"What is it, English?" Hevatha asked as they entered the town, looking around hesitantly. "What has brought these people here?"

"Gold," English replied. "They're here to get rich, to spend what they have found, to murder and cheat each other for it, to drink it, give it, and throw it away."

Hevatha had seen white communities before, but she had never seen anything like this. Five thousand people crowded themselves into the town, but few of them seemed to have anything to do but drink and shout and wander aimlessly.

"Let's find something to eat," English said. "We can sell a couple of furs, Hevatha."

"No. We will need the furs. I can find something to eat"—she nodded toward the open country beyond the town—"out there."

"No. I want ham and coffee and fresh baked bread and eggs if they have them."

"No *hootch-i-noo*," Hevatha cautioned, but English laughed at her. Something had changed in the man from the moment they entered this white town. He walked taller, seemed self-assured. He strode ahead of Hevatha and the dogs, not beside her.

"You could sell the rifle," Hevatha suggested.

"No, not yet," he answered.

"You have killing to do? I thought you did not like killing, now that you have done it."

"What?" He spoke over his shoulder, his interest held by the buildings around him, the bearded white faces. "No, I don't want to kill anyone. But I'll need the rifle."

"For what, English?" Hevatha hurried a little to catch up with him as they trudged through the mud and slush of the main street. "If we need to hunt, I have my bow, English? What do you need a rifle for?"

"Not now, Hevatha," he said, and her mouth tightened a little before it formed itself into one of her bright smiles. She had brought the man home but he would not invite her in.

"Richard English! Damn us all—it can't be you!"

Hevatha looked to the plank walk in front of the store to their right. A man with a thick chest and neck dressed in a red-and-black mackinaw and fur hat, with a flowing red mustache and toothy grin, came down from the plank walk, waded through the mud, and took English's hand, gripping his shoulder.

"Demarest," English said, "what in the world are you doing here!"

"Waiting, like everyone else. Waiting for spring. Then it's off to Dawson."

"How did you get here?" English asked, finally letting go of Demarest's hand. "How in the world!"

"Took the train, old man," Demarest said.

"The train . . ."

"There's a line through from Skagway. We reached Sitka two days after you dropped out of sight, crossed to Juneau, then down to Skagway and the rail line through to Whitehorse. Being the *chechacos* that we are—greenhorns, that is—we didn't realize that no one could get north right now. Where"—he looked at Hevatha—"in hell have you been? We figured you for a sailor's grave."

"I couldn't tell you that in a few minutes. If you can show us someplace that'll take a few furs for cash money, I'll buy you a meal and we can discuss it."

"Furs . . ." Demarest rubbed his chin. "There's nothing but furs in Whitehorse. Cash money's different. If you'll let me buy, we can eat. Place across the street isn't bad if you don't mind breakfast twenty-four hours a day."

"Anything," English said enthusiastically, "so long as it's not venison."

Demarest laughed. Then he looked again at Hevatha, his blue eyes narrowing. "Is that yours?" he asked.

"Is what . . . ? Oh, this is Hevatha. She brought me here from the coast. She speaks English."

"Speak English?" Demarest asked. "We eat now, you stay with dogs, okay?"

Richard looked pained; Hevatha broke out laughing. "Me stay," she said. "Me stay!" and then she laughed again.

"What's so funny?" Demarest, genuinely puzzled, asked.

"Your idea of how an Indian speaks English, I guess. Hevatha's a clever girl. Educated by a missionary, before the tribe bashed his head in."

"Oh, I see." Demarest looked only slightly embarrassed. "A clever girl, eh? Well, then, Hevatha, you stay here and look after the dogs, will you, while English and I hash over old times."

Demarest turned English by the arm and walked him across the street. Hevatha watched with amusement and curiosity for a time. English, happy to be among his white faces, never even looked back.

Hevatha unharnessed Tyee and sat on the plank walk before the store, arms around her knees, watching the incredible bustle of all these men who were going nowhere. Tyee groaned with boredom and rested his great head on her arm.

"I know," Hevatha said, stroking his head, "I know, Tyee."

Demarest sat smoking his pipe, eyes sparkling with voyeur's pleasure as he watched Richard English devour his breakfast, stacks of hotcakes and honey, half a dozen eggs, three slices of ham, four cups of coffee.

In between mouthfuls English filled Demarest in on his adventure.

"Nasty," the older man said with a shake of his head. He inspected his pipe bowl, poked at it with his penknife, and went on. "You were damned lucky to get away. As for making it this far, damned amazing is what it is. Too bad you didn't come in a week or so ago."

English lifted curious eyes to Demarest, gesturing simultaneously to the Chinese waiter for more coffee.

Demarest said, "You just missed Butler."

"He was here? In Whitehorse?"

"Yes, he was, and he raised quite a ruckus, they tell me. Never saw him myself. There's a flood of men out there. It seems he got up to his old tricks. A card game that went wrong, and a knife in an alley. He's gone—trying to get the jump on everyone to Dawson, they say."

"Can't make it to Dawson." English finally pushed his plate away and sat back satisfied.

"Some folks think a man could do it if he knew what he was up to," Demarest answered.

"How far is it? Three hundred miles, and the weather unpredictable. Have to go by dogsled, and I've learned the hard way that if you don't know what you're doing with a sled, you might as well carry your dogs and gear."

"Maybe so. They say Butler had three good Indians with him, Han Indians, and that's their territory. He had a good team and a good sled."

Richard shook his head. "It'll snow again, and hard. He'll be stuck in the far reaches."

"It's plenty warm now, for the Yukon, that is."

"The chinook won't last long. Hevatha says so."

"Hevatha," Demarest said meditatively. "Now, she knows dogs and sleds, doesn't she?"

English answered cautiously, "She does."

"Dogs are at a premium now. You can have horses for next to nothing, but dogs are a different matter. You can't find a white man that knows how to handle them, but that's another story. Dogs and Indian guides are what most of us are lacking. Hell, damn bunch of city men here, English." Demarest folded his big fore-arms on the table. "What do any of them know about this kind of life? What does anyone but an Indian know of it? Come spring, a thousand men will be dashing for the goldfields and Dawson. Just now"—his eyes narrowed behind the screen of pipe smoke— "I'm thinking like Butler. A man with a head start, with the dogs and the nerve to go, can beat the pack to the Upper Klondike and have his pick of claims."

English caught the drift of things. He put his hands flat on the table, examined them for a long while, and then shook his head. "A man would need supplies. He'd have to know just where he was going and what he was doing once he got there."

Demarest glanced around carefully and leaned nearer to English across the small round table. "I'll tell you something, Richard. I know both. I've been a prospec-tor off and on for thirty years. I made plenty in the California fields. Gave most of it away to a treacher-ous woman, but that's something else. I've panned and I've used a Long Tom and I've done hard-rock mining. I know color when I see it, boy.

"Let me tell you something else. I met a man named Drake who was pulling out, heading back to Philadel-phia. He was walking along the Upper Yukon when he just about tripped over something shiny. He picked it up for the hell of it. It was a five-pound rock. That's right, a five-pound nugget of pure gold. He staked his claim, took a gunnysack, and walked along the river-bank filling it with found nuggets until he reckoned he had a hundred pounds or so. He went into the nearest trading post, handed over the gold for a winter's sup-ply of food and tools. Back at the river, he got to work in earnest. Drake reckons he took two million in gold from that little stretch of river. Then he figured that was enough, that he was pushing his luck. Besides, he didn't want to do another winter in a cabin. Says he just about went crazy mad. He's gone now, back to Philadelphia."

"Lucky for him," English said, "but these stories

don't mean much, Demarest. It doesn't mean the next man is going to pull out loaded down with gold."

"Not if he don't know where he's going," Demarest said, drawing even nearer. "I do."

"How could you? What do you mean?" Interest had begun to show in English's eyes.

"I told you I talked to Drake. I asked him if he was going back and he said never. For a bottle of bourbon and a hundred dollars he gave me this."

Demarest carefully unfolded the paper he took from his inside pocket. Crudely drawn, the map was nevertheless detailed and embellished with distances and small notations.

"Drake's map. Drake's claim," Demarest said.

"If it's his claim . . ."

"Not a legal claim," Demarest said. "There aren't many dead legal claims up in that country. What you're supposed to do is stake up and then register at the police barracks at Fort Selkirk. That's nearly a hundred miles from Dawson. There's not many who find a good claim and then are willing to up and leave it, trek to Selkirk and back just to make it legal. Stake claims are generally recognized as good. But Drake has no further legal claim on that stretch of river. And he don't want it."

"When spring comes—" English began.

"When spring comes, English, there's going to be a thousand men walking that river, driving stakes into everything they see. I don't intend to sit here and rot all winter. Look at you—what are you going to do here in Whitehorse? Do you know what that breakfast cost? Twenty dollars. A man without a poke is dead in Whitehorse, a man *with* one hasn't got long to live."

"I can get a job."

"There's twenty men in line for every job. Mostly they hire the Chinese because they'll work for nearly nothing. The riverboat is shut down; the train won't be making a run after the snow starts again. Look at it twice, English, what choice do you have? I'm willing to share my claim with you. All I want's your team and your squaw."

"I don't know. I'd have to talk it over with Hevatha."

Demarest shrugged. "I had the idea she'd do just what you told her to do. Ran away from her people to bring you here, didn't she?"

"It wasn't quite like that." English could hear the wind working against the rickety building. He lifted his eyes to the greasy window and saw a little snow drifting through the air. Whitehorse bustled and froze and cursed and chafed at the bit. Beyond the town limits the wilderness began again, the endless wilderness. "I don't know if I have it in me to go back out there, Demarest. To be honest, I just don't know if I can do three hundred miles. My thoughts only carried me as far as Whitehorse."

"You had Dawson in mind. You had the goldfields in mind, Richard, otherwise you wouldn't have come to the Yukon. There's no other earthly reason for a sane man to be here. Anyway . . ." Demarest stretched and stood, his chair scraping the floor. "You think it over. Rest up a day or two. But don't wait any longer. I'm going north and I'm offering you something you'll never again in your life have offered. You won't make it alone, English, but you will with me." Demarest winked. "I won't promise you two million, but I'll promise you gold."

He had started away from the table before he stopped to add, "Besides, Butler's there. I had the idea you'd want to see Aaron Butler again."

"I don't know," English said quietly. He looked at the rifle in his hand. "I don't know if I want to see him again at all."

"He tried to kill you! He did kill Landis."

"Yes, he did." And English himself had killed a man, a Nahani Indian. It had been an accident, a mistake, but that didn't make it any less horrible. The long trek had destroyed his urge toward violent revenge against Aaron Butler. If he went to Dawson, it wouldn't be to track down the man. If he went to Dawson . . .

He opened the door to the restaurant, following Demarest into the street. A cool wind was blowing,

occasional snow falling from a slate-gray sky. It was
still warm, not much below freezing. If they could get
an early start, they just might be able to make Dawson. English looked around at the milling, drinking
mass of gold hunters, men who would leave Whitehorse
at the first sign of spring and like a trampling herd
make their way to the Upper Yukon River, pursuing a
common vague but golden dream.

Richard looked across the street to where Hevatha
still waited patiently. A couple of prospectors stopped
to look at the dogs, their intentions unclear, but Tyee
lunged toward them, snapping, and they backed off
quickly.

Hevatha stood and waited for English. When he
reached her she asked, "Now you are not hungry?"

"Full," he said happily. It took him another minute
to realize why Hevatha was looking at him the way she
was, smiling, eyes deeply amused. "But you haven't
eaten."

"No, English."

"I'm sorry, Hevatha. I wasn't thinking."

"No, English."

"I saw Demarest and forgot completely. It was good
to see him again."

"Yes, English."

"We'll find you something to eat." He looked around
distractedly. There was no more money in his pockets
than there had been an hour ago. How he was going
to find Hevatha something to eat was a mystery.

"I will eat," she said. "Let's make a camp outside of
town. There's no place for us here with all these
people doing nothing. There's no air to breathe."

There wasn't a lot of choice. English followed
Hevatha to the outskirts of Whitehorse to a spot where
barren, skeletal poplars lined the half-frozen river.
There Hevatha unpacked venison and began building
a fire to roast it over. English stood watching her,
lifting his eyes occasionally to the river.

"That was thoughtless of me, Hevatha. I'm sorry."

"Everyone is thoughtless, everyone forgets. I didn't
want to go into that cookhouse anyway, English. I

smelled the food, it was nothing good to eat. I sat and watched the men. It kept me amused. All those pale faces, empty eyes, wanting something they've forgotten and are waiting to remember."

"I want to go to Dawson," he blurted out, turning toward Hevatha.

"Why?"

"It's just important that I get there, Hevatha, believe me. Will you take me?"

"Why would I want to go to Dawson, English?"

He was silent for a moment. The wind had freshened and it nudged his body with cool fingers. "There's no reason. No reason for you to go. Demarest wants me to go with him. We need a dog team and a guide."

Hevatha didn't answer him. She returned to her cooking. Why would she want to go? To travel again with this yellow-haired man, with this one who knew nothing, who traveled slowly. What was there in Dawson for Hevatha? She didn't want gold. She didn't want to live in another white town like this one. There seemed to be no reason to go with him at all, but she watched him as he stood there staring at the river, watched his sensitive mouth and pale, searching eyes, and her heart gave her the only reason she needed.

"I have nowhere else to go," Hevatha said lightly. "I will take you. This Demarest, doesn't he know that soon the chinook will end and the winter will start?"

"He knows it," English replied.

Hevatha only shrugged. "We will go, then." She cut off a sliver of half-broiled meat and gave it to Tyee. The other dogs howled in anticipation. "We will go, English, and see what it is in Dawson that makes white men mad."

"I'll go back into town and find Demarest. If we're leaving, we should start as soon as possible."

There was a curious energetic impetus to English's words now. His movements were suddenly short, almost frenetic. He walked back and forth before the fire, which weaved in the blustering wind and cast sparks into the cold sky and snow to die.

Hevatha tended her broiling meat, only occasionally

glancing at English. Richard paced and spoke his bursts of thought aloud. "He'll have to find the supplies of course—I assume he has the money—cash is short but Demarest talked as if he had some. If the chinook holds—how many days, Hevatha?—say, a week. Three hundred miles . . ."

And the woman watched him, knowing then that English had the white disease, the disease of gold. While he had been with the Tlingit, while they had fought their way across the white mountains, he had shown few signs of it, but it was only gold that could have brought him north in the first place, and now, with other concerns behind him, the strange demanding lust for gold was again paramount.

"Do you want to go into Whitehorse with me, Hevatha?"

"No, not again. I have seen it. There are men there who want the dog team, English. A good team draws all of their eyes. It's better I wait out here."

English agreed almost absently and started trudging away toward Whitehorse. Hevatha cut herself a piece of meat and chewed it as she looked around her at the young trees. She would need sapling wood and sinew. Some sinew was saved from her deer on the sled. Snowshoes would be needed, and Hevatha walked among the trees choosing her material.

She stood near the river. It was nearly white, only distantly blue, as if holding a far memory of its origins. Icicles, dripping their melt into the river now, clung to the banks and to the roots of the trees. She stood and watched the river moving grandly, sedately from out of the barren northern lands, carrying its promise to the white men in the south.

When English and Demarest returned, they weren't alone. Another white man was with them, and two Indian men, both in middle age. They wore stocking caps and heavy sweaters with bright zigzag designs woven into them. Hevatha watched them come.

"Tutchone," she said under her breath. They may have been wearing white-made trousers and boots, but she knew them for Tutchone Indians.

Outside of their age and similar clothing, they weren't much alike to look at. The taller one had a sharp, cagey look about him. One eye was colorless due to an accident. He stood looking at Hevatha from the moment they entered the camp. The other man was shorter, rounder, constantly smiling, framing his mouth and eyes in deep weather- and laughter-cut wrinkles. Their names, Hevatha learned, were Sasak and Nadgi. Nadgi stood rubbing his hands together, nodding at Hevatha and Tyee, apparently full of good spirts and high expectations. The white men would pay him well.

Sasak's one good eye remained on Hevatha except when it shuttled almost surreptitiously to the sled, perhaps wondering what was under the furs.

The white man's name was McCulloch. Not exactly *halo skookum,* perhaps, but not long in the north. Tall, hairless, as Hevatha saw when he briefly removed his fur hat, ruddy, and hawk-nosed, he seemed humorless.

Hevatha signaled to English, who was in high spirits, and frowning, he walked aside with her. "Who are these people, English? You said only Demarest was going."

"True McCulloch is Demarest's banker—more or less. He's got the hard money to buy supplies."

"These other men . . ."

"McCulloch hired them to guide him north."

"They are Tutchone," Hevatha said.

"Tutchone Indians, yes. What's wrong with that?"

"I don't like them. Once the Tutchone took a bale of skins from the long rover while he ate with them in their lodge. They are thieves."

"These two? Or all Tutchone?"

"All Tutchone," she insisted.

"Nonsense. We'll need some good men anyway. I can't tell McCulloch to send his two away."

"They are Tutchone," Hevatha repeated, shaking her head. "There will be trouble."

English patted her shoulder and walked away from her. Hevatha had no more arguments for him, none that he would understand. These two were bad, at least the one called Sasak. She felt it inside of her belly. English would not understand that, and so she had told him that all Tutchones were bad. It wasn't true, but she had believed English would accept it.

The story about the fur bales was true. The long rover had told her of his narrow escape from the Tutchone camp.

English found McCulloch talking to his Indians in some strange pidgin tongue. "What's up?" he asked.

"Sasak just wanted to know if we should take a woman. A woman might mean trouble," True McCulloch said.

"Not Hevatha."

"They were wondering what sort of Indian she is," McCulloch told him. "They said her clothing was Tlingit, but she's not Tlingit."

"Coast Tlingit," English said. "By adoption. I believe she's Cheyenne originally."

"Cheyenne? Butchers," McCulloch said with distaste. "I was in the cavalry, old man. Dakota territory. Under General Lord. I saw some Cheyenne, by God."

"Hasn't got anything to do with here and now, True," Demarest put in.

"No," McCulloch said, recovering himself. "Nothing at all. I'm still trying to find another dog team, English, but it looks pretty bleak. Had a pack of unbroken malamutes offered to me for fifteen hundred, but that's robbery and the dogs won't take to harness anyway. As of now it looks like all we've got is your team, your sled. My boys here will do camp jobs, break trail, hunt. Your woman can handle the dogs—God, what is that big brute?"

Tyee had been in the trees; now, snuffing at the air like a prowling bear, he moved forward, his shaggy coat bristling. "That's the lead dog," English said, "and Hevatha's pet."

"Looks like a woolly ox. Is it tame?"

"Not tame enough that I'd offer it a hand to sniff," English said. He thought about warning them further, remembering the death of the Iht, but decided against it.

"We're going to have to keep it quiet that we're pulling out," Demarest cautioned them. "There's half a hundred men in Whitehorse who'd give us the knife for what we've got. The team's been seen. How about the supplies?"

"The Indians are bringing them out on the sly."

"Old packs," Sasak said. He had a voice so soft that English had to lean toward him to hear. It was a voice of flannel, half-conspiratorial, half-mocking.

Nadgi's voice, by contrast, was harsh and broken. Loudly the round little Tutchone added, "Old packs—they think we have rags, they think we have firewood, they think we have nothin', Indian stuff. No one knows."

"All right. What time, then?" Demarest asked. He glanced at his Belgian silver watch.

"How much time do you need?"

"Let me get my spare blanket and some more cartridges. That's all I need. An hour, say."

"English?"

"If the dogs are ready"—Hevatha nodded—"I'm ready anytime."

"In somethin' of a hurry, is he?" McCulloch asked Demarest with a wink.

"What are you talking about?" English demanded.

"I've heard of Aaron Butler's little trick."

"That's over," English said. "If I get the chance, I'll turn him over to the police, but that's the extent of it."

"Sure." McCulloch winked again, gestured to his Indians, and started back toward town.

"Does everyone know?" English asked.

"Everyone seems to. Maybe I talk too much. I figured you were dead and it didn't matter." Demarest lifted one shoulder. "They figure it's up to you to make things even. Landis can't. The police will never find Butler."

"Then neither can I, and that's all right with me."

"That's not the way I'd look at things. Once in Sacramento—"

"Spare me the old tales, Demarest. I don't intend to kill Butler."

"Why in blazes are you bothering to carry a gun, then?" Demarest asked with some heat. "In the Yukon there's little law, son. Someone owes Landis and his widow something. Someone owes Butler a blood debt. I figured it was you."

"It's not," English said stubbornly.

"Well, then . . ." Demarest lifted an eyebrow with surprise and disapprobation. Reaching into his pocket for a match, he lit his pipe and stumped away through the snow.

"English?"

"Yes, Hevatha."

"We are going with these men?" she asked.

"We are. It's decided."

Hevatha shrugged. There was nothing to say. She looked to the skies, wondering how long the good weather would hold. Not long enough, she suspected. Did any of these white men know what it would take to survive a winter out there without a house, without their white supplies? Did they know what the long snows would bring when there was no sound at all of a living thing in the forest and the rivers slept and the sap froze in the trees? She knew they didn't, but the Tutchone did. They knew, and so Hevatha did not believe them. She didn't believe that they meant to go through to Dawson at all.

When McCulloch returned with his Indians, Hevatha packed the supplies. There were too many of them, but the load would be quickly lightened by hunger. Sasak stood near the trees, watching her, always watching.

He knows, Hevatha thought. He knows that I have seen into his soul. Nadgi tried to make friends with the dogs, but had little luck. Tyee ignored him except for an occasional low growl. Hahtik, the black dog, snapped at him. The others allowed him near as long as he gave them tidbits.

"You watch," Nadgi said. "They will be my friends— all dogs are Nadgi's friends."

Demarest arrived a little later, carrying a pair of snowshoes, Nahani-made, and a blanket roll slung over his back. He carried a repeating rifle as well.

For a time the three whites stood together in silence, staring northward, toward Dawson; then McCulloch said, "Let's go. There's nothing to wait for, plenty to reach."

Hevatha waited until English signaled to her; then she lifted the dog team to its feet, and with the wind stiffening out of the west, the skies clearing, they started out of Whitehorse, following the white Yukon River northward.

The tundra was half-frozen, patched with snow. Sedge and heath began to appear, but still there were aspen and poplar growing densely in isolated stands. The St. Elias Mountains to the west stood massive and blue-gray against the pale sky. Tyee led the team across the bogs and fields of snow, yapping and bounding, urging the other dogs on to greater speed. Hevatha ran beside the team, guiding it. English hadn't rested for long, but the trek from the coast had hardened his leg muscles, strengthened his heart, and he ran better than at any time before. Demarest tended to lag, but for a man his age he was remarkable. McCulloch was the one who worried Hevatha. Often they had to slow the sled so that he wasn't left behind. Within ten miles he had already begged a ride and Hevatha had let him stand on the sled, slowing it too much.

"We aren't going to run all the way to Dawson, are we?" McCulloch demanded.

"Got to make time," Demarest panted.

The man on the sled shook his head. "We won't make much if we drop dead on the way."

Hevatha said, "We will drop dead, all of us, if we don't hurry. Soon the snow will come, a very long snow."

The bald man virtually ignored her. He peered ahead and then looked back to where Sasak and Nadgi jogged behind them. Hevatha too looked at the Tutchone Indians. She knew what they wanted. They wanted the whites to tire, to sleep deeply, and when they awoke they would find they had no supplies, no dogs, no sled.

"I know you, you devils," she said, and then she laughed. She laughed because they knew Hevatha had seen through them. They didn't like having her there at all.

The whites insisted on stopping at noon to eat. Already they wanted to eat. What would they be eating in a week? Hevatha stood near the dogs during the entire meal, feeling Sasak's eyes on her.

I know, you devil thing.

After lunch they went on more slowly, following a crude trail through a stand of white spruce and pine. At a distance they saw a herd of caribou making its slow way south before the winter came. The river had narrowed and Hevatha saw beaver in the tributary streams, and now and then mink splashing into the water, swimming away from the approaching men.

Looking back, she could no longer see Whitehorse. The mountains behind them grew smaller, the Pelly Mountains ahead grew larger, darker, more fantastic in their snow-streaked raw form.

The long line of Indians appeared before them like dark specters. Hevatha slowed the sled, stopped it, and waited. The whites drifted toward each other, their rifles held higher now. The strange Indians simply stood and stared.

"What the hell do they want?" Demarest said.

"Sasak!" McCulloch waved his Tutchone guide forward. The Indians continued watching. There were ten, all carrying bows and arrows. Behind them the trees shifted coldly in the wind. Hevatha went forward to stand beside and behind English.

"Sasak, dammit, what do these men want!"

"I don't know, sir. Very difficult to say, sir," Sasak said in his muted, nearly whispery voice.

"Want what we're carrying, I suppose," Demarest said around his pipe. "Damned if they'll get that. Not against three repeating rifles."

"Why don't we find out instead of speculating,"

English said. "Can't Sasak talk to them? They're his people, aren't they?"

"Not my people, sir," Sasak answered. "These men, they are Nahani."

"Nahani." English looked to Hevatha, his stomach tightening. She could only nod.

"Can you talk to them, Sasak?"

"Maybe a little. I'll see. Keep the guns with you."

McCulloch said, "Don't worry about that."

Sasak went forward uneasily. When he was within twenty yards of the Nahani he began to speak. Immediately the Nahani started to gesture. There was an occasional shouted demand. Sasak returned, wading through the melting snow.

"What do they want, some kind of tribute?" McCulloch asked.

"No, sir," Sasak said. "They want this one."

His finger pointed at English, and McCulloch, eyes puzzled, narrowing, glanced that way. "What for, for God's sake? What are they talking about?"

"They say he killed a man and must be punished. They say they know his boot tracks. They followed him across the mountains. This is the man. This is the one that killed a big Nahani chief."

"English?"

"Dammit, it's not true, is it?" McCulloch demanded.

"Richard?" Demarest asked.

English took a slow deep breath before he answered. "It's true. It was more or less an accident. I thought he was another man."

"You killed him!"

"I killed the Nahani, that's right."

"Damn all, boy"—McCulloch slapped the side of his own head in frustration—"why didn't you tell us about this!"

"It didn't seem to matter. I thought it was over."

McCulloch said, "It doesn't seem that it is now, does it?" He looked to Demarest. "What do we do, Floyd?"

"Do?" Demarest lit his pipe. "Tell them to go to

hell. If you think I'm turning a white man and a friend over to a band of savages, you're crazy."

"They'll kill us all!"

"They won't. They might try," Demarest said, working the lever on his rifle, cocking it, "but they won't."

He turned and fired the rifle into the air over the heads of the Nahani Indians. They didn't scatter at once, but slowly, gradually, they sifted back into the trees.

"Now we've had it," McCulloch said bitterly.

Sasak didn't like what was happening. "Maybe better give them the yellow-hair, sir. Maybe the Nahani follow us and pretty soon kill us all."

"Maybe someone will kill you," the woman's voice said. "Maybe you will die soon."

Sasak turned slowly, his one good eye fixed on Hevatha. He looked at her and he knew that she was serious, knew that the yellow-haired man had found a squaw with spirit.

Hevatha was angry. She knew what Sasak wanted: to set the white men at each other's throats. Perhaps they would kill each other or send English off to be killed by the Nahani. Then his thievery would be easier.

Demarest broke it up. "We're traveling together. We're partners. We're not going to leave anyone behind if the going gets tough, and we're not going to turn anyone over to any pack of savages that wanders in demanding his scalp. The Nahani will see that we mean business and they'll give it up after a while."

"They won't give it up, sir," Sasak rasped. "All of us will die because of Mr. English."

McCulloch was shaken. He looked to Demarest for leadership and Demarest shrugged it off. "It's all talk, True. They won't try anything against our rifles."

Hevatha stood in puzzlement, watching True McCulloch. He was supposed to have been a cavalryman once, an Indian fighter. Where had he done his fighting, from inside his lodge? Perhaps age had drawn off his courage. She looked at McCulloch and then again

at the sulking Sasak, and then she laughed, walking
away.

"What in God's name could be funny?" McCulloch
demanded.

"Maybe," Demarest said softly, "she sees us for
what we are. Come on, let's get going. With a little
more caution. It might be a good idea to send your
Indians out ahead to scout around."

"Yes, you give me a rifle," Sasak said, "and Nadgi
and I will proceed ahead, sir."

"No rifles." Demarest was firm on that.

"The Nahani will kill us."

"They're not going to kill anyone. They'll skulk
around for a while and satisfy their honor and then
they'll go back to wherever it is they came from,"
Demarest said.

"The Nahani will kill us," Sasak repeated dismally.
He glanced at McCulloch to see if that had any effect
on the tall man, but McCulloch's face showed nothing.
Sasak wandered off to crouch with Nadgi in quiet
conversation in a language only they understood.

Demarest went to English, rested a hand on his
shoulder, and said, "I wish you'd told us, Richard."

"What would that have changed? Nothing, if you
still wanted my dog team!"

Demarest was thoughtful. "I suppose not. Look,"
he said in a lowered voice, "I don't quite believe what
I told McCulloch myself. Those Indians didn't follow
you a hundred miles to give it up and go home. Keep
your eyes open, Richard. I like you. Hate to see you
get killed up here."

Later, after the team had started on again, Hevatha
said to Richard, "Ganook."

"Ganook? What do you mean?"

"Ganook will not forget either, Richard English. He
will not stop either. He wants to kill you too."

It was absurd. Ganook had been left far behind.
The Tlingit would have had to travel many hundreds
of miles over rough country into alien territory. Ganook
had forgotten them. The Tlingit could not be back
there.

Still English spared a backward glance toward Whitehorse, now lost in the distance, toward the white mountains, low and uncertain against the horizon. Unconsciously he began to run faster, breathing small curses against his fate and the northland.

Somewhere the Nahani watched and somewhere behind, if Hevatha was right, Ganook still prowled. Ahead was the vast cold wasteland of the Yukon and somewhere Dawson with its promise of gold and salvation.

English trudged on, noticing that the wind had cooled, that the forest had become suddenly still. Two hours later the clouds that had hovered over the western mountains began their slow march toward them, and before they had covered another five miles, it began to snow in deadly earnest as the Yukon winter returned from its brief banishment.

7

IT snowed and they walked on through a darkened world like roving spirits seeking a lost home. They moved through the forest hearing the shrieks of the wind, their heads jerking toward each falling branch, never knowing if the Nahani had returned to keep their promise.

English, lost in endless snow-veiled corridors, stayed close to Hevatha and the team. Demarest wore a scarf across his face, obscuring everything but his eyes with their frozen lashes. McCulloch staggered drunkenly along, gripping his rifle with both hands. The Tutchone were there, but silent, almost ghostly, perhaps waiting for their chance.

"How long can we keep this up?" McCulloch called out at the top of his lungs, but the wind muffled his shout to a smothered gasp. "We've got to stop sometime."

But they didn't stop. They walked on through the endless white night, the snow falling heavier by the hour. Hevatha broke out her snowshoes and began to break the trail for the dogs, which were bogging down in the deep drifts. Moving ahead of the team, she tramped a path through the deep, soft snow.

The arrow flew through the air, nicking English's parka, embedding itself in the pack. He spun, dropping to both knees. He started to lift his rifle and then halted.

Demarest was shouting something English couldn't make out. Richard looked to the older man, saw his rifle spew red-yellow flame from its muzzle, and heard the dull thunk of a bullet impacting with flesh. The

Nahani fell dead on the ground, blood from his throat coloring the snow crimson.

"Dammit, boy, why didn't you fire!" Demarest yanked English to his feet. "Wounded?"

"No." English shook his head dazedly.

"Didn't you see him, Richard?"

"I saw him." English looked with curiosity at his rifle, unfired. "I saw him."

Demarest's rime-fringed eyes stared out bleakly, questions passing through them in a rapid parade. "Better keep moving," he said finally.

English stood a long while longer staring at the inert, twisted form pressed into the snow.

The Iht had said the death word and now English walked with death. Two men had died because of him. He carried the death word with him. It clung to his heart like some tenacious parasitic organ. He carried it into the wilderness, and the wilderness became a place of dying.

"English?" Demarest was watching him with concern. "I said let's go."

"All right." English nodded and tramped away from the dead man, feeling a sawing motion against his heart, Death reminding him that they shared a common destiny.

"English," Hevatha said, "I am glad you did not kill him."

"But I did," the young man answered quietly. "I did, Hevatha."

The snow fell like diamond dust from a bright sky. They crossed a frozen river, hearing it mutter beneath the ice. The trees became fewer and then there were no more for as far as the eye could see, only the tundra thick with snow and sedge and heath.

"They won't be able to follow us so well now," McCulloch said. "The Indians will turn back."

Hevatha looked at the tall man. McCulloch, she decided, was more of a fool than she had thought. How could the Nahani turn back now, with another of their tribe dead? How could they return to their village and tell their elders that they had given up their chase?

When they camped they stood close to the small fire Hevatha had built, their eyes constantly searching the empty land. The dogs were growing tired and surly. Hahtik tried to bite McCulloch's hand off when he gave them a scrap of meat. For a moment it appeared that McCulloch would shoot the dog, but the angry impulse faded quickly. He was too tired, too cold to stay mad.

It snowed again, heavily. They trudged doggedly northward through walls of snow. From just behind the sled Richard couldn't see the lead dog. People appeared and disappeared eerily. They had long gone past exhaustion. They simply moved on, trotting at first, then slowing to a leaden walk. Hevatha moved ahead in her snowshoes, packing the fresh snow. The others walked behind the sled. The wind had begun to drift the snow, and now it stood in pyramids and cornices, a frozen white sea beside their trail.

"What's happened now?" McCulloch panted. The sled had come to a stop. Ahead they could see Hevatha, a dark, shadowy figure moving about in apparent aimlessness.

'I'll see." English moved forward and the others followed. It was difficult to breathe now that they had stopped. Frozen air overwhelmed the lungs. English's feet were numb and heavy.

He found Hevatha standing, staring out at something vast and flat and gray. She turned to English as he plodded toward her, the others at his heels.

"What is it, Hevatha?"

"A lake, Richard English. We shall have to go around."

"A lake!" Demarest boomed. "What lake! Why didn't she know it was here?"

The question was pointless; Hevatha didn't answer it. Her arm lifted as she described a proposed route. "Around through the forest, past the broken hill. We can go that way."

McCulloch peered into the wind, trying to make out

what she meant. "That's ten miles!" he exclaimed. "Maybe more."

"Yes," Hevatha said, "there is no help for it." Her lashes were white with frost; her eyes shifted from the distant trail to English. "We must go that way."

"The hell with that," Demarest said angrily. "It's frozen, isn't it? Look out there. Frozen solid. Sasak! Can't we cross that lake?"

Sasak looked carefully. He showed some concern himself, but he told Demarest, "I think so, sir. Good crossing. Good ice."

"No," Hevatha insisted. "I smell water under the ice."

"Good God!" McCulloch shouted, waving an arm. "She can smell water under the ice! I can't smell it, but I know there's water there too. What's she talking about?"

That was a direct question for Hevatha. McCulloch had the habit of asking English what he wanted to know, as if he had to interpret for the woman.

"The ice is thin. I smell water," Hevatha said again. "Sasak?"

"Thin. Strong enough for us," the Tutchone said. He had moved even closer to the lake's edge.

"That ice should be two feet thick," McCulloch observed. "Cold as it is. In Michigan . . ."

Hevatha shook her head. "No. We must go around."

"It'll cost us another day, the way things are going. The lake can't be more than a few hundred feet across." Demarest looked to English. "Well?"

"If Hevatha says go around, I'd say go around."

"Dammit all!" McCulloch said sharply. "We'll freeze trying to make a decision. Why should one Indian know any more than the other? The dogs go first, don't they? If they break through, we haul them out and retreat. But we can't stand here!"

"I say go across," Demarest said. McCulloch nodded agreement.

"I go," Sasak said. "If the woman is afraid."

"We'll all go. Cautiously, that's all," Demarest said. "Eh? McCulloch? English?"

Hevatha looked to the ice with apprehension. There was no way she could explain to these whites what she felt. Beneath the ice, water moved, dark and swirling, groaning as it shifted. The ice was too thin. She could smell the water, nearly taste it as they moved cautiously forward onto the frozen lake.

Snow drifted past. The stand of tall hemlock trees along the shore swayed in ghostly unison. English glanced at her encouragingly. McCulloch had moved out a little ahead of the others, walking to the left and just behind the team. Tyee, his massive paws slipping on the ice, led the dogs forward.

"You see," McCulloch shouted, "it's—" And then Tyee went down. Sudden jagged fissures opened at his feet and a slab of gray ice tilted up. Struggling, howling, Tyee dropped into the murky water, dragging the rest of the team after him. Hevatha looked in terror for one moment, then leapt for the sled, dragging it back. Demarest was beside her, his face brilliant red beneath the snow pallor.

English was running toward the gaping, widening hole in the ice and Hevatha yelled at him. English heard her but kept running. He leapt into the dark opening in the ice where Tyee thrashed and howled pitiably. English's right foot caught on the lip of the solid ice and bent backward. There was a sickening crack, and sudden violent pain shot through his thigh as he sank into the water.

English had his knife in his hand as he lunged toward Tyee, who was sinking rapidly now. He grabbed for harness, slashing at it with his knife blade. Tyee rolled into him, a paw raking Richard's face. Numb from the water, English was barely able to stay afloat. The knife slashed out again and Tyee was suddenly free. He scrambled up onto solid ice, shook himself, and ran in a wild circle, trying to warm his body.

English was clinging to the broken edge of the ice. Demarest and Hevatha were running to him, but they seemed to move in slow motion.

"Get back," he tried to call out, "you'll fall in too," but his chattering teeth twisted the words into a meaningless jumble of broken sounds. Hevatha was flat on her belly, her hand stretching out toward English as Demarest held her ankles. Richard felt her hand on his wrist then, her fingers so warm that they seemed to burn his frozen flesh.

"Fool, fool," she was saying, and Richard tried to grin in return. They pulled him out of the icy water, dragging him back toward the shore, where he lay on his back, trembling from head to foot, frozen to the bone. His heart leapt and danced in his chest. Hevatha was stripping his clothes from him, shouting something angrily to the others.

Then the world went dark briefly and English knew nothing, felt nothing. When he opened his eyes again he was lying next to a blazing fire, the others crouched around him. He had no body. Somewhere below, useless limbs dangled and the bellows of his lungs drew in air and expelled it in a mist, but he felt none of it until the fiery shaft of pain roared through his leg.

"Dammit, dammit all!" he shouted. "I've broken it. Broken my leg."

"We know, old man," Demarest said, his broad red face concerned, fearful. "Your squaw's splinted it but there's not much else to do. I've got some whiskey, if . . ."

"Break the damned stuff out," English said savagely. His head rolled from side to side. His body, numb, absent moments ago, had returned to his possession and it was an aching, frozen, battered thing through which firestorms coursed at intervals.

"Fool," Hevatha said, stroking his brow.

"What was I to do?" English demanded.

"Just a dog. Tyee is just a dog."

"He was going down . . ." Pain caused English to clench his teeth and bite off the sentence. Demarest had returned with a metal flask of whiskey. He propped Richard's head up and poured the liquor into his mouth. It was tasteless going down, searing as it reached his belly.

"Easy, old man," Demarest said. "Take it easy.

Damned sorry about this. Should've listened to the squaw, I guess."

"What are we going to do now?" McCulloch was whining, slapping his shoulders. It was snowing again, lazy flakes swirling down as the wind drifted across the frozen lake. The fire bent and twisted. "We can't turn back to Whitehorse!"

"We haven't got much choice," Demarest answered impatiently. "You want the boy to die?"

McCulloch didn't answer. His eyes indicated that the thought of English dying didn't seem such a bad alternative. "We can't stay here, either," the tall man grumbled.

Tyee barked then, rose from the ground, and turned savage eyes toward the trees. The Indians came forward slowly, half-lost in the fog of snow. Demarest cursed and cocked his rifle. Hevatha rose.

"They've found us. Now we're in for it."

"They aren't Nahani," Hevatha said quickly, touching Demarest's arm. McCulloch had moved up beside them and the Tutchone.

Sasak agreed, "Not Nahani. These are Han Indians, sir."

"Tell them to get out of here and mind their own business," McCulloch growled. He had had enough of Indians, any Indians.

The Han had paused. Now they came forward again. They were men and women in equal numbers, ten in all, towing sledges across the snow. On the sledges were firewood and the carcasses of two caribou. A child in furs rode on one.

"These people mean no trouble," Hevatha said.

"Let them keep going, then," McCulloch answered sharply.

"Hello, hello!" a round-faced woman called in English. Despite the cold, she had her parka hood down. Her gray hair, tightly wound around her wide skull, caught the snowflakes and glistened with them. "We are Han, good friends. Hello, hello!"

She was smiling broadly, showing good white teeth. The rest of the Han Indians smiled as well, apparently greatly pleased to find this party of whites and their Indian guides.

"My name is Hevatha," the Tlingit woman said, going forward.

"Yes, yes." The Han studied her, the smile deepening. "I see—Moon Walker. Yes, happy. All of you must eat and stay a winter. Very much food. Happy."

Hevatha was smiling in return. McCulloch looked as if he would like to shoot them all for being so happy. Demarest was wary, as if fearing a trap. English groaned and yelled for more whiskey.

"A hurt man."

"Yes. He broke his leg. We were trying to cross the lake," Hevatha explained.

"Yes," the Han woman said, her face becoming momentarily grave. "The ice is bad. All Hans know that. This lake is a hungry lake. It swallows people. It swallows dogs—"

"Can't you shut the old hag up!" McCulloch demanded. "We're freezing, stuck here, English has broken his leg, and the woman's got to babble on. Can't they help us? Give us food, a sled? I'll buy it."

"Shut up, True," Demarest said. "You've got to go slow with these people."

Hevatha asked, "What is your name, woman?"

"My name is Kawchot. Everyone knows me. I am the teller of sticks." She smiled again, apparently pleased with her name, her title, and her place in the world.

"My man is hurt. Is there a warm bed for him in your village?"

"Oh, yes. A warm bed. Warm beds for everyone. We will not eat your dogs," she promised.

"How far?" Demarest prompted. "Ask her how far their village is from here."

There was no need for Hevatha to ask the question again. "Very soon," Kawchot answered, lifting her arm. "Very soon after the trees. Come and see what beds we have, come and listen to us sing."

McCulloch didn't want to hear anyone sing and said so explosively. Demarest shut him up. "They're going to give us food and shelter, True. Keep your mouth shut."

"Where's all this leave us?" McCulloch shot back. "What about English? He can't go on, and it's his dog-sled, isn't it? These people don't seem to have dogs. If they did, they wouldn't be dragging those sledges around themselves, would they?"

"We'll find out. Keep yourself calm, will you? English is hurt. He needs a place to stay. This is a godsend for us."

"Come on, come along. Oh, there is a fine big dog," Kawchot said, spying Tyee. "You, Moon Walker, put your man on the sled and bring him to us. We will keep him fed; you will keep him warm. Then he will smile again."

English had been listening to all of this through a hazy consciousness. At times everything was clear, at other times he could hear nothing, see nothing. Pain and utter numbness alternated. He felt himself being lifted onto the sled and after what seemed an interminable wait they started on, plodding through the snow, which was falling in earnest again. The trees formed a dark, moving canopy against a gray-white sky. Tyee barked and Hahtik joined in. Hevatha was walking beside him, looking straight ahead, her face lovely against a dreary background. She seemed to feel his eyes on her, and smiling, she took his hand, walking on beside the sled.

The Han village was in a small valley beyond the trees. Smoke flavored with the scents of broiling meat rose into the sky. Children like bundles of fur with legs came running to greet them. Their homes were made of skins over bent saplings. English was aware of a gabble of voices, of many strangers around the sled, of being lifted, and then he was unconscious again.

After a brief, swirling descent into the frozen lake of dreams, he again opened his eyes, seeing little at first. A fire burned softly, its grace touching his frozen body with comfort. He was shirtless, but furs, soft and thick, had been placed over his body. His leg throbbed, but the pain was distant. His fingers and toes tingled

as they warmed again. Hevatha was there. He saw her
before the tiny fire, feeding it pieces of fuel a stick at a
time, as if she were feeding some bright animal. Her
hair was loose now, bunched at the middle of her back
with a rawhide tie. She had a cloth dress on. She
seemed to be speaking softly, or perhaps the words
came from someone else's lips, someone far distant.

"Hevatha."

She turned, smiling, and Richard felt his heart swell.
He saw something in her smile, in her fire-bright eyes,
that he hadn't seen before, something that—fool that
he was—had eluded him.

She came to him on her knees and bent low to
stroke his hair, to kiss his forehead. She rose, her
hand still on his head, and English took her hand.

"You are well?" she asked.

"Hot now."

"You need to be hot for a time. Very hot. You are
lucky you aren't dead, English. For a time I thought
. . . You are lucky someone did not have to take off
your toes or fingers with a good steel knife. Could I
have done it? You were foolish to go into the water,
to cut Tyee free."

"He saved my life once, didn't he?"

"Only a dog, he is only a dog with a dog's instincts."

English shrugged. "I am only a man." He squeezed
her hand. Hevatha looked at him quizzically and stood.
Now English could see that they were inside a Han
house. Weapons and tools stood in one corner. A
woven blanket with a hole in the center lay around the
fire. Something shifted at Richard's feet and he lifted
his head. Tyee's yellow eyes were watching back.

"He has been there since we brought you in here.
This house," Hevatha said, "is Kawchot's. Do you
remember her? She is a good woman who tells sticks."

"Some kind of fortune-teller?"

Hevatha repeated, "She tells the sticks."

A hand drew back the skin flap of the house. Behind the man who entered, snow twisted down past
the village and the surrounding trees.

"He awake?" Demarest asked. At Hevatha's nod

the big man came in, hat in his hands, his red beard curling around his jaw like flames. "How you doing, English?"

"I feel all right." English touched his leg. "I guess I'm done as far as Dawson goes, eh?"

"Looks like it." Demarest nodded, crouching down.

"Sorry. I mucked it up. I muck everything up."

"Just bad luck, that's all." Demarest pointed out, "If you hadn't cut that lead dog free, chances are the whole team would have followed it down. Maybe the sled too. Where would that have left us? Just bad luck. Well"—Demarest looked around—"this isn't much, but you'll be comfortable for a time . . ."

"What's on your mind, Floyd?" English asked. He smiled faintly as he asked the question. He knew what Demarest wanted. "No need to hold back. I can see how things lie."

"That's right," Demarest said with a relieved grin. "No need to hold back. We're still partners. We've still got Drake's claim and his map. We've still got the jump on the rest of those *chechacos*."

"Weather's turning nasty, Floyd."

"Yes, it is, English," Demarest said, tugging at his beard with two fingers. "McCulloch and me, we figure we can beat the worst of it to Dawson if we start now, though. Sasak thinks so too."

"Sasak lies," Hevatha muttered from near the fire. Demarest glanced at her.

"You want the sled and team," English said.

"Yes." Demarest's relief broadened. "That's it, English. The team and the sled. I'd like the squaw too, but I guess . . ." He looked at Hevatha and swallowed the rest of the sentence. "It's not that we're deserting you, Richard, but you see how it's got to be. Don't worry about us cutting you out of anything. I'll put it in writing if you want."

"We've already shaken hands," English replied.

"Yes, that's right, we have!" Demarest went on, "We've got to get to Dawson. Someone jumps that claim in the meantime, and none of us gets anything. You're living up to your part of the bargain anyway.

Your share was the sled and the dog team. I figure McCulloch and I go on ahead with the two Indians and wait out winter in Drake's old shack. No one can touch the place if we're living there. Come spring, you'll be healed up. McCulloch and I will have plenty of work done by the time you get there. Save you some labor, eh!" Demarest lifted a hand, which he nearly slapped down on Richard's broken leg. He looked at the hand and shook his head.

"It makes sense," English said. "I can't travel. No sense you two being stuck here all winter."

"That's the spirit. You won't be sorry, English. Floyd Demarest never forgets a partner, never forgets a promise. The lead dog . . . I guess he stays too. No one can handle him but you and the girl, I expect."

"You're right. There's the black dog, Hahtik."

"That one's a devil, but he's savage enough to keep the others in line, I suppose. Nadgi knows the dogs. He's learned their ways. He can handle Hahtik. Well . . ." Demarest rose. His head nearly touched the roof of the skin house. "If there's anything you want off the sled . . ."

"Hevatha will look." He rolled his head toward Hevatha. She was facing away from him, still staring into the quietly shifting flames. She nodded her head. "My rifle . . ."

"Looks like your rifle went into the lake, Richard. You won't need one here."

"I suppose not. I was thinking of the Nahanis."

"Hardly think they'll bother you in this village. If you really need a gun—"

"No, never mind, it's all right," the blond man answered.

"We'd stay a few days to make sure your leg doesn't get worse," Demarest said, "but . . ."

"No. Try to beat the weather, Floyd. After all, I've got a lot riding on that claim too."

"All right." Demarest tugged his fur hat on and stuck out a hand. English took it in both of his own hands. "We'll get on the trail, then. Have your woman take what she wants from the sled." Demarest didn't seem to know how to say good-bye. He still seemed embarrassed by events, by his decision that he and McCulloch had to press on northward toward Dawson. Finally, with a last few mumbled words of farewell, he backed from the Han lodge. English was almost happy to see him go, almost happy to be left behind. Outside, the snow fell and the hard wind blew. It was a long, long trek to Dawson over bad country through rough weather. The Nahani were out there somewhere, still angry over the murder of two of their people.

Here it was warm and quiet, the fur bed soft, folding arms of comfort around English. Hevatha was there, and Tyee, and the fire flickered hypnotically.

"You trust those men?" Hevatha asked.

"Of course."

"Then it is good." She shrugged.

"It'll work out. Come spring, we can make our way to the claim, start in working, and just maybe make our fortune."

"You still want gold," Hevatha said.

"Gold?" English seemed to have to think about it. "Yes, I want gold."

"I did not know if that was what brought you here. You came to the north and sometimes you tell me you have come for this, sometimes for that. I think that you don't know why you are here, English." She paused. "Maybe you have come for me."

Her eyes couldn't meet his as she said that. She turned half away. English's hand stretched out and touched the hem of her skirt, and when she looked back, his pale eyes were on her, deeper now than usual, showing distant light.

"Perhaps," he said. "Perhaps that is why I am here, Hevatha."

"I will see to the sled." She went quickly out, as if English had offended her, and he could only lie there watching the shadows the fire cast on the skin walls of the house.

The pain returned sometime later, stronger than it had been for a while, and English closed his eyes, wanting to drift off to sleep, where the pain became only a hollow echo cast down the well of unconsciousness from some unreal world above.

He slept fitfully. Many-armed Indians in fox hats pursued him across a frozen lake, and he fell through the ice, to be attacked by fish with wolves' heads. Another Richard English standing apart from this watched and said, "I am lost. The planet spins and I cling to it. There are deep fissures everywhere. Beneath my feet there are horrible things. There is nothing at all to cling to, no reason to swim or run or fight."

He awoke. Before the fire Hevatha stood naked, her hair free of its tie, her eyes deep with woman-knowledge, and she came to him as he watched, his body warming at the sight of her, his arms reaching up to her.

She turned back the furs and crawled in beside him, her body molding itself to his in a way mysterious and perfect and beyond pleasure.

Hevatha held him gently. His leg had been broken; he was tired and sick and cold, and whether he knew it or not, quite lost in the white world of the north.

She cradled his head in her arms, holding his cheek to her breast, which rose and fell in deep swelling motions like the sea. His hand rested on her thigh, and their flesh seemed to bond at that point. Now and then his fingers moved, slightly and perhaps not deliberately, as if wanting to cling to her, yet afraid to. English remained flat on his back. With his leg broken he could not roll to her, but it was still good, for she had waited a long time for him to touch her, a long time while she fought back the wishes of her body, her heart, and her soul.

Now he was against her, solid and pale and needful, and it was good. She held him and felt his hair against her cheek, felt the steady pulsing of his body, the closeness of his heart while he lay still and comforted and very young against her breast. The snow twisted down outside and the wind rippled the walls of the hide house. They were untouched by the storm, by the cold, by the drifting, changing, darkening world.

"This, Richard English," Hevatha whispered, "is why you have come north."

He could not hear her. He was sleeping again, sleeping differently, more soundly, wrapped in her comforting warmth, sharing the peace which demands two, male and female. She kissed his hair so lightly that he could not have felt it. She wanted to wrap her arms around him more tightly, to draw him to her, into her, to shelter him and give him her strength, to take from him, exchanging comfort, but he was weary and hurt and lost.

Hevatha held him as the storm and the world drifted past. Life was centered here where he touched her, where his breath brushed her breasts like a warm summer breeze. Her heart swelled and beat more rapidly; it became a joyous, needful thing yearning for the man beside her.

"The storm," Hevatha whispered, "must never end."

English was confined to his bed for long weeks, growing restless and more uncomfortable. Hevatha went out more often as he grew stronger and more cantankerous. She walked among the Han villages, a happy, guileless people she felt at home with immediately. She fished with them through the ice of the long lake, bringing home sturgeon and trout to smoke on the racks the Han built over their fires. She hunted and trapped, surprising and delighting the Han with her skills.

"You are our guest," she was told. "You don't have to work for your supper."

"A good guest does. Besides, I am not a guest while I am here. I am one of you."

Tyee ventured out more now that English was better, and he was an object of both fear and admiration. The Han in this village had no dogs, although other bands did. Kawchot explained simply, "We eat them all. So we walk, but we have full bellies!" She smiled expansively and rubbed her own round belly.

The weather was changeable but never warm. At times the temperature dropped to the point where nothing could move outside. No Han or caribou or bird stirred in the wilderness. To venture out was to die, and so the Han stayed in, huddled around small fires as they always had.

On one hard, bright, frozen day Kawchot told the sticks for Hevatha. The women sat alone in Kawchot's house. She lived alone, two husbands had been lost, one in war with the Nahani, one torn apart by a grizzly bear named the Winter God, who had only three feet and a temper formidable and savage even for a rogue grizzly.

"So my husband, whose name was Tashak, went out for wood to bring home," Kawchot said, "and he saw a pile of furs lying on the snow. 'Ho,' he said, 'someone has left a great pile of furs out to freeze. I will take them to my house so they are not ruined.' And Tashak went to the furs, a huge pile almost over his head, and he put his hand on the top fur, which was very coarse, and ho, it was not a pile of furs at all but the Winter God sleeping in the snow, and the bear was angry with Tashak for awaking it and it rose to tear off his head and eat it. So I had no husband again." Kawchot looked suitably saddened briefly. "This was many years ago, before I told sticks. If I had told sticks then, I could have warned Tashak not to find a pile of furs and disturb it."

The old woman was unwrapping a bundle of sticks which had been rolled in the fur of an ermine. The ermine's head was still attached to the fur, as was its tail.

"The ermine knows many things. It listens underground. The ermine knows how to change its coat so no one can see it. White in the winter, brown in the summer. The ermine knows where the wolverine keeps his teeth."

The sticks in Kawchot's hand were four-sided, painted a different color on each side. Red, yellow, white, and black. Symbols had been cut into some of these sides.

"Now I will tell you, Hevatha, what you will find. Now I will show you something. Now I say your name twice: Moon Walker. That is your name to the Han." She repeated it: "Moon Walker."

The sticks were cast and Kawchot watched them in silence for a long while, her leather-colored, deeply seamed face intent. "Now," she told Hevatha, "I will tell you why your name is Moon Walker. You maybe do not know about the moon. Maybe the Tlingit know nothing, I don't know. I will tell you. The moon has the secret ways. It is day and night at once there. The people live in gardens and walk around eating gooseberries. They always smile because they never have to work. Just eat berries from the gardens.

"They always are walking, though. Always walking because night is just behind them. They walk from garden to garden, eating gooseberries."

Hevatha found herself smiling, and Kawchot said, "See—you are always smiling, Hevatha. You never cry. You are always walking. You go from one place to another. You are a happy woman, pleased with your own body, pleased with your own strength. The night cannot capture you. You are always walking from darkness and into the sun, as the Moon Walkers do."

Only now did Kawchot begin to interpret the sticks. "A long walk, a very long walk," the old woman said. "A long hunt and a troublesome man. Peace and much work. I see you living long, but your world will be different from any you have known . . . maybe"—the old woman shook her head—"maybe a world with white people in it. Maybe a world with much happiness."

Kawchot was pleased with her telling of the sticks. Perhaps she had invented it all, but there was no harm done. Everything she had said could be true. Hevatha looked away briefly and then glanced back. Kawchot's expression had changed greatly. Her chin seemed to have grown so heavy that it tugged her mouth down. Her eyes were hooded. In her hand was the ermine skin with the sticks wrapped in it. All but one stick, the one which still rested on the earth, pointing directly at Hevatha. Kawchot saw Hevatha's eyes on her and she scooped the stick up with a rapid, mechanical smile.

"What does the dark stick mean, Kawchot?" Hevatha asked, placing her hand on the Han woman's wrist.

"Dark stick? Means you are a Moon Walker, very happy."

"The truth?"

"Means something, but it is not for you. I dropped it by accident."

"No you didn't, it was there all along, Kawchot."

"Oh, no! I think not."

"Is it bad, Kawchot?"

"Just sticks," she said, "just sticks. You will walk very happy."

"All right," Hevatha said, letting her hand fall away from Kawchot's. "It doesn't matter if you don't wish to tell me."

The old woman put the sticks away in a small woven basket. "Just sticks."

"Death?' Hevatha asked, guessing. "Does it have something to do with death, Kawchot?"

"Maybe." The old woman shrugged. "What does it mean, anyway, death? Shadows beneath the trees, that's all. Sunlight comes and shadow comes. Death is the shadow of every living thing."

"You don't want to tell me?" Hevatha asked.

Kawchot answered carefully, "You have already told yourself. I have nothing more to say."

Then Kawchot's smile returned and she launched into a long story of a summer rice harvest, a story which Hevatha felt sure was designed to distract her. It was an unnecessary diversion. Hevatha did not fear death; as the Han woman had said, it was always there. You could not shake it any more than a woman can shake her shadow.

She did not think of death with English, nor of despair or illness, nor of darkness or winter. Only of life. He was in a warm and burgeoning spring, he was light and comfort.

During the long nights of the winter, during the gray and blustering, earth-darkening storms, she would lie beside him, lie and feel his nearness until she was nearly trembling with the need to roll to him, to slide her thigh across his leg, to feel him stir as he placed his arms around her neck and pulled her face to his, as he tasted her shoulders and her ears, her long dark hair. He would kiss the inside of her wrist, the hollow at the base of her throat, and his hands would take her firmly, gently, and he would press his body to hers.

His hands seemed made to know her body, tutored in their gentle caresses by some primitive force. His fingers ran across her back, along her spine, revealing his knowledge of Hevatha's own womanliness, through her abdomen, her loins, across her breasts in tingling ripples.

His touch was something her body had always craved, needed, expected as her birthright. It had been so long in coming and it was so good and natural that at times Hevatha laughed out loud with unadulterated joy, holding him to her, loving him.

There were times when Richard withdrew from her during the long winter, times when he seemed to be struggling against something dragging him back into the unhappy mists of his past life.

He would sit brooding by the fire, massaging his healing leg or simply staring, arms folded, head bowed to the flames. He saw things distant and valuable in the golden-red flames, but he couldn't bring himself to discuss them openly with Hevatha and she had to guess much of the time, unable to fully fathom the intricate puzzle of her yellow-haired man with the lost blue eyes.

Her own English grew much better. She forced herself to learn the words, even those tongue-twisting, impossible words he sometimes used with strange intonations and hidden meanings. She forced herself to learn because she needed to know what he thought, she needed to be closer to him, a part of him. Even when he brooded, he was necessary to her, as necessary as air itself.

Hevatha had never needed anyone, never wanted to need anyone. It was a strange, sometimes disconcerting feeling. Often she kept silent as he ranted, at other times she cajoled him, teased him, or simply lay back silently, being a woman so that he forgot his ugly thoughts and went to her, his lips following the line of her thigh, brushing her abdomen, his hands lifting her, drawing her against him. He would kneel before her, holding her until his arms ached. Then he would shake his head and go down to her, smothering her mouth with his until their mingled breath was heated and rapid.

"Are you tired of this alien land?" Hevatha asked him. The fire was on his face, reddening it, netting it with shifting shadows. He did not lift his eyes when he answered.

"My dreams, Hevatha. I am tired of my dreams. They are the most alien land I have ever walked."

"Dreams of gold, English?" she asked, going to him on her knees, one hand resting on his bare shoulder.

"Who knows what dreams are about? I can't remember."

"You are tired, that is all, tired of being inside, of the winter, of inactivity. That is all normal, English. And I want you to tell me these things, to tell me how you feel."

"How I feel?" English turned his eyes abruptly on her and laughed out loud. "I feel nothing. I am only echoes and shadows."

When he was like that, Hevatha said nothing to him. He was drifting down some dark river that only he understood. Perhaps he was only winter-weary, perhaps he needed his own kind. Maybe it was work he missed, good work. But then, English hadn't been a worker for a long time. He had written words for other people to admire or laugh at or despise. He hadn't done that since he had come north, perhaps not for years. He seldom discussed that with Hevatha.

Richard did not always brood. Usually he was alert, alive, and happy, laughing with Hevatha. As his leg grew stronger, he went out into the village to meet the

Han, leaning on Hevatha's shoulder, Tyee bounding
behind them. They visited Tan Yuolo, who was the
chief of the Han band, and Cuah, who pretended to
speak English in front of his tribesmen. Hevatha and
English pretended to answer him, and everyone was
impressed.

They spent time with Kawchot, letting her cook for
them, give them gifts of blankets and buckskin shirts.
Kawchot liked them both and promised to adopt
Hevatha before they left.

"And now," Kawchot said, reaching for her ermine
skin, smiling broadly, "I must read the sticks for the
white man."

"No!" English's hand unexpectedly shot out and
folded over Kawchot's. "I don't want you to."

"You do not wish to now your fate, English?"
Kawchot asked, perplexed and disappointed.

"I know what it is. I don't want anyone to say it,
that's all." He held Kawchot's hand so tightly that he
hurt the woman. "I'm sorry," he muttered, drawing
his hand away quickly. "Hevatha, let's go out. I want
some air."

Kawchot watched the man go out, followed by
Hevatha. She considered throwing the sticks now that
he was gone, reading what lay there, but she shook
her head, putting her bundle away again. If he did not
want them to know, then she would not ask the spirits
to reveal the white man's fate in secret. Kawchot
walked to the door of her house, rubbing her hand.
She looked out and saw them walking, this fine young
woman, proud and beautiful, and her man.

It was good. They were meant to be together. The
stars had said it, the sticks had said it. Yet something
lay between them, something unseen, solid, like the
pure ice in a pond. Something unhappy, dangerous,
and perhaps evil.

Kawchot thought of Hevatha's black stick, shook her
head, and returned to her house.

On the hill above the village, the children of the
Han were screeching and yelling, tumbling and dancing in the snow. They slid down the long slope on

frozen hides, spinning, fighting, shouting, throwing snowballs at one another. It was a long trudge back up the slope with the hides, but the Han children seemed never to tire of the game.

Hevatha stood holding English's hand, watching. She burst out in laughter as two hides crowded with children raced at breakneck speed down the slope and the small warriors on board pummeled each other with snowballs. One Han boy bounced from a hide and tumbled downward in a flurry of snow, the others jeering at him.

"Well?" English said.

Hevatha laughed, shaking her head. "Yes! You against me. See who is the better warrior."

"The better . . . ! I'll show you who the best warrior in the north country is, Hevatha. Come on, now. Up the slope. Anything goes." He leveled a finger at her and she laughed.

"Anything."

At the top of the hill English was panting. He hadn't done any walking to speak of for months. Three small Han boys stood around him, staring with curiosity and a shadow of resentment.

"Come on now, lads, give me a sled!" English took a frozen hide from their hands and examined it carefully. "Good workmanship there, this'll do. Hevatha?"

She too had a hide, and now the children understood what was happening. They began to leap around and cheer and make snowballs. "No rocks inside those," English shouted. "No rocks!" He moved forward to the edge of the slope, alone but for one small girl. Around Hevatha a virtual crowd of Han children had gathered.

"Here!" English cried, stroking his yellow beard. "What's going on here?"

"They're going to be in the fight," Hevatha said.

"Well, that's all right enough, but why are they all with you, Hevatha?"

"This is my army," she said, looking around with haughty dignity. "That"—she pointed to the single

small girl with the vast snowball in her chubby hands—
"is yours."

"Oh, no. No, we don't! Why are they over there,
because I'm white? No." English shook his head and
bent his arm, making a muscle no one could see beneath his parka sleeve. "Men against the women. See
this, boys." He tapped his muscle. "Big warrior. Fight
with me, not the women!" He pulled one boy to him
and then another. They laughed and changed sides.
The small girl still stood looking up at English, her
round face shiny and snow-scratched. "No, there you
go, child, you're with the girls." English bent to tell
her that again, and she hurled the huge snowball into
his face.

"That's it!" English yelled as the children roared
laughter. "War. It's war now!"

English and Hevatha dragged their skins to the top
of the snow-covered slope. The snow, packed down
and glazed by the sledding, was a sheet of ice between
flanking drifts.

Alongside the icy slip the Indian children lined themselves, hurriedly making snowballs. The girls waited
along English's side of the slide, the boys along
Hevatha's.

"Are you ready, woman?" Richard shouted.

Hevatha laughed. "For the honor of the Han
women!"

"For the great warriors of the Han tribe—small
size," he added.

"And the fox clan?" she suggested.

"Yes, and the fox clan!"

"Ready, then?" Hevatha asked, and before English
could answer, she started down the slope, her dark
hair flying, her laugh rising into the winter skies as the
frozen hide began to spin, and along the snowy gaunt-
let the boys began to fire snowballs at her, some of
them bursting in air, showering her with snow, others
striking nearer, and occasionally smack on target.
Hevatha, waved a fist and shrieked. Behind her English was claiming a foul.

"That wasn't a fair start!" To catch up with her he

took a running start and went to his belly, the frozen hide accelerating like an arrow out of a hunting bow, racing dizzyingly down the slope past a fusillade of snowballs aimed at English by the legion of squealing Han girls.

Hit smartly on the cheek, English wiped at his face, lost control of his hide, and went careening off to Hevatha's side of the slide. He looked up, saw her eyes open wide, and then his sled slammed into hers. English's shoulder met Hevatha's body as his hide skidded out from under him and sailed on down the slope. Hevatha lost her sled as well, flopped over onto her back, and slid on headfirst down the icy bank, English cartwheeling after her until they crashed into the mound of snow at the bottom of the slope. Hevatha went in headfirst, and came up sputtering, wiping snow from her hair and eyes. English, on his back, lay still, holding his belly.

"English?" She got to her knees and peered down at him. Snow dropped from her head onto his shoulder. "Are you all right, your leg . . . ?"

His hand went behind her neck and he drew her to him, kissing her deeply with lips warm and comforting. When she drew away, English laughed. He lay there laughing as the children stormed down the hill, cheering and leaping; and Hevatha lay beside him in the snow, her head on his chest, her own laughter ringing.

They stood, dusting off the snow. English ducked one last snowball, pretended to chase the girl who had thrown it, and then halted, breathing hard now, waiting for Hevatha. He put his arm around her shoulder and walked with her toward the village.

They were within sight of it when Cuah came running toward them, wearing only his elkskin trousers and a woven shirt. He was pointing and waving, shouting something. Cuah had no need now to pretend to speak English. They understood his words well enough anyway.

"Nahani!" was the word he repeated over and over, pointing back toward the village. His fine dark hair fell into his eyes. He wiped it away angrily and gesticulated wildly. "Nahani, Hevatha!"

English glanced at Hevatha. Together they hurried on toward the village. Kawchot was standing in the middle of camp near the fish, which stood in a frozen silver line on stakes waiting to be smoked. She caught Hevatha's hand.

"They are coming. Many Nahani. You must hide."

"We'll hide in the forest," Hevatha said.

"No. They will find you. Stay here. We will hide you."

The place chosen was in Kawchot's own house. English and Hevatha were placed prone in the corner and covered with furs. Several small children, Kawchot's grandsons and granddaughters, were placed on the furs or before them, playing a game of hoops and snakes. Kawchot herself started a cookfire and busied herself over it.

It was hot and airless beneath the furs. Hevatha lay still, touching English's hand once. They could hear voices outside. The Han and the Nahani were speaking. Hevatha could make out only a few words. They were enough.

"White man . . . his woman. He killed a great man . . ." Kawchot was nearer the furs now, and as she stirred her bowl of fish-and-leech chowder, she translated in a low voice.

"They say they are friends of the Han. Say they do not want a war, we have not had a war for many years. They say we are a small band, we have no guns. They say we know where you went. A white man, a woman, a huge dog."

Tyee! Hevatha's heart constricted and began to thump heavily. Her throat was dry and tight. They had forgotten Tyee. Where was he? If they saw Tyee they would know. The Han had no dogs, and if they had one, they would eat it.

"The dog," Hevatha whispered. "Tyee!"

Kawchot made a hissing noise, sharp and anxious. They heard her whisper something to one of the children and then go to the door of her house to stand watching the Nahani warriors, who spoke to Tan Yuolo, the clan chief of the Han.

Tan Yuolo kept saying "No" to something. Hevatha silently thanked all the Han for their protection. The Nahani were a larger, fiercer tribe and quite capable of destroying this small band of Han, yet Tan Yuolo and the others defended their friends.

One of the Nahani cried out with savage delight, and Hevatha felt her hands form into fists. "There," the Nahani shouted, and then something she didn't understand.

She didn't need to. She heard the deep-throated growl, the sudden slashing snap of powerful jaws, and knew they had found Tyee.

Tan Yuolo was repeating his "No" endlessly. The Nahani grew very excited and spoke rapidly in their own tongue. Tyee growled again and then Kawchot was speaking, answering a question in a voice which was deliberately stupid.

"Good dog, big dog. We make for dinner. For all the people. Come now. I will cook him up good and the Nahani will eat with us."

The Nahani made a disgusted noise. Kawchot said, "We find him not long ago. Make him fat to eat."

The door to Kawchot's house opened and she came in. Peering out from under the furs, Hevatha could see Tyee. He cocked his great head and looked at his mistress, walking to her to sniff at the furs.

"Go away," Hevatha hissed. "Go."

Tyee, having discovered where Hevatha and English were, decided that they were playing some human game he knew nothing about and indifferently walked to the fire to flop down beside it. Kawchot had a steel knife in her hand. She peered out the door and called, "Come eat good dog, friend Nahani!" For good measure she added, "Eat it fresh and raw and bloody."

The Nahani remained awhile longer but eventually they drifted way from the house and out of the Han village. It was a long while before a runner came in, grinning, and gave the message to Kawchot that the Nahani were gone.

"Come out now, come out!" Kawchot said, throwing back the furs.

"Gone?" English asked. He was stiff and half-suffocated. Tyee waddled to him and Richard scratched his ear. "I thought you were going to cook our friend. What if the Nahani had accepted your invitation to dinner?"

"Nahani don't eat dog, English. They say it is their fathers." She paused thoughtfully. "Maybe so, maybe so."

"They'll be back, won't they?" English asked.

"No, I don't think so," the Han woman answered.

"I think they will be. At least they'll be watching. They haven't forgotten yet. They won't forget. Hevatha, we'll have to go," Richard said.

"Yes, English, we will have to go."

"We are not afraid of them . . ." Cuah and Tan Yuolo had entered the house. "We will hide you all the time. Until there is no snow except in the mountains."

"No, it won't do," English said. "You've been kind to us, all of you. We won't have you hurt or troubled on our account."

"I can make a sled today," Hevatha said. "We will travel very light. Tyee can pull it alone."

"Stay, stay," Tan Yuolo was saying, but the chief of the Han had a knowledge of imminent danger in his eyes. He knew that it was best for their guests to leave. He was watching English curiously, however. He asked finally, "They say you killed a great Nahani, English. This is true?"

"I killed a man, yes," Richard admitted.

Tan Yuolo pushed out his lower lip and nodded his head thoughtfully. English had gained stature in his eyes, apparently. Richard didn't bother to explain, to tell the Han that it had been an accident, that he had fired out of fear, fired on a man who had suspected nothing.

Kawchot was already busy making up a small sack of supplies. Cuah had gone out and returned with a pair of badgerskin gloves, which he gave to English. In two hours they were on their way, Hevatha had gone into the forest and cut saplings for her light, makeshift sled. It weighed next to nothing and with their few possessions Tyee could draw it easily.

The snow had drifted away, the wind had died. The cold disk of the low sun gleamed like pale gold through the glittering white forest behind the Han camp.

Hevatha hugged Kawchot good-bye and the teller of sticks whispered something that made Hevatha laugh. Then with half the village standing silently, motionlessly, Hevatha started Tyee forward across the bleak tundra, Richard limping beside the sled.

After an hour they could see nothing of the village, nothing but the empty length of snow-covered land and ahead the ivory slopes of the mountains, and beyond them, somewhere, Dawson.

"Walking again," English said. "Pursing something. Running from something."

"Eating gooseberries," Hevatha said, and she smiled.

"What?" English asked with some irritation. He was in no mood for riddles.

"Nothing. Walking on, I said, walking away from the night. With my good man, with my pleasure." She glanced at English, but he seemed not to have heard her. His mind had already run ahead of them, the scout of anticipation. It had flown across the tundra to Dawson, found gold, grown rich. He was already lost to the beauty of the wilderness, already lost to her. She lifted her eyes to the distances, bent and formed a snowball to toss at Tyee, and walked on, never glancing back. The darkness might have been gaining.

8

THE country began to change, to grow mountainous and wooded, tangled gorges where white water rushed and carved deep scars in the face of the wilderness. Twice Hevatha and English were forced by weather to stop and build temporary shelters; English had chafed at the restrictions of a capricious winter. He had sat and glowered and cursed in his own tongue. The gold was in his eyes. He saw nothing else, not even the soft light in the eyes of his woman. He held her as if she were a distant thing, and Hevatha accepted it. At other times, in the dead of night he clung to her like a small child. This too she could accept. She could accept any of it so long as he was near her.

It was clear for three days running and the snow on the peaks had begun to melt, flooding the gorges with wildly boiling, evil-tempered rivers which undercut the slopes and uprooted entire stands of full-grown pines, sweeping them away to form dangerous log-jams in the narrows. The jams might well break free at any time and send a sea of water roaring downstream.

It was clear and warming, but still in the deep valleys where Hevatha and Richard traveled there was snow, and Tyee earned his share of their rations. The big dog seemed tireless as he trudged on, great paws punching deep impressions in the snow.

They saw the Tutchone Indians long before they met them. A sled loaded high with furs and hides drawn by a ten-dog team appeared at the far end of a narrow wooded valley. English grew alert but they had no reason to fear these Indians. They acted like what they were, a trapping and hunting party returning home with a good harvest.

The Tutchones, three of them, wore beaded elk-skin jackets lined with bear skin. None of them carried weapons. Hevatha and English had determined to simply pass the south-bound Indians—until they saw the dog.

"Hold up!" English ran in front of the Tutchone sled, holding empty hands in the air. The Indians looked puzzled, the driver of the team stopping it with difficulty as the dogs snapped and snarled and fought the Indian's braking.

Hevatha had halted Tyee to one side, and now she came to where English stood before the Tutchone, who watched him as if he were a madman.

"What is it?" one of the Indians asked.

"That dog," English said, pointing. The dog, the black dog, was Hahtik. Evil, sneaky Hahtik, Demarest's lead dog.

English realized that he was taking a chance. Suppose these men had killed Demarest? They could as easily kill English and Hevatha. Yet they had no guns and seemed only bemused at Richard's wild questioning.

"Where did you get him? Ask them, Hevatha. That was a white man's dog!"

Hevatha asked the leader of the Tutchone where they had gotten Hahtik. The man turned and pointed up the valley. Using sign language and an occasional English word, he told Hevatha. "We lost three dogs and so we traded for these."

Hevatha, who now saw that two of the team dogs were those given to Gunyah at potlatch, two of those white dogs which Hevatha and English had taken, asked the Indians another question.

"These dogs. You traded for them?"

"Yes, we traded. A dozen good otter skins, two bear skins."

"What does he say?" English asked impatiently.

"He says they traded for them."

"Traded? In Dawson?" English demanded.

"In Dawson?"

"No," the Tutchone said. "Long River." He tilted his head eastward.

"From a white man?" Hevatha asked.

"No. Not a white man." The Indian grew cautious now. He looked again at English, apparently relieved that Richard carried no firearm. "Tutchone Indians traded to us."

"That damned Sasak!" English exploded. "Sasak and Nadgi. They've killed Demarest."

He stalked toward the leader of the Tutchone. "It was Sasak, wasn't it? Sasak. Hevatha was right. We shouldn't have trusted them. What else did he trade you? Have you got Demarest's gun, his coat? Maybe the map. Have you got anything else?"

English whirled and went to the shed, trying to untie the lashing which held the Indians' goods on. Hevatha touched his arm. "English, no!"

"They've got Demarest's gear. Maybe the map."

"Richard!" She yanked at his arm and turned him, and English stopped, his arms hanging limply. The Tutchone were scowling. One of them had produced a knife, which he held beside his leg.

Hevatha said urgently, rapidly, "You're going too far with this. These men are trappers and traders, nothing more. If they are something more, we can do nothing against the three of them Let us go while we can."

"Demarest is dead. They killed him."

"Is it Demarest you are worried about or the map?" Hevatha said sharply. English had an answer ready to fling into her face, but he clamped his jaw shut and stamped away instead. Hahtik snarled at him and snapped at his leg, and Richard kicked the black dog savagely. Hahtik came at him again, held back by the harness and the other dogs' weight.

English stood near their improvised sled with Tyee, seeing Hevatha speak a soothing word or two to the Tutchone, seeing one of the Indians lift his finger and tap his skull significantly. Then the Tutchone went on their way, Hahtik leading the dog team southward, following the grooves Hevatha's sled had made in the snow.

English stood and waited and when Hevatha reached him he turned his head away. "He's dead," was all English said.

Demarest was dead, and McCulloch, and the map to Drake's claim was gone. Sasak and Nadgi had turned on them, stolen what they could, and left the whites for dead. The map—what would it mean to the Tutchone? They couldn't sell that or eat it or trade it. It probably had been thrown in some campfire or left to rot beneath the winter's snow.

They had walked and run this far for nothing. For month after month they had worked their way northward, or sat waiting for the chance to travel on, fighting Indians and hard weather, half-starving, freezing. For what?

Still, there was no other direction to go but northward, and so they went on. They were following the Klondike River now, moving north from its turbulent juncture with the Stewart. English spoke little, no matter what Hevatha did to cheer him up. And when he did, it was with the strange, self-pitying words of his books. She found herself wishing that they could have stayed with the Han.

Those last few weeks he had been bright and happy, pleased with the healing of his leg, content to play with children or listen respectfully to the old, to lie with her and take the comfort of her body, undriven, unhaunted, simply living.

"Where do you travel when you travel without me?" Hevatha had asked him once.

He had looked up slowly from the firelight and said gloomily, "I walk many trails. My interiorized lives flourish in deep vaults." He touched his heart and then his head. "I live my many lives."

"There is only one life, Richard English, and it is not within you but around you, outside of you. With me, with the moments of time nature has given us. The rest of it is dark dreaming, and you harm yourself with it."

"The rest of it is my reality, Hevatha. I don't like things here, above ground, very much."

"Then your eyes are closed," Hevatha said, scooting to him, to take him, turn his head, and lift his face to hers. "It is a beautiful world. Dangerous and difficult, but filled with brightness, with the mirrors of light on the snowfields, with the glitter of winter forests, the long flights of ducks and geese, the bite of cold air at the lungs, the romping of Tyee, the laughter of children, the feel of our bodies together in the warmth of the night. Why would you hate it, why would you wish to be alone?"

"I simply am," he said in a defeated tone. "I live with my own stink."

He wanted to tell her then, to explain about Laura, to tell Hevatha that there were other sorts of women in the world, those a man was proud to walk beside, who delighted the eye and raised the envy of other men, but he couldn't do it. He couldn't bring himself to discuss Laura, not with Hevatha, who was so distant from his lady, his one woman; with Hevatha, who walked in moccasins and wore skin skirts and knew nothing of sophistication or reserve; who laughed as if all the world were amusing and worked like a man; who could not read, write, or speak the English language properly; who was nothing but someone who sometimes, temporarily, prevented the memory of Laura from overwhelming him. These thoughts were nothing English was particularly proud of. "I am," he repeated, "simply alone."

"Even with me, English?" Hevatha asked.

"Yes," he answered, "even with you."

"Then it is another woman," she said.

"Yes. It is another woman. A faraway woman."

And then there was nothing to say to him. Something had hurt him, someone had marked him. She could only pity him at times like that—and love him very much.

They came upon the mining camp suddenly. The

river bend was sharp, a jutting bluff concealing what lay on the other side until they were nearly upon it.

A cabin of unbarked pines tilted crazily toward the river. The windows were covered over with oiled paper. A pile of tin cans stood behind the hut in the snow. A man in a red-and-black mackinaw walked past them, scarcely glancing at the stranger, his woman, or the dog. Across the camp other dogs, huge packs of them by the tumult, howled to the Yukon skies. Hevatha and English went on, and the cabins, the wagons and sleds, the numbers of men grew larger. Along the riverbanks was a scene of vast and malignant devastation. Everywhere the earth was ripped open, dark earth piled up in oozing mounds. Gravel piles, like useless levees, and endless trenches blocked their path. The river had been diverted from its channel and it flew into the air over half-efficient multiple dams, trickling into sinks and over low ground to form cold, steely puddles the size of small lakes. The hill had been stripped of its trees for over a mile and the peeled timbers stood in palisades forming dams or ran alongside trenches or buttressed shafts dug into the earth. Beneath the old riverbed the earth was stripped to its gray bedrock.

Everywhere were men, an army of men, slovenly, mud-spattered, bearded, working with shovels and picks and sledgehammers, guarding flumes and gravel heaps and tailings, screening gravel and panning the hundreds of tributary streams which flowed off the denuded hillsides. It was a vast and hungry regiment, eyes fixed on their work, fingers swollen and broken with weather and icy water, faces red and grim and gaunt or swollen with insect bites, a furious scurvy-ridden, valiant and mad army.

"This?" Hevatha said in awe. "This is what you would do, Richard English?"

"For a time, for a month, for a year—and then work no more. Ever."

In his eyes Hevatha saw the same dark, cunning, avaricious light as she saw in the eyes of the others.

They watched each other suspiciously, not daring to leave their mound of gravel or section of river.

They moved through the camp, avoiding pits, mountains of soil, and working men. A little man with a torn hat sat on an overturned section of wooden gravel chute and watched them come.

Gray hair stuck out over his ears in curly knots. In his hand was a brown bottle. Richard asked him, "How far to Dawson?"

"Dawson? There's a lot of men want to go to Dawson, son."

"Can you tell me how far it is?"

"Just follow the river." The little man took a drink from his bottle and corked it again.

"*Hootch-i-noo*," Hevatha muttered.

"That's what it is, young lady. A lot of men drink it up here, you know."

English couldn't decide if the man was drunk or crazy. He had removed his torn hat to scratch at a hastily plastered knot on the side of his head. Seeing Richard's eyes on him, he explained. "Took a tumble. Bleeding pit. At night."

"I'm looking for a friend of mine. If he's alive, he might have come through here. A big man with a red beard, nearly sixty, but solidly built."

"A lot of men come through this way, son," the little man answered. "Some got red beards, some are old, some young."

"His name was Demarest."

"Nobody tells me their names."

"Come on, English. He has *hootch-i-noo* fever. He can tell us nothing." Hevatha tugged at English.

"I'll tell you this," the man said. "I'd keep traveling was I you. That's a nice-looking woman there, nice-looking Indian woman. A lot of men here don't have a nice Indian woman."

"All right," English said. He might as well have been talking to an echo anyway. "Dawson?"

"It's on ahead, son, on ahead."

"Idiot," Richard English muttered. Still, the man

had been right about one thing, the miners were watching Hevatha in a way English didn't care for at all, and it was best to move on.

It was almost a relief to clear the camp, which they deduced from a broken sign above a trading-post door was called Cabin Strike. Beyond Cabin Strike the trees flooded the valley once more, blue and deep green and flourishing. The river flowed clean and bright. English sighed, glanced at Hevatha, and trudged on.

"At least," she said, "you did not want to stay in that place and drink *hootch-i-noo* and have gold craziness with the old man."

English turned on her, his finger lifting for the coming lecture, but she was laughing happily, pleased with Richard's reaction, and he shook his head, laughing himself.

They passed other miners, most of them afoot, a few with mules, great packs on their backs, trudging down the riverside trail toward Cabin Strike. Now and then one of them lifted hopeful eyes or asked the way, but for the most part they just filed past, walking southward to join the army of the dead, each one seeing himself as the one with the big strike ahead of him, the vast field of undiscovered gold surrounded by his claim stakes.

"You see," English said, "they don't know what they're doing. And in a few weeks all those men from Whitehorse will arrive to crowd the place even more. No wonder they have shootings and knifings up here. They hardly have room to walk around each other."

"You have a different plan," Hevatha said lightly. There was a faintly mocking tone to her voice, but English ignored it.

"That's right. I have Drake's claim, a proven claim."

"Demarest is gone."

"That doesn't matter," English said brusquely. "I'll poke around and find out where it is. I've a fair idea from Demarest's description anyway."

"Then you will be rich."

"Yes, dammit, I will! Maybe I don't know anything about gold mining, but I'll find someone to help me.

Look at those people back there." He jerked a thumb across his shoulder in the direction of Cabin Strike. "Do you think half of them knew what they were up to?"

"No, I imagine only those with gold knew what they were doing."

"Yes." English put his hand on Hevatha's neck and walked beside her, their hips bumping. "But I'll learn what I'm doing, I'll find the old claim. I'll be one of the few who succeed up here, Hevatha." He added with more intensity, "Because, by God, I will not fail!"

Dawson, when they finally reached it, was an unlikely-looking mecca. Like Whitehorse, it was composed of buildings thrown up with whatever was at hand, thousands of jerry-built miners' shacks, tents, the streets muddy and nearly impassable. But it was larger, much larger. Thousands of people wandered the town or made hasty preparations for departure to yet another strike, rumored or real. There were signs of a future, permanent community. On a low hill a church was going up, complete with steeple. The town hall, where miners gathered for news of fresh strike or to raucously vote on some town ordinance, was a large two-story building on the main street. There was a police constable with several deputies, whose main duties seemed to involve staying out of the way of brawling, drunken, whiskered men.

Here and there Hevatha saw women, not only Indians but also English and Chinese and French, dressed in silks and furs, satins and lace, indications that they had achieved the upper echelon of society, for which there was only one qualification: your man had to have struck it big.

A lady in a red-and-black dress stood pouting at a corner, waiting for some gentleman to help her across the muddy street. She didn't have to wait long. A vast miner with a black beard covering nearly all of his face suddenly scooped her up and waded through shin-deep mud to the far corner while the lady daintily pummeled him with her parasol.

Hevatha led Tyee up the muddy street, dodging freight wagons and mules, horses and other dog teams that barked a warning or a greeting to Tyee.

"Where to, Richard English?"

"The town hall." English pointed to his left, and they crossed the street just in front of a skidding high-wheeled beer wagon. The driver leveled some good Anglo-Saxon curses at them and popped his whip at the ears of his team of Belgians.

Tyee was slipped from his harness and allowed to sit on the plank walk, which was unevenly frosted with snow and muddy goo from the boots of passersby. English strode into the town hall with Hevatha behind him, entering a dingy, smoky, clamorous room where miners milled and shouted.

Hevatha looked into their faces, seeing gold fever everywhere. Those men had come from far away, and they were all bold men or they wouldn't have been in Dawson, far away from their civilization and its comforts. They were strong men, not evil, but single-mindedly devoted to their one goal, growing rich.

English crossed the room, Hevatha trailing after. She wore the Han dress Kawchot had given her, and over it a buckskin jacket and skirt. Her hair was in two braids worn down her back. The miners glanced at her but she seemed to have little interest for them. Not while gold was in their minds.

"Rock Creek," someone said excitedly. "Amos Drew staked a hundred feet and took out ten thousand the first week."

"Up along the Clinton they're still picking up nuggets with their bare hands. Stuffing them in their pockets until a man can hardly walk."

"United's moving in there. Jasper Cartwright sold out," another man countered. "Can't fight those combines. Best to strike out east again."

The conversations were about gold and claims and nothing else. English had stopped in front of a huge map that covered half of a small wall. Blue lines wavered southward and northward. Red circles or green ones dotted the map. From the shape of the blue lines

Hevatha knew they were rivers. The Yukon, the Stewart, the Klondike. The red circle was Dawson itself. English was studying the map intently. Small, irregular boxes had been drawn along the rivers and streams, indicating claims. Smaller numbers identified each one. In the front of the room a huge leather-covered book sat on a table surrounded by a dozen men. In it the owners of the claims were identified.

"Looking for something special?" a man in a twill suit asked. His eyes briefly surveyed Hevatha and then ignored her. He was dark and oily with small weasel eyes. He wore a round hat such as Hevatha had never seen. She didn't like a thing about him.

Apparently English didn't either. "Nothing special," he answered.

"If you need help, let me know." He handed English a card. "Bertram St. Ives. I'm a surveyor."

"Thanks," English said, taking the card. His eyes reflected immediate mistrust. When St. Ives had walked away, whistling, Richard said, "I never saw a working surveyor dressed like that."

"Can you find what you want, English?" Hevatha wanted to know.

"No, dammit, I can't. Not without the map."

"Men are reading names in that book," she said with a nod toward the table.

"Yes, I know, but I don't want to let anyone know what I'm looking for."

Hevatha shrugged.

"Dammit, if we only had the map and the claim papers."

English was behaving in a strangely childlike manner, she thought, as if they could simply run out to wherever this claim was and fill sacks with gold, returning wealthy by dark.

There was a murmur and movement at the other end of the hallway, men moved aside, lifting their stained hats from their heads. Hevatha stood puzzled by it all until the woman appeared, passing through a corridor of humanity. The men watched in respectful awe, with some darker, more carnal gleams in their eyes.

It was no wonder. She was striking, blond, erect, slim, and she walked with ease and grace despite the high heels of her green leather boots. She had a small uptilted nose and green eyes. Her eyebrows were arched and perfectly formed in a way Hevatha knew was not natural, though how the woman had accomplished that trick, she did not know. Her skin was smooth and very pale, her lips a light red. She wore a green skirt and jacket over a white blouse that blossomed with lace at her throat and cuffs.

"How do, Mizz Penner," a miner said, and she nodded distantly, like a royal lady forced to acknowledge a servant's presence.

She swept through the room, and the riotous conversation, the cursing, halted. Jewels glittered on her hands, and at the base of her throat a great multifaceted diamond sparked with cold fire.

She walked to the front of the room, glancing at English, dismissing him. She walked to the table where the big book rested, and the men there stepped aside as a man in a brown suit rushed up to help her, bowing, patting at his face with a folded handkerchief.

English asked a man nearby, "Who is that?"

The miner looked at English as if he had dropped off the moon. "That's Sarah Penner, son. Widow of Satchel Penner. Satch had the fourth claim filed on the Upper Yukon, and in those days they didn't worry about a hundred-foot staking. Satch brought in something like ten million in a single year. Killed himself doing it—or, some say, he was killed—but the lady he brought out from Philadelphia is still here. Maybe she likes being a big frog in a small pond, maybe she wants to stay close to the source of her money, I don't know. She and our other matron, Hanna Sue Blythe, are Dawson's society—all we got of it."

The woman had finished her business and now she walked from the table toward the door, a sudden smile brightening her face. The men standing, watching, smiled back in an automatic response.

Hevatha noticed English's eyes. They were just a little more than curious as the blond swept past them again, a vague, sweet scent trailing her as her little green boots clicked against the planking.

Then she was gone and the murmur rose to its roar of minutes ago, the shouting and pushing began again. At several small tables men were buying and selling paper, at others disputing miners were angrily thumbing through a book on Yukon mining law.

"Is there anything else to be learned here, English?" Hevatha asked. "I can hardly breathe."

"No," there's nothing more, I suppose. He stroked his beard absently. His eyes were still on the door where the white woman had exited. Hevatha looked at her man and smiled, shaking her head.

"Let us go, then. Perhaps we can find this claim by ourselves. From what Demarest said, Drake was a well-known figure."

"We can try." English looked despondent, but Hevatha refused to let him remain so.

"We will find it," she said confidently, "if it pleases you."

Still English's eyes were on the door. He knew her. He knew Sarah Penner without ever having seen her. He knew her erect carriage, gracefully swaying hips, the smile. He had known her all his life. It was Laura who walked through the crowded room, Laura who caused the men to step back deferentially and gape, to worship her with their eyes. English felt Hevatha take his arm and he looked at her like a man waking from a dream.

"English?" she asked with a smile. "You are all right?"

"Yes, all right."

"She is a beautiful woman, is she not?"

English didn't respond. He took her hand and tugged her after him. "We have things to do."

They worked their way through the crowd of milling miners to the front door and stepped out. Without warning, English was face-to-face with the last man he wanted to see.

Aaron Butler was walking in the door to the town hall as English was coming out. The two men recognized each other instantly and they halted no more than a foot apart. English's face was taut, his eyes flashing; his fists had bunched. Butler looked at him in a deliberately taunting manner. He wore a yellow-and-black mackinaw, a wide-brimmed hat, and twill pants. His mustache, unwaxed, unruly, splayed out from the corners of his mouth. He was wearing a pistol in a waist holster, smoking a dark, thin cigar.

"Hello, writer," Butler said. He made no attempt to keep the sneer out of his voice. He knocked the ash from his cigar and blew smoke skyward toward the thin, shifting clouds over Dawson.

"You bastard. You murderer!" English said. His voice was so strangled by emotion that Hevatha hardly recognized it.

"Murderer?" Butler turned the word around in his mind as he rolled his cigar between his thumb and fingers. "I don't care for that kind of language, English."

"I don't care what you like! You killed Charles Landis on board the *Cormorant,* damn you! And you did your best to kill me. We'll see what the law has to say about this."

"The law won't say anything, English. There's no one else alive who was on deck that night. Your word against mine. I'd keep my mouth shut if I were you."

Butler was trying to make his voice pleasant, perhaps, but his pocked face was drawn savagely down, his dark eyes alight with cold, warning light.

"I don't need the law," English decided suddenly, and he leapt at Butler, going for his throat. Aaron Butler grabbed his pistol from his holster and slammed it against English's skull. The blow started bells ringing in Richard's head. Pinwheels and skyrockets flashed hotly through his consciousness. He saw Hevatha make some movement, saw her be hurled aside. And then English was on his back in the foot-deep mud of the street, staring up blearily at Butler and the miners who had crowded around him. English tried to rise, slipped, and fell again as the miners laughed. Butler still had the gun in his hand and for an instant English thought he would use it, but there were too many people around. He holstered the revolver instead, turned his back deliberately, and strode into the town hall.

English lay there propped up on his elbows. The humming in his head was like a swarm of hornets. A dull, throbbing ache had begun at the base of his skull. Hevatha stepped down to him and helped him up. Dripping mud, English got to his feet and leaned against a hitching rail, holding his head with muddy hands.

"Come on, English. Let us go away."

"I could kill him," English said from out of pain.

"Or he could kill you. Neither is good, English."

"No good," English panted. "It's no good. But that's the way it's going to be in the end, Hevatha. I'll have to kill him or he'll kill me."

"Then let us go away from here," she said.

"No!" he said passionately, his head lifting to the door of the town hall. "I'm dammed if I will. Besides," he said, his voice lowering as his head did, "where would we go, Hevatha, where could you and I possibly go? Fugitives . . . fugitives from some crime we never committed, from some crime of the soul."

"I am not a fugitive," Hevatha announced. "Nor are you. You are sometimes a silly man, Richard English. Too many books in your head, I think. Maybe you should get them out so that you can think better, so that you can go on with living."

English grinned. It was a crooked grin that allowed a little blood to trickle from the corner of his mouth, but it was a grin and everything was all right.

Straightening himself, he tried to wipe most of the mud from his arms and legs. Hevatha worked at his back. Tyee sat watching them as if all the goings-on were beneath his canine dignity.

Someone in the street shouted and English turned to see an enclosed carriage making its tortuous way up the street. It was painted green, striped with gold. Specially fitted fenders had been bolted on over the

wheels in a vain attempt to keep the elegant coach
from being spattered by Dawson's mud. Drawn by two
matched dapple geldings, it swept past and they had a
glimpse of Mrs. Sarah Penner. English watched the
coach with a thoughtful, complex expression.

The coach turned left and then was lost from sight
until a minute later it could be seen making its way up
a knoll to a huge white house with corner turrets. It
was still under construction apparently, but it stood
alone and aloof on its knoll, pretentious and yet superb.

The coach vanished behind a stone wall and then
was gone. Hevatha shrugged. "That is where she lives.
Her and her people."

"She lives alone there, I think."

"Alone? A hundred people could live there!"

"She lives there alone," English repeated. "Gold
bought that. Gold made her what she is. Gold. . . .
And I'll have it. I'll have a house like that, larger."

"To live in alone, English? It must be cold in a large
house alone."

He didn't respond. He stood watching the house for
another minute, mud falling from him in clumps. Seeming to awake from some distant golden dream, he took
Hevatha by the arm. "Come on, let's go."

"Where?" she asked as English hurried her along
the plank walk, leaving the sled and Tyee behind.

"The constable. Butler's not going to get away with
murder. I'll let the law handle it."

It took them five minutes to find the building hous-
ing the town constable, although it wasn't a hundred
feet from the town hall. The building, of gray clapboard with a tarpaper roof, had no identifying sign.
Inside, smoke from a glowing iron stove filled a small
office. Beyond the office another door opened onto a
corridor fronted with cells. From there a man's voice
rose and fell in a pitiable moan. Richard rapped loudly
on the cluttered desk.

It was a minute before a man in long johns and
suspenders, wearing a blue cap, emerged from within.
A badge hung negligently from a suspender strap.

"What do you want?" the constable asked, his mouth shifting to one side as he spoke and examined the Indian woman and the man in buckskins.

"My name is Richard English and I want to speak to you about a murderer who's running around loose in Dawson."

The constable nodded, went behind his desk, picked up a pen, which he toyed with, and finally said, "So you finally showed up, did you?"

"Showed up?"

"Yes, I've been expecting you. I've spoken to Mr. Butler about you. Said you might show up trying to make trouble." The constable's expression was placid, his pale face highlighted with two red spots on his cheekbones. He yawned and tossed the pen down on his desk.

"Making trouble," English repeated slowly. He was incredulous and suddenly furious. "*Mister* Butler is a well-known San Francisco cutthroat. On the way north aboard a ship called the *Cormorant,* he killed a man named Charles Landis, a well-known man, I believe, a lumber-mill owner. He was killed over a card-game loss. Since I saw the murder, Butler tried to kill me. I went overboard, surviving, somehow, through the grace of God. I show up here only to be assaulted by Butler, and when I come to the law, all I hear is that I'm making trouble!"

The constable nodded slowly. He might have been watching a very dull stage play to which he knew all the well-worn lines. "I have discussed this with Mr. Butler, as I say. Now," the constable said, leaning forward, "the fact is that Mr. Butler is a man of substantial means, well on his way to becoming more than substantial, a partner of Bertram St. Ives, who's our local surveyor and also a claim purchasing agent. You are . . . some squaw man."

English objected violently, but the constable, a slow-tempered man, simply raised a hand. "Some sort of wanderer come looking for gold like the other ten thousand men outside that door. I know . . . once upon a time, Butler says, you wrote some kind of book for ladies to sit by the fire with, but it was no great shakes and maybe you expected the world to fall at your feet, but it didn't." The constable yawned again. Wood popped in the belly of his iron stove and the three of them glanced that way.

The officer of the law went on. "I don't know all of that for a fact. I say Mr. Butler is a substantial citizen, and he is. That doesn't mean that I believe substantial citizens always tell me the truth. On the other hand, I can't credit every wild-eyed tale I hear, not in the Yukon. You apparently are a young man with a lot of imagination and a lot of emotion inside you—"

"That doesn't mean I'm not telling you the truth," Richard said with vehemence, moving toward the constable's desk another step.

"No," the constable replied softly, searching his pockets for something he never found. "It don't mean that." He scooted around in his chair, looking for a comfortable spot. "What it means is this: I can't arrest a man on your say-so. What kind of evidence have we got against Butler?" He spread his hands. "I got no idea what happened aboard that ship coming north. In the Yukon I can't arrest him without a warrant, and I wouldn't get one. We'd be laughed out of court, or rather, you would. I don't intend to get involved, not on the unsupported word of a man who obviously had a grudge against Butler."

"I see," English said stiffly.

"I hope you do. My advice would be to steer clear of Butler, son. I don't know exactly what he is, but I know this—he's a tough man who could break you up eight ways from Sunday with his bare hands."

"You think so, do you?"

"Yes, son," the constable said softly, "I think so. Now," he went on, "this is the second time I've heard this story from someone who wants me to get up and arrest Butler, and I'll tell you exactly the same thing I told Floyd Demarest—"

"Demarest! He's alive, then?" English asked excitedly.

The constable nodded. "Yes. You know him, I understand. He's alive. I told him what I'm telling you. A problem like the one with the Indians, the murder of McCulloch, I can handle."

"McCulloch was murdered?" Richard asked. It was numbing, although he had almost resigned himself to the fact that both of his partners were dead. He hadn't liked McCulloch much, but that did nothing to erase the distaste he felt.

"You haven't seen Demarest yet, I take it. Yes, McCulloch is dead, pretty brutally killed. Those two Indians you men had hired on are pretty well known in this region as bad ones. Being *chechaco*, you wouldn't have heard their names. They cut up McCulloch, thought they had killed Demarest. They showed up in Dawson, believe it or not, strutting and cocky, with too much money for an Indian. Demarest wasn't far behind them."

"You caught them?" English asked.

"You bet," the constable replied. "Want to see them before we hang them?"

English's eyes lifted to the cells down the corridor. "They're in there?"

"Them or two other cutthroats named Sasak and Nadgi. You know, it was the little one, the smiling one, that did the knife work on McCulloch." The constable pushed back from his desk and rose, inclining his head. "Come on, have a look at them. In this case, maybe your corroborating testimony can be of some use. They were guiding McCulloch and Demarest north?"

"That's right. The last time we saw them, the four of them were together."

The constable nodded. He walked heavily toward the cells, his boots barely clearing the floor. It was an odd shuffling gait, stolid and implacable.

Hevatha followed, not liking the smell of the place, of man-sweat and *hootch-i-noo* and vomit and burned food. Sasak was standing in his cell, his head turned sideways, birdlike and savage, his hands gripping the bars. He smiled as he saw English and Hevatha. Smiled and spat at them.

"Here, mind your manners, Sasak."

"I spit on whites," the Tutchone said virulently.

"Yes, you'll spit on us till we hang you, you devil," the constable replied.

Nadgi was sitting on a bunk on the far side of the darkened cell. He saw Hevatha and rose to his feet, smiling. "Hello, hello, how is the big dog?" he asked cheerfully.

"You killed McCulloch," English said, and Nadgi looked at him as if he were mad.

"The man had things we wanted. Goods, dogs. Rifles. So we killed him. I should not have missed the other one. I should have smashed his head with a rock. Then we would be free, Sasak and me. Free and wealthy, eh?"

Nadgi was smiling still, and the constable turned to English. "See? They don't understand right and wrong, none of 'em. Indians . . ." He looked at Hevatha and fell silent. "But here they are," he said, rocking on the balls of his feet. "Here they are and soon we'll teach these two right from wrong. With a rope."

Sasak spat again and the constable turned away. "I quit hitting him. Don't do any good. Seen all there is to see? Come on back into the office."

"About Butler," English began as they reached the superheated office again. "He—"

"Forget it." The constable had opened the door to his iron stove, burning his finger. He cursed and sucked at his finger. "I've told you how that stands. Leave well enough alone before you get yourself in serious trouble, son."

"Like getting myself killed?"

The constable turned his head. Firelight bled across his face. "Just like that." He poked at his fire and closed the door again.

"Do you know where Demarest is now?"

"Upriver. Six miles or so. At least that's where he said he was going." The constable rose heavily, holding his back. "Sometimes it's hard to get a fix on men around here. Nobody wants to tell anyone else where he's poking for color. I thought Demarest was telling me it straight, though. I've got a close mouth. I wouldn't tell you except he said you were his partner."

Outside, the skies were heavily veiled in gray clouds, but they were thin, containing no rain or snow, no blustering promise of thunder and lightning. Dawson continued to groan and shriek and grumble and race and hoot and bluster and surge beyond the office door.

"I shall get Tyee and the sled," Hevatha said. There was no need for her to ask English what he was going to do next. Demarest was north along the river. Gold was north, along the river.

Maybe English would find his gold quickly and lose his fever. Maybe he would find enough gold to build his big house where no one lived. Perhaps he would even buy Hevatha a green dress and a coach to match. She pictured herself tottering along in high boots and laughed, shaking her head.

"Not for us, Tyee. You shall wear no diamond around your neck."

Tyee's flat pink tongue lolled from the corner of his mouth as if he enjoyed the joke. He walked to the sled with Hevatha and was harnessed once again. They were joined by English, still mud-caked, the side of his head now developing a knot.

No matter, he looked content, eager to be away. He spared only one brief hostile glance at the town hall and then they were off again, walking out of Dawson toward the wide river beyond.

The mining camps they saw were fewer and smaller than Cabin Strike, and by the time they reached Drake's camp on a wide bend in the river they had seen no one for a mile.

The silver-white Yukon River was half a mile wide at this point, forming a vast sweeping arc as it flowed southward. Pines and cedar trees clogged the hills rising above the river. A long island in the river's center was similarly forested, appearing deep blue-green far out across the water.

There seemed to be no activity at all along the river's gray gravel beaches, at least nothing like the hungry depredations they had seen farther south.

There might have been no one living there at all, except that from the stone chimney of a low log cabin set back among the trees, smoke rose into the gray sky.

"It's Demarest," English said with a grin of relief. "Let's find the old redbeard."

Approaching the cabin, they saw the door open cautiously; then it was swung wide and Demarest appeared, hands on hips, stubby pipe in his mouth, hatless.

"Well, boy, what took you so long?" he shouted, and then came down the path to shake Richard's hand warmly. "Long winter, eh?" the miner asked.

"Too long." English looked around in puzzlement. "Where's the claim?"

"It's here. Impatient, are you? Don't blame you. Come along to the house, I want to show you something. Hevatha, come along. Bring the brute if you want." Demarest slung an arm around English's shoulder. "The claim's not on the river proper, son. I've staked a hundred feet out for myself and worked it a little for appearances' sake, but that's not where the gold lies. The Yukon's too quick for panning, too big for damming."

"Drake said—"

"Drake was sly. I mean to be just as sly. There's a creek out back, Richard," Demarest said, stamping the mud from his feet before entering the cabin. "Well . . . I'll show you."

The sack was under a floorboard in the cabin, and when Demarest lugged it out, they could tell it was very heavy. English knew, knew before Demarest carried the sack to his puncheon table and opened it, lifting out a handful of soft, bright dust.

"How much?" English asked, leaning nearer, as if he wanted to breathe in the dust.

"Two thousand, I'd say. My scales are small and I haven't bothered to weigh it all out. At first I had to mercury it up and I figured Drake had taken the cream and given me a dud, but last week I found a rich bar. Scoop it out with your hands."

"Two thousand."

"Two. It took me most of a month, but now we're into the rich sand."

"How rich?" English asked in a croaking voice. "How big a strike do you figure, Demarest?"

Demarest tugged at his beard thoughtfully. "I wouldn't want to give you any false hopes." He grinned. "I'd say a million easy. If we protect it, watch ourselves . . ."

English hadn't heard anything after the word "million." He placed his fingers gently into the sack of gleaming, coarse gold dust, letting it seep through his fingers.

"Half of that is yours, Richard," Floyd Demarest said.

"Half?" Richard's blue eyes lifted.

"We're partners. McCulloch is out of it now, poor devil. If it hadn't been for you and your sled, we wouldn't have made it this far."

"You panned it out," English pointed out.

"That's right. To tell the truth," Demarest said, closing the sack, returning it to its hiding place beneath the floorboard near the hearth, "I'm not much concerned about a thousand here or there. Not after what I've seen."

"No one else can find it?"

"I don't think so. It's way upslope, well concealed. When I see someone coming, I make for the river edge down below, and I show them some color—not enough to interest anyone—show them my stakes, and they move on. One thing we can't do," Floyd Demarest said, "is go into Dawson and start spending fast. I'll take half a pound or so in now and then for supplies, but I keep my mouth shut. That's the way we have to do it until we're ready to pull out."

"I understand," English said.

"There's big money here, son, but we're only partly

legal. If they get wise to us . . . well, there'll be trouble."

"They won't get it from me," English swore.

'I know they won't." Demarest sat at the table and relaxed a little. "Now we've got someone to keep watch while we work. That's slowed me down some, handling things alone. I didn't dare hire anyone on. Not after that business with the Tutchone."

"I talked to the constable. I saw Sasak and Nadgi."

"Changed a bit, haven't they? Dirty bastards. Hevatha here had them figured, like she had the lake figured. We should have listened to her."

"The constable seems to like to keep his feet away from the fire. I ran into Aaron Butler."

"Did you? Yes, I saw him there too, the devil. Well, the law here is a little reluctant to make more trouble than it can handle. Generally the feeling seems to be that if it didn't happen in the Yukon it doesn't matter. There's half a hundred men in Dawson who are wanted somewhere else. Boxer Thrush is a good-enough constable, I suppose, but past history is just that to him. They say Boxer had some trouble of his own back in the States."

"When the Indians did a murder," Hevatha said quietly, "then he was quick to catch them."

"Yes," Demarest drawled, "I guess you're right there, Hevatha, but there wasn't much doubt as to who was guilty there."

"One man saw it—you. One man was dead—McCulloch," she pointed out. "When this Butler killed, one man was there—English. One man was dead—Landis."

"Well, damn me," Demarest said, scratching his head, "there is a parallel there, isn't there? But, like I say, Boxer Thrush is only hired to take care of criminals who do their dirty work in the Yukon."

"The law is the law," Hevatha said stubbornly.

"What happened anyway?" English asked. "How was McCulloch killed?"

"Dead of night, middle of a snowstorm. The Indians got up and hitched the dogs. McCulloch never had a chance. Nadgi got him with a knife. Stabbed him maybe a dozen times. Mac called out once and I took off at a run. Didn't have my rifle in bed with me, and that's the last time I won't. Nadgi, or Sasak, one of 'em, threw something at me. Maybe a war club, maybe just a rock—all I know is, it hit my skull and sent me flying. Right over an embankment. I fell maybe forty feet, but there was snow below and I survived the fall well enough. I suppose it was too much trouble for 'em to climb down and see if I was alive. They just took the team and our goods and mushed. I had me a long walk into Dawson, but I reached it in four days.

"The day after, believe it or not, into town comes Nadgi and Sasak, wanting to buy hootch and bullets. Boxer Thrush walked up to 'em and cuffed 'em."

"The constable said they had long records," English said.

"So it seems. Well"—he shrugged—"I'll know better next time. I'll listen to Hevatha."

"Will you listen to me now?" she asked softly. Her eyes were bright and intent.

"Now?" Demarest scratched his head again. "About what, Hevatha?"

"About all of this," she said. "About the gold. Leave it now. You have two thousand dollars. You have money to go home. You have your lives. The gold will bring something bad to you, Demarest. It will bring something bad to English. Leave it. Go home."

Demarest smiled. "She's gone suddenly fey on us, Richard. Leave it, girl? Not on your life. There's a million, maybe a lot more waiting for us up along that creek. They can pull my teeth and tie me to a stake. I'm not leaving. As for Richard . . ."

"I'll leave when you do," English said intently. "Or maybe not then. We came north for one reason; now we've got it. We've touched it, seen it, smelled it. I know what I want. Hevatha is tired. Hevatha is a cautious person."

Hevatha walked to a window and peered out it at the long, broad river. Maybe she *was* tired. Something within her was slowly growing, taking a little of her energy. Maybe it was also making her cautious, but she felt that something evil was close to them, something that would touch them all and perhaps destroy English.

Gold cast long dark shadows. It was too bright not to. It promised much: happiness and wealth and contentment. But standing behind the bright promises were the darker things. The dark of the moon, a black stick, death.

9

THE creek was a quiet, rambling thing which wound its way through the deep pine forest to join the Yukon. The water ran slowly and was nearly clear. Beneath its surface the sand glittered oddly. Demarest dipped his pan into the sand and washed it, swirling it around as he raised it so that the lighter particles drifted over the rim of the pan. What was left was gold.

"It's rich, English," Demarest said, grinning around the stem of his pipe. He had his shirt cuffs rolled up; his collar was open due to two missing buttons. The shadows of the pines wrapped themselves over his body, following the bulky contours. "Very rich."

"A million, you say?" English asked. The word had many connotations in his mind. Shining jewels and slender blond women. Respectability, purchased with the labor of his hands.

Demarest crouched. "If it has depth. The bed's narrow all along its course." A stubby finger jabbed downstream. Through the trees English could see the Yukon, placid and powerful at once. "I've taken a plumb here and the sand is old and deep, maybe ten feet to bedrock. Farther along it should follow suit. At any rate, English, there's gold here and it's ours. Drake got out rich. I figure we'll do the same."

English had taken off his coat and rolled up his own sleeves. He was going to be rich and there was only one way to begin. He took the pan from Demarest's hands, tugged up his wading boots, and went into the stream.

Hevatha could no longer see the men working. She

had climbed the pine-strewn slope and crossed to a tiny
high valley. It was a rich, quite beautiful place where
caribou grazed on the sedge and cotton grass. Butter-
flies in swirling clusters hovered over the flowers dot-
ting the heath. She had seen mink skittering away into a
small, quick-running upper stream, and the sign of a
black bear among the blackberries. White spruce and
birch in new spring growth budded extravagantly, shoot-
ing forth bright green leaves. In the short growing
period of the far north, everything burgeoned furiously,
life rushed along, each living thing expanding, flower-
ing, growing, blossoming while winter and shadow and
snow were briefly held in abeyance.

Hevatha's people, the Tlingit, had lived in the same
way. When the herring came, there was a furious rush
to harvest them. When the salmon ran, they were
harvested. They would come only once.

A lynx bounded away through the cotton grass,
once turning its head with its long tufted ears toward
Hevatha long enough to emit a warning hiss. Hevatha
laughed and walked on, enjoying the feel of sun on
her body. Had it been so long since the sun had
shone?

Hevatha stopped to pluck a columbine and place it
against her cheek. Crouched there she saw the footprint, a child's footprint, and she lifted curious eyes to
the mossy stretch of ground. Rust red, yellow, and
green, it extended to the base of a deep stand of trees
beyond.

Hevatha walked that way, seeing the child's mocca-
sin prints here and there. Entering the forest, she
stopped to listen, heard laughter, and went on.

The Han had their camp in a broad grassy valley
beyond the trees. The valley folded in the center,
funneling a sun-bright rill downslope. Above and beyond
the forest-ringed valley, craggy gray mountains, still
streaked with snow, jutted into the summer sky.

There were children and hide houses, smoke racks
and all the scents of an Indian camp, broiling caribou
meat, oil, and green hides being scraped for clothing.
And there was Kawchot.

The teller of sticks peered at Hevatha, shading her eyes with her hand; then a broad, delighted grin split her dark face.

"My Moon Walker! My adopted daughter, Hevatha!"

Kawchot ran toward Hevatha, her heavy hips rolling, her laughter bubbling from her lips. Panting, exhausted, she hugged Hevatha tightly, stepped back to arm's length to study her face, and hugged her again.

"What are you doing here, Hevatha!"

"And you, Kawchot?" Hevatha patted the old woman's sun-warmed hair. "What are the Han doing here?"

"Here!" An arm described an arc. "This is our hunting ground, we have come here forever, since I was a child. When the summer sun lifts its face above the horizon and the ice on the long lake begins to break, we travel northward." She had her arm around Hevatha's waist now, walking her back toward the camp. "Come sit with me, Moon Walker, come sit and eat and tell me how you have come to this hunting place."

Across the camp Hevatha saw Cuah and he called out to her, "Hello, then, Hevatha!" The rest of the words were English as Cuah imagined it to sound, and Hevatha laughed, answering him in English.

"You are learning more and more of the white tongue!"

Tan Yuolo was there, and the old chief took both of Hevatha's hands. "A winter guest returns. That is good luck. Look here. Hevatha, a grandson yet so small it is pink."

From the arms of a young woman with wide, shy eyes the chief of the Han band took a blanket-wrapped bundle of living flesh, toothless, thatched with a flourishing crop of dark, flyaway hair. "My grandson," Tan Yuolo said, "soon a great hunter. Very much a joy!"

Hevatha uncovered the baby and admired it, wrapped it up again, and handed it to Tan Yuolo's daughter.

Kawchot asked, "And you, Hevatha, when does your baby come?"

"My . . ." Hevatha was briefly stunned; then

she broke into a deep smile. "How did you now, Kawchot?"

"It is in your eyes. I see it all. Boy or girl? I do not know. Maybe the sticks will tell me. A white man's baby. Which white man, I wonder?" Kawchot said impishly, tapping her chin meditatively. Then she hugged Hevatha again. "Come inside. Have tea and food and talk to me, daughter."

Kawchot took Hevatha into her house, and while they sipped their tea from horn cups, Kawchot talked. "Now, I do not understand where all these whites have come from, Hevatha. I do not understand what they want. All they do is foul the rivers. All they do is dig holes. Kiptah is Tan Yuolo's daughter, the one with the little baby. She told me that they come for gold. I know what gold is, I know the white men trade it for what they want, but why don't they stay home where the sun is high and pick up their gold?"

"They have no gold, Kawchot, and so they covet it. It is rare to them."

"Do they have caribou or muskrats?"

"No."

"Maybe then they would trade for caribou meat and muskrat hides," Kawchot said thoughtfully. "Now, this Dawson. I have seen it. Men build their houses there, of wood so that they can't transport them when the snows come. That means they mean to stay here. Why—all for gold?"

"All for gold, Kawchot."

"That is all very strange," Kawchot said. "We don't need gold to live. If we want furs, we go and find otter and bears and beaver. If we want food, we fish or hunt or dig roots."

"It is," Hevatha answered, "a different world they live in." Very different, she thought, recalling the woman with the pale eyes and her green dress, her empty house. Something moved uneasily in Hevatha's heart, a tinge of jealousy, perhaps, remembering English's eyes on Sarah Penner. It was an unworthy feeling and she pushed it away consciously. At home, wherever that was, somewhere where the sun was high, English had another woman, Hevatha knew that. A woman, she thought, who had scorned him because he had no gold, a woman who had read his written words as Hevatha could not, and found them lacking.

"Now," Kawchot said, "I know why you are here, Hevatha. You follow your man. But why is he here? Is he another gold seeker?"

"I'm afraid so," she answered, but she shrugged as she said it. Who was she to say that having gold was bad? The Tlingit had none and so she had never learned to value it, as English had never learned to value the good *eulikon* of the Tlingit.

"Then"—Kawchot rose—"we know how to make that man happy. Come along, Hevatha."

Hevatha got to her feet and together the women went out into the bright day. There were few men in camp, for it was hunting time, but the children, loud and fluttery as a flock of crows, leapt and shouted everywhere. Some called to Hevatha.

Kawchot led her adopted daughter out of the village of the Han and along the river which made its way through the folded valley. Blueberries were thick along the river's edge and so were soapberries. A snowy owl, his winter plumage changing to a dull brown, was startled from his sleep to fly away on broad wings, hooting crankily.

The land was grassy; tall yellow flowers swayed in the wind from the west. Hevatha hiked her skirts up and followed the Han woman over a little hillock to a place where a second, smaller stream joined the first.

"What is this?" Hevatha asked.

Kawchot just crooked a finger. "Come now." She beamed. "I will show you."

They slid down a grassy bank to the sandy beach of the smaller stream, and there Kawchot showed Hevatha what she had brought her there for. "Do you see?" the Han woman asked, crouching. When she stood, she had a nugget in her hand, a nugget the size of a partridge's egg. Hevatha took it and turned it over, weighing it in her palm. Then she tossed the nugget away into the river, where it disappeared.

"Do you not wish to tell your man?" Kawchot asked, bewildered. "Do you not wish to make him a present of this gold so that he can be happy?"

"No," Hevatha answered. She brushed the hair away from her eyes and crouched, watching the river. The gravel in the shallow water was bright with gold. Nuggets and shifting dust. "I do not wish to tell him."

"But, Hevatha!"

"We will not tell him, we will tell no one." Memories of Cabin Strike came to her mind and she imagined the valley, the hunting grounds, the rivers torn to muck and gaping pits, fissures and sinkholes, overrun by an army of dirty, bearded, gold-hungry men.

"Tell no one. They will come, Kawchot, and take this land from you."

"No one can take it from us," Kawchot laughed. "It has always been ours. If your man wishes gold, though, he may have it." She looked more deeply into Hevatha's wide brown eyes. "You do not want your man to have gold, Hevatha? Why is that? If he has gold, what will happen?"

"I don't know." Hevatha flipped a pebble into the river, watching its ripples.

'Do you think he will go away to his home? Do you think you will lose him?"

"No, of course not," Hevatha laughed. She stood and watched the river for a long while. Kawchot was silent. Maybe, Hevatha thought. Maybe Kawchot was right. She had never considered the end of this journey with English, the time when he might find gold, when he might go south with his respectability. What, then, would become of Hevatha? She ached with the thought. Her womb fluttered at the thought. *It isn't that,* she told herself with stubborn, violent insistence; but something deep inside said that it was as Kawchot believed.

"If he finds no gold," Kawchot said, "he may go. If he finds all he wants, then he may go. Only your love can hold him, nothing else."

"For now," Hevatha answered, "we will say nothing. He has his gold, other gold. He needs no more. I tell you this: from what I have seen, if the whites find this, they will come for your gold."

"Don't be concerned, Hevatha. This is our land. Even the white government has said this. After a war they wrote down where we might live. By the big lake to the south in the winter; here in the summer. This is ours." Her broad smile gestured widely. "No one can take it. To a friend like English we can offer the gold. But to no one we give up the earth and the creatures on it. Those are Han."

When Hevatha returned to the cabin, she found English and Demarest finished with their day's work. English was jubilant, exhausted, filthy.

"Where've you been, Hevatha? Lord, what a day! Give us a month and we'll be ready to pull up stakes and retire wealthy men," he said.

Tyee rose, walked to Hevatha, and brushed against her. "It was a good day, then, Richard English?" she asked, and English laughed.

"I'll wager we took out a thousand. Demarest?" He looked to the red-bearded man, who was leaning over his scales, dipping gold dust from a rawhide pouch onto the pan.

"Double that, English. Double it. Worth it, wasn't it? All of this trip north, the long winter, broken leg and all."

"Worth it, yes," English said. He walked to Hevatha and squeezed her shoulder. She could smell the whiskey on him and she glanced at the table, seeing the jug beside Demarest. "I'll dress you up splendidly, Hevatha," English promised. "All in red. In red, Floyd?"

Demarest glanced up and grunted.

"Yes, all in red. Red dress, red shoes, red hat . . ."

"Not for a while, English," Demarest cautioned. "We can't be showing too much gold."

"No, not for a while."

"They'll be all over our claim. I've seen a lot of shady work in a few months up here. Men cheated out of their claims, men disappearing, if you get me. Our old friend Aaron Butler has accumulated a lot of gold without ever getting his hands dirty. Him and that rat St. Ives."

"If the law won't take care of Butler," English said, patting Hevatha's shoulder before walking to the jug, pouring himself a tin cup full of whiskey, "then we will. Men disappearing, huh? Maybe Butler will disappear one day."

It was empty talk, but a dangerous mood, Hevatha thought. She had seen men boast themselves into impossible situations before, vowing to kill, being forced to do it eventually. English swallowed his whiskey. His eyes watered and he coughed once.

"Hevatha doesn't seem happy today," Demarest said, returning to his old habit of speaking about her as if she weren't there or couldn't speak English.

"She's happy enough, aren't you, Hevatha? She just doesn't understand what this all will mean."

"I understand, Richard English," she replied. Then, as he filled his cup again, she went out of the cabin with Tyee to watch the sunset bleed crimson smears onto the wide Yukon. She walked to the water's edge, watching Tyee leap away in pursuit of a hare. She watched the river and listened to its dark mutterings, watched it grow dark and obscure.

"I understand," she said under her breath. And then English was beside her, turning her face to him, and he kissed her. Hevatha's lips parted, her knees trembled. He was there and strong and happy, wanting to share his joy with her, to share his life force, to be with another as all healthy creatures wish to do, and she let him kiss her and lead her to a hidden place among the pines.

There she undressed, and while English watched her, she hollowed out a sleeping place beneath the pines, shifting the pine needles until she had formed a hollow where they could lie and share warmth and existence.

He went to her as she watched the coming stars

blink on through the pines, as the Yukon flowed past. He was naked in the night, naked and male and sure of himself again. He had found his gold, his strength, and he lay beside her, his hands warm and urgent on her thighs, her breasts, his face distant, familiar, eager in the darkness.

What did he feel at these moments? He spoke only a little when they made love and came together. Was she only a warm spot in the dark universe, or did he feel what she did? Could any man? Was she what he was to her, a need, a reason for all of time and existence, a dream and a reality at once? Did he feel as she did, that without him there was no life and no death, only an empty wandering through the shadows of eternity?

Now, as he held her and clung to her and kissed her throat, there was no gold on his mind; now, as he rolled to her and she clutched at him and he responded, male and warm and single-minded, there was no northland and no land of the high sun, no other woman with yellow hair and green shoes, and Hevatha stroked his head, taking him to her as a mother takes a child, as a woman takes a man, as the pale soul accepts the dark, completing the circles of existence.

She wondered for a time longer what he was thinking, but then she was carried away by her body's own needs, by her soul's own wishes, and she only responded, leaving thought and reason far behind.

It was time to tell him she had a child growing within her, an independent, living, striving thing, but she could not bring herself to say it. She only held him, drawing her skirt and his coat over them as the night grew cool, and his body, warm against her, provided all that Hevatha needed to exist, all of her joy and worth.

She loved him. It was that simple. The rest of the world could fade to night, to nothing. There was nothing beyond their sleeping place. There was no other world.

The days went by, the cache of gold beneath the floorboards of the cabin grew bulky. English grew restless. Demarest could see it in him, as could Hevatha. He was drinking too much, talking too much, worrying a little.

"Thin, it seems thin, Floyd."

It was the sand he meant, the gold-bearing sand in the creek. Day by day the amount of gold dust they brought back to the cabin diminished—only a little, but enough to measure. At first English had thought he had slackened his work without realizing it, and so he had begun work when the dawn first touched the skies, worked until sunset ended in darkness. Later he had tried lanterns hung from the trees along the creek so that they could pan longer. Demarest had called a halt to that folly himself. A man can work only so long, so hard.

"Thin."

"We'll find it again." Demarest puffed placidly on his pipe, seated at the table, the firelight behind him. The red-bearded man's face showed no tension, no concern. "English, we've got fifteen thousand there." He nodded toward the floorboards. "We'll get out with twice that easily. Fifteen thousand will last me the rest of my life in San Francisco. We haven't done badly, if worse comes to worst."

"A million," Hevatha and Demarest heard the blond man say. "That's what we were looking for."

"A million might come, might not. We've had more luck than nine out of ten. I've been rich, I've been dead broke. I'll accept something in between."

English said something else, and then the word "million" was uttered again.

Demarest poured himself a cup of whiskey and said, "You're tired, that's all. Take the day off tomorrow, walk with Hevatha in the hills."

"So you can grab it off while I'm not looking!" English said, his mouth cynical, his eyes hard.

"Don't be a damn fool. We're partners."

"Yes, I know—a handshake. A handshake was fine when we had nothing, Floyd."

Demarest was briefly angry, but he drank from his cup, wiped his beard, and replied calmly, "We can put it on paper here and now if you want, Richard."

"What's a piece of paper?" English answered.

A long silence settled in the cabin. The fire popped; Tyee yawned and rolled over. Hevatha went to the window to stare out.

Demarest went on, "A million dollars gold, English. A man can't spend that much in a lifetime. A house, a couple of suits of clothes, a stock of good whiskey, roast beef and oysters every night. I don't need it anymore."

"I do!" He said it like a fervent convert to some golden religion, rising to bang on the table, turning haunted eyes to Hevatha and then to Demarest, who calmly rocked on his heels before the fire. "I do," he repeated softly, running a hand over his yellow hair. He sagged into his chair then, like a man exhausted.

English worked harder yet. The gold beneath the cabin grew, but the stream itself seemed to be depleted as they worked upstream and down, looking for new bars of gold-bearing sand. Hevatha watched or visited the Han or walked alone across their long valley, sometimes arriving almost unconsciously at the juncture of the two creeks where gold shimmered brightly, gold no one but the Han had ever seen.

Still she did not tell English. Was she wrong? Demarest seemed to think they had done well enough. It was Demarest who made the suggestion one night.

"How about Dawson, Richard? We're going to go crazy out here, you know."

"Dawson?" English said, as if such a place existed only in imagination. "What for?"

"What for? For anything Dawson's got to offer," Demarest said brightly. "Something to eat that we haven't cooked ourselves. A set of underwear that'll hold together, a pair of gloves, a shot of whiskey, a cold beer! Use your imagination, man."

The idea seeped slowly into English's mind. Demarest encouraged it. "We need another pick, salt and flour.

We've been at this long enough. Break out a hundred in dust. That won't tip anyone. Get yourself a decent hat."

"And a red dress for Hevatha," English said with more enthusiasm, turning to take her arm and pull her onto his lap.

"I don't want a red dress, English," she objected.

"An egg!" Demarest said, rubbing his hands together. "What would you give for an egg or a quart of cow's milk?"

"Cream. Ice-cold cream from a pewter mug, nearly frozen."

"And a steak, English. Not venison, but cow meat. A half-pound of lemon drops or horehound."

"An apple, Floyd! My God, a juicy apple. Hevatha's never had an apple."

"That's right. An apple—tinned peaches if we can't find fresh fruit. Tinned peaches in a bowl of ice-cold cream!"

"Can we do it? Can we risk it?"

"Sure. Dust is the usual currency in Dawson. Take it easy, spend fifty, a hundred dollars. No one thinks anything of it. A tin of peaches goes for five dollars anyway, the cream for the same. An egg, maybe a dollar apiece if we can find 'em, but, English, old man, we deserve it. And," he added with a wink, "we may just see a white woman. Have a chance to talk to someone besides ourselves about something besides the claim." He seemed to have forgotten Hevatha was there. Now his eyes lighted on her. "I . . ." he began, and faltered. The apology, if that was what it was, died in his throat.

English didn't notice it. He had already gone to the floorboard to remove one of the concealed sacks of gold. "Prices being what they are, I'll take two hundred, Floyd, all right?"

Demarest's eyebrows lowered a little. "It's your gold, Richard. Take what you want."

"How about a shave, Floyd? What do you think of that?" English pulled at his long curling yellow beard with two fingers. "How'd you like to see my face again, Hevatha?"

"If you like," she said.

"What's the matter, Hevatha?" Demarest asked. "Not thrilled about going into town? Not much for you to do there, I suppose."

"I am happy to go to town," the woman said. "I'll make the sled ready."

"No, let's walk, all right, English? Walk and leave Tyee in the cabin to keep watch."

"All right." English was still trying to decide if he ought to have his beard taken off in Dawson. Sure, hot towels and bay rum. That was luxury. He tied his poke onto his belt and put his faded mackinaw on over it.

Hevatha slipped into her parka without buttoning it. It was cool outside, but the sun was bright, there was no snow and little wind. "Tyee"—she crouched by the big dog, rolling his massive head between her hands— "you stay here. You sleep and watch the cabin so that no one gets in."

"Not really much chance of that," Demarest said, tugging on his hat with the earflaps. "I haven't seen anyone for a week up this far. Still, I feel better with the big fellow in here." He looked at English. "Ready?"

Richard patted his gold sack. "I am that, Floyd. This is the best idea you've had since . . ."

"Since I got the map off Drake, huh?" Demarest was pleased with himself. If English wanted a million, Demarest was content with what they already had. He was no longer a young man; he had been wealthy once, and he had been poor. Poor was all right for a younger man, but Demarest had a fear of dying sick and broke, finishing up in some poorhouse. He considered telling English now, but he decided to hold back. Demarest was through—let English have the claim. He was going to book passage to Seattle and get out of the Yukon before winter came again, get out like Drake had, not with a million, but with a decent bankroll.

"Let's go," English said. He opened the door, turned to glance at the floorboards, at Tyee, who was lying, head on paws, directly over the cache. "Come on, Hevatha, we'll see what pretty things they have in the Dawson stores." He put his arm around her waist and walked out with her to stand breathing in the cool pine-scented air as Demarest fastened the latch on the cabin door.

Dawson rollicked on through its long party. There was nothing to do in the Yukon territory but spend gold or look for it. If you had it, you spent it. A day-long saloon party was *de rigueur* after a good strike. Those who had, spent; those who didn't, waited for someone else to strike it. Some plotted ways to take it from the newly rich. Back-alley stabbings and crooked card games were part and parcel of gold-country life. Stealing dogs was considered bad form, lifting a poke was not viewed as moral, but both were understood. So was the hanging which followed if a man was caught. Normally a man was apprehended, tried, and punished in the same day—it was that or build a larger jail. Selling worn-out, nonexistent, or already staked claims to *chechacos* was a booming business. Many worn-out miners got their going-home poke by doing that. Dawson was larcenous, brawling, and bloody. Defeat was seldom evident. Dawson's men were ever optimistic; how could they fail to be, when every week converted some ragged, stubborn gold seeker to a polished, spatted, tailored millionaire?

Not all of those with money showed it. Secretiveness was as common as eccentricity. A man telling his sad tale of failure to an equally battered, shabby gold hunter might find a sack of dust left behind as a parting gift. Of course that poke might be taken away with a smile by the next man he met.

Prices were sky-high; a good steak was forty dollars. Anything on the side boosted the price still higher. Eggs at a dollar apiece were considered a good bargain. The profiteers had pounds of dust in their safes. The richest men in Dawson ran the stores and the saloons.

There wasn't much excuse for being broke in Dawson unless you were newly arrived. You struck gold or you left—or froze to death out on some godforsaken claim where the icy winds blew and there was nothing at all to eat. Despair was uncommon, but it was there to be seen on certain tragic faces. Handsome McClintock had sat in the Renegade Saloon for over a year, begging for drinks. For the price of a glass of whiskey you could hear his story of misplacing fifty thousand dollars in gold dust during a week-long binge of celebration. For nothing at all you could hear tales of claims nearly purchased, of strikes just missed, of the wrong sale at the wrong time, of dirty-dealing and murder.

Gold was the topic of every conversation, from the polished walnut tables at the Yukon Bank to the scarred, dilapidated tables of the Renegade Saloon. And the stories were believed, or half-believed. In a time and a place where men made their fortunes practically overnight, you never knew who was lying, deluded, or just well-informed. A whisper could start a gold rush, a nugget a stampede toward some distant, barely accessible canyon. There was nothing unusual about seeing fifty men rush out of town in the dead of night on the strength of a boastful lie.

Hevatha knew all of this, but she had no interest in it. Madness, gold madness, she called it. The whites had two great weaknesses so far as she could see: gold and *hootch-i-noo*. They seemed to feed on each other.

English and Demarest had stopped first for whiskey, leaving her outside. There was a sign on the door of the place which read "No Indians, no Chinese." Hevatha sat on the plank walk and waited patiently. Soon her man and his partner would emerge from the saloon, their cheeks glowing a little more, their voices a little louder, English's emotions a little closer to the surface. But they had worked hard and it did little harm.

The door opened and a rush of sound briefly touched Hevatha. A man in high boots and faded shirt staggered past, looking at her. She turned her head deliberately away. The man laughed at something and went on.

It was another half-hour before English emerged, tugged Hevatha to her feet, and said, "Let's go shopping now! Let's find you a red dress, Hevatha."

"I don't want a red dress, English," she answered, but again he ignored her.

"I wonder what size you'd be? I haven't bought a woman anything to wear . . . in years." He briefly returned to his past, shrugged away whatever thought had come to him, and led Hevatha down the walk, Demarest following, his pipe spewing tobacco smoke. Both men were happy, warm with whiskey fire.

"This is it for me, Richard," Demarest said as they passed the restaurant. "I'm eating. Eating everything they have on their menu. Maybe the menu as well. Join me?"

"Later. I'm shopping. I'm going to buy Hevatha a red dress."

Demarest lifted a hand and went in through the green door, a small brass bell tinkling. English led Hevatha on, crossing the muddy street to a small unpainted building which advertised "Ladies' Garments for the Discriminating" on a weathered sign.

The inevitable sign was on the door: "No Indians."

"The hell with that," English said recklessly. "You're going in!"

"For what, English. To make trouble? I don't care to make trouble. I don't care for a red dress!"

"You're going to have one. They won't tell me . . . Very well," he said, looking into her eyes, "wait here and I'll buy it myself."

He staggered just a little as he let go of her arm and started toward the door. Hevatha blew out an exasperated breath and then broke into a smile. If he wanted her to have the dress so much, let him buy it. If it pleased him, she would wear it.

She leaned against the wall of the building, arms folded, to wait.

English passed through the door of the dress shop

and slowed his uneven advance. The clerk was an older woman with pinned curls that had been dusted with powder. Her cheeks were sallow, her lips dry and pursed.

The lady with her was Sarah Penner. The blond turned her head only slightly. There was fire in those green eyes and a hint of mockery; a patrician profile was shown to English and then turned away as the two women examined a bolt of white lace.

"Perfect for the outer skirt, Mrs. Penner."

"It's not perfect at all," Sarah Penner said, her voice modulated to convey displeasure without edging into peevishness. White-gloved fingers dropped the lace onto the counter. "I suppose that's all you have."

"Yes, Mrs. Penner. The way things are here . . ."

"Yes, I know. Well, then, I'll take it."

"The entire bolt?" the older woman asked with surprise and pleasure.

"I wouldn't want anyone else wearing the same lace, would I, now?" Sarah Penner asked with a smile that could have melted ice. English was nearer now. He knew he was gawking but couldn't help himself. The flush in his cheeks had grown hotter. Sarah Penner turned suddenly, her smile growing even more radiant.

"Yes?"

"Forgive me." English straightened, feeling obscurely ashamed of his clothes, mud-daubed and worn, of his run-down boots and scent. "I once knew a woman very like you, Mrs. Penner."

"Did you?" The green eyes searched English's face. The smile lingered but it had altered, becoming bold or challenging but definitely enticing. "You know my name; have we met?"

English moved nearer yet, unable to hold himself back. He was aware now of her powder, softly scented. Her complexion was smooth and without blemish. She was nearer to thirty than twenty, but time would always be kind to this woman. English stood staring, aware that he appeared to be exactly what he was then, a shabby gold-rusher with a drink too many. If the lady was discomfited by that, she didn't show it. Maybe too many men had stared at her. She was a rare sight in the Yukon.

English realized that he hadn't answered the lady's question, realized that she was waiting, coolly amused. "No. I've seen you, of course. All of Dawson seems to know you."

"Yes," she said without false modesty, "all of Dawson knows me." Sexuality smoldered in those eyes, teasing or inviting, amused or deadly serious.

English blurted out his next sentences, half a lie. "My name is English, Richard English. I'm an author researching the gold rush in the Yukon. I apologize for my appearance, but I've been in the goldfields myself."

"An author, how interesting," the lady said, as if it really were. "And what are you researching in this shop, Mr. English? How Yukon ladies dress?"

"No." English grinned. "My Indian guide—a woman—I promised her a red dress."

"A woman guide? You must have had an interesting time of it out here," Sarah Penner said, the corners of her mouth twitching without becoming a smile.

"Everyone has an interesting time of it in the Yukon," English answered.

"Yes? You don't know the people I know, then, Mr. English." The shopkeeper had returned with the bolt of lace wrapped in brown paper. She placed it on the counter, and as Sarah Penner gestured with her hand impatiently, the woman simply went away. People like Sarah Penner didn't have to pay cash for things. She picked up the bolt, and then, as if it were an afterthought, asked, "I did invite you to the party, didn't I, Mr. English?"

"A party, no. You hadn't said anything."

"Authors are always amusing. People keep asking them about their books and they keep drinking." A sweet smile dulled the acid edge of her words. "Come along tonight. Do you know where my house is? Good. If you have something else to wear . . ."

"Yes," English said hastily, "I do."

"Good. Good-bye, then. Send a bill, Rose!"

"Yes, Mrs. Penner," an unseen voice answered. Then, her head held high, Sarah Penner glided out of the store. The cold of the day briefly flooded the store and then was gone.

"May I help you?"

English turned to find the storekeeper, Rose, behind the counter. Her face was stiff and her eyes weary. "I'm looking for a dress for a woman. A red dress. Scarlet, perhaps."

The storekeeper's face showed distaste in the lines that formed around her mouth. She didn't bother to ask what kind of woman wore scarlet. There were other miners in Dawson who had come looking for bright dresses, for black stockings, other apparel in dark lace.

"I may have something. Will we need a fitting?"

"What?" English's eyes were still on the closed door of the shop. "Oh, I don't know. No, I suppose not." He was suddenly impatient and the storekeeper had the idea she could have sold him anything at all and he would be pleased with it. Still, she was polite. In Dawson, you never knew. Look at Sarah Penner's late husband. Hadn't he come in with mud to his waist, booming that he wanted to buy the shop for his new wife?

Rose led English to a wall rack where dresses colorful enough to form a rainbow hung in neat ranks. She removed the brightest red dress she could find, in silk with black lace at the cuffs and hem, and held it up for English, spreading the skirt.

"Yes." He barely looked at it. "All right."

"The size, sir?" Rose asked. "This is a twelve."

"All right. Fine." English had a sack of dust out, weighing it in his palm. "You have scales?"

"Yes, of course. Wrap it up, sir?"

"Yes. Wrap it up. Tell me, where's the nearest men's clothing store?"

"Two doors down, sir," Rose said. She read his eyes, her mouth tightening a little more, and she sighed

inwardly. Sarah Penner could be elected mayor of
Dawson in the morning if she wanted it. The men
around here . . . But then, they were lonely men,
weren't they? Her late husband . . . Rose's mind drifted
away into her unhappy past and then snapped back to
business. She withdrew a brass scale from beneath the
counter and weighed out fifty dollars' worth of dust
while Richard English drummed impatiently on the
counter with his fingers.

Carrying the brown-paper-and-string-wrapped parcel, English went out into the main street of Dawson.
Hevatha rose, dusting off the back of her skirt, and
walked to him.

"Here," he said. "Just as promised." He kissed her
lightly, very lightly, on the temple and then turned
her. "I want to get a shave, Hevatha. Seen Demarest?"

"Still eating," she answered. "Aren't you hungry
now, English?"

"No, not now . . . A shave and then a new suit of
clothes. We'll both get dressed up and parade around
town, all right, Hevatha?"

"Yes, English." Hevatha clutched the parcel with
both arms and walked along behind English as he
strode toward a barber shop on the corner. She was no
fool—she had seen the yellow-haired woman come out
of the dress shop. English had her on his mind again.
She wasn't angry or even annoyed. She felt sorrow for
him.

At the barber shop a line of men stood outside the
door, all of them bearded and impatient. A bottle
changed hands from time to time. English fell in behind them.

He told Hevatha, "Look, you may as well eat. You
can find a place in one of those Chinese restaurants.
Put your dress on." He held her by the shoulders,
smiling. "I want to see how you look. You won't even
recognize me, I'll tell you that."

The man with the constable's badge pinned to his
heavy coat strode up the plank walk and the miners
moved aside for Boxer Thrush. "English," the lawman

said, "haven't seen you for a time. Demarest here too?"

The two men shook hands. "He's stuffing his face across the street," English said. "I'm going to get cleaned up. I'm invited to Sarah Penner's tonight."

"You don't say?" The constable studied English with new consideration. "How'd you break into society?"

"Told a few lies," English said with a smile.

"I see. By the way, we won't need you or Demarest for witnesses in that Tutchone case."

"Good. That's all settled, then?"

"More or less. They broke jail."

"They what?"

"Broke jail. One of 'em got away. Nadgi won't be doing any more mischief in the Yukon. Tom Kite saw him sneaking out the back window and shot him through the head. The other one, Sasak, got away. He'll run south as fast and as far as he can, I suppose. His own people will shelter him. Damned Indians . . ." Boxer Thrush glanced at Hevatha and shrugged. "Guess I'll see how Demarest is doing. You boys doing all right up there, are you?"

"Just about making expenses," English said blandly. The constable, who never believed a miner's statements about his fortunes, nodded.

"Good. Say, Aaron Butler's still in town, English."

"Don't worry about that. I don't want any more of him."

"All right. It might be a good idea to just steer clear of him, anyway."

"I intend to. I've other things on my mind, constable."

"Yes," the constable drawled thoughtfully. "Have fun. Don't do anything you could get locked up for. We've got a waiting list at the jail."

Then he looked again at Hevatha, fleetingly touched his hat brim, and walked off, swaggering just a little, calling out to those he passed.

The line of miners shifted slightly. Two men with freshly barbered hair and beards came from the barber shop, smelling of lilac or bay rum, and the waiting men hooted derisively, whistling and catcalling.

English shuffled ahead with the line, which had grown by three men. Hevatha, still holding her package, inched along with him. "This is no fun for you. Go and and get dressed. Get something to eat," English told her.

"I want to see your face naked again," Hevatha answered.

"Soon enough. I'll catch up with you. Did I give you any dust? Here." He gave her what was left in a small pouch, moved forward with the line again, and waved a hand.

There was nothing for Hevatha to do but wander off. The day was cool. She looked at Dawson with amused eyes, wondering what fate had pushed her here, far away from her home. She missed Aunt Godak. Missed the sea in its frothing, furious beauty, the long rocky beaches and the offshore islands where Yakwan lay. But the Iht had been there, and Gunyah and Ganook. She had as many unhappy memories as good ones. Her home in the Cheyenne lands had so faded and dimmed that it seemed she never had had a mother, a sister, a father.

But, she told herself, straightening her shoulders, she had come into brightness, into a true life. She had her man, English—foolish, alternately strong and weak, mysterious even now. She had her man and she knew, if he did not, that English needed her yet. He was a boy at times, at others an old man.

He was only a man and he needed his woman. If he wished her to wear the red dress, she would. If he wished her to lie down with him, she would. In time he would see her face, see in her eyes all that Hevatha was.

She stopped on the street and opened a corner of the package, peering in at the dress. She shook her head and laughed out loud. The dress was ludicrous; she would wear it.

She walked the streets of Dawson, holding the package to her breast. Once, above a saloon she saw a

woman lean out a window and laugh almost frantically. A miner, shirtless, laughed as well and tugged
her back from the window. The white woman was
wearing a red dress. So that was what they liked; so
she would be as he liked.

Stopping in an alley behind a blacksmith's shop that
reeked of sulfur and slag, Hevatha placed the package
on a covered rain barrel, opened it, and slipped the
dress on over her buckskin shirt and cotton blouse.
Her parka she held in one hand as she twisted and
fumbled and tried to figure out how a white woman
buttoned a dress in the back.

To accomplish that took her almost fifteen minutes,
and even then they all didn't seem to be in the right
buttonhole. Hevatha removed the wooden cover from
the rain barrel, and peered into the dark water, seeing
her reflection. Braided hair, red silk dress, half-smiling
mouth, wide brown eyes, and she shook her head.

"English, will we ever understand each other?"

Putting her parka on again, she walked through the
alley to a ramshackle building which said simply "Food"
above the door. A Chinese man, no taller than
Hevatha's shoulder, came out, dumped a basin of
water, and bowed to her, holding the door. Inside it
was warm and close despite the emptiness of the dining room.

"Yes, to eat?" the man asked with a broad grin, and
Hevatha smiled in return. The Chinese had a face like
an Aleut, uncomfortably like Koosh's face. "Yes?" he
asked again.

Hevatha answered. "Anything. Whatever is good.
Whatever does not cost too much gold."

The small man scurried away and returned in a few
minutes with fish, good sturgeon, not burned as a
white man might like it, but filled with juices, tasting
of the lakes and the deep. He offered her caribou
meat, deeply smoked, and honey and bannock, and
Hevatha ate until she was full, too full in her tight red
dress.

Going out, she found the skies over Dawson flushed

with summer sunset. The town continued its unending, fitful revolving. Men trying to forget themselves roamed the streets, staggered into and out of a saloon, or sat aimlessly staring on the wooden benches before the stores and restaurants. Ghosts. The ghosts of men came to the Yukon.

Hevatha walked to the barber shop and peered in its small, oily window. English was not there. She crossed to the restaurant where Demarest had been eating. Crouching, she looked in there as well. He was not among the bearded, unwashed miners collected at the long plank tables.

Two men walking past looked her up and down, seeing the silk skirt billowing out from beneath the parka, the moccasins below, and they laughed. Hevatha couldn't help but join in, looking down at the strange layers of clothing. At her laugh the men's laughter changed from mockery to enjoyment, and they lifted thick, callused hands in farewell.

The sky was growing dark and finally Hevatha remembered that English had been going to buy new clothes, so she walked up the street to the clothing store. It was locked now, dark and empty. The ladies' clothing store was still open, however, and she returned there. The sign on the door kept her outside, but through the windows she could see he was not inside. An older white woman with a full figure and a rigid spine was jabbing her finger at something on the counter while the storekeeper nodded abjectly.

Hevatha turned from the window, looked up and down the street, and then sagged to the plank walk to sit, arms around her knees, waiting.

The sky went darker yet and the lanterns along the main street were lighted. The hoots and hollers of the miners grew louder as the whiskey flowed. Now and then a horse-drawn wagon, a dog team, or a man on muleback came up the road and passed.

The door to the shop opened and Hevatha glanced that way. The woman she had seen inside emerged, holding a large parcel. She had auburn hair, a face beginning to go fleshy but still showing fine lines, pale eyes which were at once amused and cynical. She wore a dark blue dress and a matching jacket edged with fur. Mink, Hevatha thought. The woman looked impatiently up and down the street.

"No carriage. Fool's drunk again, I suppose," she said, and then she glanced at Hevatha.

"Lost my driver. Waiting for a man yourself, I suppose. What a life. We spend all our time waiting for them."

"Your man is gone?" Hevatha asked.

"My driver, honey. My *man* is long gone." The woman glanced at a watch pinned to her bodice and frowned with disgust. "All the same, all unreliable." She added, "But not unpredictable. A glass of whiskey or a woman. Maybe cards as a third choice. Why do we rely on them at all?"

"Because they are men," Hevatha said. She got to her feet, stretching her arms, yawning widely.

"Yes, I suppose that's it. Lost your man, did you?"

"He will be back for me," Hevatha answered.

"Sure. If he doesn't get into something more interesting. Where in God's name," the woman asked, "did you get that hideous dress?" She went to Hevatha, lifted the hem, and smiled. "Don't tell me—your man bought it for you. You're wearing it to please him."

"Yes." Hevatha liked the woman's candor, her strength. "I am wearing it for him."

"I hope he's worth it, honey. You've got no idea where he is now?"

"I thought here. But I heard him say there was a party somewhere. At a lady's house."

"Not Sarah Penner's party, I hope! God, I'm trying to get there, though why I'd go, I don't know. Posturing, artificial thing. Well, we get along with our neighbors. I'm Hanna Sue Blythe. You call me Hanna. Is that where your man went? To Sarah Penner's fancy ball?"

"I don't know," Hevatha answered. "I think maybe."

"And you accept that? Woman, you can't let him

treat you like that. You sitting on the cold street waiting. If I could have a word with him—"

"He is a good man," Hevatha said.

"Yes, I know. They're all good until the next woman comes down the street. Don't you just sit here, young lady. I've had four husbands and I'll tell you the way to lose them: let them go where they want to go. Give them their freedom, be generous with them. That's how they wander, honey."

"I will wait."

"You'll wait, all right, wait until he's ready for you. Don't be foolish. You think he's gone to Sarah Penner's party, do you? That's where I'm going—if Ford ever sobers up and figures out that I'm waiting for my carriage. Durn him, if I have to walk . . . Spent a lot of time walking in my time, and some of it behind a mule. Second husband was a dirt farmer. Poor farmer, great man for loving . . . Wait a minute . . . come on, come with me."

The older woman took Hevatha's hand and started tugging her toward the door of the now-closed dress shop. Hevatha held back. "What do you want, woman?"

"Told you to call me Hanna." The woman kept on tugging.

"The signs says 'No Indians.' "

"Yes, and it says 'Closed' too, but signs are put up to please the clientele, and I'm the clientele, honey." Hanna Sue Blythe began pounding on the door, and before long Rose, looking more weary than annoyed, answered, swinging the door open. Hanna pushed on through, practically dragging Hevatha after her.

"Now, then," the older woman demanded of the shopkeeper, "what are we going to do about this?"

"Do . . . ?" The woman in charge of the store spread her hands.

"You sold this dress, didn't you?" Hanna demanded. She lifted the skirt of Hevatha's red silk dress accusingly. "What sort of woman do you think this is? She don't . . . doesn't want this damned thing, Rose."

"But, Mrs. Blythe!"

"I know, a man bought it. A man! What would he know about dressing a lady?"

"She's *Indian*," Rose said with something nearing anguish.

"Right. I'm Scotch-Irish with a touch of Portugee. What's that got to do with clothes? Rose, break something out, in white, I think. Lacy and white. Go good against her complexion. The lady's going with me to Sarah Penner's ball. A special guest of mine. White lace, yes, that'll do it." She moved along the wall, examining the remnants of lace. "This won't do at all, Rose, is this all you have?"

"Yes . . . well, that is, I did have needlepoint lace. Mrs. Penner wanted it over her own dress. Couldn't wait for me to do it for her." Rose sniffed. "I suppose she'll have some servant without a lick of skill or sense attack that. That was all I had. Mrs. Penner bought it all."

"She did, did she?" Hanna Sue Blythe asked, growing taller, her voice louder. "Expensive, wasn't it?"

"It was," Rose said in a smaller voice. "Three hundred dollars the bolt."

"Profitable. Now, let me ask you this, Rose. How much is a second bolt? Don't answer. You'll say you don't have more, but I wouldn't believe it. Five hundred, say? Five hundred dollars for the exact lace."

"Mrs. Penner—"

"Mrs. Penner wouldn't know where the stuff came from. I sure wouldn't tell her. Look at this poor girl in this godawful crimson sinner's dress. White lace we want, and don't tell me you haven't any more, Rose."

"Mrs. Blythe, you know we promise exclusivity here."

"Sure. And I promise you I'll shop somewhere else if I can't find what I want now. Hold on there, girl!" Hevatha had tried to ease toward the door, but her new benefactress towed her back.

"It's possible that I have some needlepoint lace left in the back. I'd have to look," Rose said in a hushed voice.

"It's possible. Why don't you look. What was Mrs. Penner going to wear under the lace, Rose?"

"Organdy," the shopkeeper said in a voice that cracked.

"We're not planning a murder here, Rose!" Hanna said boisterously. "I'm just asking what the lady was wearing tonight."

"White organdy and needlepoint lace. French," she added automatically.

"Who made the dress? You?"

"Yes," Rose answered, "but, Mrs. Blythe—"

"How much?"

"Mrs. Blythe! If Sarah Penner ever saw—"

"I asked how much?"

"It cost three hundred dollars, Mrs. Blythe."

"I'll give you five hundred to make one just like it."

"Mrs. Blythe," the woman called. "You'll ruin me!"

"I'll ruin you if you don't do as I ask," the older lady said. Hevatha was inching toward the door again but Mrs. Blythe pulled her back. "No you don't. We've a mission tonight, a noble mission."

"It will be trouble," Hevatha said, and Rose nodded in vigorous agreement.

"That's right, but I can stand some trouble. I don't like Sarah Penner and her high-toned ways. I don't like women content to fool with other women's men, nor women who scorn others like you, Hevatha. My God, you're twice as good-looking as Sarah Penner and a notch younger, I'd say. You let your man go off into her den! I've got a score anyway that I mean to settle. Rose—the dress!"

"Mrs. Penner's dress took two weeks to make, Mrs. Blythe."

"Yes, I'll bet it did. I'll also wager you could whip one up in an hour if you really tried. Try! Who's that out there now? Ford with my coach? Durn him! He'll have to sit and wait now. Rose," she said, sitting on a chair, crossing her arms, "get to it. A thousand for the whole job—see if that won't put some scurry in your bustle."

"Mrs. Blythe!" the dressmaker wailed again, but she went off in frantic search of material and pincushion, needle and thread.

"I don't like this," Hevatha said. "I don't want to make trouble."

"Why not?" Mrs. Blythe snapped. "Why let those like Sarah Penner make it all? Why let the men do as they like? We'll show 'em something, dear, we'll show 'em." She patted Hevatha's hand, and as her driver poked a sheepish head around the door, she snapped, "Ford, sober up! You'll have some driving to do tonight. This lady and I are going to Mrs. Penner's party. I'd appreciate it if you didn't look like somebody recovering from a back-alley beating."

"Yes, Mizz Blythe," the driver said, bowing out.

"He'll be going for another drink," Hanna Sue Blythe commented. "Sit, girl, sit—and for God's sake, take off that dress. You'll be a lady tonight and I'll wager you this: when the men of this town see you, you'll be queen of Dawson of the Yukon—not Mrs. Sarah Penner."

10

IT was a long walk on a cold night up the road to Sarah Penner's lighted house, and Richard English stopped once to take a drink from his newly purchased flask filled with good dark rum. He wore a dark blue suit, string tie, and black hat. His new black boots hurt his feet as he started on again, over the frost-glazed mud underfoot.

There were three carriages in the yard, rarities in the northland, and half a dozen horses, again rare. But Dawson's finest citizens were expected to display wealth in such small ways. The money, when it came to the lucky few, sometimes came so fast and in such abundance that it was virtually impossible to spend it, and so if it meant that the carriage might take six months to arrive from Seattle or San Francisco with a team of matched bays, useless except for the summer months, it mattered not at all. If the house Sarah Penner lived in had twenty-four rooms and a mere three of them were actually used, it was looked upon only as a minor extravagance. If Yule Travis, who had been a railroad engineer the year before, now wanted to take his baths in a solid gold tub and wear silk pajamas from New York, well, that was within the boundaries of good taste for Dawson.

English scraped his boots on an ornate iron scraper and tugged at the cord of a doorbell. A man in a clawhammer suit and white tie, a butler who looked more like a prizefighter, opened the door, looked English up and down, made an attempt at a bow, and allowed English to enter the foyer, which was lighted to brilliant white by a chandelier with a hundred candles. English handed his hat to the butler, wiped back his yellow hair, touched his newly shaven face, which now was ornamented only by a full blond mustache, and entered the main ballroom, where Dawson's elite, such as they were, stood in small circles sipping from crystal punch glasses, wearing their finery.

The language was a little coarser, the voices a little louder, the subject more earthy, but it might have been a San Francisco dinner party at the house of Dr. Wentzel. Richard half-expected to see Laura, cool, blond, haughty, descending the marble staircase, but Laura Wentzel was far away, asleep in her cozy bed, her head filled with dreams of stocks, bonds, and country homes.

English didn't see his hostess. He knew few of the others there. Bertram St. Ives, the surveyor and manipulator, was in close conversation with a red-haired man who just shook his head stubbornly. Joseph Carmody, the mayor of Dawson, whom English had seen but never met, was standing very close to a matronly woman in blue, swallowing glass after glass of punch.

English wandered across the room, seeing men in walrus whiskers wearing dress suits, barrel-chested miners in tight-fitting store-bought tweeds and twills. Probably each man he passed had enough gold dust to bury himself in. Dawson society was very democratic—as long as you had the gold to be admitted: former saloon girls, married to tough miners who had struck it rich; the former railroad engineer, Yule Travis, wearing a pirate's gold earring, his hair to the middle of his back; a dainty French lady imported by mail order by her gold-rich husband, lately a fireman from Vancouver.

English passed a small alcove with a single door opening off it. The ceiling was vaulted, the walls painted eggshell white. He stepped into the alcove, lifted his flask from his pocket, and took a deep drink.

"Needful, ain't it?" a voice asked. In a red velvet chair sat a whiskered man.

"Sorry, didn't see you," English apologized.

"No one pays me much mind, son," the man said,

stretching his arms as he yawned. When he stretched, the cuffs of his suit rode eight inches up on his lanky arms. The man had gray-streaked, pomaded hair. A bent nose lent character to his lean face.

English walked nearer to the man, who sprawled on the delicate chair uncomfortably.

"Hell of a thing, these shindigs," he said to English. "I'm Gage Power."

"English. Richard English."

"My old lady drags me along," Powers said, rubbing his fleshless jaw. "Wants to snoot with the highfalutin. Wants a house like this." Powers looked around in dubious survey. "Why, I don't know. Guess I'll get her one. Have to be bigger, if I know Penny." He looked at English again. "Mind passin' a flask, son?"

"Not at all. Seen our hostess, have you?" English said as Powers took a long drink of the rum.

"No. I'd like to. I'd like to see her . . . Nice-looking woman," Gage Powers said, moderating his thoughts.

"You know these people, do you?" Richard asked.

"Most of 'em. Knew most of 'em when they had nothin' but a dog team and a Winchester. Now they forget that, think of themselves as mag-nates."

"Once they get a few dollars, you mean."

"It ain't necessarily the money. Look at Yule Travis—you can still have a drink with him and talk like men. Me, I reckon I'm worth near to ten million now, and I like to think I'm still human. Some of these others . . . You should've known Satchel Penner—used to be a man till he struck it. Then this widow of his drove him to his grave, I'd say . . . well, no sense dredging that up while I'm under the lady's roof."

English had another question but the door in the alcove snapped open and a dark, scarred face peered out. "Ready for some cards, Gage?"

"I'm ready. It's that or pink punch and pleasantries. Come on along, English."

"I'll stay out here, thanks."

"Waiting for the hostess?" Gage asked. "If I know Mrs. Penner, she'll make her grand entry in an hour or so. Likes to keep the men waiting, you know."

English hesitated. "Come on, Gage!" someone shouted.

"We're short a man," the man in the doorway said.

"I'm not carrying much money," Richard admitted.

"Low stakes," Gage Powers said. "Nothing like that game Shanghai Pierce got into. Lost a million and a half, he did. We're playing to kill time, son, for the conversation. Hell, I'll stand for you if you get into trouble."

"Gage!"

"We're coming'!" Gage wrapped an arm around English's shoulders and walked him in through the door to a round table with five chairs huddled around. Three men sat waiting, one of them idly shuffling a deck of red-backed cards. He was Aaron Butler, and English stiffened, halting Gage in his tracks.

"Trouble?" Gage Powers asked.

"No trouble," English said through tightened lips.

"Young man knows me," Aaron Butler said, looking at the cards he spread on the table and not at English. "Doesn't like me."

"That don't leave him alone," Gage Powers said, and Butler snorted.

"No." He lifted his black eyes. "Willing to sit in a card game with me, writer?"

"I recall the last one we were in together."

"Do you? I was the loser, wasn't I? Ought to give you cause for optimism."

Every word of Butler's, each casual gesture, was a challenge. It was sensible, logical, to turn on his heel and walk out, but English was drawn by the challenge, urged along by Gage Powers' arm, and before he really was aware of having made a decision, he was seated at the table between Powers and a man named Curt Collins, looking across a poker table at the pocked, hard face of Aaron Butler. The fifth man was Yakima Brown, another millionaire, one who lived in a shack up along Clinton Creek with six hired, heavily armed Ingalik Indians and refused to spend a single cent except on whiskey and cards. He had a tangled black beard, a sleepy-eyed expression, weather-scoured hands, and seemingly endless patience.

Butler shuffled, each man anted up a hundred dollars, Yakima Brown cut, and the cards glided to the waiting hands of the miners.

English didn't play well and he knew he wasn't. His eyes, his mind, were on Aaron Butler, waiting to catch him cheating, bottom-dealing or thumbnailing a card to mark it. In the meantime he neglected to fold, played recklessly or absentmindedly, overraised, and called too soon. He was out five hundred dollars in gold before he had had time to warm his chair.

Gage Powers saw English heft his sack of dust, and the millionaire asked, "Can you play on?"

"There's more at home," English said tightly. Aaron Butler was smoking a dark cigar, watching him with cynical amusement.

"I'm standing for the boy until he refills his poke," Powers told the table, "or," this with a wink, "until he's skinned us all and gotten it back."

That settled that. Gage Powers was good for more than anyone could count. The cards floated out again, the game shifting to five-card stud. English won back two hundred dollars and then the game moved to draw poker as the deal passed from Butler to Brown to Collins, who played with his tongue thrust out of his mouth, his eyes screwed up as if he were in intense pain.

The butler came in with a tray containing two bottles of whiskey and five glasses. Collins asked, "What's going on out there? Madame come down yet?"

"No, sir, not yet."

"Good," Collins grumbled, opening a bottle and pouring. English took a glass as well, though he didn't need it. His own Cuban rum had been working on his head. He sat glowering, needing more than anything in the world to beat Butler, who seemed to win at everything. English was down five hundred dollars again, a reckless amount for him, but he had it. He had plenty. Not as much as Brown or Gage Powers, but enough to give Butler a beating.

He lost another five hundred on the next hand, tried doubling up the next game, and lost again. He took another drink of whiskey and settled in, his face flushed. Butler's face was a wooden mask, weathered and pocked. Gage Powers and Brown exchanged stories and laughed at the loss of a few thousand dollars. English was in over his head and realized it.

"Everything all right?" Butler asked with oily concern.

"Deal. All I want from you is cards, Butler."

"That's all you'll ever get from me, English," Butler assured him. "Sure you want to stay in the game?"

"Deal, I said."

"Sure. You want to ante?"

English had nothing on the table before him and he looked at Gage Powers, who nodded amiably. "I'll pay you back, Gage."

"No problem. Take minted money, will you?" he asked, taking a dozen fifty-dollar gold pieces from his vest pockets.

English accepted the money, tossed in one coin, and poured another drink. The game was five-card stud. English got a king in the hole and a king up. The third card was a seven. Butler was betting now. He had two sixes showing. English glanced at the other hands on the table, guessing his chances for a third king. There were none showing. Collins gave it up, throwing his cards in. A six? Hadn't Collins been showing the six of spades? English's next card was a four. Gage folded and Yakima Brown followed him, leaning back to light a cigar.

That left Butler and English. Butler, on the strength of the two sixes, still led. "Five thousand," he said quietly, and a sack of gold dust followed by another plunked to the center of the table.

"Five thousand," English said almost to himself. Five thousand of Gage's money. But English had Butler beat on the table—unless he had a third six in the hole or drew one next time. Collins had had a six showing. One six left in the deck. Twelve-to-one odds.

"I'll see that," English said. He stacked the gold

coins neatly and pushed them into the pot. Butler's face still showed nothing.

Two pairs, English thought frantically; he's got two pairs. No, he was trying to bluff, hoping for another six. Maybe he already had the third six.

Butler flipped English his last card and English held back his smile. The six of hearts. He had Butler. Butler would try to bluff English, try to convince him he had another six, but he damn well didn't. English peeked again at the facedown six of hearts and managed to smile.

"Your bet, Butler."

"You got nothing left," the gambler pointed out.

"Not with me. Gage? You'll let me stand on you again?"

"Go ahead, this is gettin' interesting," Powers said.

This is it, English thought. This is where he tries to bluff me out of the pot. He hasn't got three sixes. I know where the other two are. English took a drink, a deep drink, which stung his throat and caused his eyes to water. He took another look at the king he had in the hole and another peek at the red six, the six Butler needed to beat him.

"Ten thousand," Butler said, and English nearly laughed out loud.

"I was expecting that," he said. "I'll see you, Butler. Let's see if you've got enough to beat these."

He flipped the king of diamonds over to lie beside the king of clubs and leaned back, beaming. Butler's expression still hadn't altered.

"I've got the sixes you see," Butler said, and then he flipped his hole card up, "and one you didn't see."

A *six.* English snapped forward, his hands spread, shaking his head back and forth. "No you don't! You must have cheated."

"Easy, boy," Gage cautioned.

"But I've got the six of hearts! And Collins . . . he had that card. He threw away the six of spades." English lunged across the table and turned Collins' unplayed hand faceup. Seven, deuce, five of spades, and the *nine* of spades.

Aaron Butler was looking at him steadily, coldly, from beneath his heavy dark eyebrows. He glanced at the other players, who nodded, and then raked in the gold.

"Nine does look like a six, I guess. A man shouldn't drink when he's playing cards. Doesn't do much for the memory," Butler said, and then he laughed. He laughed and English could have thrown himself on the gambler and strangled him. Gage was holding him back, he realized. In his hands were crumpled cards.

"Easy, English, this don't do any good. You got the money?"

"I've got it, Gage." English, pale and unsteady, wiped back his blond hair. "I've got it. I swear you'll get it, Butler."

"Sure. I wouldn't worry about it. Just get it."

The butler opened the door again and called in, "Mrs. Penner is making her entrance, gentlemen."

" 'Bout time," Yakima Brown said with a yawn. He rose, studying his engraved gold watch.

Butler had risen and now with a cigar in his teeth he strode past English to the door. Beyond the door, the guests, some of them wearing masks now, had moved toward the foot of the great marble stairway.

"Gage?" Yakima Brown said.

"I'll catch up in a minute," Gage said. Brown shrugged and he and Collins went out, closing the door.

"He cheated me," English said, standing with his head hanging, a card still in his hand.

"If he did, I don't know how it was done. No one saw it. The money, son, if you don't—"

"I have it," English said, his head snapping up, his face flushing. "I have it and I'll pay the bastard!" He looked at the card in his hand and slowly opened his fingers, letting it flutter to the floor.

"All right," Gage said soothing. "Let's go out now and join the party."

"The party . . ." English said absently. He shook his head. "No, I haven't got the heart for that now. I'm going to go get the man's money—your money."

"All right, English." Gage Powers patted his shoulder once, and then the lanky millionaire strolled out of the card room, leaving English to stand brooding, staring at the cards, at nothing.

He had the money, all right, if he took all of his cache from the cabin. If he took all of Demarest's as well. And that was the only way to do it. Floyd would understand. Maybe. He could have English's share of everything they took out of the creek until they were even. There was still plenty of dust in that sand downstream. But English was broke, flat broke, and maybe there wasn't enough left in their claim to ever replace what he had lost.

He turned and looked at the closed door, hearing applause from the ballroom. Butler had cheated him. How, he didn't know, but he was convinced that Aaron Butler had skinned him. And he knew he would never be able to prove it. He turned back to the table, lifted the quart of bourbon that hadn't been touched, put it into his coat pocket, and started out. The butler was in the doorway, going to clean up, maybe. Beyond him Sarah Penner, radiant in a white dress, was moving through the throng of guests.

"There another way out of here?" English asked.

"Yes, sir . . . you're not feeling well?"

"Not well at all. Show me."

English was taken to the kitchen, where four Chinese worked over steaming caldrons, chattering away, waving spoons. It was hot, very hot in there, and very cold when he stepped outside into the night. It was going to be a long walk upriver and back. English opened the bottle of whiskey with his teeth, spat the cork away, took a deep drink, and started unsteadily into the night.

Inside, Bertram St. Ives was politely applauding, his pink hands barely touching each other as he watched the lady glide into the center of the floor, take the mayor's hand, signal with a nod to the band, and lead the first waltz.

"Not dancing?" Aaron Butler said casually.

"Oh, it's you," St. Ives said. "What's going on?"

Butler handed him a folded note. "Give this to Jimmy. Tell him to take my horse and get down there quick as he can."

St. Ives opened the note, scanned it, and frowned. "Hardly worth it, is it, Aaron?"

"It is to me."

"You shouldn't let things get personal. I never do. Men get hanged when they let it get personal."

"You want me to find Jimmy myself?"

"No." St. Ives tucked the note in his pocket. "I know where he is. He and a couple of her ladyship's servants are drinking rye in the library."

"Then give him the note, Bertram," Butler said, and this time there was warning in the man's eyes. St. Ives nodded and walked away, working his way around the hall toward the library while Butler, smiling darkly, watched the dancers on the floor swirling around the centerpiece, Mrs. Sarah Penner.

Outside, the bay horse lifted its head. A narrow, slightly unsteady boy of eighteen was loping toward the animal, frightening it a little.

"Easy, Spellbinder," Jimmy Waley said. He swung aboard and heeled the horse roughly. It was a good horse, big and fast. It was only the second time Waley had ridden Spellbinder, the fourth time he had been on a horse since he had come to the Yukon. Come, failed, and then luckily attached himself to Aaron Butler and Bertram St. Ives, where he was well treated and trusted. They knew Waley had a close mouth. They also knew he had a murder on his record in Oregon. That had been an accident. Jimmy Waley wasn't a violent person. The man he was delivering the note to was, and he shuddered a little despite the whiskey in his belly and the heavy lambskin coat he wore.

The little shack was on the north of town, on the property St. Ives owned and was building on. There would be a land office there one day if St. Ives' plans went right, and St. Ives' plans usually did.

Waley slowed the horse to a walk, whistled once,

and approached the shack cautiously, reaching for the fifty-dollar gold piece St. Ives had given him.

Swinging down from Spellbinder, he walked to the crooked shack's door, knocked, and turned his back, folding his arms on his chest, blowing out clouds of steam. He turned back as the door opened and its inhabitant peered out. Starlight gleamed on something cold and metallic in the man's hand and Waley felt a shiver creep up his spine.

"Here," he said, handing over the gold piece. "Mr. St. Ives wants you to do something."

"What?" the man in the shadows asked, and Waley handed him the note. Sasak took that too and then closed the door, leaving Waley alone and glad of it.

Sasak lit a candle and hunched over the note. He read English but it came slowly. He moved his lips as if the operation were a painful one. When he had finished, he straightened up, touched the paper to the candle flame, and watched the note burn to ash. Then Sasak placed the gold coin he had been given in his boot and went out.

He would need a horse, but that was no problem. St. Ives kept two of them in the barn across the lot. Sasak was a fair horseman. He didn't quite trust animals that large. They bit you or kicked or threw you off. But in dry weather they were as good as a dog team, better.

He saddled a lanky blue roan in the barn and rode out, upriver, following the Yukon northward. When he reached the cabin, it was as the note had said. No one was there. It was dark inside. No one moved. Still the Tutchone watched for a while from the pines before moving toward it.

Find the gold these miners had hidden and take it to St. Ives. And suppose some got lost on the way, as it would? Sasak was growing very rich. Nadgi should have lived to share this wealth, but then, Sasak reflected, he would be only half as rich.

Sasak speculated on where the gold would be. Under the floor, beneath a mattress, behind loose stones in the fireplace. There were only so many places. They never buried gold outside. They wanted to sleep with it near.

Sasak stepped onto the porch, the boards cracking softly underfoot. He put a hand on the latch string, tugged it, and went in.

The thing hurled itself out of the darkness, a savage, razor-fanged hideous fury weighing as much as Sasak did. Sasak cried out in terror, knowing what it was. He threw his arm over his face and the wolf-dog clamped onto it, savaging the arm as Sasak pawed at his belt sheath, groping for his knife.

His arm was filled with flame. The huge dog twisted his head violently from side to side and Sasak screamed again. His hand found the rawhide handle of his knife and he slashed out with the blade. He felt steel meet flesh, but nothing stopped Tyee's assault. He stabbed again, the knife glancing off the sled dog's skull. Still the beast held his tortured arm, tearing at it.

Sasak stabbed with frenzied force, slashing, cutting, trying to reach the vital organs beneath the thick coat of fur. The blade cut flesh and hide and then struck heart muscle and the great dog groaned with pain, still holding the intruder's arm. Sasak twisted his blade and ripped outward with it and Tyee sagged back, his jaws unclamping. He fell heavily to the floor, tried to rise, and fell back, his breathing strangled by blood.

Sasak kicked at the body. Once, twice, holding his arm as his boot thudded against Tyee's skull.

He staggered to the lantern on the table and struck a match. His jacket was ripped to shreds. Meat hung from the bone of his forearm. Blood smeared the floor. Tyee's chest still rose and fell and with a feral cry the Tutchone Indian threw himself on the great dog, stabbing at its throat until Tyee no longer twitched and the yellow eyes stared out blindly at the lanternlit interior.

Sasak began ripping the cabin apart, hurling things everywhere. Pain had brought madness to him and he slashed at the mattresses, emptied the cupboards, sending a canister of flour to explode against the floor. Looking down at that, he saw what he wanted.

The flour had begun a sift through the join of two planks. Sasak crouched, panting, growling with pain, his left arm useless, blood hot as it trickled into the palm of his hand. He placed his knife blade between the two planks and pried up. The gold cache was underneath.

He tugged the bags of gold dust out with one hand, grunting and swearing. He found a burlap bag and, one-handed, placed the smaller rawhide bags inside it. He shouldered it, got to his feet with extreme effort, and staggered toward the door. He paused to spit on the body of the big dog and then stumbled out into the night.

He fell from the porch and was a long time rising. By the time he reached the trees his knees were wobbly, his head spinning. Blood soaked his sleeve and pants leg.

Sasak found the horse but he could only lean against it at first, his breath coming in gasps, knotting in his throat. By the time he finally got into the saddle, he could hardly see, barely remember which way Dawson was. Did he have the gold? Yes. He was rich. Why give any of it to St. Ives? He could ride south to the Tutchone lands and be welcomed as a prince.

The horse had started on by itself. The reins dangled. Sasak clung to the saddle horn, watching the stars whirl in a magic sky. Where was Nadgi? Stupid Nadgi would wander off when he knew Sasak needed his arm bound. See if Nadgi got any gold.

Sasak held on as the horse walked into a wooded gully and crossed a small creek. He heeled the horse. Get along, faster, he thought, but the words wouldn't rise to his lips. His head was empty, filled with buzzing hornets. He heeled the horse again and the horse leapt. Sasak fell to the earth to lie in a deep patch of brambles.

He lay dazed, looking at the swirling sky. There was a roaring in his ears. Did he have the gold? His hand stretched out and touched the burlap sack. Yes. He smiled. It was all right. He still had the gold. And then Sasak thought nothing more at all. The swirling stars stopped their motions and blinked out one by one.

*   *   *

Richard English stopped beside the river. His head rang. It seemed that someone had cried out in pain. He listened, but it didn't come again. He lifted the bottle he held to the stars and saw that it was half gone. He took another long drink, which lifted his stomach briefly, and then started on.

"Damn Butler. Damn Butler. Throw the gold in his face. The cheat."

He was alone and cold. Hevatha hadn't been in town when he returned. English couldn't remember when he had last seen her. At the barber's? She must have come home. The cabin was ahead, seeming to bob with each step English took now. The Yukon flowed past, muttering, whispering, chanting.

The cabin was dark. Maybe Hevatha was asleep. English paused for another drink. His forehead was beaded with cold perspiration. He was going to be sick, very sick in the morning.

He walked the path to the porch, paused to take a series of slow breaths, and started up. Even in his condition he knew something was wrong. What?

The door stood open. That wasn't right. "Hevatha? Hevatha?" he called, but no one answered. There was an unhealthy scent in the cold air, unidentifiable, vague.

Some deep, primitive sense in English warned him. He stood staring at the door, hand clenched. He called out again, "Hevatha," but his voice was only a croak.

He went onto the porch and stood staring at the planks underfoot. A dark, sticky pool of something . . . He knew what it was before he crouched to touch it.

Hevatha! He lurched toward the door and went in. The body lay crumpled on the floor and English felt bile rise in his throat, felt his pulse hammer at the temples. He crouched.

"Only Tyee." Only Tyee, sleeping. "Wake up, Tyee, lazy son of a wolf."

He bent, stroked the fur, and felt the same stickiness. "Tyee?"

English wiped at his face with a bloody hand and

went to the table, fumbling for a match. The lantern
flared up and revealed the ravaged cabin interior, the
empty gold cache, the cooling body of Tyee.

He stared toward the hole in the floorboards, turned
helplessly, hand hanging in the air, and walked to
Tyee. He made it to the door before he was sick, as
sick as he had ever been in his life, as sick as any man
can be.

It came finally, a second cry, the cry of a man in
anguish. It was a long time before English realized
that the cry was his, the fear his, the anguish only his
in the Yukon night.

"When," Hevatha asked, "do we go in?" It was
cold in the carriage without her good parka, with only
a white dress of organdy and lace to keep her warm.
Inside, the lights blazed and there was laughter. "I
want to see English."

"Be patient, dear," Hanna Sue Blythe said. "Did I
give you your mask yet?"

"I have it," Hevatha said. She held up a black
mask, which covered her face from forehead to chin.
She didn't understand why the whites would wear
these masks tonight. They weren't celebrating any great
feast; they were not wearing the masks of their clans.
The masks seemed to be simply to hide their faces.

Hevatha looked toward Sarah Penner's house. The
band had struck up and they could hear applause now.
"That'll be our queen," Hanna said. "Now we can go
in."

"Will he like this?" Hevatha asked, running her
hands over her skirt. "Are you sure English will like
this? He asked me to wear the red dress."

"He'll love it, honey. You look like a princess, just
like a princess."

Hevatha looked to the house, sighed, and stepped
down from the carriage behind Hanna. The older
woman had a mask carried on a stick, which she held
before her face as they walked, lifting their skirts with
one hand.

"Wait a minute," Mrs. Blythe said. She straight-

ened Hevatha's mask, which was tied on with a length
of black ribbon, looked her protégée over once more,
and then nodded. "All right."

"What are they doing, dancing?" Hevatha asked.

"Yes, dancing. And if I know our queen . . ." The
butler emerged to open the door for the two women,
and through the foyer they could see the whirl and
glitter of the ballroom, see the woman in white smiling, swirling, the center of attention, the hub of the
party.

Hevatha looked around in wonder from behind her
mask. Such a house. Larger than she had thought,
grander. A hundred people danced in its ballroom,
moving to the strange music. She could not see English anywhere. Mrs. Blythe held her arm as if afraid
she would flee.

They waited until the music stopped and then they
started forward, Mrs. Blythe nodding to the people.
Eyes turned, masked faces followed Hevatha across
the room to the vast table where a crystal punch bowl
with floating slices of oranges rested between two whole
roasted pigs and thinly sliced roast beef.

"Have something to eat, honey," Hanna said cheerfully, but Hevatha shook her head.

"I want to find English. Who can I ask?"

"Just a minute, dear, be patient."

A man and a woman without masks walked past and
they stared at Hevatha, the woman laughing behind a
fan. They went on, the woman's head turning back
toward Hevatha. The band had struck up again, and
again Sarah Penner led the dance. She was in the arms
of a tall man with silver mustaches, smiling at him as if
he were the only thing in the universe worth admiring.

Slowly the dancers made their turn around the floor,
the music drifting above them, the chandeliers in the
ballroom glittering, catching sparks of fire from the
candles, casting them off into the corners of the room,
striking here and there on a face, a hand, a necklace.

A woman shrieked hysterically. Hevatha turned
sharply. Someone was hurt, she thought at first, but
that wasn't it. The woman uttered something not audi-

ble above the music of the orchestra. The dancers had stopped and now the music staggered to a halt as Sarah Penner came forward, her hand trembling as she lifted a pointing finger and leveled it at Hevatha.

"You! Who are you!" she demanded.

Hanna stood smugly to one side, holding her mask in front of her face, peering over it now and then as the blond woman, her perfect smile twisted into rage, advanced on Hevatha.

Someone tittered and a man suppressed a coughing laugh. The reason for Sarah Penner's fury was evident to everyone. Sarah Penner, the exclusive Sarah Penner, who had spent two weeks and three hundred dollars having her ball gown made up of the rare white needlepoint lace and underskirts of white organdy, was looking at a woman who wore exactly the same dress.

Hanna lifted her mask again as Sarah Penner came nearer. The chandeliers caught the diamonds at her throat and they gleamed with cool fire.

"I asked you who you are!"

"Sarah . . ." the man with the gray mustache said, touching her arm, but she shook him off violently.

"You!" Sarah took another step toward Hevatha and the trembling hand shot out, ripping Hevatha's mask from her face. "An Indian!" she shrieked. "An Indian in my dress. An Indian at my party!"

Sarah was beside herself. As Hevatha backed away into the punch table behind her, Sarah Penner clutched at the sleeve of Hevatha's dress. "An Indian! Get her out, out!" The sleeve, hastily basted on by Rose, ripped at the shoulder seam.

"For God's sake, in my own house! My own ball." The blond's face was twisted, ugly. A drop of spittle had appeared at the corner of her mouth. She reached again for Hevatha, but had her hand slapped away.

"I will leave," Hevatha said.

"You're damned right you'll leave. You'll leave, Indian!" Before anyone could stop her, Sarah Penner had snatched a carving knife from the table. "And you'll leave that dress. My dress!" Whether intended to slash the dress or to actually stab Hevatha, she had the chance to do neither. As her arm lifted, Gage Powers stepped in and caught her wrist, barely escaping a knifing himself as Sarah Penner thrashed around wildly.

"Easy, Sarah," Powers said, taking the knife from her, but nothing was going to halt Sarah Penner's fury.

"Indian. A squaw in my dress! An Indian—"

Hevatha erupted. "Indian—crazy, dirty Indian. Crazy mad Indian!" she shouted, laughing wildly. She looked around, picked up the massive punch bowl, and threw it at Sarah Penner. Red punch like thin gore showered over the woman, washing her hair into her eyes, turning her prized white dress to a deep pink. The punch bowl itself crashed to the floor. Hevatha, hands on hips, head thrust forward, continued mockingly, "Who brought this white woman here in my dress? Who is to blame for this! Crazy woman." She swept a platter or roast beef from the table, and Sarah Penner, sodden, stunned, could just stand and watch. "Here, here is some more entertainment from a crazy Indian!" Hevatha shouted. She yanked and tugged and ripped the tablecloth from beneath the food remaining on the table, sending one of the roast pigs to the floor to stare up blindly at them.

"Young lady!" the older man said to Hevatha, coming forward.

"Yes, yes, I know—go home! I am going. Dance, eat your meat. I am leaving, the crazy Indian is going." She turned then and walked toward the door. Someone laughed out loud. Yakima Brown bowed low was Hevatha, her feet thudding against the floor, sleeve torn, hair disarranged, stamped out. In her wake was Hanna Sue Blythe.

She caught up with Hevatha on the front porch. "Hevatha, wait!"

"I am going home."

"Wait. I'll drive you into town," Mrs. Blythe said.

"Why? Why drive me? Give me my clothes from out of the carriage. My red dress and my buckskins."

Hevatha was turned by the arm. Hanna Sue Blythe

looked down at her and said, "I'm sorry, honey. I didn't know—"

"You knew everything. You hate that woman and so you used me to make her a fool. You made me a fool too."

"I didn't . . . Ah, hell," Hanna said, leaning against the carriage. "I did it, I'm sorry. It was worth it, too—except I shouldn't have used you. Shouldn't have."

"It is done," Hevatha said, and then she smiled. "Her dress—when I threw that bowl at her. Did you see her eyes?"

"She was a sight to see," Hanna said with a sigh, and then she laughed out loud. She laughed and Hevatha joined in, leaning beside the woman against the carriage. "I guess it was a dirty trick on you. I'm not sorry for doing it to Sarah Penner, though, not a bit. But how can I make it up to you?"

"Just give me my clothes. It doesn't matter. I didn't see English, did you? He wouldn't like what I did. He would be ashamed, I think."

"Well, no reason for him to be. You did what any woman would have done if she had your nerve. I do want to do something for you, Hevatha," Hanna said seriously.

"I want nothing. Take me to town. I will walk home . . . in the red dress. That will make English happy."

"All right. Where's that driver of mine?" she asked, looking around. "Never mind, I'll drive myself."

"You are going home too?"

"Not on your life! I'm coming back up to enjoy the aftermath. It wasn't exactly good clean fun but it's the most I've had in months, and it'll be a long while before Sarah Penner has another ball."

"You should help that woman who makes dresses," Hevatha said as Hanna snapped the reins and turned her carriage.

"Rose? Don't worry about Rose. She made plenty off me tonight, and I'll give her plenty more business in the future. Sarah Penner'll fume but eventually she'll go back to Rose too. She's the only seamstress in town who knows what she's doing."

"I think, Hanna Sue Blythe," Hevatha said, "that you are an evil woman."

"Honey," the woman answered with a wink, "you're damned right."

Hevatha tugged at the sleeve of her dress and it came off completely. She pulled it over her hand and held it up like a battle pennant. "Evil," she repeated, and then she laughed, and Hanna joined in as the carriage rolled down the dark road to Dawson.

The white dress was left in a trash barrel. Hevatha had put her buckskins on again, over them the red dress, over that the parka. Hanna waited as Hevatha changed in the alley behind the dress shop. It was cold and both women shivered a little.

"I owe you a favor," Hanna said. "Can I give you a little money?"

"No money," Hevatha said.

"A ride home?"

"The trail is too narrow for horses and carriage. I would prefer to walk anyway. Go back and enjoy your party, Hanna Sue Blythe. Tell them that a crazy Indian is sorry."

"I'll tell them nothing of the sort." Hanna climbed into the carriage, reached out to pat Hevatha's hand, and then snapped her reins, lifting a hand in farewell before the carriage disappeared around the corner of a building. Hevatha stood silently for a minute, shaking her head. Then she glanced at the trash barrel, at the red dress she wore, and she smiled. She started on, out of Dawson, away from this white town and its crazy people. She wanted to find English, to lie down with him, to hold him and make him happy. It was a night for it, cool and deep, seeming to hold many mysteries. The river was dark and strong; the trees silent in deep ranks.

English was waiting for her in the cabin.

Or was it the ghost of English? A man was sitting on the bed, hands clasped, arms hanging between his legs. He lifted his head as Hevatha entered, but his eyes showed no light. They were only shadowed hollows in his face. Hevatha walked to the lamp on the table. There was no fuel in it and she had to fill the lamp before lighting it. When she had done that and adjusted the wick she turned back to the man on the bed.

"English, what is it?" Hevatha asked, going to kneel beside him, her hand on his knee.

"I buried him. Just outside."

"Buried him? Demarest! He is dead?"

Richard's eyes lifted, taking on the fire of the lantern. "Not Demarest, Tyee."

"Tyee is dead?" Hevatha sat on the bed beside her man. His suit was muddy, bloodstained, dusted with flour. He smelled of sickness. Hevatha put an arm around his shoulders and stretched out her legs. Her red dress showed beneath her parka and English stared at it blankly.

"Dead," he said again.

"Yes. I heard you."

"You don't seem to care much!"

"I care, English. I care. Tyee is dead. But he was just a dog, English, only a dog. What has happened here?" she asked, looking around the cabin carefully for the first time. The planks above the cache had been removed, she saw, their food supplies scattered, their mattress ripped to shreds.

"I don't know." A helpless hand waved in the air. "Someone broke in. They killed Tyee."

The porch planks creaked and they looked up to see Demarest in the doorway. He began a story that broke off immediately as he saw the cabin interior, the two bedraggled people on the bed. "I had me a few . . . My God, what's happened?" the big man looked bewildered, lost. He walked to the center of the room and turned in a slow circle.

"Robbed, Demarest. They killed Tyee."

"Who?" Floyd Demarest demanded.

"No idea."

"Damn. I need a drink."

English took what remained of his whiskey from his pocket and handed the bottle over. Demarest drank deeply. "The gold, all of it?"

"All of it."

"All of it—gone." Demarest took a wooden chair, uprighted it, and sat shakily. "My gold. I didn't tell you . . . wanted to pull out, English. Wanted to go somewhere warm and give this up. My gold . . ."

English glanced at Demarest. By lamplight Floyd Demarest looked smaller, older, tired. "I was going to take it anyway, Floyd," Richard said from somewhere far distant. Floyd Demarest's head swiveled slowly toward his partner.

"What are you talking about? You drunk?"

"Drunk? Not now. I lost the money in a card game, all of it. I was going to take your gold myself."

Demarest didn't answer. He couldn't. He took another drink of whiskey and sat staring at the hole in the floor.

English couldn't help himself; he went on, "I lost it all to Aaron Butler. I was going to pay you back, give you all my dust until I caught up."

"We're just about out of color along the creek," Demarest said as if to himself.

"There's enough to make up what we lost!"

"Is there? Is there, now? And what about the time we've lost? Who's going to pay me back for that when winter comes and I'm stuck here?" Demarest practically leapt to his feet, his eyes wild. "I'm getting old, old. That was my stake, English! You have the nerve to tell me you'd rob me of it!"

"I would've paid you back," English muttered, his voice dropping as Demarest's rose. The red-bearded man stood near the hole in the floor, fists clenched, his jaw working involuntarily.

"Who was it? Who was the thieving bastard? What about that damned wolf-dog? What was the use of leaving him here if . . . ?" And then Demarest saw the blood on the floor and he remembered. He looked at English and Hevatha again and then returned to the table to sit, his head in his hands.

"We'll make it back, Floyd," English said, but his partner didn't answer him. English suddenly lurched to his feet and stalked out into the night and Hevatha followed him.

She found him near the river. He stood and watched the Yukon flow, just stood there. Hevatha was beside him, and without looking at her he said, "What kind of fool am I, what sort of child? What am I doing?

"When I look at myself I see nothing. I used to be called brilliant, ambitious. I'm nothing but a child. What in God's name has happened to me, Hevatha?" He turned and clung to her. She said nothing; she did not move. "Stupid," English said against her shoulder. "I wanted to teach Butler a lesson. I did that, all right!" He laughed harshly. "This is the end of everything."

"Or a beginning," Hevatha said, speaking softly. She put her hand on his head and held him to her.

"What sort of child," he asked again, "have I been?"

Then he did not want her near him. He wanted no one to share his shame. He pulled away and walked northward along the river, and Hevatha let him go. She watched him and said to the dark and constant river, "Only a dog, English; only gold."

Early the next morning English was up and working. His skin was chalk white, his eyes very red, but he looked determined as he attacked the sandbar below the falls where he and Demarest had decided their best chance of a rich new strike lay. It was hardly rich so far, but English had built a diversion dam and was doing fairly well. Demarest, by contrast, seemed to have given up. He stood on the bank and watched English. It was difficult to tell if his constant glower had its origins in anger or frustration or simple sadness.

Hevatha watched her man work and from time to time she lifted her eyes to the highlands, to the valley of the Han. She nearly told English one day, seeing the desire, the need for gold on his face, but she kept the secret in the end. The land above was Han land; let English work out his repayment below.

That was exactly what he intended to do, work it all out, repay Demarest, and then, surprisingly, "get out."

He told her that as they rested one noon beneath a huge, shifting pine tree, pocked by generations of woodpeckers. "I'm going to repay the man and get out. Gold," he said, tossing away the pine needles he had been braiding, "I don't want it. Let the other fools have their try."

"What will you do then, English?" she asked, keeping her eyes on the ground.

"I don't know. Anything. Go back to the States, stay in Alaska. Hevatha . . . would you go with me?" he asked, and his blue eyes were distant.

"Richard English, I love you. I will go anywhere with you. I want to do everything with you, always."

"Yes. I've been a fool about you too, haven't I?" he asked, and he smiled, lying down with her on the pine-needle-strewn earth, the pine moving overhead in the breeze. He touched her lips and kissed her lightly, let his finger trace the arch of her eyebrow, and then he squeezed her so tightly that she thought she would burst.

It was time then, finally time, and so she told him, "Be careful, Richard English. Perhaps the baby does not like to be squeezed so hard."

He simply stared at her. He sat up sharply and stared again. English got to his feet and she reached for him. Maybe she should have said nothing. He turned and walked away, directly into the icy stream where he had been working. He walked into the stream until he was to his waist in quick-running cold water and then he ducked under the surface. When he rose again his arms were thrust skyward and he shouted out madly. Hevatha sat, hands around her knees, watching. English was running through the creek, sending up fans of silver water. He yelled like a madman and then fell, going under the water again. When he arose, sputtering and gasping, his emotions had cooled. He walked back to the beach, his heavy clothing sodden, and came to Hevatha.

His blond hair hung in his eyes. His skin was bluish with the cold. He took her hands and said, "I love you, Hevatha. You have made me happy. That"—he nodded back toward the river—"is the last of a boy you will ever see in me. It's time for me to grow up and face my manhood. You need a man; the baby will."

And then he lay beside her for a time, shivering, until Hevatha prodded him to his feet. "Change your clothes, my *man*, before the baby has no father."

Demarest was sitting on the porch of the cabin, staring aimlessly into space when English, soaking wet, elated, arrived. "What in God's name . . . ?" Floyd asked.

"Floyd, kiss me! Hevatha's having a baby. Grin, you old sourpuss, grin and dance me a jig!"

Demarest just sat there as he had done for the past few days. English tossed his coat on the porch, kicked off his boots, and went inside, rummaging for dry clothing.

He stood stripping off his shirt as Demarest entered. "A baby," the older man said. "You two are going to have a baby?"

"That's right, Floyd, what do you think of that?"

"A baby," Demarest repeated. "Damn me."

"What do you think, Floyd?" English asked, tugging off his socks. "Isn't that the best news in the Yukon?"

"The very best," Floyd Demarest said with feeling. He knuckled a tear out of his eye, went to English, and shook his hand warmly. "English, congratulations . . . and I'm sorry."

"Sorry?"

"For acting like a fool, sulking. I'm through with that now."

"You had the right, Floyd. It's all right. I'll be glad to have you back working with me, though. You know, I haven't been doing so badly. I've got almost half your dust back."

"And how much of yours?"

"I threw mine away. You'll have yours first, as I promised."

"And let the baby go naked, I suppose. No, you won't, English. I'm calling us even. I'll make up my poke, you make up yours. We're partners, aren't we? Let's act it again."

"Floyd," English said, putting a hand on Demarest's shoulder, taking his weathered hand, "there's never been a better partner, anywhere."

"Get dressed, then, damn you," Demarest said gruffly. "We've got work to do! What are we lyin' about for?"

Hevatha had come to the cabin and she smiled as she heard the two men. It had been eating away at English, festering in Demarest. They were friends and both hated the grudge.

"English?" she asked. "Would it hurt your feelings if I do not wear the red dress again?"

"Hurt my feelings? No! I don't know what in God's name I was doing buying that. Why didn't I just get you beads and baubles? What are you going to do with it, burn it?"

"I think give it to a friend."

"Do that. I'll get you a new dress. Any dress you like. One to be married in."

"Marry a . . . ?" Demarest fell silent.

"You wish to marry me, English?" Hevatha said.

"I wish to. I will. I love you, Hevatha. It's just that I'm a little slow at saying things, at doing them."

"Then"—she shrugged—"we will be married." She took the red dress from her trunk, folded it, and kissed English. Then she went out again.

"Think twice, son," Demarest said. "You sure you wan to marry an Indian?"

"No," English answered, buttoning his dry shirt. "I'm sure I want to marry that woman. I want to marry Hevatha, and I will."

"Then I guess I'll have to break out my suit again, because you won't be married without me as best man. I won't stand for it."

"Floyd," English said quietly, "thanks."

Demarest grunted in response. English was nearly dressed and now Demarest grabbed his old leather cap with earflaps. "Let's get out there and get to work, English. We've both got something to work for now, don't we?"

"I always did, Floyd, I just wasn't smart enough to recognize it."

"Few of us are, English. Damn few of us."

Hevatha had gone out and turned toward the creek. She crossed it on a sandbar and climbed through the pines to the high valley. She found the Han camp busy, happy, prosperous. There were many caribou hides, much meat, many fish.

Hevatha walked to the hide house near the big split boulder and called out. "Kiptah?"

"Who is there? Come in," Tan Yuolo's daughter called back.

Hevatha ducked inside to find the young woman nursing her baby. It worked furiously at the nipple, tiny fists clenching and unclenching, eyelids softly fluttering.

"Hevatha"—Kiptah smiled with deep pleasure—"I have missed you. See the baby, how he grows."

She stroked the infant's head and Hevatha got on her knees beside them. "Such a hungry little boy."

"Yes. It takes all my milk to feed him. He will be a strong man, a great hunter like Poduk, his father."

"Poduk is not here?"

"Hunting. Or so they say. Sometimes I think the men go out with their bows and sleep in the sun on some good flat rock."

Hevatha laughed. "Perhaps they do, but you have plenty of meat."

"All salted and smoked. It will be a good winter."

"I have brought you something, Kiptah. Only a small thing. If you do not want it, tell me."

"What?" Kiptah's eyes gleamed. She rose, holding the baby, rocking it. "What have you brought me?"

"Only this poor gift," Hevatha said, and she brought out the red silk dress.

"Oh!" Kiptah put a hand to her mouth She placed the baby on its bed and covered it and came to Hevatha, fingering the silk, holding the dress up. "Such a beautiful thing. Where could it have come from?"

"It is a white dress," Hevatha said. "Maybe you can make something pretty out of the cloth."

"Cut it up?" Kiptah was aghast. "Never, never." She stood, holding the dress before her. "How can you give such a thing away, Hevatha!"

"My belly," she said, rubbing her abdomen, "is beginning to swell. I cannot wear it."

"How can you give it away? Oh, thank you, Hevatha, you are good to me. I have never seen anything like it, never." She turned, letting the dress fly out at the skirt.

"It is all right?" Hevatha asked.

"All right?" Kiptah said blankly.

"Poduk will not mind if you wear it?"

"Poduk will say nothing. How can such a dress be made? Feel how soft and smooth it is. Look at the color of it, Hevatha." Tan Yuolo's daughter held the dress up, her head slowly shifting from side to side, her eyes wide with pleasure and astonishment. The baby cried, but Kiptah didn't seem to hear it.

"I am happy that it pleases you," Hevatha said, rising. "I think I will visit Kawchot now."

"Thank you. Thank you, Hevatha. You are my friend, a good friend."

Hevatha went out then, leaving Kiptah still holding the dress to her body, stroking the silk, her eyes bright with pleasure. Hevatha paused outside the hide house, feeling momentarily uneasy, but then she saw Kawchot across the camp and the feeling dissipated as she waved and called out to her adopted mother.

When Hevatha was gone, Kiptah slipped from her buckskin skirt and shed her coarse blue blouse. Then, reverentially she put the dress over her arms and let it slip down, caressing her body with its silky smoothness. She tugged the skirt down and turned, running her hands across her thighs, lost in the sensuousness of the material, the feel of it next to her skin.

It was a long while before Kiptah realized that someone was watching her. Poduk was there in the doorway, his eyes flinty. His flat, somewhat fleshy face was smothered with anger.

"What is this thing, woman?" he demanded.

"A new dress," Kiptah, startled, shot back.

"Who gave it to you?" The warrior came forward, his eyes sweeping up the dress to his wife's face.

"Hevatha."

"It is a white dress. Take it off. You need no such things." Poduk looked around. "Where is the baby? Sleeping? Where is my supper? Take that dress off!"

"No, why should I?" she asked petulantly. "When you married me, you promised me things. You promised my father that a chief's daughter would not want. What have you given me? A bone necklace, green hides to make my own clothing from, an otter fur now and then."

Poduk was through discussing it. He stepped to his wife and yanked at the front of the dress. It split in the back, buttons popping. Poduk looked at his wife, standing before him, half-dressed, her milk-ripe breasts exposed.

"Make me my supper," Poduk said, and with that he was gone, throwing his bow into the corner.

Kiptah stood, her eyes blazing, her lips trembling with violent replies, her head humming with anger. She stepped finally from the dress, picking up the buttons, examining the torn seam with dismay.

She placed it carefully on her wicker basket and dressed again in her buckskin skirt, her Han-woven blouse.

"I will keep what I wish to keep," she muttered. She would tell Poduk she had thrown the red dress away, but she would not do that. She would mend it and when Poduk was on a hunt she would wear it. Carefully Kiptah folded the dress and placed it under her sleeping baby's blankets. When she was through she pushed back her long black hair and got to work preparing Poduk's supper.

11

THE following day Boxer Thrush rode out to the gold camp on the Yukon River. The constable was astride a jenny mule, wearing a long black coat with his badge pinned prominently on the lapel. He swung down before the cabin as English and Demarest were setting out for work, standing stretching the kinks out of his back as the mule wandered off, looking for grass.

" 'Morning, Thrush," Demarest called out. He glanced at English. "Kill anybody, Richard?"

English coughed out a small laugh. "Not lately."

"You men got time for a bit of conversation?" Boxer Thrush asked. His tone indicated that they should make time.

"Sure," Floyd said, "Come in and have some coffee, Thrush."

"I would, Demarest," Thrush answered, walking to the miners, seeing the Indian woman in the doorway, watching, "but this is a little more than a visit."

"Oh?" Demarest fumbled with his pipe, patted his pocket, searching for a match, and squinted at the constable. "What's up, Boxer?"

Boxer looked at English, reached inside his long coat, and pulled out a sheaf of folded papers. There was a red wax seal, broken, clinging to the heavy ivory-hued paper.

"It seems," Boxer said, clearing his throat, "that a Mr. Richard English is in what we call a state of indebtedness to a Mr. Aaron Butler and a Mr. Gage Powers in the amount of fifteen thousand dollars."

Hevatha had come down off the porch to stand just behind English, her arms folded, her eyes alert. Boxer Thrush turned his head to spit.

"What I'm here for is to collect that money," the constable said. "One of these here"—he shuffled his papers—"is a collect warrant from the court." He handed it to English. "Duly served." He glanced at his watch.

"He'll get his money," English said. "We were robbed, Thrush, or he'd have it by now. He'll just have to wait."

"That's something to settle with Butler in or out of court. I'm just an officer of the court. As far as Gage Powers goes," the constable told them, "he don't care to make a fuss one way or the other over a few thousand, but I suppose Butler is a different story. Thought I told you to stay away from him, English."

"I tried. It didn't work out." English was scanning the legal document, scowling.

"We can nearly make it, Richard," Demarest said. "We've got some dust, and a few days—"

"Take your stake again?" English said. "No. Not on your life."

"Partners, aren't we?" the red-bearded miner replied.

"It wasn't you who ran a pair of kings up against three of a kind."

"You boys do the best you can. Go down to the courthouse and see what kind of an extension you can get," Thrush advised them. "Now, then," he said, shuffling his papers again, "this is the painful one. I'm sorry, men."

"What is it? More bad news?" Demarest asked, taking the document the constable gave him. Demarest scanned it and then exploded, "Dammit, no!"

"Afraid so," Thrush said, spitting again. "You men should've filed on this claim. Someone else did, down at Fort Selkirk."

"Who? No one else even drove stakes up here?"

"I just had a look, man. There are stakes in place along the river. A man named George Pease has legal title to the frontage and to the cabin."

"Who in hell is George Pease? We've seen nobody around," Demarest insisted. "How could this Pease, whoever he is, have driven stakes up here and filed in Selkirk at the same time!"

"You don't have to file in person, Demarest. Nor do you have to drive your own stakes. An agent can do it on your behalf. George Pease owns this cabin. Where's the . . . ?" He dug into his papers again. "There's his notarized title. You men sign on the bottom that you've been served with notice to abandon this claim."

"I'll be damned!" Demarest said, his voice rising, quavering. "I'll not sign that."

"I hope you do, Demarest," the constable said. "And I hope you move out peacefully. I don't want to bring a couple of deputies out here and do things the hard way."

"You'll have to!"

English gripped the man's arm. "Floyd," he said, "we don't have any choice."

"Who is this Pease, where is he?" Demarest demanded. "By God, I'll have a talk with the lyin'—"

"Pease, from what I understand," the constable went on placidly, "has sold his claim and quit the Yukon."

"Sold it!"

"To Bertram St. Ives," Boxer Thrush told them. He looked at the last paper in his hands. "Mr. St. Ives—I talked to him yesterday afternoon—wants you off the place immediately."

"St. Ives! That weasel, what does he want our little claim for? Butler's behind this, behind it all."

"Could be," the constable acknowledged, "but that won't make it any less legal, men."

"Hired some down-and-outer to file a claim, slipped him a few bucks' getaway money, and purchased the claim. You can only file on so much land, but you can buy up all you want. St. Ives is a leech, a weasel, a crook—"

"Easy, Demarest. It's not worth it. I've looked at your claim down there. What in hell you're bothering to work it for, I don't know. What St. Ives wants with it, I couldn't guess, but that's the way things stand. Take my advice, get off."

Then Thrush tucked away his papers and went after

his jenny mule, whistling and shouting at it. They watched him swing aboard and ride out. Demarest's fist was bunched around the legal papers. His face was red, eyes dull.

"They can't do this to us."

"Looks like it's been done, Floyd," English said quietly.

"And you're going to take it!"

"What else can we do?"

"They've got the river claim—why, I don't know, just Butler trying to get even with us, I suppose—but they don't know about the creek."

"With someone around, Floyd, we can't work that. We don't have legal claim up there, either."

"I've got a legal claim. A Winchester rifle. They won't push me off, by God. If Butler—"

"Remember your advice to me, Floyd. Butler's trouble."

"I'll tell you this—it's a guess, but let's hear you deny it—Butler was behind that robbery the other night. He wants to teach us a lesson for speaking up against him. Maybe," Demarest said, "maybe I'll just teach *him* a little lesson." Fuming, he spun on his heel and stalked back to the cabin. English watched him go in and bang the door shut.

"What does this all mean, English?" Hevatha asked.

"Mean? It means we're done. We've lost the cabin and the claim. I'm in debt. Butler's got us over a barrel."

"You cannot take gold from the creek anymore?"

"Just until whoever's coming out gets here, Hevatha. As soon as they see us, they'll move in . . . not that there's that much gold left anyway. I only hope," English said, looking at the cabin, "that we can somehow come up with enough to pay Butler what I owe him and have something left over for Floyd. He's a big tough man, but he's scared. You can see it growing in him. He's scared."

The sun had risen above the dark ranks of pines across the Yukon now and a mist rose from the water, drifting across them. The dew on the pines sparkled

and danced. Hevatha asked, "How much gold does
Demarest need?"

"A couple thousand. Five pounds." English looked
at the paper in his hand and shoved it angrily into his
pocket. "I'll see if I can get him out of this mood.
Once we get to work, he'll be better off."

Hevatha was listening but she wasn't watching English. She watched the river flow, the mist rising ghost-
like from the water. English gave her a kiss and left.
Slowly Hevatha turned and looked to the hills to the
west, toward the Han land. There was still that gold,
but had she the right to take it? Only a little, perhaps,
enough to help Demarest. But they would want to
know where it came from . . . if they knew she had
brought it.

If they didn't know . . . ?

Hevatha turned and started walking westward. She
circled around the Han camp, feeling some shame
about her mission despite the fact that she had been
offered all of the gold she wanted.

Coming to the place where the two creeks merged,
she climbed down the sandy bank through the black-
berry vines and went to the river's edge. It was there,
gold, and a lot of it. Five pounds. Just a little. It could
be taken in nugget form here, simply picked up, pock-
eted, and taken back to the camp. If she went out at
night, she could dump the gold into the creek, or
perhaps pretend to find it along the Yukon. She
crouched and picked up a nugget.

"What are you doing, Hevatha?"

Hevatha turned guiltily. It was Kiptah, alone, wearing the red dress. She walked toward Hevatha, hands
behind her back, hips swaying gently.

"Just taking a little gold," Hevatha aid. There was
no point in lying.

Kiptah stood swaying back and forth, perhaps waiting for Hevatha to admire her in the dress. "What will
you do with the gold, Hevatha?"

"Give it to my man."

"Your white man?"

"Yes. You look very nice in the dress, Kiptah,"

Hevatha said, and the girl smiled with pleasure. "Where is your baby?"

"Home with grandfather Tan Yuolo." Kiptah came forward to crouch beside Hevatha, who was scooping up other nuggets. Most were the size of an elk's tooth, some as large as an egg. "Why does your man want gold? They say that in the white town you buy things with gold, but no one will let me buy things. Did your man buy this dress with gold, Hevatha?"

"Yes, Kiptah," Hevatha answered with barely concealed impatience. "But this gold is not for buying things."

"Do they have red moccasins, Hevatha, the white women?" Kiptah asked.

"Yes, Kiptah," Hevatha sighed.

"Tan Yuolo won't let me go to the white town. I would like to see red moccasins."

Hevatha's parka pockets bulged with gold. Kiptah's eyes were fixed on them. "You wouldn't like the white town," Hevatha told the young woman.

"You have been there?"

"Yes. To that one and another. There is nothing for an Indian woman there."

"That is what Tan Yuolo said," Kiptah replied sulkily. "Poduk told me that if I ever went to a white town he would beat me. What do they know about white towns?"

"Listen to them, Kiptah."

"Yes; but you go."

"Not because I want to," Hevatha said.

"No?" Kiptah's eyes were skeptical. "Are you coming to the village, Hevatha?"

"Not today. My man is having trouble. I want to be by him."

"And give him gold. Does that make him happy?"

"He needs it. I don't think English is crazy for gold anymore."

"Good-bye, then, Hevatha. Come and see the baby."

"I will. Tell all of my friends that I wish them well."

"Yes," Kiptah answered, "I will."

Hevatha started homeward and Kiptah watched her

go, walking downstream to the second creek, crossing it, climbing the bank beyond. Hevatha lifted a hand and was gone then, into the forest of cedar and pine.

Kiptah stood musingly by the hill. Glancing again to the place where Hevatha had disappeared, Kiptah crouched. She crouched and picked up a large nugget, turning it over in her hands. She kept it in her hand as she turned and started thoughtfully homeward. First she would have to change her dress so that Poduk would not beat her; then she would go home and nurse the baby. Then she would make Poduk's supper. After that she would have to nurse the baby again, and by then it would be nearly dark. Kiptah looked again at the gleaming, heavy object in her hand. It shone dully with promise. Laughing out loud, Kiptah hurried on toward the place where she had left her other clothing.

When Hevatha returned to the creek she saw Demarest and English working upstream. English was moving very rapidly, almost feverishly. Demarest was sluggish, almost indifferent, it seemed. English was right: Demarest was becoming a defeated man.

Hevatha paused beneath the trees where the jays complained noisily. She could go no farther with her pockets bulging as they were with Han gold. Looking upstream again, she reached into her pocket and tossed the large nugget into the stream, where it vanished in the shallow water. She repeated that process, her eyes on Demarest and English. They were too busy panning to notice her.

When her pockets were empty, Hevatha walked through the trees, circled back past the cabin, and walked to where the men worked, crouching down, her arms looped around her knees.

It was a long while before English noticed her. "Hello, Hevatha, where have you been?"

"Walking. It is good to walk a lot with a baby growing," she answered.

English paused and smiled, "Yes. The baby." He waded to the shore, carrying his pan in both hands. He sat down on the ground beside Hevatha. "Sometimes I forget about the baby, and then I remember and something glows within me."

He put his arm around her and pulled her head to his shoulder, kissing her hair.

"Slacking off again?" Demarest called. It was a joke, but there wasn't much humor in Demarest's tone.

"Walk with me, English," Hevatha said, rising, tugging at him.

"Now? You've just been walking. How much does the baby need?"

"I want to talk to you," she insisted, and he rose, waving at Demarest, who just nodded.

They walked along the shore beneath the great pines, the sun warm, falling between the gaps in the trees. "Winter will be returning, English," Hevatha said.

"How long? A few more weeks?"

"Very soon. We have no place to live, English." They had come to the spot where Hevatha had placed the nuggets. "If the men come and take the cabin away, then we will be without a home."

"I know it." English rubbed his chin. "Maybe we'll just leave the Yukon before winter comes."

"That would take money, wouldn't it? We can't walk south again. Where did you want to go, English?"

"I don't know. I was just thinking . . ." Out of habit he had been watching the creek flow past; now Hevatha saw his eyes change expression. "Just a minute!"

English went to the water's edge and peered down. Then he waded in and scooped something up. Hevatha tried to look blank and then suitably surprised as English held up the egg-sized nugget.

"Damn me," he said. "And here's a few others. Never saw anything like this along here . . . sand must've shifted. Demarest! Demarest!" Richard waved an arm and waded ashore. "Must be five pounds of nuggets . . ." He stopped and looked at Hevatha. "Just about five pounds . . . If I didn't know better . . ." He stood looking into Hevatha's eyes but she gave nothing away. Demarest had arrived and English showed him what he had found.

"Here?" Demarest took the largest nugget and examined it. "Unlikely spot. I'll get the screen. We'd better see what else we can find."

Demarest started briskly back upstream. English was studying Hevatha's face, sensing something, not knowing what. "I guess," he said finally, "that'll have to be it for the walk, Hevatha. I've got to help Demarest do a little screening. We'll talk about a winter home another time."

"All right, English. I know you must work." Then she went on tiptoe and kissed him. She was smiling when she turned and walked away, humming to herself. English, puzzled, watched her for a few seconds, but by then Demarest, looking more excited than he had for some time, was back with a shovel and a framed screen, and English turned to help his partner work.

In an hour they had found no sign of any other gold, and Demarest suggested they give it up. "Just a fluke. Thought maybe we had a big strike. Not that it would have done us a lot of good now, with the vultures hovering. At least," he went on, removing his cap to wipe his forehead with his wrist, "you'll be closer to paying back Butler."

"No. This gold is yours, Floyd. I owe you, remember?"

"And I told you you didn't have to pay me any more."

"Take it anyway. I'd feel better."

Demarest didn't argue anymore. "All right, I'll stow it. It's my getaway money, English. I've had it with the Yukon."

"You mean it, don't you?" the blond man asked, shouldering their shovel.

"Yes, I mean it. I won't wait out another winter. Besides," he said as they started toward the cabin, "it's one thing when you have a proven claim like we did, and a house. To go wandering around the country after know-not-what like these other boomers is a different story. What do we do? Slog up and down the hills, sleeping out, waiting until the first big storm pins us down somewhere? Not for me, English. I had my try. I didn't come out like I expected, hoped to, but that's enough for me. What about you, English?"

"Hevatha and I were just talking about that. Things don't look real promising, do they? Still, I might stay on another winter. I have those debts to clear up. If I could find a little dust somewhere to do that, and enough to take me out, well, that would be all right."

"Winter's long," Demarest said.

"Damn long. I've got Hevatha, though. She knows how to live out here. Baby's on the way, so I hate to travel now." English stopped and watched the creek run for a moment. "Where would I be going anyway, Demarest?"

"Home."

"I've forgotten where it is."

"Well, whatever you decide, you know I hope things work out for you . . . Dammit!" He was looking toward the cabin, visible downslope through the trees. "They couldn't even wait a day!"

They could see three men, a pack mule, hear voices. Demarest looked back toward the creek and their claim, but there was no way to disguise what had been going on there.

"Let 'em have it," English said. "There's not much left to take out anyway."

"Damn that Butler," Demarest said. He was rigid with emotion, staring down at the cabin.

"Easy, Floyd. It won't do any good to get mad. We made a mistake and it caught up with us."

"I'll tell you the mistake we made, Richard: not killing Aaron Butler when we had the chance." Demarest took a long, deep breath and finally seemed to calm. "Well, let's go on down and get our gear and our poke."

The three men were all strangers. Two had dark beards and red-and-black mackinaws; the other was narrow, clean-shaven, bald. "You the men that were squatting here?" the bald one asked. His eyes were like a fish's. His mouth was thin and twisted into a cynical smirk.

"Squatting!" Demarest boomed. "Why, by God, I'll—"

English grabbed the big man's sleeve, tugging him back. "That won't get us anywhere."

"Where's this George Pease who's supposed to have staked our place out?" Demarest demanded. English was still holding him back.

"Who? Never heard of him. Place belongs to St. Ives Land Company now. We're representatives of that company." The man rocked on his heels with satisfaction, thumbs hooked in his belt.

"Hired trash," Demarest muttered, and one of the bearded men took a half-step forward, eyes narrowing, mouth tightening menacingly.

"Do you boys move or do we start throwing your stuff out?" this one asked.

"You just try that," Demarest said.

"Floyd . . ."

The bearded man said, "You're a little too old to be talking so tough, Pappy. Look in your mirror sometime. Maybe you used to be something—you're big enough—but you're over the hill. I wouldn't try getting tough. We might just have to dump you in the Yukon."

They all heard the two sharp clicks of the Winchester's lever action being cocked, and they turned as one man to see Hevatha standing at the corner of the cabin, the rifle ready.

"English," she said, "let us take our things and go."

"Yes." English looked at the three men St. Ives had sent up and then at Floyd. "Let's get our gear, partner."

"Tell that squaw to be careful with that rifle," the fish-eyed man said. "It might go off."

"It might at that," English replied thoughtfully. "Hevatha, I want these three to stand right here until we're through packing. If they move, you just shoot them."

"I will, English," Hevatha answered, and they believed her enough to stand still and silent while Floyd and English went into the cabin to take what they could carry. The gold, a sackful of food, blankets, and a few utensils.

Demarest was stony-faced, furious as he threw things together. English tried a few times to calm the big man, but nothing worked. "Butler," Demarest muttered. "I'll get him yet. You were right, wanting to fix him."

"I was wrong, Floyd. Wrong, and you know it. It wouldn't have solved anything. It won't now."

"He'll get his back," Demarest responded. Then he stood, looked around the cabin, and kicked the table over, sending the lantern flying. "Damn this place, damn Dawson, damn the Yukon!"

Outside, the three men still stood motionless, silent. Hevatha gave Demarest his rifle and they walked past the land-company men southward, toward Dawson.

It was a silent walk for the most part. Demarest was in no mood to talk to anyone. Hevatha did ask, "What will we do in Dawson, English?"

"I'm going to the courthouse, for one thing. Then we'll see if we can find a tent. They're usually at a premium, but maybe with winter approaching we'll have better luck."

"And then?"

"And then," he said, taking a deep breath, looking to the sky, "we'll find a place with just a little gold, enough so that we won't starve, and build a cabin, a small cabin, just big enough for the two of us."

"The three of us, English," Hevatha said quietly, and his hand reached out to wrap around hers.

Dawson stood under gray skies. Clouds were building, promising cold rain. Demarest hadn't spoken to them all the way, but had been muttering under his breath, and now he lifted red, angry eyes to the gold town.

"Sooner I shed this place, the better I'll like it," he said.

"We'll miss you, Floyd," English said.

"Miss me, you two?"

"Sure. We've traveled a way together. We'll miss you, Floyd."

Demarest looked again at the two of them, the tall blond mustached man and the beautiful Indian woman who was carrying his child. "Not *too* much, I'm thinking," he said, managing a small, crooked smile.

They split up at the courthouse, Demarest going to see if a horse could be purchased in town, English leaving Hevatha to watch their gear as he entered the domed wooden building.

Hevatha waited, watching the miners pass. They might have been the same men or a hundred different ones, she couldn't tell. There were fewer now, with winter coming back to the north country. They would return home or find holes to wait out the hard weather; then, like a hibernating, many-armed thing they would emerge from their dens in the spring to again tear at the earth, to flood it and mar it, to gnaw, dig, and devour.

English was back, looking relieved. "It went well?" she asked him.

"Well enough. I was able to pay Butler back. Gage Powers doesn't mind waiting for his, it seems. That puts me under more of an obligation to see that he's paid quickly, somehow."

"Now we will find a tent?"

"Yes, if we can. I'll need a saw and a few other tools as well." He had shouldered their sack of provisions and now he paused to ask, "Is this crazy, Hevatha? Can we do it? Build a place to stay, try it on our own?"

"There is nothing crazy about building a shelter. There is nothing crazy about a man living with his woman."

"Yes." Something seemed to adjust itself in English's mind as he stood looking down at her. "My woman. It's not enough. I promised you you'd be my wife. Let's marry now, while Demarest is still here, while we're in Dawson."

"If you wish it, English."

"You mean you don't, Hevatha? You mean you don't care?"

"I was your wife from the first time you laid me down, Richard English. I will always be your wife."

Nevertheless English was determined to do it properly. The new church, its steeple now half-painted, rested on a low hill to the south of town. Up the muddy road they trudged, English carrying their belongings. Overhead, flocks of geese, many hundreds of them, winged southward, honking.

The minister was in his rectory reading a letter. A balding, red-faced man with a cast in one eye, he rose to greet English, taking one of his hands in both of his.

"I'm Dr. Smythe," he said, "the Reverend Smythe."

"English. Richard English." He placed his sack on the floor and swept his stained hat off his head.

"What can I do for you, Mr. English?"

"You can marry me to this woman."

"I see." Smythe nodded, his expression unsettled. He cleared his throat. "An Indian woman."

English's smile froze on his face. "That's right," he answered.

"You know, Mr. English, when a man is a long while away from home, sometimes the body seems to dictate to the mind. Have you thought this through?"

"From one end to the other," English said woodenly.

"I see." The minister looked at Hevatha again. "I assume you are both Christians."

"Christians? Does it matter?"

"Very much, I'm afraid. Has the woman been baptized?"

"I don't know. Hevatha?"

"You mean getting down in the water? The missionary did it to Aunt Kawclaa, but the rest of us laughed. It was too funny."

"Funny!" Dr. Smythe repeated, his color deepening. "There is nothing at all funny about the sacrament of baptism, young woman. It is the difference between salvation and the death of the soul!"

"Then it was not funny," Hevatha said. "It looked funny, though."

"Look, Dr. Smythe," English said, "they didn't understand what was going on. They didn't mean to mock anything, it was just something outside of their culture. It seemed odd to them."

"Yes." Dr. Smythe wasn't quite mollified. He was a man accustomed to leading other people who felt exactly at he did.

Recovering his professional ease, he sat behind his desk and made a note on a blank piece of yellow paper. "We can solve this, of course, Mr. English. All that is necessary is for the young woman to go through a period of instruction in Scripture and our beliefs. Then, after she has come to understand the faith, accepts Christ, she can be baptized and the ceremony may be performed."

"What is he talking about, English?" Hevatha asked.

"He won't marry us until you believe everything he does," English said bitterly.

"Young man!" Smythe was incensed. "I will not marry a Christian to a pagan, or perhaps you aren't a Christian either."

English didn't bother to answer. There were too many things he could have said, none of them constructive. "Isn't there a Catholic priest in Dawson?" he asked.

"Father Connelly, but if you think the Roman church will allow you to marry without her conversion to Catholicism, you have no understanding of their canon either."

"I guess I don't," English said.

"Of course, there is a justice of the peace, if you decide to marry outside the laws of God and church, but I understand that in the Yukon it is illegal for a white man to marry an Indian anyway." That seemed to please Smythe. He sat back, rolling a fountain pen between his palms.

English stood silently watching. Abruptly he turned, snatching up his sack of provisions, taking Hevatha's hand. He led her out, letting the door to the church bang behind him.

"What happened, English?"

"He won't marry us."

"Well, then that is all right." She smiled. She stopped him, placed both hands on his chest, and looked up at him. "I told you, I am already your wife, Richard English."

"Yes." There was still anger in English's eyes, but it softened now. He put his arm around Hevatha and walked slowly with her down the road to Dawson.

"Now we will find a tent?"

"We'll try. Corcoran's store, I guess. He sells used mining gear. Quite a business, buy out a miner who's given it up, who's desperate, broke, buy for next to nothing. Then sell the gear to a *chechaco* who has arrived with gold fever, who hasn't thought about pans and picks and shovels. He'll have a tent if anyone does. I'll pick up a hammer, nails, and a saw."

"You have built a cabin before, English?" Hevatha asked.

"No." The smile was self-mocking. "But I suppose I can do as well as some of the shacks I've seen thrown up around Dawson. Just so the roof doesn't fall in."

Hevatha saw her then, or thought she did. In an alley they passed, a woman in a red dress scurried away from them. Hevatha held back, trying to look into the ally. English still had her hand and she had to jerk free.

"What is it, Hevatha?" he asked.

"One minute, English." She returned to the head of the alley and peered into it. Muddy earth, stacked empty barrels, trash and iron, rusting on the ground. The woman was gone. She turned back to English who was puzzled.

"What did you see?"

"I thought, just for a minute . . . But it must have been another woman. I thought I saw Kiptah in that alley."

"Kiptah?"

"Maybe you do not remember her. She is Tan Yuolo's daughter, English."

"A Han? What would the Han be doing up here?"

"They have a summer camp here, English. They have been here for a long while."

"And you never told me? I would have liked to see them, especially Kawchot and Tan Yuolo. I could have talked to Cuah; he makes me smile with his white man's talk." He stopped and held her by the shoulders. "You never told me, Hevatha. Why?"

"You were so busy working, I did not want to bother you."

"And that," he said tolerantly, "is a lie."

"Yes," she agreed with a smile. "It is a lie. Call it a woman's whim, an Indian's whim."

"All right . . . you're not going to tell me anyway. I suppose you've got a good reason. Let's find a tent."

With winter coming on, Corcoran's store was glutted with stock, remnants of golden dreams. Still, he was a hard man to deal with, knowing there was no place else to go for equipment. Finally English settled with him for a patched two-man tent and some used hand tools. Hevatha stood outside the store—the inevitable sign hung on the door—and watched the streets, puzzled and worried by the apparition in the red dress.

Up the street, something was happening. She saw men running toward the alley beside the blacksmith's shop, heard a man call out, someone hurrying toward the constable's office. Hevatha hesitated, opened the door to the store, and called in, "English, something has happened to Kiptah!"

Corcoran looked up furiously; English dropped the dust he had been giving the storekeeper to weigh out and rushed from the store.

He caught up with Hevatha halfway across the muddy street. "What happened?" he shouted.

"I don't know. Kiptah . . ."

They reached the head of the alley and forced their way through the mob of miners there. The body lay crumpled, bloody against the dark, damp earth of the alley. But the body wasn't Kiptah's. It was Floyd Demarest; someone had cut his throat.

English halted, arms dangling, mouth open as he gasped for air. He looked at Hevatha and then turned away to be sick. The voice of Boxer Thrush could be heard now. "Get out of the way. What's going on here? Out of the way, Ned!"

Thrush made his way forward. Glancing at English, who was leaning against the side of the building, he went to the body.

"Dead," he said unnecessarily. Demarest's face was

contorted and blood smeared his throat and face, his thick hands. "What happened, English?"

"Someone killed him!" English shouted. "What do you think happened, Thrush?"

"Take it easy. You didn't see it?"

"We just got here. Does he have his poke?"

Thrush was searching the body, turning the pockets out, removing Demarest's pocketknife, handkerchief, and pipe. "Nothing on him of value."

"He had several thousand."

"Robbery then, I expect. Happens every day. You don't see it; I do. He flashed his poke in the wrong place in front of the wrong man." Thrush rose, wiping his bloodstained hand on his trousers. "Damn shame."

"It was Butler," English said intensely, "Aaron Butler."

"Easy, English."

"I know it was. He hated Demarest."

"Aaron Butler doesn't need to cut a man's throat in an alley to get a couple of thousand dollars."

"No, he's got other ways! Legal ways, like taking a man's claim from him."

"That's right," Thrush said quietly. "He's got other ways."

"He did it, or had it done. I know he did."

"You don't know a damn thing, young man. You liked Demarest; he was your partner. You don't like Aaron Butler. Those two facts don't make Butler a murderer. And if you shoot off you mouth enough, you'll find yourself in court on slander charges."

"Slander!" English laughed bitterly. "How could anyone possibly slander a larcenous, back-stabbing, murderous bastard like Aaron Butler? The blackest thing you could say about him is true. Hevatha, come on."

He took her hand and walked through the gathered miners, trembling with emotion. He stopped with her on the street, taking slow deep breaths, trying to calm himself. "Let's get our gear, Hevatha. Let's collect our supplies and get out of this white town."

"As you say, English. But I would like to find Kiptah."

"You sure it was her?"

"I think so."

"Chances are it wasn't. Even if it was, what difference does it make? She just wanted to look around probably. It's going to rain, Hevatha," he said, looking to the skies. "Let's go home . . . wherever home might be."

She nodded her head and took the sack of provisions as English carried the tent. Then they started out of Dawson, but Hevatha paused twice to look back. It had been Kiptah, and Hevatha was worried.

Poduk was tired and cold. The rain had come in quicker than they had thought. The fishing was not good. The wind was cold and strong.

And now Kiptah was not home to make his supper. Poduk scowled, stripped off his wet clothes, and slung a blanket over his shoulders, poking at the fire. Where was the woman? Where was the baby?

He stood at the entrance to his hide house watching the rain slant down over the summer village of the Han. If the woman had the baby out in this rain, Poduk swore he would beat her.

He beat her often, but it seemed to do no good. What was the matter with Kiptah? What did she want? He was a good hunter, a strong man; he had given her a baby. He would talk to Tan Yuolo when the rain stopped. He would ask the chief of the Han if he should beat Kiptah more.

Poduk looked around for something to eat. Smoked sturgeon and bannock was in the food basket. He chewed on a bannock cake as he watched the rain.

Where was his son? If the baby got cold it would die. He stood over the baby's empty wicker cradle, missing his son. One day the baby would be a boy; Poduk would teach him to hunt, he would teach to fish. They would wrestle and then in years to come the boy would win at wrestling; then he would be the hunter for the family and Poduk could be easy in his mind, knowing that in his old age a young Han would feed him.

The narrow colored thread caught Poduk's eye. There was a crimson thread against the baby's brown blanket. Poduk snatched up the top blanket and saw the red dress beneath it. He picked it up and scowled at it. The woman had defied him again. She had promised to throw away the white woman's dress, but she hadn't.

Kiptah was a bad woman. Poduk walked to the fire, which had come to life, and he placed the dress on the flames, which slowly poked through the red material, curled around it, and devoured it. He went back to the baby's bed and took off the second blanket.

What was that? More bright things. Poduk crouched, holding his blanket around his shoulders with one hand. A string of glass beads. A necklace made by white men. He held it up, seeing the firelight gleam on the blue and green beads. Angrily Poduk snapped the necklace, letting the glass beads roll across the earth floor of his house.

More white things! Was Hevatha bringing them to his wife? He didn't think so; no one had spoken of Hevatha for days. She hadn't been in the Han camp. Poduk looked at the ground, at a glass bead which lay there, and he stepped on it, deliberately slowly, crushing it to powder. Then he walked to the entrance again and stood gloomily watching the rain.

Across the camp the baby cried out and Poduk, without dressing, started from his house, bowing his head to the storm that darkened the sky. The muddy earth was cold against his bare feet. He paused, heard the baby cry again, and went on, his pulse hammering in his throat, his vision blurred by anger and the constant rain.

Reaching Tan Yuolo's house, Poduk threw back the hide flap across the entranceway and went in to stand dripping water, his teeth chattering with the cold.

Kawchot sat rocking the baby, which cried with frustration, trying to nurse at the air.

"Where is his mother?" Poduk demanded, but the teller of sticks could only shake her head. In the corner Tan Yuolo lay, blankets and furs heaped over him. Poduk started to ask Kiptah's father the same question, but he could see that something was wrong. The Han chief's face was blotched, his open eyes stared at nothing.

"Tan Yuolo is ill?" Poduk asked.

"A fever. A bad sickness," Kawchot said. She let the baby grip her finger. It tried to nurse on it, failed to find milk, and cried out with tiny anger.

"He will live?" Poduk asked. He was genuinely concerned. Tan Yuolo had been his father's best friend. Tan Yuolo had chosen him from among all of the Han's best young hunters to marry his daughter.

Kawchot didn't answer. Her eyes lifted to Poduk's and he knew that Kawchot had asked the sticks, that Tan Yuolo would die. "She should be here," Poduk said, his voice softening briefly. "Where is she? Where is Kiptah? Tell me, Kawchot, did Hevatha take her away to the white town?"

"Hevatha? No, Poduk. Hevatha has not been here. She would never come to our camp without visiting me, she is a good daughter, our Moon Walker."

"Then where is she?" Poduk sank to the floor beside the fire. The baby continued to cry; the breathing of Tan Yuolo grew more ragged and labored. "Where is she?"

Jimmy Waley turned the lamp down. He liked it a little dark when he was with a woman, although he wasn't exactly with this one yet. The Indian girl sat at the table in Sasak's old shack studying the things he had purchased for her. Purchased with her gold. She wasn't allowed in the stores and so she would peer in the windows and point.

That was where Waley had first seen her, peering in the window at Rose's dress shop. She had been wearing a red dress. She had a weakness for red, it seemed. That day Waley had bought two more for the girl.

Her name was unpronounceable to Waley and so he called her Kippy. Now, spread out in front of Kippy were hand mirrors, beads, a cheap imitation silver bracelet, a Spanish-style hair comb of tortoiseshell, a length of black lace, and a little red hat. On Kippy's feet were red boots, which she wobbled in.

"You got enough gewgaws now?" Waley asked, moving nearer to her to put his hand on her shoulder and peek down the front of her dress at the full golden brown breasts of the young woman.

Kiptah turned to look up at him. "They have other things. I saw a doll with glass eyes. I saw a necklace which shined; I saw a blanket, red and gold."

"Yeah, but you've got plenty of stuff. You've left and come back twice. Where do you go to get that gold you spend?" Waley asked.

"Home," Kiptah said with a shrug. She put the Spanish comb in her hair and held the hand mirror up to study herself.

"Yeah, but where is that? Have you got a lot of gold there? Much gold?"

Kiptah shrugged. Waley had moved behind her chair to let his hands slip around and cup her breasts. Kiptah seemed not to notice it. Waley bent and kissed her neck and Kiptah shook her head, forcing him away.

"Do you like this comb in my hair, Waley?"

"Sure, I like it," he said sullenly. "You know what I'd like more," he said, moving to her again.

When the door popped open Waley leapt back. Kiptah looked up to see the big man with the black mustache and pocked face standing there. He strode in, his eyes hard and knowing.

"This her?" Aaron Butler asked.

"Yeah. Yes, sir," Waley said, looking at his hands as if they could betray him.

"What is she, Han?"

"I don't know, sir. Guess so."

Aaron Butler looked at his employee with disgust. "You Han, girl?" he asked Kiptah.

"Yes, I am Han," Kiptah answered, taking the comb from her hair, picking up the bracelet to try that on.

"Speak English? You speak it?" Butler asked.

"My friend taught me. Hevatha. Moon Walker."

"That makes it easier," Butler said. He looked scathingly at Waley, removed his bowler hat, and slung it onto the trunk in the corner. Then he reversed a chair and sat facing Kiptah.

"You like those, do you? Like those pretty things?"

"Yes." Her eyes rose only briefly. She could sense the power in this man, the dark power which lay subdued just now like a caged animal. "I like these things."

"Don't have anything like them where you come from, do they? Only skins and furs and bone things."

"Yes, that is all."

"You want more things?" Butler asked. Her reached over and took hold of the silver bracelet. Kiptah held the other end of it and tugged at it.

"That is mine," she said.

"Yes, and I asked you a question. Do you want more?"

"I will get more. I will bring gold and buy more. Waley will take me."

"Waley won't take you," Butler said firmly. Kiptah's eyebrows drew together.

"He has told me this," Kiptah insisted.

"Listen to me, woman," Butler said, yanking the bracelet from her. "Waley won't take you anymore. Waley does just as I say. I'm Waley's chief, you understand that?"

Kiptah glanced at Waley, who shrank into the corner. When she met Butler's gaze again his eyes were friendly. He let go of the bracelet, took her hand, and then fastened it around her wrist.

"You see, I'm your friend. I don't want to take anything away from you. What's your name, girl?"

"Name's Kippy," Waley said.

Butler shot a hard glance at Waley and the kid shrank just a little more. He knew Butler well enough to know that he had been told to butt out. Maybe Waley had found the girl, discovered she had gold, and sent for Aaron Butler, but now the boss was here and there wasn't any need for Jimmy Waley to do anything but shut up.

"Now, Kippy, I'll tell you how it is. I'm a big chief in Dawson, understand me? Big chief. If I tell someone to let you buy something, they do it. If I tell someone that you can't buy anything, not even an old blanket, then you won't."

"Another white man will sell me things," Kiptah said. Butler's hand shot out. He took hold of her chin, his thumb digging into her jawbone.

"No one will sell you anything. You'll be lucky if they don't set the dogs on you." His expression softened, his hand stroked her cheek. "But you and I can be friends, you understand me, Kippy?"

She was frightened now and she tried to rise, but Butler yanked her down, keeping hold of her arm.

"I have a baby," she said. "I must feed him."

"All right. In a minute. You have a baby? Has he got plenty of warm blankets, has he got a nice shirt to wear, has he got a little bonnet?"

"He will have," Kiptah said uncertainly.

"Sure he will." Butler let go of her arm and leaned back, searching for a cigar in his vest. Kiptah sat fascinated by his raw power, his apparent strength, his controlled fury. He was not like Poduk. Poduk grew angry too; Poduk was very strong, but Poduk had the anger of a child. When he didn't get what he wanted, he grew savage. This one, this white, was powerful and confident.

Butler lit a match, touched it to his cigar, and began to smoke. "Come on," he said finally, rising.

"Where are you taking me?"

"Shopping, where else?"

"I have no gold left," Kiptah objected. Still she allowed Butler to hoist her to her feet.

"I've got gold, don't worry about that."

"You would spend your gold to buy me things?" she asked in amazement.

"Of course," he said, "why not? We're going to be friends, aren't we?"

Kiptah nodded her head dubiously, hopefully. Waley still hung back in the corner, sulking. He had found the Indian girl, he had been curious enough about the gold she had to keep her on the hook until Butler arrived. Butler now stuck a hand in his pocket and pulled out two fifty-dollar gold pieces. He flipped them through the air to Waley and all of the young man's animosity disappeared. He beamed. "Thank you, Mr. Butler. Hope this works out."

Butler didn't answer. "Come on, girl," he said to Kiptah, "we're going shopping."

She walked toward the door, moving carefully like an animal in unfamiliar surroundings. Butler was smiling again, but she had already decided that meant nothing. All that mattered was his true intention. Was he really going to buy her things? Tan Yuolo and Poduk said you couldn't trust whites to do what they said; that they were changeable and perverse.

Butler led her outside, buttoned his coat against the cold wind, and marched uptown with Kiptah trailing. Now and then he glanced back to her, offering her one of those brief, meaningless smiles.

"Where do you want to go?" he asked her, and she lifted a finger to point at Rose's dress shop.

"I want to go there, but they won't let me in."

"Don't worry about that. They'll let you in, all right, if you're with me. Didn't I tell you that I was a big chief here?"

Kiptah nodded doubtfully. Waley had told her she couldn't go in. Butler seemed confident, but Kiptah was dubious, dragging her feet as they approached the store, stepping up onto the plank walk.

"Come on," Butler encouraged her. He walked directly to the door and swung it open, waiting for Kiptah, cautious and slow, to come through.

Rose looked up from a dress form draped in green satin and stood, shaking her head nervously. "Oh, no, no Indians in here," she said.

"Shut up," Aaron Butler said. "The girl's with me. Want to throw me out, Rose?"

The woman looked as if she would like to if she had the physical strength, but she just shook her head. Butler unbuttoned his dark coat and dug into his pockets again.

"Here's five hundred, Rose. If she goes over that, send me a bill."

The dress-shop owner showed the same respect for

gold as Jimmy Waley had. Rose took the money and
tried a smile. "Yes, Mr. Butler. I suppose we can
make an exception this time."

Butler looked smug, bored. "Help her out, will you,
Rose? That way," he added, "you can steer her to
your most expensive stock."

Rose, miffed, kept her mouth shut, tried momentarily for that elusive smile, and tight-lipped again, began
guiding the Indian girl around the shop.

Kiptah was lost in a glow of wonder. She had entered some paradise where anything was possible. The
lady gave her dresses of green and blue, and of red.
Two more of red. There were shoes with rows of little
buttons and small hats with ribbons and veils. There
was cloth of all sorts to be used for whatever you
wanted, silk and satin and lace and crinoline. They
had petticoats which made Kiptah laugh and bloomers
which made her laugh even harder. Still she bought
them, and the woman kept piling up her purchases on
the counter.

Butler watched like a benign father. There was a
dark light in his eye, but Kiptah had come to accept
that in this white warrior already. He was a man of
moods, but now he was in a generous frame of mind.
If he wanted to beat her later, that was all right, she
would at least have her new clothes, many new clothes.

They were in the store for an hour. Most of the
clothing had to be left behind. "I'll have it sent over to
the shack, the house where Waley took you, all right?"
Butler said. A new red dress was in Kiptah's arms,
wrapped in brown paper.

"Why are you good to me?" she asked once.

"Because we're going to be friends, Kippy," Butler
answered.

"Because you want more gold?" she asked.

Butler roared with laughter. "That's right, Kippy.
You're not so dumb, are you? I want to show you what
you can really do with gold. Not just come in and buy
a trinket or a red dress, but how you can live, with my
help, the help of a white chief."

Butler had stopped before a shop which smelled of

hot oil and powder and flowers. "Come on, we're going in here."

"What is it?" Kiptah asked. She hesitated and Butler towed her along behind him.

"A hair salon. You have beautiful hair, Kippy. Don't you want them to fix it up for you, to curl it and pile it on top of your head? Then," he said, pausing to stroke her shoulder, to look into her round, childish face, "you'll be more beautiful than any white woman, the most beautiful woman in Dawson or the Yukon. Come on."

The faded yellow-haired woman who ran the shop looked up with dismay. She pointed to the sign on the door, but Butler with bullying and bribery brushed aside the objections. Kiptah was placed in a tall chair and the yellow-haired woman with her scissors and curling iron and pins got to work on the long glossy black hair of the Han girl.

That wasn't the end of it. By the time Kiptah had had her hair fixed and put on her new red silk dress, Aaron Butler was back again with a horse-drawn surrey. He helped her put her new shoes on and led her out under the scornful eye of the hairdresser.

He held her hand as she hoisted her skirt and awkwardly clambered aboard. Settling back, she let Butler drive her from town without asking where they were going. It was a good dream she had entered and she let it envelop her. She did not have to cook for Poduk or scrape hides; she didn't have to sneak to wear her nice dress. The white men on the street turned to look at her with different eyes, very different eyes, as Butler drove her up the street past the lighted saloons and hotels. She thought with a pang of the baby as her breasts began to ache and leak milk, but the baby would be all right until morning. He might cry a little, but he would be all right.

And Poduk would beat her . . . She put that out of her mind. She wished to live in the dream.

The dream had just begun. Butler drove a little ways out of town to a vast white house where lights blazed from the windows. Inside there was a massive

stone fireplace with logs the length of a man burning
brightly. No one could be cold in this house; the wind
did not seek out the bad seams in the hides, dampness
did not leak onto the floor and freeze there if the fire
went out. Butler had men to watch his fire, to close
the doors, to bring food when they sat at a long table
where candles glowed on silver.

"So much," Kiptah said softly.

"All bought with gold, Kippy," Butler said, leaning
back as one of his soft-footed servants poured liquor
into two glasses. "Do you see what I'm trying to show
you? Look at the way you live, the way your people
live. Look what they could have." Butler's arm moved
in a flourishing gesture which included the high-ceilinged
dining room, all of the house, and the town of Dawson. "Gold, Kippy. And I'll help you. I'll help you
and your people to get rich."

"And you will get richer," she said shrewdly.

"That's right," Butler answered. "The gold is on
Indian land, I take it?"

"There is gold," she said hesitantly. The soft-footed
man had given her wine. It glowed in the candlelight
and when she sipped it her belly warmed.

"A lot of gold?"

"There is gold," Kiptah said uncertainly.

Aside, Butler said to his serving man, "Send someone over to Bertram St. Ives' house. Tell him I want
to see him tonight. Now." The man bowed and glided
away, carrying a tray.

"Do the Han own that land? Or are they just living
there?" Butler finished his wine and poured more
from the carafe. He tasted that and leaned forward
toward Kiptah, folding his arms on the table.

"It is our land," she said rapidly. "The government
gave it to us to hunt on in the summer."

"Hunting grounds? You don't live there all year
around?"

"No, we live by the big lake in winter."

Butler turned that over in his mind, rotating his
wine goblet in his hands. St. Ives would know where
they stood legally, how to bend the law a little if it had

to be bent. Bertram wasn't much physically, but he knew the law and he knew where to settle a bribe so that it would do the most good. There were millions of acres out there; the damned Indians could hunt anywhere.

Kiptah drank her wine. The uneasiness she had begun to feel drifted away as it reached her head. She wished the people of the tribe could see her now, wished her father could see her in her red dress, her hair pinned and curled. Poduk! She could imagine him barging in, yanking her dress off, humiliating her and slapping her. But that couldn't happen, not with Butler here. He was more than a match for Poduk.

"We'll go out tomorrow," Butler was saying, "and you show me the gold. I want to see what you've got."

"Tomorrow I will have to go to my people, my husband, my baby. I should go tonight . . ."

Butler had gotten to his feet. He walked to her and practically jerked her from her chair. He held her, and her head lolled on her neck. She was limp in his powerful arms. Strength radiated from the man; perhaps it was evil strength, but it caused Kiptah's legs to tremble, her belly to go hollow.

"Tonight," Aaron Butler said into her ear, "you're staying here. With me. If you want, you can stay with me always, and I'll see that you always have pretty things, soft beds, good food, a warm fire. What do you want to do, Kippy? Go back and let your man beat you and work you until you're old and dried up?"

Kiptah's lips parted and Butler pressed his mouth to hers. The wine spun in her head and she felt him scoop her up and carry her off, farther into the dream.

12

THE river had no name. A tiny tributary of the Yukon, it flowed through a time-cut gorge above the long meadow, then fell to race through the pine forest, sending mist into the air to spray and gloss the trees. When it reached the valley it slowed, becoming temporarily placid before the land once more tilted downward and it began to hiss and sing again, racing to meet the Yukon.

The tent stood back in the pines on a narrow grassy bench where a single cedar tree bent curiously away from the prevailing winds and the grass was always strewn with fresh mushrooms in a dozen hues.

Beside the tent the cabin was slowly being constructed.

English worked on it only part-time, although winter was fast approaching. The mornings he panned in the creek, taking out less than fifty dollars a day. He and Hevatha ate in the early afternoon and then together worked on the cabin. The first few rows of logs had been trimmed, notched, and caulked with mud. English had installed a roof beam to help them crudely winch the upper wall logs into place. The work was difficult, frustrating, and slow.

"But it is a beautiful cabin, English. Stand back and look at its beauty," Hevatha said.

Instead, perspiration streaming down his face, English looked at the woman with the wind-tangled hair, the healthy smile, the dark, shining eyes.

"It's ugly as sin, square and crude and a little pathetic," he answered. He took a bandanna from his pocket and wiped at his face. In the pines ravens called to each other and from time to time took to slow, circling flight.

"Beautiful. You made it. We made it. It is our home, English."

"Yes," he said at last, rolling down his sleeves, "I guess you're right after all. You see something half-done; I see something half-incomplete. You see accomplishment and I see more work. But I'm trying, Hevatha, trying to learn to see the world the way you do."

"I don't want to change your world, English," she said, "I just want to make it brighter."

"You do, Hevatha, you do." During the long nights when she was next to him, laughing or touching him, her softly swollen belly pressed to him, her breasts warm and comforting, her kiss gentle, knowledgeable, her eyes bright with love, she made the world bright, she made herself essential to him.

"Looking back," he said once as he lay on his back in the tent, the furs and blankets piled around and over him as Hevatha traced patterns on his chest, "I can see that you gave me a new life. How could it take me so long to realize that? The Iht would have killed me if not for you; the wild country would have defeated me. I would have sunk into myself and let myself grow dark and cancerous.

"Baptism. Remember Dr. Smythe—that tickles, Hevatha—and his need to baptize? I was baptized in the sea, reborn on the beach. But I carried memories of a previous life, too many memories, cherished too dearly."

"Memories of yellow-haired women," Hevatha said, leaning low so that her breasts touched his chest, her lips met his.

"Yes, I suppose. Whatever she was. Whoever. And then Sarah Penner. God, what I thought she represented, I don't know. My old life, a life I was clinging to without having evaluated it. You never actually talked to her, did you, Hevatha?"

"Only once, English." Hevatha sat up and wiped back her hair. Her laughter was sudden and deep.

English propped himself up on an elbow and stared at her curiously.

"What's so funny now?"

"Shall I tell you about the time I talked to Sarah Penner?"

"Yes, certainly. Where was this?"

Hevatha lay beside him, holding his strong arms, and she related the tale of the fancy ball, how Hanna Sue Blythe had dressed her in the same dress as Sarah Penner and taken her there. "Cruel," English commented. "That Blythe woman is a vixen."

"She wanted to offend Sarah Penner. I was there. She took me. Anyone would have done as well." Hevatha went on; by the time she reached the incident with the punch bowl, English was laughing so that tears streamed down his cheek. He drew her down to him and kissed her throat, the angle of her jaw, her ear. Then he drew the furs up higher and took her in his arms.

Outside the winds blew and the new storm blustered. Lightning struck so near to their tent that they could smell its sulfurous charge.

"O-Ai-No," Hevatha said. "The North Wind is mad and it comes to chase away the people from the land. O-Ai-No's big voice says to the people, 'Go away now, I am back from the distant sky. Now I want my land back, go home to the south."

English grinned. "You don't really believe that, do you?"

"Believe what? That North Wind is coming back to his land?" she asked.

"That this O-Ai-No—is that what you called him?—is a real living thing?"

"Oh, yes, he is real. How could North Wind not be real. There he is. Hear him?"

"But it's just the wind, Hevatha."

"Just the North Wind, O-Ai-No, coming to tell the people to go south."

"Just the wind."

"That is what I said, English. You are a funny man."

English could do no gold panning the next day. The river, swollen with new rain, roared past their home site. In the afternoon the storm broke briefly and they moved three new logs into place. It was numbing work in the cold. By the time they retreated to the tent their fingers were stiff, their faces masks.

"The baby kicks, English," Hevatha told him inside. "Come and put your hand on my belly, come feel it kick. A strong baby. What is it, do you think—a boy or a girl? Kawchot could tell us by casting her sticks."

"Kawchot could *not* tell us. She could make a guess and have a fifty-percent chance of being correct."

He walked behind her as she lifted her blouse. His hands, still cold, touched the warm mound of her belly. It was a long while before the baby kicked again, but eventually it did, and English felt a thrill pass through him, a sad, poignant, amazed thrill. They had done this thing together. Somehow they had made a life. He turned Hevatha and held her and she smiled up at him, seeing the dampness in her man's blue eyes.

"And so, what shall we have to eat?" she asked. He kissed her in response. Outside, O-Ai-No blustered.

"English," Hevatha asked him as he stood at the tent flap, watching the cold rain fall, the river, white and gray and violent, rush past, "why aren't you doing what you want to do?"

He turned toward her, puzzled. "And what is that, woman?"

"Write your words. That is your work, isn't it?"

English shrugged. "It used to be my work."

"When they gave you gold for it?"

"It's not that. What have I got to say? If someone isn't listening, why speak?"

"I listen. You said other people listened."

"Maybe. Fantasies. I give them fantasies and they dream with me. What's the value of that?" he asked.

"Fantasy? A dream, you mean?"

"Something like that, Hevatha, and I don't have room for fantasies anymore. I have you and you are my reality."

"Dreams are real, English. You are a strange man indeed. Don't you know that when you share your fantasies you are sharing something real? Tell me what the difference is, show me."

"I've given up trying to understand the difference," Richard said flatly. "One thing I have decided: all this *art* of mine, this need for something beyond life, is just a schoolboy fantasy. You are art, Hevatha, the baby, the winter storm."

"Then tell them that, English. Tell them that the winter storm and the coming of spring are art. That it is both—fantasy and reality. We are all dream-seekers, and what is wrong with that?"

"You just don't understand, not really."

"No," she admitted, "not really. Why should I understand your dreams?"

"I'm nothing when I work, nothing when I do not."

"Yes?"

"Just a perspective from which to view existence, that's all my work is."

"What I think," Hevatha said, "is that you confuse yourself with every thought. You have me, you have the baby, you have life, you have work. Breathe it all in. Rumble back at the North Wind, shout at those who have offended you. Make yourself content. Write your words and tell them to me. No one else can share them; no one else knows you; no one else loves you as I do. But do not give it up. That might even make you hate me in time, English."

"Hate you?" he said, and he said it with wonder. "How could that ever happen? It won't. That is all I can promise you, Hevatha. I will always love you."

"And that," she replied, "is all that a woman ever needs to know. I want no other promises."

English brooded, but it wasn't the old dark mood where he lost himself in a house filled with old dreams, the ghosts of wanting, of needing. Now he retreated into himself to try to understand who Richard English was. He *had* been reborn and he had become a creature he did not yet fully understand.

He had changed greatly. Hevatha could see it, hear

it, feel it. It was in the way he talked, in the way he spoke. His body had grown hard and lean; his eyes looked out at the sky and judged the weather, he heard the animals in the forest and knew which they were, if they hunted, mated, scolded, or foraged. He was closer to Hevatha, so close that at times they seemed one; he was impatient for only one thing—the baby. He no longer felt frustration, suffered from the idea that his world had slipped away, that his white woman had scorned him, that it was necessary to fill his pockets with gold and return to the south to show them that he had worth. He loved his Hevatha.

She found the poem near their bed and she didn't know if he had left it deliberately for her to find or not. Slowly she worked through the words, and when she was finished, she laughed out loud.

"And what's so funny?" English asked. He had been just outside the tent, skinning the hares he had snared. He ducked his head inside. The snow fell beyond him; the river flowed.

"This, English. How you tease me!" she said.

"Tease you?" He was confused. "What, that poem? Throw it away, it's nothing."

He had come in to sit beside her and reread the little poem. "I don't see what you mean."

"Read it aloud to me," she coaxed.

And he did.

> The storm from the North
> When it came in, stamping feet
> Reduced the world with its thunder

English looked up at Hevatha. "What I mean is that the violence of the storm makes us all seem smaller, trivial, that a storm distracts us, shifts our thoughts to larger things instead of small musings. The crackle and boom of a thunderstorm lifts our heads and seems to close off the rest of the world briefly."

"Oh, I know all of that," Hevatha said, still obviously amused by something. "Yes, a storm closes the light out. What was that new word—isolates us."

"Then just what, if you understand it, is so amusing

about it? Or is it just that poor an expression, Hevatha?"

"What?" she laughed again. "The storm has feet, English."

"It's just a manner of speaking. An image."

"A storm has *feet*, English! Now you tell me North Wind is nothing real. Just wind and rain. Now you tell me O-Ai-No is not a real thing, now you tell me it is nothing at all . . . and then, Richard English, you give it feet!"

English could only scratch his head and grin. He looked at the small poem and then at his woman and he laughed out loud, tossing the paper away as he went to Hevatha and took her down into their bed. "Woman," he told her, "you know too much."

The building of the cabin advanced despite worsening weather. English had managed to build up his cache of gold dust so that he estimated he had enough to pay back Gage Powers. One fall day when the sun suddenly broke through the dark clouds, spraying the earth with gold, glittering off the river and the patched snow, he told Hevatha, "I think I'd better go into Dawson while I still can. Do you feel like going with me?"

"I feel like being with you always. Do you mean because I am getting to be a fat woman?" Hevatha asked.

"That too," English said, putting his hands on her abdomen. "How is he today?"

"He. Now it is a son. Is that what you wish for, English?"

"I don't know. I want a baby, someone to live on as a memory of our love."

"The baby will be its own person, English, not only a memory of us."

"Yes, I know that. Funny how poorly I express myself for a man who was once supposed to be a writer."

"A girl would not offend you?" Hevatha asked.

"A baby girl? Why would that offend me?"

"Among the Tlingit a boy is always hoped for, a

warrior, a hunter to help the tribe through hunger and battle times."

"We aren't among the Tlingit."

"No. Maybe," she said brightly, "there will be one of each. A boy and a girl."

English frowned slightly. "That's right, you were a twin, weren't you? Are there other twins in your family?"

"English, I do not even know. I am not a Tlingit, but a Cheyenne. Have I ever told you this? My mother was not a Cheyenne Indian. What she was, she did not know. The Comanche raised her after finding her beside a trail where a thousand lost Indians walked. Her mother had died."

"Finding her? In Comanche country? Where would that be, then—Texas, perhaps?"

"I do not know."

"The Trail of Tears," he said, but Hevatha didn't know what he meant. "The tribes of the Southeast, from Georgia and Florida, among other places, were forced to walk to reservations in Oklahoma—Indian Territory, they called it then."

"My mother had a dream that her father was a tattooed man," Hevatha said.

"Seminole?" Richard guessed. "Possibly." An idea was developing in his mind. He paced the floor, his head bowed as always to clear the low roof of the tent. "How would you like to find out who your grandmother was, who her mother was?"

"That can't be done, English. They are lost in time."

"Maybe, maybe not. Your mother was Cheyenne. She lived on a reservation?"

"After the great war."

"Then there would be a record," English said enthusiastically. "And a record of your sister and brother— if they survived."

"Not many survived the battle, English."

"Maybe they did. Maybe they are still alive. Perhaps they know who your grandmother was—or perhaps there's a record of her in army files somewhere in the South, in Florida or the Indian Bureau in Oklahoma. Maybe your grandfather is alive . . . how old would he be? Or a cousin, an uncle, someone who knew them. Think, Hevatha, we could turn back the pages of their lives and discover who they were, what they were."

"For what purpose, English? They are gone."

"They are gone. A lot of Indians are gone. Maybe one day the Han will be gone, I don't know. There ought to be someone, something to witness their passing. I can't write now; you know that. I can't write because I don't want to write about poor empty Richard English and his small problems. Like a damned fool, I've been looking past what matters in the world, the source of art and drama and tragedy and courage. The people themselves. The Indian people."

"My people, English, are gone. Their courage is gone, their tragedy."

"Then we'll bring it back to life! But it isn't gone, Hevatha. Think of the signs you see in every Dawson store—'No Indians.' Don't marry an Indian, don't try to learn about their culture. If they won't be white and Christian, annihilate them. . . . I'm here, standing beside the great tragedy of this world, and I haven't even seen it. Well, Hevatha, shall we do it? Shall we find out where you have come from, what has happened along the long, long trail?"

"If you wish, English," she said quietly. She went to him and held him. "All I care about is you. If this is your dream, it is mine. If it brings you to life, I wish to go with you."

"Yes, yes," he said, and Hevatha felt her heart flood with joy. It had been a long winter, but her man had finally risen from his frozen slumber, from his self-induced hibernation. She had never seen him so intense, so intoxicated with an idea. It would be good; they would do this thing together.

"If we go to Dawson," she said, "I wish to go through the camp of the Han. I wish to see my mother, Kawchot."

"And let her tell the sticks?"

"Yes. Let her have that joy. Let her touch my belly

and tell us if is a girl-child or man-child I carry. Soon
they will be going south, Richard English, maybe we
will not see them again, and they have been our
friends.''

"Yes," he answered, "they have been our friends
and I've not told them that. If a white community had
taken me in and fed me and given me a house to live
in for a winter, I would have been forever grateful.
But I haven't told the Han that. It is time, Hevatha.
Time I awakened to many things."

They set out while the sun still shone brightly, striking brilliant images against the river's face. English
carried his gold inside his coat in a buckskin sack tied
around his neck. He gave the gold little thought. An
idea had sprung up inside his mind, an idea which
seemed to demand his attention, to demand action.
The gold didn't matter. He could work his way south,
work his way across the country. He had done hard
labor before and now he was probably in better condition than at any other time in his life.

They could travel to Dakota first—could they make
it before the snows came? Likely not, he had to admit—
and then to Texas and Oklahoma. There could still be
some of Hevatha's people alive, those who remembered her family. And they would have tales to tell,
tales which no one wanted to hear just now, but which
they would one day care about.

"They are still here," Hevatha said with relief. Below them the Han camp sat in the folded valley. There
wasn't as much activity as usual, probably because the
hunters had not been out with the snow. There would
be no meat to smoke, no hides to prepare, no fish to
salt down.

"Do you realize, Hevatha, the Han are as close to a
people as you have, as I have? I haven't any family at
home; I don't like to think of myself as a Yukon man.
You were Tlingit, but no more. These," he said in a
sort of wonder, "are very nearly our family."

"Yes, English, I know. You must think very deeply
sometimes, for it often takes you a long time to discover these simple things."

English smiled and then pinched Hevatha. She squealed once, turned as if to fight him, laughed, took his hand, and walked with him down the hillside to the Han camp.

Kawchot was in her house, alone. The old woman's face reflected some sadness they couldn't guess at. She rose slowly, took Hevatha's hand, and kissed her cheek. "And English comes too, a rare gift. Thank you."

"What's the matter, Kawchot?" English asked bluntly. "Your face reveals a sadness."

"Yes? Then my face knows. There is a sadness. Sit down and I will tell you. Have tea, have bannock. Soon we will see each other no more. Soon the Han travel south again."

Kawchot told them, "Tan Yuolo has died."

"No? I'm sorry, I liked him," English said.

"He was our good friend. What happened?" Hevatha asked.

"A fever. He burned away."

"Now he is happy," Hevatha said, finding, as usual, a way to make tragedy palatable. "He walks with his fathers and laughs and makes a good hunt."

"Yes, now he is happy," Kawchot said, but she sniffed, tears welling up in her eyes—faded eyes, English thought. "Cuah is chief of the band now. Good Cuah."

The flap to the hide house opened and English turned his head. Poduk stood there, his mouth pulled down, his chest rising and falling with emotion, his clenched fist extended toward English and Hevatha.

"They must go!" he said wrathfully. "Why are they here? How can you allow such things to come into your house?"

"Go out of here!" Kawchot snapped, getting heavily to her feet. "This is my daughter and her husband. What are you interfering for, Poduk?"

"You know why. She, evil thing, cannot come here. I don't want to see her face or this white face. I will kill them if they come again. Hear me, Tlingit woman! I will kill you."

Kawchot advanced upon him, her round body

hunched and purposeful, but Poduk turned abruptly, turned and stormed out into the day, leaving English and Hevatha stunned, Kawchot apologetic.

"He is a stupid thing, stupid with anger. I am sorry," the teller of sticks said.

"What is he so angry about?" Hevatha asked. "So angry that he would threaten to kill me, to kill English? What has happened, Kawchot?"

The old woman settled to her blanket again with a sigh. "Kiptah, his wife, has run away. She has run off and left her baby here."

"The baby . . ."

"It is well. Tama's wife is nursing it along with her own baby. Poduk is in a fury."

"Why does he blame Hevatha, for God's sake?" English asked. "And what do I have to do with it besides being her husband? I haven't seen Poduk but three times in my life, and we've never argued."

"It is," Kawchot said, "the red dress."

"The red dress?" Hevatha and English exchanged a puzzled glance. "What are you talking about?"

"It is this way," Kawchot explained. "Poduk says his wife was content with him, happy with the new baby, until Hevatha came and gave her a red dress. Then she decided she must have more white things. Then she began to lie to Poduk and sneak around, leaving the baby alone. Poduk burned up her white woman's dress, but Kiptah went and got another one. Then she got beads and bracelets. Then she didn't want to be Poduk's wife anymore. One time she went off to town and didn't come back. Someone has said she is living with a white man who buys her everything."

"A white man?"

"Yes, so it is said, so Poduk hates white men now, and he hates Hevatha, saying if she hadn't given Kiptah the red dress, then he would still have his wife at home where she belongs." Kawchot shrugged heavily, as if her shoulders burdened her. "Kiptah's father is dead now; there is no one to talk sense to her." The teller of sticks glanced at the corner where Tan Yuolo had spent his last days.

"Maybe she'll come to her senses and return," English said.

"Maybe. Then Poduk could beat her and everything would be all right again; but I do not think she will come home. Soon we will be leaving this place, going back to the big lake. If Kiptah does not come soon, she will not come at all."

"Where did she get the money to buy these things?" English asked. "From the white man?"

"I think I know," Hevatha said. She looked at English and gave her head one rapid shake. Her smile was apologetic. "The Han have gold, English. Much gold."

"The nuggets I found and gave to Demarest!"

"Yes. I should have told you, but I didn't know what you would do."

"At that time," English admitted, "I might have gone after it myself."

Kawchot didn't know what they were talking about. Hevatha explained. "The man with the red beard, English's partner, needed money to go home and live out his days. I took some gold from the place where the two streams meet and gave it to him. I did not tell them where it came from. Kiptah was there that day, wearing the red dress. She must have thought I took gold and bought pretty things with it."

"I see." English was silent. "In a way, it is our fault, it seems, Hevatha. Mine and Demarest's for wanting gold, mine for buying you that red dress."

"Yes," Hevatha said impatiently, "and the fault of the lady who made the dress and all of the men in Dawson and O-Ai-No for letting the Han come north."

"I don't see what we can do about it, though. Dragging Kiptah back wouldn't do any good if she's got her mind set on living with a white man. I wonder . . ."

"What, English?"

"I wonder what would prompt a white to take her home and buy her things."

"She is a pretty girl, English," Kawchot said.

"Yes, but still . . ." He looked at Hevatha. They

both knew. It was the gold, the damned gold. Kiptah could show the white man where it had come from.

"All of this has to do with the gold, English?" Kawchot asked.

"Yes, I'm afraid so."

"The man was tricking Kiptah?"

"It seems that's what happened, yes."

"Then it is good. I was concerned about it, but it is good then," the teller of sticks said.

"What is good?" Hevatha asked.

"That Cuah has gone to talk to the white men, that Cuah has gone to trade the gold for goods the Han can use."

"He's done what?"

"Gone to talk to white men at the streams. They wish to buy the land from us. Cuah said it is a good thing. Cuah said that we can have our hunting camp anywhere. In the Long Meadow east of us there is a good hunting camp. Let the whites have the gold; they will give us blankets and rifles and many things."

"They'll rob you blind, you mean," English said, standing. "Don't you realize what's happening, Kawchot?"

"How can he sell the land?" Hevatha asked worriedly. "It is treaty land, isn't it? The government won't let them sell."

"The white man explained that," Kawchot said. Now she too was worried. Had Cuah made a terrible mistake? "He wrote a letter to the government and the government agreed to the sale so long as the white man gives us payment."

"Who in the hell . . . ? What was the white man's name, Kawchot? Tell me." There was urgency in English's voice. For a moment a befuddled Kawchot couldn't recall the name of the man with the funny hat, and then she did.

"It was St. Ives, English. A man named St. Ives."

"St. Ives. Yes, it would be."

"Who is he, English?"

"A manipulator, a lobbyist, a surveyor, a cheat. You say Cuah has gone out there now to talk to St. Ives?"

"To him and other whites. I don't know who they are. The council went with him."

"Hevatha, we've got to go over there," English said.

"Yes. What can we do, though, English?"

"I don't know, maybe nothing."

Kawchot asked, "English, why is this so important? They have promised that we can have other hunting lands, any we like. They have promised to give us payment."

English crouched down to answer the woman. "They'll give you something, but it won't be enough. The gold is Han gold, or should be. Right now the Han people might not want gold, they might not need to buy white goods, but everything is changing in the world, Kawchot. There are forty thousand people in Dawson. They are pushing, squeezing. They will give you a hunting ground and then perhaps take that away. Your children and grandchildren will have nothing, while a few whites grow richer."

English rose. "Hevatha?"

"I am ready, English."

"I only hope . . ." What was there to hope for? It was none of their business, and St. Ives would be the first to tell them that. It was between Cuah, the council, and the white speculators. Still, they had to try.

Hevatha was already nearly out of the house. English looked again to a worried Kawchot and caught up with her. "How far is it?" he asked.

"A few miles. St. Ives, English, he is a friend of Aaron Butler, isn't he?"

"His partner. That's enough to tell us that this stinks."

They hurried on, speaking little, across the meadows through the tall, rain-heavy grass. When they reached the juncture of the two streams they found a hundred people there. Cuah was beaming, wearing a derby hat and a new coat. The Han council stood by, each man holding a rifle or a string of beads. Payment for tens of millions of dollars in gold.

English searched for and found St. Ives, smoking a cigar, speaking to a man in overalls and a yellow mackintosh, pointing to the stream. Aaron Butler stood beside a carriage, looking smug and content. In the carriage sat Kiptah, wearing a fur coat and fur hat.

"Look, English! There is the white who took Kiptah into his house. Butler."

"Yes," English said through his teeth. "That figures, doesn't it?"

Various dignitaries in tall hats and dark coats stood by the streams. Crates of goods had been placed on the earth near Cuah and the council.

Cuah greeted them as English and Hevatha walked to him. The Han smiled and gestured. "Welcome, friends," he said in English, and then his words became gibberish. Cuah still pretended to know the English language, and this time he might have ruined his people with that pretense.

"Cuah," Hevatha said in the Han tongue, "what has been done here?"

"We have made our fortune. Look at these goods. And more to come. Much more to come. The whites have fooled themselves."

"Cuah, don't you understand what has been done?"

"Yes. We have sold our hunting ground. No matter, we shall have another."

Hevatha looked at English, who turned sharply and walked to the small gathering of dignitaries. He didn't know it at that time, but these included a man from the Bureau of Indian Affairs, an officer of the Interior Department, a member of Parliament, a judge, two lawyers, and a representative of the governor-general. St. Ives had done everything legally, although his methods might have been open to question.

Bertram St. Ives turned his head to frown at the approaching white man and his Indian wife.

"English," was all he said.

"What in hell is happening here?" English demanded. St. Ives was furious, but he kept his emotions suppressed.

"We have concluded a purchase of Han lands in the interests of the Yukon Territory and the Indians alike."

"I can see that," English shot back, nearly shouting

as a pair of top-hatted men drifted nearer to listen.
"How much have you paid them?"

"The amount was substantial."

"Yes, that looks like a substantial amount," English
said wildly. "A million dollars' worth of goods easily.
Five million?" He looked again at the crates of cheap
goods the land speculator had given the Han. "Or
something like five hundred dollars?"

"Who is this man?" one of the top-hatted figures, a
man with a lantern jaw, long lean head, and tiny eyes
under a shelf of brow, asked.

"An American," St. Ives answered, waving his cigar. "A failed prospector, once a writer, I believe. His
name is Richard English, Judge Talbot."

Judge Talbot simply cleared his throat and turned
away.

"Why don't you clear out, English. What do you
want here?"

"I want to see that the Han have their due."

"In what capacity?"

"I'm their friend."

"I see." St. Ives was amused. "Your wife is Han,
perhaps."

"No, she isn't."

"Then I assume you had your eye on this gold.
Sorry, it belongs to me now. For the good of the
territory. I've been given a license and lease to explore
and develop the resources of the basin known as Wild
Rose Canyon. Would you care to see the treaty?"

"That man—their spokesman, Cuah—doesn't even
speak English!" Richard shouted. Heads turned. The
dignitaries, all quite pleased with themselves, stared at
this madman who had appeared from nowhere. To
English's right there was movement. Aaron Butler was
strolling toward them, Kiptah on his arm.

"He spoke well enough to understand what we were
offering him, to sign over his tribe's mineral claims to
this land," St. Ives said sharply. "Now, if you will
excuse me, I have other business to see to."

"Wait!" English grabbed St. Ives' arm. A crowd
was beginning to gather around them. Aaron Butler,

appearing placid and self-assured, stood only a yard away. "You can't do it. What are you leaving these people?"

"Young man," Judge Talbot said, "I have no idea who you are or why you see fit to interrupt peaceful and fruitful negotiations between the Yukon Territory and the Han tribe, but I suggest that you are a disruptive element and verging on illegality in your interference with a lawful and amiable exchange."

"You are a judge, aren't you?" English said, annoyed at the stilted language.

St. Ives had wisely turned his back and moved away; Aaron Butler, enjoying this, had come even nearer. He was virtually at English's shoulder. Kiptah, smiling prettily, clung to him.

"Go home to your people," Hevatha said. "What are you doing here with this man?"

"I go where I like," Kiptah said haughtily. "Are you the only woman who may have a white man? And my man has much money."

"What's the trouble?" Butler asked the judge.

"This man, I can't recall his name. He seems to have some ax to grind. If he has a complaint about the procedures, I suggest he settle it in court. I don't understand what he wants or why he's come here."

Butler smiled at the judge. He placed a hand on English's shoulder. "Maybe you'd better wander off, friend. This is none of your business."

"You dirty, scheming bastard," English growled. Butler continued to smile and English swung a fist at his face. Butler was backing away, but still it clipped his nose and for an instant the killing animal in Aaron Butler flared up. His eyes grew feral, his mouth twisted with dark pleasure.

Butler might have come forward, but the judge had beckoned two men to him from the ranks of the observers. One was a huge Indian in a blue suit, the other Boxer Thrush.

"I don't know what's going on here. I'm afraid this young man is mad," the judge said, "but"—and his voice began to tremble—"I want him out of here."

Boxer Thrush was amiable but firm. "Come on, English. All you can do is get yourself into trouble here."

"Don't you see what's going on here!"

"Nothin', so far as I can see, that concerns me much, or you, English. All I can tell you is if you don't take off, they're going to have me arrest you, and I'll have to do it."

"Boxer, this is a crime. There's a crime here larger than anything you've ever looked into, including murder."

Thrush looked briefly skyward. "Yeah. You going to leave now, English, or do I have to take you into custody?"

"I'll leave." English looked around him, seeing the mockery in the watching eyes, the amusement and pity. "I'm leaving. Hevatha?"

"That is all we can do?" she asked.

"That's all." He added under his breath, "For now."

They walked away then from the gathering, hearing a few derisive comments, laughter, jeers. English's ears burned with anger and humiliation. Hevatha held his arm and walked silently beside him.

"We can't allow this to happen," English said.

"What is there to do?"

"I don't know. The government is happy, Cuah is happy, Butler and St. Ives are happy. Still it is rotten. The Han are going to lose millions of dollars. They're going to barter away their future, and no one seems to care."

"The Han do not understand, English; Cuah does not understand. He is like Kiptah, who thinks she has found wealth and contentment, who hates us for telling her different. Butler—paagh! How could she live with that thing? She sees nothing, a bit of red silk, a fur hat, yes. But she does not see her future. The Han cannot either, English. They have been poor upon the land, a hard land. A few things to brighten their lives, to make it easier to exist, are all they can see. It is up to us to change this. Who is there to care but us?"

"Caring doesn't seem to be enough just now," English said despondently. They could see Dawson now, and they trudged on.

"Only the law can help," Hevatha said.

"What law? That was the law back there."

"That was a part of the law," Hevatha said. "The whole of the law, the whole of the white government, cannot be so blind, so willing to take from the Han."

English stopped and turned toward her. "What are you suggesting? That we take them to court?"

"Before the council, the judge, the court, whatever you might call it. Can this not be done, English?"

"I don't know . . . Maybe. Why not?"

"If the law can take from the Han, it can give to them."

"Possibly. We'll need some help, though. Someone who knows a lawyer willing to take this on. Someone to tell us how to go about filing a suit. It's more difficult because the Han aren't at all unhappy with the settlement. I don't know anything about law. Can we even file suit?"

"They are being cheated, English. If the law allows that, then the law is no good."

"We need help. A lot of help."

"But we will try, Richard English?"

"How can we not?" He took her arm. "The Han are our people, aren't they?"

Still, it seemed improbable that anything could be done. English felt ignorant and impotent. What was needed was a strong lawyer with a sense of moral indignation. If there was such a man in Dawson, English hadn't heard of him; and how would such a man be paid?

Instead of going to the courthouse to settle the debt he owed Gage Powers, he went to the new house Gage was building for his wife. Four stories of house with a stable and servants' quarters, a ballroom, dining room, sewing room, den, library, eight bedrooms, and ten baths.

Gage himself was standing in a state of wonder, watching the shingles be tacked to the roof of one of the four towers. He turned toward English, frowning at first until he recognized the blond man, and then he grinned, thrusting out his hand.

"Something, ain't it," Gage Powers said, a little embarrassed. "I grew up in a cabin with three rooms and six brothers. Penny, she wanted a fine house. Had to beat Sarah Penner's place, outshine that gingerbread nightmare Hanna Sue Blythe lives in, have more gold fixtures than Yule Travis' monstrosity. Me, I don't care. It's only money and if it keeps Penny busy, keeps her happy . . . What brings you this way, English?"

"This." English untied the gold sack from the thong around his neck. "We can weigh it out, if you like, but I'm pretty sure it's right."

Gage Powers looked more surprised than pleased. "I won't say I've forgotten about it, English, but I know how it is. A man has good intentions, but in the Yukon it's tough to get the wherewithal sometimes. Sure you don't need it yourself?" he asked, hefting the bag in his hand.

"It's a debt owed, Gage."

"True," the lanky miner said thoughtfully. A bundle of shingles slid from the cupo_laed_ roof of one of the towers and smashed against the ground, and their heads turned that way briefly. "Monstrosity," Gage muttered. He seemed to notice Hevatha for the first time and he smiled. "This is your woman, is it? Pretty thing—wait a minute," he said, his eyes narrowing and then sparkling with humor. "I've seen you before, haven't I, woman? At Mrs. Penner's house the night of the grand ball?"

"I am afraid so," Hevatha said.

"Sure. Spunky woman, this is," Gage Powers informed English. "Got yourself a good match. Say, you two want to come in and take a look at how good sweat-earned gold can be squandered? Sure you do, come on," he said, hooking their arms with his, "we'll have us a whiskey, English. You can tell me how things are going out back. I've been town-tied so long I can't remember what's out beyond the city limits."

He took them up the steps to the front porch. Paint-

ers' drop cloths were everywhere, inside and out.
Entering through a half-wallpapered foyer, they came
to the ballroom, imitating but surpassing Sarah Penner's. Two huge fireplaces flanked the room. A spiral-
ing gold-and-white staircase rose to the upper floor,
where the cool blue sunlight fell through three arched,
leaded windows.

"Home—how the hell can you call something like
this home?" Gage Powers asked, his voice dropping as
he glanced around. "The old woman is liable to hear
me. I've promised to say no more about the house.
Come on into the kitchen, the only room we can keep
warm. Got a gaggle of Chinese in there half the time.
Been meanin' to learn the Chinese tongue. Bothers
me, them being here from across the sea, not know-
in' a thing about who or what they are. Got to be
more to them than what we see."

They went in through a broad white door, their
arms still linked. The kitchen at this hour was empty,
all white tile and copper with a central counter for
preparing food.

Gage Powers walked to a back cabinet, opened it,
removed a jug of corn whiskey and toed the door shut
again. "Set," he said, indicating a small table to one
side. "Lady drink? No? Well, that's as should be.
Don't like to see a woman drink unless it's sipping a
little wine, just enough to put the roses in her cheeks.
A drunk woman—rather see an Apache with a war club
in his hand and fire in his eyes. And I've seen some of
those too. Me and old Bill LaPlante used to scout for
the army, Crook's army, down south. Bill's likely still
at it. Crazy about the desert. Me, I got the wanderlust."

The jug was placed on the table, two crystal glasses
following. Gage Powers frowned at the glasses and
said, "Wonder what these cost me?"

When he had seated himself and poured a drink for
English, one for himself, he asked, "Now, then, what's
happening out back? I saw a dozen or so government
types in town yesterday, men that don't belong. They
were tight-lipped as hell, so I figured it had to do with

gold and somebody trying to sew it up for private use. Did I guess right?"

"You guessed right," English said, and then he explained to Gage Powers what was happening.

"And the Han are going along with this, are they? Damn shame." He emptied his glass and refilled it from the jug. "How the hell could they know what they're sitting on? Who's behind it—never mind, there's only one man in Dawson who could rig this. Bertram St. Ives, or am I wrong?"

"You're not wrong."

"Wondered." Gage pulled at his chin. "Wondered when I heard that Aaron Butler was living with a squaw—beg pardon, miss. That's far from his style and inclination."

"You know this St. Ives well?" Hevatha asked.

"Too damned well. Tried to beat me out of my claim once. Couldn't outtalk my shotgun. Known him since he drifted in and got cozy with Sarah Penner . . . this is before old Satch died." Gage hesitated. Then he shrugged. "Some folks say St. Ives got rich on that."

"On Satchel Penner's death?" English asked.

"Yeah. Some folks say," Gage Powers replied, drinking from his cut-crystal goblet.

"What folks?" Richard asked.

"Well . . . maybe folks like me."

"I don't understand this story," Hevatha said. "What are you telling us, Gage Powers?"

"The woman gets to the heart of things, don't she?" Powers asked with a chuckle. He leaned forward, gripping his bony knees. "All right, then. At the time, I was a down-an-out sourdough and no one would listen to me. Now I'm somebody, by virtue of a bank account, but by now things have kind of drifted into the past, you know what I mean?

"To my mind," Powers continued, "there was always something funny about Satch's death. You'd of had to of known Satch. He was Pennsylvania stock, shrewd and close with the dollar. He had hit it big out back, along the Little Chase Creek, but he wasn't spending. Like Yakima Brown, you see. Yak, he'll

spend money on gambling and whiskey, but everything else is nothin' to him. Yak will live on beans
when he's got the price of half a million Texas cows in
his cache. He'll wear used clothing when he's got
twenty thousand in his pocket. Satchel Penner was like
that. Except his new bride didn't think much of it."

"Sarah Penner."

"That's right. She was Philadelphia society. Her
daddy was in railroads and she liked spending money,
figured it as her female pre-rogative." Gage again
looked at Hevatha. "Apologies again, miss."

"He did not give his wife gold?" Hevatha asked,
glancing sideways at English as he took a drink of his
hootch-i-noo.

"Well, Satch gave her some, but not near what she
expected to get from him, I suppose. Wasn't so much
that Satch was cheap, but he didn't figure building a
house in Dawson when he was planning on going back
to the States, didn't see the sense in a woman having a
hundred dresses when she could only wear one at a
time. Like that."

"You mentioned St. Ives. Where did he come in on
this?" English asked.

Powers considered the question. "Where exactly? I
don't know. All I know is that one day Satch was
dead, heart attack they say, out on the Little Chase,
and next thing you know, his widow's building this
house, buying clothes and jewels in numbers that
would've choked old Satch; then this cheap grifter
named St. Ives that we used to see round buying up
worthless claims, selling them to *chechacos*, he's wearing pin-striped suits and driving a carriage, spending a
lot of time with Mrs. Penner, consoling her, like."

"Are you hinting that Mrs. Penner and St. Ives
might have murdered Satchel Penner?"

"I don't know enough to hint at nothin'," Gage
Powers said. "All I'm sayin' is what I saw. Only man that
might actually know somethin' now is an Ingalik Indian
named Toskobe. He was mighty close to Penner for a
hired Injun. Penner paid him good, treated him good,
drank with him, swapped yarns."

"Who is this Toskobe?" Hevatha wanted to know. "Dead also?"

"No, but he's been mighty shy of people, white folks especially, since all this happened. You want to know where he is?"

"Yes."

"Why? What can you find out from Toskobe that could help you with what you're trying to do?" Gage Powers asked.

"That St. Ives and Butler are crooks," English answered.

"Hell," Power said, "no one's ever doubted that. But I'll tell you where he is. Works for my friend Yakima Brown. Sits with a rifle on a ledge watching over Yakima's claim from dawn to dusk."

"Would he talk to us?"

"Couldn't say. He's Indian."

"You see what I'm after, Gage," English said.

"Sure, I see. Discredit St. Ives and Butler. Get them tried for murder maybe, claim-jumping at the least. But evidence, son, will be mighty hard to come by. Say Toskobe saw the murder—doubtful, since he's still alive—so what? No court will listen to an Indian. Say St. Ives and Butler were convicted of something, even spitting on the street—what's that got to do with the government taking Han land? I think you're walking a dark valley without a match."

"Maybe. I want to know anyway."

"Listen, maybe I talk too much. I don't *know* anything, English. I've been in the Yukon for a time; I've heard things, that's all. Maybe I shouldn't drink whiskey. I don't want to steer you two off to where you're likely to get in more trouble than you can handle."

"We asked you," English said, "and you answered us." He rose, leaving half of his glass of whiskey. "Hevatha and I are going to do something about this if we can. You can't stop us, can't be blamed for it. But maybe you have helped us. Maybe."

"Well, I hope so. I feel a little ashamed for having encouraged you to get into that poker game with Aaron Butler. Hope I've—"

They were interrupted by an ululating squeal which sounded like a seal having its throat cut by a Tlingit hunter.

Powers winced. "That's Penny. She was a hog farmer's daughter. Christ, can that woman yell. Coming, Penny!" He added in a lower voice, "Probably found a faucet leaking. You people be careful. Need help, you come back to old Gage Powers."

They promised that they would. His wife called again from somewhere upstairs and Gage turned, swallowing his last inch of whiskey before shuffling off into the interior of the massive house.

Outside Hevatha stood watching the building clouds. English was as silent as she was. The only noise was the rustle of the wind, the hammering of the roofers.

"They killed Satchel Penner," Hevatha said.

"I know they did. How we could prove it, I don't know. What difference it would make, I don't know, but they surely did kill him, Hevatha."

"I think," she said quietly, "we should talk to this man, this Toskobe."

"Yes. This is dangerous—you know that, don't you, Hevatha? If Butler and St. Ives get onto us, they'll kill us."

"You do not want to do this?" she asked.

"I want to do it," he answered. "Butler killed Charles Landis. I think he also killed Demarest. Maybe Satchel Penner as well. If he got the opportunity, he'd murder me without thinking much of it. I've been a thorn in his side for a long while. I want the man put away or hanged, so that he can't kill again. St. Ives is a crook, if not a murderer, and from what I've been hearing, I'd say he's both. Right now those two thugs are threatening to do more damage than they've done in their lives, dooming a people who should be rich to poverty. I can't think of any way to stop what they're doing to the Han except stopping Butler and St. Ives permanently."

"Then it is for the Han that you wish to do this, English? Not out of a need for revenge?"

English had to think for a moment, but he answered, "It is for the Han."

"What about the law? Should we try to see a lawyer?"

English put his hands on his hips and breathed in slowly. "Yes. We have to at least try that."

That course of action was nearly fruitless. Dawson had five lawyers. English and Hevatha talked to all five of them, and the response was unanimous. A sleek, copper-haired young man named Alexander Polite told them, "You haven't got grounds for a suit. You're talking about misrepresentation and larceny here. The people you want to try are not only Butler and St. Ives—difficult or impossible to convict in Dawson, I'd say, since they know what jury tampering is—but you also want to accuse and convict the Territory of the Yukon and the Dominion of Canada. You tell me what sort of a chance you think you have, Mr. English. A man would be crazy to take this case. I'm presumed to still have most of my mental equipment; no, thanks."

"We will not let them steal," Hevatha said.

"You don't have a lot of choice, young lady. What you have told me, if true, speaks badly for the way the Indians are going to be treated, but as a legal matter it's entirely a moot point."

"English?"

"He won't represent the tribe, Hevatha. Very well, what if we take it to court ourselves? Can we do that?" English asked the lawyer.

"Legally any citizen can file suit against any other citizen, organization . . . or the government anytime he or she wishes, Mr. English. However, it's seldom done and even less seldom successful."

"We don't seem to have any choice, do we? Will you tell us how to go about filing?"

Polite sighed and stared at his desk for a long minute. "I would like to help you, English, but it would be the end of my law career in the Yukon. You understand that, don't you?"

"I understand that. Will you tell us how to file suit on behalf of the Han tribe?" English repeated.

Polite leaned back in his chair, spreading his hands. "If you wish. I can tell you that this is an exercise in absolute futility, however. You don't stand a chance. Let me ask you one thing: do the Han want to take this to court?"

"No."

Polite sighed and turned his eyes to the corner of the room. "May I then ask what you're bothering for, Mr. English? Idealism? Profit? Notoriety?"

English's mouth tightened a little. Before he could answer they heard an uproar in the outer office. A woman speaking loudly and with authority.

"My one-o'clock appointment," Polite said, looking at his silver watch. "You'll have to excuse me now. Get back to me."

The door opened behind Hevatha, and Mrs. Hanna Sue Blythe swept into the room trailing a boa. She wore yellow, carried a fur muff, and had a delicate, tiny black hat pinned to her hair.

"Polite, it's past time. I don't sit waiting . . . Hevatha!" She smiled with delight and hugged her. "I didn't know you were in town. And you didn't come by to see me. Of course I wasn't home. There's this wretched business with Ford. He got drunk and ran down someone with my carriage. Only a miner, can't see why people make trouble over these things. And this is the elusive Mr. English, who buys red dresses for young ladies and leaves them sitting on the sidewalk."

She was smiling as she said that; her right hand, soft and ringed, emerged from her muff to shake Richard's hand. "Whatever are you two doing here? Claim dispute?"

"Something like that," English said.

Polite had risen as if to escort English and Hevatha from the room. Hanna Sue Blythe turned on him. "Sit down, Alex. I want to talk to my friends for a minute. Have you taken care of their problem?"

"No, Mrs. Blythe. Frankly, they have a problem the law can't do much about. A moral consideration."

"Moral? What's the Yukon know about morality?

What exactly is the problem?" She dropped into a padded leather chair and sat waiting. Hevatha explained the situation while Hanna Sue Blythe listened thoughtfully, occasionally pursing her lips to form words which never emerged. Finally she spoke.

"St. Ives and Aaron Butler. Slugs. Leeches. Both of them ought to be hanged on general principles. What's the matter with you, Alexander? Why don't you help these people out?"

"I really don't see the basis for a lawsuit, Mrs. Blythe," the lawyer answered crisply. "However—"

"However, hell! You're scared."

"I beg your pardon!" Polite drew himself up, placed his thumbs in his vest pockets, and scowled.

"I said you're scared. Taking on the territory and two of the Yukon's biggest swindlers scares you. How much does it scare you, Alexander?"

"I don't understand you," the lawyer answered.

"I'm asking you, darn it, how much it would take to get you interested in this case. It's got to hold some fascination for you, doesn't it? Standing up to the land grabbers, challenging the territory. Worried about your career? What if you win this case, Polite? Have you considered that? You'd be set for life, wouldn't you?"

"It's not winnable," Polite said unhappily.

"Nonsense. Any case can be won. Fair means or foul. The lawyer who talks the most carries the jury."

"Yes," Polite said skeptically. "Take this case before a jury of miners, men who want to get in on the rush for the Han gold, and tell me what kind of luck you think you'd have then!"

"Then we'll take it before the judge. Turnbull? I know Howard Turnbull, too. You've seen him, Hevatha, at Sarah Penner's party. Tall man with silver mustaches and sideburns which look like he wears 'em to keep his face warm. He's a decent man."

"No matter how decent he is," Polite argued, "he can't hand down a decision outside of legal precedents!"

"Ten thousand?" she asked in response, and Polite gawked at her. "Twenty thousand?"

"You'd be throwing your money away," the lawyer said, but his eyes had begun to reflect interest.

"Write down the fee you'd accept," Hanna Sue Blythe said. "Or steer us to a colleague who can use the money and isn't afraid of the case."

"This is not what we were going to discuss, Mrs. Blythe," Polite objected.

"No. For that other business, give the man whatever he thinks is fair. Ford ran him down."

"Mrs. Blythe . . ." Polite mopped at his forehead as if it were perspiring. He continued to argue but Hevatha noticed he had seated himself at his desk, drawn pen and inkwell to him, and written a number on a sheet of heavy paper. He folded the paper and walked with it to Hanna Sue Blythe. "You understand, if I fail in this, my career in the north would virtually be ended." With some shame he handed the paper to Mrs. Blythe, who only glanced at it and stuffed it into a pocket.

"Well, then, that's settled. Quickly, Mr. Polite. Those dignitaries are going to be leaving Dawson soon."

"It will take awhile to organize my brief, to find time on Judge Turnbull's docket."

"I'll talk to Howard Turnbull, don't worry about that. The morning," she said, rising, "will be soon enough. You get to those lawbooks of yours, Alexander. You find some way to save the Han land for them."

The young lawyer could only stand and look dismayed. Hanna nodded to Hevatha and English and with them swept out of the office. "He's a bright young man," Hanna told them outside. "He'll come up with something. He's got enough inducement to keep him at it."

"Why are you doing this?" Hevatha asked.

"Why? I owe you still, dear. Besides, it stirs things up, and I like things stirred up. Now, you two come up to the house and we'll have something to eat."

"We can't do that," English answered. "We have some other business to take care of."

"Anything I can help with?"

"I don't think so. We're going out to Yakima Brown's claim to talk to a man who works for him."

"About the Han gold?" Hanna asked.

"About the murder of Satchel Penner," English answered.

"I see." Hanna was silent for a long minute. Dawson bustled around them and roared past in heavy wagons, cursing and shouting. "Somebody's finally going to take a look at that."

"You have your suspicions?"

"Suspicions, yes. Let's walk a little, all right?" They turned east and walked up the plank walk past the hurrying townspeople.

Hanna said, "You know the story, that Satch Penner had a heart attack on his claim out at Little Chase Creek. Could have been, the way that man worked to keep his Philadelphia bride in the style she demanded, but it struck some of us as odd. One thing—within a week the bride was fooling around with Bertram St. Ives. Nothing too obvious, mind you, but he was seen at her house. Servants can see and talk too, you know. The other point that always struck me was that the widow wanted her husband buried where he was, out at Little Chase. Said that was where his heart was, or some such foolishness. Well, maybe so, but you know Sarah Penner. She wouldn't pass up the chance to do things in a big way. Ostentatious funeral, some kind of mausoleum for old Satch, in marble with angels standing on it."

"No one investigated?"

"Investigate a heart attack? The only law officer we've got is Boxer Thrush. You know Boxer, he's no coroner and he wasn't given cause to look into things. The widow was satisfied, no one else kicked up a fuss. Boxer, he wasn't going to go out of his way to make trouble."

"Gage Powers says there's an Indian named Toskobe who might know something about it."

"Toskobe? Don't recall that one. Maybe so. You're out to nail Butler one way or the other, is that it?"

English replied slowly, carefully, "I suppose so. I

hate to think it's personal, but it is. I don't like the man, I don't like what I've seen of St. Ives. I don't like to see the Han cheated."

"I'm going to do everything I can to help you out. My reasons are personal too, I guess. First off, I owe Hevatha something. Second, I'd hate to think that Sarah Penner got away with murder. Maybe our motives aren't so pure, but if we get the right results, well, it'll be of more benefit than sitting around with noble spirits having done nothing."

"I hope so," English answered.

"You know," Hanna said, stopping at a corner, "they won't let you do this without trying to strike back. St. Ives and Butler play rough. You're putting yourself and our young lady in danger."

Hevatha answered with a smile, "If we do not go ahead, what are we?"

"Well, I don't know. Me, I'm a natural coward. I said English and I didn't have such pure motives. You, Hevatha, you do, don't you? You want to do this for the Han, only for them. You're a saint, darlin'. English," she said threateningly, "you take care of this lady or you'll answer to me."

Then she was gone, walking straight across the muddy street, holding up an imperious hand to stop traffic.

"And now, English, what do we do?"

"Now we find Toskobe. Hevatha, I don't want you hurt. Are you worried about what they might do to us?"

"I have you, English," was all she said.

"Yes?"

"My life has been full," Hevatha went on. "I have no fear of death, only of life without purpose and love and justice."

"Yes. Without purpose, without love." He only stood there for a time, looking at nothing.

"You are silent. Listening?"

"Just listening," English answered. "To echoes of my life without you, Hevatha. Without purpose, without love." He grinned then and put his arm around her shoulders. "Let's go now. There isn't much time to waste."

Kiptah crossed the parquet floor to the dining room, hesitated, and went in. Aaron Butler sat alone in shirt sleeves with a bottle of brandy before him, toasting the empty room. She went to him and put her arms around him from behind. The man stiffened at her touch.

"Still here? I thought you were going shopping."

"Not yet. I am tired of shopping. I want you to touch me as you used to."

"Touch you," Aaron Butler said tonelessly, refilling his brandy glass.

"Yes, you made me happy. Everything you do makes me happy," Kiptah said, nuzzling his ear. Again she felt Butler go rigid. "Are you angry with me?" she asked.

"No." Butler didn't turn toward her. He drank his brandy and took a cigar from the neat row of dark cigars he had on the table before him. "Do you know, girl, that I've done what I came to the Yukon to do? I'm going to be one of the richest men in America. It took a long time, a lot of work, and some cleverness. Now I've got it, and I'm going to hold tight to it."

"We will go somewhere and spend all of the money."

"I think I'll stay on one more year and make sure everything's under control. Then San Francisco. I'll build a house there on Nob Hill. New York and Europe. A nice slow tour of the Continent. Run for office, maybe. State senator from California."

"And I will be with you," Kiptah said.

"You?" The question was virulent and mocking.

"I am your woman," Kiptah said, backing away a little, leaning around to look into Butler's dark face.

"Sure. Up here."

"Always."

"Look, Kippy, you can't be that stupid. I have ambitions. It won't do me any good to parade an Indian mistress around, and I don't have any intention of doing it."

"'What do you mean?" She sagged into a chair at the head of the highly polished table and sat, head cocked, watching Butler. Her pulse had begun to flutter in her throat.

"We've had fun, we've spent some money. That's all there is to it," Butler said casually.

"I am your woman! I showed you the gold. You took me to your bed! I left my husband and my baby, my people."

"You didn't leave them for me," Butler said, his face growing darker. "You left them for pretty things. All right, you've got your pretty things."

"What are you telling me?"

"You stupid squaw, what do you think I'm telling you?" Butler demanded, coming to his feet to stand unsteadily over her, weaving slightly, his eyes bright. "You got what you wanted. I got what I wanted. All right, it's over. Go on back to your husband, maybe he'll take you back."

"I cannot."

"Then go where you damn well please!" Butler said savagely.

"You only wanted to use me," Kiptah said, clutching her throat.

"Yes, and you didn't want to use me. Why, you stupid, grasping, ignorant thing. We had a partnership, you might say. The partnership is over. You've been paid for your trouble."

"But I love you!"

"Love me!" Butler spat. "You . . ." He lifted a hand if to hit her, looked at it, and lowered it again as if it were too much trouble. "I'm in a good mood now. Clear out. You can't have thought there was anything to this. No one could be that stupid, not even an Indian."

Kiptah rose shakily. She started to speak, started to shout, started to cry. She did none of those things in the end. She turned and walked away very slowly. From across the room she said, "But I love you."

"Get out," Butler said.

"If I don't . . . ?" Kiptah responded, coming nearer.

Butler stood and whirled in one motion and the fist at his side slammed into Kiptah's face. She fell to the floor, sliding across the polished parquetry. Dazed, she tried to rise and failed. Braced on her arms, she looked up at Aaron Butler.

"Get out now. I'll tell you in another way you'll like even less."

"I will go," Kiptah said. "I will go now. What do I do with my pretty things? Where can I take them? How will I live? My people won't take me back."

"Still got a red dress, don't you?" Aaron Butler asked. "You'll find a way to live."

Then he returned to the table and sat there drinking his brandy as Kiptah, leaning heavily against the sideboard, got to her feet and unsteadily started away toward the great staircase.

"Something wrong?" Jimmy Waley had appeared from the kitchen. He kept his distance from Aaron Butler, seeing the look in those eyes.

"Nothing. Get upstairs and help the woman pack, Jimmy."

"Kippy?"

"There another woman living here? Do it and get her out of my house. Now."

"Yes, sir." Waley stood there for a moment longer, watching Butler pour yet another glass of brandy. Then, moving silently, he crossed the room and went to the staircase.

Butler continued to sit and brood. His ambitions grew larger as he drank and his cold fury seemed to feed on the alcohol. Sasak was gone. Waley wasn't any good for what he had in mind . . .

"Bastard," Butler muttered to no one. Bastard English and his squaw. Went up to the Han hunting grounds and made trouble. In front of everyone. Bastard was always making trouble. What was he after, the gold? No. "Just wants to cut me down," Butler told himself. "He'll get what Demarest got. The two of them."

The anger came and then drifted away in a haze of brandy and cigar smoke. Upstairs someone threw something. Butler smiled. Well, it was time the squaw was gone. No sense beating around the bush with her. Sure, she had been useful, and she wasn't all that bad in bed, but he didn't need an Indian tagging along. Maybe Sarah Penner was tired of St. Ives by now. What kind of lover could he be? If not Sarah Penner, well, there were lots of lovely society girls in Frisco, in New York. For a man with gold . . .

The front door banged open, banged shut. Bertram St. Ives stormed through the house, calling Butler's name. When he found his partner, Butler stood, smiling. "Have a drink, St. Ives. Don't want to celebrate by myself. We're rich, my man."

"Rich, yes. You know what's happening?" St. Ives threw his hat down on the floor.

"What's happening?" Butler asked from out of the fog of brandy.

"English. English and that Indian woman of his. My God, Butler, they've filed suit against us over this Han thing!"

"Filed suit? Ridiculous."

"Maybe so, but they've done it. I just saw Judge Turnbull. The old fox was enjoying it, enjoying telling me about it. They'll have us in court, Butler."

"So what?" Butler said. "Everything's on the up-and-up."

"Is it, now? Legal, maybe, but they'll have us in court, have us in the newspapers. Some of our friends in the capital are liable to bail out and let us take it on the chin."

"They can't take the land lease back!" Butler grunted as the implications of a trial sank into his mind.

"I don't know." St. Ives ran his hand through his hair and reached for the brandy decanter. "I don't know what they can do. I've talked to George Greenwood. His legal opinion is they don't have a chance. But you never know. But think about this: if we have to appeal or have a delayed decision, what happens? The Han are pulling out. That country will be crawling with prospectors overnight. We'd have to hire an army to keep them out. Once it comes out in court that the Han land is a rich strike, the poachers will kill us!"

"The Han are pulling out, you say?" Butler asked.

St. Ives was scowling. "What's that got to do with any damn thing?"

"This—there's only one man who gives a damn enough to carry through with this, isn't there?"

"English, sure, but—"

"Then," Aaron Butler said with a soft smile, "don't worry about it, Bertram. Richard English will never see the inside of that courtroom. Don't be so nervous. Have a drink. I'll take care of English."

"The way you always take care of our problems."

"That's right," Butler answered, "the way I always take care of things."

13

IT was already nearly dark when English and Hevatha returned to their cabin on the little creek. In the hazy, half-lighted sky the aurora borealis dueled with the low amber-colored sun. Rosy waves of coldly brilliant light streaked with coruscating bars of greenish white blotted out the northern stars. Across the forest, wolves howled in protest or appreciation or primitive accord.

Smoke still rose from the cabin. The tent was a wind-drifted collection of canvas and ash. Nothing stood, nothing remained. The camp was gone, supplies, bed, blankets. And the cabin. The frustrating, demanding, tilted, ugly collection of logs that was home was gone. There was nothing left.

"Lost," English said. He appeared numb and perhaps frightened. Hevatha touched his arm. "They wouldn't even let us have that."

They crossed the stream, splashing through the cold, shallow water. Numbly English surveyed the cabin, walking through the ashes. He kicked at a small, scorched section of canvas which had been a wall of their tent and stood staring at the northern lights, cold, bright, unreal.

"Demarest lost, Tyee lost. McCulloch. The gold, the Han land, the cabin. Everything lost, Hevatha. *Enfants perdus.*"

"What did you say, English?"

"Lost children. You and I. How can we form this world, beat them?"

"We will keep fighting, that is all."

"And lose again?"

"We will keep fighting," she repeated.

"He knows now. Butler knows we're taking him to court."

"And he is worried," Hevatha said. "He is worried or he would not have had this done."

"That does us a lot of good."

English was gloomy, feeling half-defeated. Hevatha rubbed his neck and stood near him, her face shining oddly in the strange light of evening.

"Let us make our bed, English. Let us sleep and worry about these things tomorrow. The house is burned. We will build another house. Our blankets are gone; we will find another blanket."

"Make our bed? Where?"

"Anywhere. We will hollow out a sleeping place, you and I, beneath the pines as we have done before. We shall make a bed of pine boughs and cover ourselves over with their warmth. I will cling to you and you will be with me, among me, and the night will be warm, as it will be forever for the two of us."

"The three," English said.

"Yes, the three of us. Don't fear for the baby. He is warm and safe and loved and protected. Don't worry for me. I am not a woman who demands much, English, you know that. I only want you. And don't worry for your own sake. I am here; I love you; I will keep you from the night, always."

There was one blanket left, the corner of it burned. With that and nothing else they made their bed in the trees. They scooped out a hollow and filled it with pine boughs cut from the surrounding forest. With the blanket over them they covered themselves with more boughs. They were a crude but effective insulation against the chill of the night, crude and ancient, developed by the Indians in the times before houses, before blankets. As was Hevatha's method of warming her man, of keeping the night and its cold, its dark fears away.

She lay beside him and she held him and her body was warmth and comfort, her breath the breath of spring against his cheek and his ear, her hands gentle and comforting as she clung to him. English could look upward through the pines and see the night stars, the faint glow of the aurora, the softer light of the burned-out sun to the south. She touched him and there was no other necessary warmth in the world, no need or aspiration, no hunger or want. He had his Hevatha and the rest of the world could sink to snow and ash and stone.

The stars misted and doubled and drifted crazily and Hevatha touched his cheek. "A tear, Richard English? For me?"

He didn't answer; he wasn't sure that he could. He simply drew her nearer and let the night pass, unable to sleep even when Hevatha's gentle breathing, the slight involuntary movements of her body, told him that she was asleep and dreaming and content. He hugged her tightly, kissing her hair, and then, afraid that he would disturb her sleep, he lay back, one arm under his head, to watch the night, the universe, and his time and hers shift slowly, inevitably toward its end.

With the morning they rose and started toward Little Chase Creek. Yakima Brown himself was sitting on the porch of his cabin, rocking back and forth in a rickety rocking chair, watching the snow drip from the roof of his shack and from the surrounding pines. He lifted a hand but did not rise as the two of them walked up the path to his cabin.

"English, ain't it? What brings you this way?" Yakima asked.

The two shook hands and English said, "We wanted to talk to a man who's supposed to be working for you."

"Which one?"

"His name is Toskobe," Hevatha said.

"Toskobe?" Yakima scratched his neck. "If you can get that one to talk, you're doing something. He don't speak much. Matter of fact, I used to think he was mute."

"He worked for Satchel Penner, didn't he?" English asked.

"Yes, he did." Yakima's eyes grew curious. "That what you're interested in, Satch's death?"

"Well . . ." English decided to be forthright. He had a feeling the millionaire prospector would know if he wasn't. "Yes. I think Satchel Penner was murdered."

"Been talkin' to Gage Powers?" Yakima asked. A crow swooped low, cawing loudly, and Yakima Brown glanced at it.

"Yes."

"Gage always held that somethin' was wrong there. Me, I don't know." The bony shoulders lifted in a shrug. "What causes you to be curious about this?"

"I think Bertram St. Ives or Aaron Butler, or both, did it."

"Still feudin' with Butler?"

"It's more than that, but there's no need to go into all of it."

"No, I guess not." Yakima pointed toward the trees. "See that man? The Indian. He's got a Winchester and a dead eye. I've got six of 'em around me. Know why? St. Ives and Butler. They won't try Yakima Brown's claim. I don't intend to have no accidents. You're right about 'em, they're bad and the Yukon would be better off with both of 'em planted deep. As far as talkin' to Toskobe, well, you're welcome to if he wants to talk. You'll find him up near the mule shack. See that gray building through the cedars? Let me know what happens, will you?"

English promised he would. With Hevatha he started toward the weathered building among the trees. The man called Toskobe was leaning against a sun-warmed wall, watching them with narrow eyes. He wore a fur hat, badger-skin jacket, twill pants, and fringed black boots.

"Toskobe?"

The Indian didn't respond. Hevatha and English walked to him, English stretching out a hand, which the Indian only glanced at.

"We want to talk to you about something. About the death of Satchel Penner."

The Indian simply stared. Silence was his way of dealing with the world, of avoiding white men's problems and their repercussions.

"Hevatha? Maybe he'll talk to you."

"Maybe. What shall I tell him, English, what shall I ask?"

"Tell him what this means to the Indian, to the Han and others. The Ingalik Indian too, perhaps."

English withdrew a little way. He watched Hevatha, watched her approach the man and ask him something in a soft voice. Still the Ingalik was silent. Then, astonishingly, Hevatha began to berate him, to jab her finger at him, to yell at him. Toskobe, startled, grew angry and then thoughtful and finally he answered Hevatha, saying something English could not hear. Hevatha laughed and Toskobe actually smiled.

It was another minute before Hevatha walked back to where English waited, Toskobe behind her.

"He wants to talk to Yakima Brown," she said.

"You learned something?"

"Maybe. He's afraid of being entangled in white affairs, of being locked up in jail. He says his brother reported a white man for stealing his dog team and the brother, not the white, was locked up while the court decided what to do. In the end the white went free and Toskobe's brother lost his dogs."

Toskobe needed reassurance. "These people want something," he said to Yakima Brown. "I don't know what. Do you want me to talk to them?"

Yakima, in his rocking chair again, studied English and Hevatha. "I think we can talk to them, Toskobe. Want me to come along and listen in?"

"You wont let them put me in white jail, Yakima Brown?"

"My best man! Why, Toskobe, if Boxer Thrush ever locked you up, we'd come and tear the jailhouse down."

Toskobe thought it over. He looked upriver to where twenty men hired by Yakima Brown worked at his claim. "Then we had better talk," Toskobe said. "Come, I will show you."

It was a long trek over the piny hills and across a grassy, snow-patched valley to the Penner Company's strike. They had given up on the streambed there and were working hydraulics, huge steam-driven pumps spraying out thousands of gallons of water against the banks above the river, toppling great trees as they washed the earth open, seeking new veins of gold.

"His grave," Yakima said, panting a little, "is next to the company offices."

Hevatha and English looked toward the two-story white clapboard building where horses were hitched and a surrey waited for its owner.

"Not there," Toskobe said flatly, and they looked at him.

"What do you mean? That's where they buried Satch. I was there," Yakima said.

"Buried there, not dead there. An empty box for the whites to pray over."

"You're sure?" Yakima asked.

"I am sure." Now that Toskobe had made up his mind, he showed no reluctance to push through to the conclusion of this business. "The old shaft, Number Two."

"Where's that?" English asked.

"Number Two"—Yakima pointed toward the hills. "Satch hadn't worked that for years."

"The men told him there was new gold," Toskobe said. He looked with some concern toward the bustling gold camp. "We will go this way, in the trees."

They followed him upward, crossed a narrow creek where fern grew among tall, moss-covered boulders, and came finally to a barren stretch of land where the cold winds blew. Tree stumps and tailings and a litter of rusted cans covered the gray earth. Ahead a massive pit had been bored into the ground.

Toskobe took them there and stood looking down. "Someone pushed earth in, caved in the shaft."

"He's down there?" Yakima asked.

"Down there." The Indian pointed. Now he looked worried again. Perhaps he didn't like being around the dead, perhaps his old fear of being involved in white disputes had returned.

"Let's have a look, then," Yakima said, shedding

his coat. English took off his coat as well. Toskobe looked around nervously.

"Hevatha will watch," English said, and the Indian gave the woman his rifle, shaking his head.

The three men slid into the depths of the pit, gravel and loose stone following them downward through the old timbers and over boulders.

Toskobe spoke in a hushed voice. "This way, I think. I saw them from the trees, but I did not see which way they went. Only the two men coming down; only the one man coming back."

"Which man?" English asked, turning toward Toskobe.

From out of the soft, cold darkness the Indian answered, "The man with the pocked face, the man with the big mustache. Aaron Butler."

"When was this, Toskobe?"

"One year. Before the first snow."

Yakima interrupted them. "Come over here," he hissed.

English hurried over the rubble, a loose stone rolling under his foot. Yakima was standing hunched, motionless. He pointed. "Sleeve of something," he said.

And it was. The sleeve of a leather jacket with something hooked, broken, yellowed poking from it. The hand of a dead man. The weather and the insects had done a clean job. There was no flesh at all on the bones. English crouched, touched a finger joint, and it broke away.

"Clear the rubble off," he said hoarsely. His own throat was choked; Toskobe made a muffled gagging sound.

Yakima did most of the work. The old prospector had seen his share of death and lifeless men. "All right," he said at last, his face ashen in the dim light. "There it is, that's it." And he bent to pick up the skull. In the back of it was a squarish hole from which fracture marks radiated. Yakima, crouching, looked up and said, "Pickax. From behind." He made to hand the skull to English, but Richard's hand refused to stretch out and take it.

"Are we sure? Sure this is Satchel Penner?"

Yakima held up a section of skeletal finger. There was a gold wedding ring on it. It was engraved inside: "S.P. from Sarah."

"I guess," Yakima said, "we're sure."

"We should not be in this place," Toskobe said, looking up toward the gray patch of sky above the tunnel. He might have been superstitious, but no one argued with him. There was an unholy sensation beneath the earth where the dead man lay, something vague, musty, and unhealthy which nudged each man's knowledge of mortality and caused them to scramble out far more quickly than they had gone in.

"Well?" Hevatha came with the rifle and handed it to Toskobe, who took it and turned away. Then she saw the skull in Brown's hands. She nodded. "So. All of it true."

"All of it true," English answered. He wanted to touch her, to hold her, to feel her life, but the nearness of death was palpable, holding him back.

"It's enough," Brown said shakily, "to maybe get Butler convicted of murder."

"But what about the Han, will it help them?" Hevatha asked.

"I don't know. There's one other point." English looked at Toskobe, who had wandered away some distance, studying the grass intently. "Butler can't be convicted unless Toskobe testifies that he went down in that shaft. Toskobe won't do it voluntarily and we've promised him he won't have to go to court. I won't go back on that promise."

"Nor will I," Yakima said. "I've seen too much double-dealing with these Indians. We can tell about stumbling across this, I guess, but what does that do to get Butler and St. Ives hanged?"

"We can at least prove he was murdered," English said, but that wasn't enough in itself and they all knew it. Toskobe paused and shot them a wary glance. "We'll see. We'll just have to see."

"Let's get away from here," Yakima said, and it wasn't apparent if he was suffering from the jitters himself for just wanted to be cautious with Penner guards around the area.

They swung far wider than they had on arriving, working their way through thick, cool forest where squirrels scolded the intruders, and once a prowling lynx moved away from their approach hissing.

Back at Yakima Brown's camp Toskobe returned to his post without a word, still obviously concerned that he had done the worst thing he could do—trust his fate to the whites.

"He'll be all right," Yakima said. He distastefully placed the skull in a burlap sack, the gold ring on his little finger.

"Thanks, Yakima," English said. 'We couldn't have done it without you." English reached out for the sack, but Brown shook his head.

"No you don't. I'm coming along. Think I'm going to miss the end of this?"

"All right." English grinned. "You're welcome to see it." He looked at the sky. "We've got time enough to get to Dawson, I think." He looked at Hevatha. "Will Hanna Sue Blythe put us up for tonight?"

"She has offered, English."

"Hanna, huh? Fine strong woman," Yakima said, and English and Hevatha smiled. Yakima muttered, "Far as women go, that is. Far as they go."

It was ten miles to town and they walked it without incident, Yakima carrying the grisly trophy. Hanna Sue Blythe herself opened the front door to her huge house when they reached it.

She hugged Hevatha, ushered her in, took English's hand briefly, and squinted at Yakima Brown. "You owe me two dances, " she snapped.

"Had to leave early," Brown mumbled.

"Got drunk, you mean. Men." She led them into her parlor which was all blue satin, white antimacassars, braided rugs, and sepia etchings. A fire glowed softly behind a brass screen. "Yakima, there's whiskey there. I'll be watchin' how much you guzzle."

Yakima walked immediately to the sideboard, speaking in undertones about women. Hevatha sat in a huge overstuffed blue chair and crossed her legs. English paced nervously despite Hanna's injunctions to sit and relax. Standing with his back to the fire as Yakima swallowed his first drink in a gulp, Richard told the lady what they had discovered.

Hanna Sue Blythe stared at the burlap sack in fascination. Since she seemed not to be watching, Yakima poured another three fingers of bonded bourbon into a lead-crystal glass and drank that on the heels of his first drink.

"It doesn't surprise me," Hanna said. "Still, when you have your worst suspicions confirmed, it's unsetting. Did Sarah Penner put them up to it?"

"It looks like it. Why else bury Satch out at the claim?"

"You'll never prove it in court."

"No. Worse, I don't think we can prove Butler did it."

"No witnesses?" Hanna asked.

Yakima glanced at English, who answered, "No, I'm afraid not."

Hanna Sue Blythe was an astute woman. "I see. Well, don't tell me, then." Her eyes narrowed and then she rose with a shrug. "Watch that whiskey, Yakima," she snapped. She herself walked to the sideboard and poured a glass of sherry. "I've talked with Judge Turnbull. He was willing to hear this case sometime in the next century. I pointed out to him that the government people would be long gone by then. I also pointed out the matter of five thousand dollars the judge owes me. We go into court tomorrow morning at eight o'clock."

"Whole thing's a waste of time," Yakima said gloomily.

"You think so?" Hanna asked.

"Sure it is. Han are gone. Indians can't testify in court anyway. We got nothing on Butler, nothing on St. Ives or Mizz Penner. They got the government on their side . . . and the law. They got the 'X' of the Han chief on a treaty. We got ourselves a situation where the best we can get out of this is a little humiliation; the worst, maybe a knife across the throat on some dark night after Butler thinks everyone's forgotten." He slugged his drink down. "And that is what I think."

"Why don't you go on home, then, Yakima," Hanna said harshly.

"And miss it? Not on your life. Besides," he said, pouring again, "I like your whiskey."

"You like any whiskey." Hanna looked again at the burlap sack, distaste and curiosity mingling in her eyes. "Well, I guess we'd better go to bed. I'll have Ford and one of the other men stand watch tonight." She touched her throat. "I'm not quite ready to have this powdered and too-wrinkled neck of mine slashed."

Hevatha and English were given a bed in an upstairs room. Hevatha looked at it in wonder, walked to it, tested it with her palms, and then plopped down on it, bouncing up and down.

"You've never been on a bed!" English realized.

"No. Not the kind that moves and bounces." It amused her.

English sat beside her. "We will sleep on other beds, we'll ride trains and steamboats, we'll do strange and wonderful things together, Hevatha, when we've finished with this business."

"As you wish, English," she said, and lay back on the bed, her dark eyes softly lighted. English went down to her and kissed her, then made gentle love to her before he fell off to sleep.

Hevatha slept too, but it was a troubled sleep. The wolves wandered her dreams, and the Iht, with a handful of black sticks. She awoke sharply once, her heart palpitating rapidly. She looked to her yellow-haired man, sleeping quietly, and she rolled to him to hold him as the dreams dissipated and became only haunting echoes in the back of her mind.

At eight o'clock the next morning Hevatha, English, and Hanna Sue Blythe entered the courtroom, Hanna brushing aside the bailiff who pointed out the "No Indians in Court" sign.

They marched up to the front of the courtroom,

where Butler and St. Ives, appearing irritable, sat surrounded by a group of government representatives and two lawyers. Alexander Polite, drawn and agitated, was watching them, hurrying them along with his eyes.

He looked at Hevatha and winced inwardly. Hanna seated herself with showy aplomb. In another minute Judge Turnbull appeared, his severe face wreathed in long silver sideburns. He glanced at Hanna as the court rose and then was seated again. The look was that of a man who had had a dirty trick pulled on him.

His eyes then settled on Hevatha, and the severity of his expression was intensified. English glanced around the courtroom, spotting Sarah Penner and Gage Powers. The attorney for the defendants was George Greenwood. He immediately moved for a dismissal of the suit.

"Even in this rural, rustic bailiwick," Greenwood said with gravity, his hands in his trouser pockets, heavy brows drawn together, "it ought to be obvious that the charges brought before this court are vacuous, substanceless, and frivolous. We have here"—he picked up a copy of the treaty signed by Cuah and the council—"a legal, well-witnessed document condoned by the territorial commission, giving over to Mr. St. Ives and his partner, Aaron Butler, of the Great Northern Exploratory Company, exclusive mineral rights to the former hunting grounds of a band of Han Indians called the Besna. The terms were understood by all parties, agreeable to all parties, duly witnessed and signed." Greenwood made a vast gesture of contempt and disgust. "The only injured parties here are our busy legislators and these representatives of Great Northern, who are being forced to waste their time enduring this folly."

Greenwood tossed the treaty down and seated himself. The judge, with a glance at Hanna Sue Blythe, refused to dismiss the charges at that point, although his expression was uneasy.

Polite was brittle and as uneasy as Turnbull when he stood and explained that the complainant, Richard English, was convinced that the Han band had no idea what they were signing away, that in effect business and government interests had deceived the Han Indians.

Greenwood spent a lot of time clearing his throat during the rather nervous speech Alexander Polite had prepared. Papers were rustled and men yawned furiously. The judge appeared more unsettled with each passing moment. His career too, he reckoned, was on the line. He might have owed Hanna money, but he could easily visualize his reputation in ashes, and the inevitable mockery.

"I ask the court to allow the plaintiff to speak," Polite said finally, and at a nod from Turnbull, the lawyer took his seat with apparent relief as Richard English strode forward to face the court.

"What we are presenting to the court," English said, "is a moral issue. I've been informed that the Great Northern company has given the Han band approximately twenty thousand dollars in merchandise for mineral rights which may be valued in the tens of millions. These are a simple people. They were given what was to them vast wealth, but the fact remains that the distance between the true worth of their land and what they were compensated for is vast and deliberately immoral. The chief of the Han does not speak English or write or understand the value of gold. A people have been deprived of their wealth so that Great Northern and the government might prosper as the land is developed."

English glanced around. His speech had no effect except to deepen the boredom of most of those present. One of the government representatives was glancing at his watch.

Greenwood rose to his feet slowly, his hand up as he objected. "Your honor!" he said, his face showing suffering caused by the ignorance of English and all of his kind. "Let me applaud this young man for his moral conscience; let me also remind the court that no part of the judiciary body is required to measure or mete morality. We have a country full of parsons who draw themselves up to the pulpit each sabbath just for

that purpose." Greenwood drew the appreciative tit-
ters he was seeking. "What we are seeking to do here,"
he said with forcefulness, "is to substantiate or ne-
gate the validity of a legal document, one that has the
laws of this territory behind it in form and substance.
What has this lecture on morality to do with this
document?"

Greenwood again slumped into his seat, outrage
and bemusement on his face. English turned toward
the court, seeing nothing but rows of blank or amused
faces. Those present had come for a show. English
couldn't even give them that. He looked to Polite, but
the lawyer had obviously given the case up before he
had even entered the courtroom.

"I will speak."

Heads turned toward the woman's voice. Hevatha
rose and walked toward the judge. "Now, I will speak."

"Your honor," Greenwood said as if he were in
pain. "I object. The laws of the territory are quite
clear about the rights of an Indian in a court of law.
It's necessary for a white lawyer to present—"

"Quite right, sustained," Turnbull said.

Hevatha hadn't returned to her seat. She spoke to
the judge, who was looking at Hanna with an uncomfortable expression. "This is a strange law," Hevatha
said. "This is a matter which concerns the Han, but
where are the Han? Someone stands to speak for the
Han, and the law says: this is another Indian, she
cannot speak." She turned toward the gallery. No one
had moved to take her back to her seat, although the
bailiff was poised to do just that if the judge directed.

"All over this town I see signs, 'No Indians.' Everywhere I go, and it makes me wonder. What if the
Indians had put up signs, 'No Whites'? But the Han
did not do that. The Han welcomed you to their land.
Their land now grows smaller and smaller. You came
and you grow wealthy while the Han grow fewer and
poorer as their hunting grounds are taken.

"Someone here said 'What has this to do with morality?' What has morality to do with your law? I
don't know. When the whites came, they first sent

missionaries and they told the Indians, 'What you are doing is not right. You must be Christian and give up your savage ways. You do not understand morality like the whites do; we will teach you.' "

"Your honor, please," Greenwood said wearily.

"One minute, Mr. Greenwood," the judge said. The signal flashed by Hanna's eyes was quite clear.

Hevatha, her head down, hands behind her back, paced the floor. "The missionaries came," she went on, "and told us not to kill, not to steal. But the whites killed Indians. But the whites gave the Han a few blankets for much gold. The men who did this knew it was wrong, they know it now." She looked at Butler and St. Ives. Butler crossed his legs and arms and looked away.

"The white way is the new way, the way things will be," Hevatha told the court. "That cannot be changed. But the Han who live in the old way must not be cheated or driven away or left behind as wealth comes to their land. The whites have told us they have a duty to the Indian, to convert him, to make him welcome in the modern world. When does this begin? When will he start helping the Han? When will his laws stop cheating the Indian? If I understand, that can be done here. It can be started here by one man. You, Judge, can say, 'A wrong is being done to the Han, let us remedy it.' But will you say it? Or will you be silent and think to yourself: 'What does it matter? They are only Indians.' "

"I really must object to all of this as irrelevant, your honor," Greenwood said. He was on his feet now, as was his silent associate.

"Irrelevant?" Hevatha said. "Do I understand this word? Do you mean that what happens to the Han, to their land, to their gold, is not important here? What else are we discussing?" she asked with a sharp laugh. "We are here to decide what is fair for the Han, but when someone mentions it, it is *irrelevant?* Is it because the Han did not write this down on paper and give it to a white lawyer, another man who would make money from them? I am sad," Hevatha said. Her

mouth tightened a little. She touched her forehead
with her fingertips and went to stand before the judge,
placing her hands on his bench.

"You are the man who must decide what will happen, whether the Han should not be given a fair por-
tion of the gold taken from their land. You are the
man who must decide if morality belongs in this courtroom, you are the man. Do what is justice."

She turned then and walked back to her seat, a
murmuring from the gallery following her.

Judge Turnbull watched her for a moment and then
shifted his eyes. He had his hand before his face when
he said, "No evidence has been presented to this court
to indicate that the contract between the Great Northern company, the Territory of the Yukon, and the
Han Indians concerning the mineral rights on the property formerly considered the hunting grounds of said
tribe is illegal, produced through coercion, forged, or
otherwise invalid. The only decision the court can
reach—" He moved his hand from his face as the back
door to the courtroom slammed open and Yakima
Brown appeared, striding down the aisle as heads
turned. In his hand was a burlap sack.

"Please, Mr. Brown!"

"Settle down, Turnbull," Yakima said. "I figured as
long as we have everybody in place here, we might as
well have a look at something I come across."

"I'm in the middle of—"

English had his eyes on Butler. Butler knew. He
knew what was in that sack. St. Ives touched Butler
on the arm, turning a worried, ferret face to the big
man. Yakima had marched to the front of the courtroom to stand there, sack in hand.

"What in the name of God are you doing!" Turnbull
asked. "Sit down or I'll have the bailiff—"

Aaron Butler leapt from his seat and with a pistol in
hand charged toward Brown. A woman screamed;
Yakima spun, flinging the sack at Butler as his pistol
discharged. The skull went rolling across the floor as
Butler fired again into the belly of the bailiff who had

drawn his pistol. People dived for the floor. English half-rose and was yanked back by Hevatha.

Butler was intent on making it to the door behind the judge's bench, the one leading to Turnbull's chambers. The judge leapt up to try to stop Butler, and Butler shot him point-blank through the head. Someone in the back of the courtroom cut loose with a wild, ill-advised shot over the heads of the spectators and his bullet slammed into the lintel over the door, spraying splinters. By then Butler was through.

There was a moment before anyone else could move; then a mad charge led by Boxer Thrush, his gun now drawn, reached the door, finding it locked. By the time it was battered down, all they found was an open window. Aaron Butler was gone.

Thrush, in a dither, talking to himself, reentered the courtroom, gun still in hand. He looked at the skull on the floor, at Yakima Brown, who looked no more disturbed than he would at a Sunday picnic.

"What's going on? What's that?" the constable demanded.

"That is what's left of Satchel Penner, Boxer." St. Ives had risen stealthily and was moving through the crowd toward the door. "I'd stop that one if I were you," Brown said. He pointed toward the blond lady in pink. "And I'd have a little chat with Mrs. Sarah Penner."

"They killed him?" Boxer asked.

Yakima toed the skull until it rolled over, revealing the square hole in back. Boxer Thrush nodded. "St. Ives? Hold up there. Mrs. Penner, please keep your seat, ma'am."

It took awhile to get organized. Thrush spoke to another judge; Turnbull was covered with his robes and finally taken away; witnesses were interviewed. Finally the court was cleared, everyone moving out in silence, bursting into rapid, excited conversation as soon as they cleared the courthouse doors.

English, Hevatha, and Hanna Sue Blythe stood aside. The skies were cloudy; it was cold enough to snow.

"Butler's finished, probably the other two as well,"

Hanna said. She glanced at Yakima Brown, who had come to stand beside them.

"The Han are finished," English said.

"What?" They almost seemed to have forgotten the Han and their treatment. English slipped his arm through Hevatha's waist and held her.

"The Han. You heard Turnbull handing down his decision. If we went to court again, we'd hear the same result, wouldn't we?"

"Butler is a murderer, St. Ives a thief."

"Yes. Maybe the government will have to take over operation of the Great Northern. Maybe Aaron Butler will finally hang. That won't do the Han a bit of good," English pointed out.

Someone called out and a way was cleared for Boxer Thrush, who walked grimly through the crowd, holding Sarah Penner's elbow. The woman was chalk white, obviously frightened. Her little pink hat had shifted to one side of her head.

St. Ives was escorted by a deputy. He complained and threatened. "What is all this? I'll have your badge, Thrush. I'll sue you and this town for false arrest. Where is your warrant?"

"I'll get a warrant as soon as I have a chance to talk to a live judge," they heard Boxer Thrush say, and then the procession was gone, the onlookers drifting away in pairs and threes.

"It just doesn't help the Han a bit," English said again.

"You two come over to the house and warm up," Hanna said. "You too, Yakima, if you'll stay sober."

"Thank you, but I don't think we will," Richard answered.

"No?"

He looked at Hevatha, who nodded her agreement. "No, I think we've had enough of Dawson. It's going to snow. We'll head south, I think, to be with our people."

"Your people?" Hanna was perplexed.

"The Han. I think we'll stay with them awhile if they'll let us."

"You're more than welcome at the house, English. Hevatha."

"English is right," Hevatha said. "We will go to the Han. When summer comes again, we will travel on."

"Travel on? Where?" Brown asked.

"To the States." It was too much to explain just then, and Brown seemed to need no other explanation.

Hanna kissed Hevatha and held her arms a minute. "It's been good to know you, Hevatha. Darn it all, you've taught me something. Not that it'll do me any good. I'm to used to being who *I* am!" She laughed briefly, shook her head, took Yakima's arm, and guided him toward her waiting carriage.

"Now we will go?" Hevatha asked.

"Yes." English looked around him at the bustling, roaring town. "Now we will go."

"I am sorry, English," Hevatha said as they started on.

He looked at her fine profile, her long lashes, those serious dark eyes. "Sorry? About what, Hevatha?"

"Sorry that you did not get your gold. You came to the Yukon wanting that, wanting to take something back with you, to seek and discover."

"Yes, and I have done all of that. All that is missing is the gold, and at this moment, Hevatha, I swear to you I'd cast it out into that muddy street and walk away from it happily. I came to the Yukon and sought and learned and lost. I miss Demarest and Tyee more than I could miss any amount of gold; I have you. I've grown, I hope, and learned, and I have you, the two of you."

"Still . . ."

"Hush." He stopped her, turned her and kissed her, having the satisfaction of watching her mouth blossom into a smile, deep and loving. "There is no 'still,' there is nothing else in the world, woman."

English felt the cool dampness touch his hand and he looked upward, watching as the snow began to swirl downward out of a September sky. They hurried on then. There was too much to do, there was a world to see.

*   *   *

He crouched in the darkness of the supply shack, a hunted thing, hearing a voice now and then, voices which caused him to withdraw deeper into the dense shadow of the shack. Where in hell was Waley?

If the kid got there with Spellbinder, Aaron Butler could show Dawson his heels. No animal alive was going to catch that big horse, and if the snow held back long enough that a horse could still travel, Butler with his hideaway fund—fifty thousand in U.S. currency—could reach the coast and be out of the North before anyone in Juneau or beyond could even be notified. Then Frisco, and on to the Dakota scheme Lou Schuyler had been hatching.

The sound outside the shack brought Butler's head up; he drew back the hammer on his Remington .36-caliber revolver. His hand was shaking slightly as he lifted the muzzle of the pistol toward the door, and it annoyed him.

Kiptah slipped in the door and closed it behind her. She wore a fur coat and hat, black gloves and boots.

"What are you doing here? How'd you find me?"

"Waley told me," she answered.

"The idiot!"

"He knew I would tell no one. I know what has happened. I have come to go with you."

"To go with me," Butler repeated angrily.

Kiptah moved to him and touched his shoulder. "You are my man. There is trouble. We will go to another white village and live."

"Are you stupid?" Butler asked. He sagged into a wooden chair, placing his gun on the table before him. "Didn't I tell you to go back to your people? Didn't I tell you I didn't want you?"

"You were angry, you said many things."

"Where in hell's Waley! I've got to get moving."

Kiptah knelt before Butler, her hand on his knee. "Now you need me; now you have only me. I will stay with you and be loyal."

Butler's hand slashed across her face, the knuckles drawing blood from Kiptah's mouth. He took her by the arms, fingers digging into her flesh, shaking her until her head bobbed and her eyes stood out.

"I want one thing from you, Kippy; get out of here! I don't want you and I never did. What would any man want with some painted-up squaw woman? You make me sick, touching you makes me sick." He threw her aside and she lay sprawled on the floor, motionless. Her fur hat had flown off to lie beside her hand on the oily earthen floor. When Butler rose, he stepped on it. A horse could be heard walking toward the shack and Butler eased to the door, peering out.

"Finally," he said under his breath. He turned back to grab his coat, hat, and gun.

Kiptah had already picked up the revolver. On her knees, she pointed the gun at Butler. The hammer was back, her finger on the trigger.

"Look, girl, like you say, I lose my temper," Butler said affably. He moved to his right a little and the muzzle of the gun followed him. "I just lost my temper. You understand," he said, speaking quickly. "You can go with me to Frisco. We can live together, live well. I'll show you a lot of sights."

"You are evil," Kiptah said. Blood trickled from the corner of her girlish mouth. Her dark hair hung over one eye, unpinned, unheeded.

"I told you how it was." Butler laughed. He glanced at the door, wishing for Waley to come in, to distract the girl. He wanted only to be on his way, to be done with this stupid woman, and off on Spellbinder. "You wouldn't shoot me, Kippy. Think of the fun we've had! Why don't you give me the gun?"

He stuck out his hand and Kiptah pulled the trigger. A ball of white-hot fire bored through Aaron Butler's belly and he staggered backward against the wall of the shack. Powder smoke, thick and acrid, clogged the interior of the building. The shot echoed endlessly in his ears. And then he heard no sound, saw nothing as sudden darkness hammered him down into oblivion.

Jimmy Waley burst through the door, uttered a small surprised curse, and crossed to where Kiptah had risen shakily. He took the gun from her hand and she leaned against him. From up the street Waley could hear shouts.

"Get out of here," he said, shoving her away. "The horse outside—get on it and ride. Now!"

"You . . ." Kiptah said.

Waley still held the pistol. Glancing down at it, he answered, "Hell, they'll probably give me a medal."

Kiptah looked again at Waley and then once at the body of Aaron Butler. Then she was gone, out the door and onto Spellbinder's back, riding away from the shack.

In another minute Boxer Thrush and two deputies appeared in the shack and Waley surrendered the gun.

14

THE snow fell steadily. They walked southward through the storm, following the trail of the Han. In the pines the snow wasn't deep and they had hopes of making the Han camp by the big lake that day. They talked little. The wind and the walking were against it. Hevatha was cheerful; there was a new world before them. A safe, warm winter among friends, and then southward into new lands. English was introspective, juggling the opposing thoughts that he had done all he could; that he had accomplished nothing at all. Maybe, however, the Han needed nothing more than they had, and the loss of the gold and its purchasing power meant less to the Indians than he believed. The Han could hunt, fish, live on. Yet the world was closing in on them. Oblivious of that, they were content with the old ways. One day it would not be enough to know how to fish and tan green hides; English could only hope that that day was a long way off.

They walked through the clearing storm and emerged from the trees to cross a long stream-cut meadow. The Tlingit seemed to rise from the snow. His face was painted; in his hands was a repeating rifle. English threw himself to one side as Hevatha yelled in anger, "It is over, over, Ganook!"

But the Tlingit had waited long for his revenge, for a chance to slay the killers of the Iht, to kill the white who had taken his woman, and the rifle spat fire. English felt searing pain in his chest, the rush of following hot blood.

Ganook had turned his rifle to fire at Hevatha, and English lifted himself from the snow, a tortured yell

rising from his throat. He ran at Ganook, seeing surprise in the Tlingit's eyes as he switched his sights
again to English, to the wounded, wild-eyed white
who was already nearly on top of him.

The rifle discharged again over English's shoulder as
he leapt at Ganook, driving the Tlingit to the ground.
He drove his fist into Ganook's face three times, feeling cartilage break as Ganook's nose shattered.

The Tlingit shoved English aside and dived for his
rifle. English scrambled after him through the snow,
dragging Ganook down by the leg of his sealskin pants.

Ganook had a bone-handled knife in his hands as he
rolled to kick out at English with both feet, driving
Richard back. By the time English could stagger to his
feet, Ganook was poised and ready to slash him with
the finely honed blade of his hunting knife, to spill his
bowels on the snow and finally finish this debt of
honor.

Thunder roared and lightning crashed close by and
Ganook stumbled backward, swatting at his back.
Hevatha stood in the snow, the rifle still at her shoul-
der, and English saw her shoot the Tlingit again.

That was the last thing he saw for a long while. The
pain in his chest erupted volcanically and the hot blood
continued to flow. English clutched his chest and pitched
forward, hearing from a great distance the sound of a
woman screaming.

He awoke hours later, shivering with the cold, the
deep, penetrating cold which threatened to freeze the
bones and stop the heart. He awoke and it was dark,
the snow still falling. Beside him, warming English
with her body, was the woman. The only woman.
Hevatha.

He touched her hair and felt her shudder, and when
she lifted her face to kiss him, he tasted the salt of
tears.

"Crying! *You*, Hevatha . . ." he said weakly.

"Every woman must cry sometime," she said. She
moved nearer to him, holding him as tightly as she
dared. "Do not die, Richard English. Please do not

die. God and the universe want us to be together and love each other for many, many years."

English touched her hair again, mumbled something that made no sense at all, and then dropped again into the void beneath him, the spinning, senseless, timeless void.

Hevatha rose and began to work, cutting pine boughs, lashing them together. "He will not die," she said to the night and the storm, "because I will not allow it."

She built a litter and with great effort rolled him onto it. Then, through the falling snow, across the black and endless land, she began to drag him, gripping the poles of her travois so tightly that her frozen hands ached. She looked to the sky, to a point beyond the sky, trudging onward through the snow until her thighs were knotted, her feet raw, her lungs half-frozen. "He will not die because I will not allow it."

When English awoke again he was burning with fever. He had furs piled over him; he tried to throw them off but the sudden movement shot jagged pain through his chest and he lay back to stare upward, his face trickling perspiration.

It was a long while before he realized that he was looking not at the sky but at the ceiling of a hide house. He rolled his head to one side and saw the fire burning softly, weaving gold and crimson fibers into a pleasant and comforting, constantly changing tapestry which held his attention for long minutes.

It was another long minute before he realized he was not alone. She sat there, sleek and beautiful and perfect, her long dark hair brushed loosely across her shoulders, flowing across her breasts; and Hevatha came to him to give him water as he tried to speak her name.

"Heva . . ." But it would not come out of his parched, knotted throat. Still she knew, she understood, and she gave him small sips of cool water, holding his head on her lap, stroking his hair until he was asleep again.

The next awakening was like a reemergence from

the tomb. He was awake, fitful, hungry, curious. His mind had shed the dark, frenzied images of fear and pain. Hevatha was there still, as she would always be there, her hair braided now, her infinite, sweet smile returned.

"Han camp," English said, trying to sit up.

"Yes. Hush. Be still. We are in the Han camp."

"Alive. It's good, so good. I am alive and you are in the world. The baby?" he asked with sudden anxiety.

"Still well. Not born yet, but soon."

She knelt beside him and helped him to eat. She told him then what had happened, of the three days through the storm, of stumbling into the camp, into the welcoming arms of the tribe. "And who is here too?" she asked brightly. "Kiptah came home. Poduk beat her fearfully. Oh, it was terrible and good. Now she has her baby and her man, her people again. That is enough to eat . . . your poor belly. Stay warm, sleep some more."

"I can't sleep. I don't want to sleep. I feel as if I've been asleep forever. I only want to look at you."

"Yes?" she asked, tilting her head, smiling down into his blue eyes.

"Yes," English answered, taking her hand.

When he was awake and alert again, they talked, talked of their own future and of the future of others. "What you wish to do, English," Hevatha said as she lay beside him in the night, "to look into the past of the Indian, to chronicle him, to give him a history, is good. Only you can do that, not I. But I can learn to do something as important, English, I can learn to teach the Indian about the future. The future comes with a rush and it is upon us suddenly like a summer storm. The Indian is here, needing to know about his own past, needing to look into the future and see where it is he is going. He needs to make decisions, English."

"Many decisions," English agreed.

"I see the Indian because I am Indian, English, and what I see is a nation, many nations, walking just a step ahead of the darkness of the moon, walking into the bright world. He must not stumble. It is important that he knows where he has been and where he is going. Is there anything more honorable, English, than that we should try to help?"

There is, he thought, nothing more honorable, and as she lay close to him, they could see the half-moon gliding across the endless sky above the land of the Han, and he could feel the next generation, feel the young Indian moving in Hevatha's womb, and he knew that his life and hers would be forever bound to the life of the Indian.

He closed his eyes then and slept, and for a little while the Moon Walker watched the bright half-disk against the dark sky. Then, after a time, Hevatha smiled. She hugged her man more tightly and said, "It is good," and then she too slept, walking a dream moon into the future.